An

Mrs. Matthew Bauer

requests the honour of your presence

at the marriage of her daughter

Diane Sarah

to

Mr. Dominic Thomas Granatelli

on Saturday, the fifteenth of June

at two o'clock

Saint Benedict's Church

St. Louis, Missouri

Dear Reader,

Everybody loves a June wedding, and this month, Harlequin cordially invites you to attend the most romantic nuptials of the year!

With This Ring is a heartwarming collection of four short stories all revolving around the St. Louis wedding of Diane Bauer and Nick Granatelli. Written by your favorite Harlequin authors, these romances celebrate the joys, heartaches and magic of that special day....

The authors of *With This Ring* are no strangers to romance fans. Bethany Campbell has written for Romance and Intrigue. Barbara Delinsky helped launch Temptation and has been delivering exemplary books ever since. Bobby Hutchinson has made a name for herself with Superromance, American Romance and Temptation. And Anne McAllister is a popular contributor to the American Romance, Presents and Romance lines. A very talented and prolific group of writers!

So, sit back, sip some champagne and enjoy *With This Ring*. Please drop us a line letting us know how the wedding went!

Best Wishes,

Birgit Davis-Todd
Senior Editor
Harlequin Books
225 Duncan Mill Road
Don Mills, Ontario, Canada
M3B 3K9

With This Ring

BETHANY CAMPBELL
BARBARA DELINSKY
BOBBY HUTCHINSON
ANNE McALLISTER

Harlequin Books

TORONTO • NEW YORK • LONDON
AMSTERDAM • PARIS • SYDNEY • HAMBURG
STOCKHOLM • ATHENS • TOKYO • MILAN

CONTENTS

Acknowledgments

Special thanks to Joyce and John Flaherty for valuable insight into the real St. Louis. With your help, the wedding went off without a hitch!

Thanks to Sue MacKenzie, gourmet caterer, for suggestions about the menu.

Bobby Hutchinson

A word of thanks to Bill McFetridge and Franklin Evarts of Ozark Film and Video Productions, for technical advice on camera work.

Bethany Campbell

I'd like to thank Ethel Calcagno, Susan Huntley and Mary Lou Bockert for input on St. Louis; Gary Ross Mormino for having written a whole book on *The Immigrants on the Hill;* and H. E. Clark, Aine, Sieve and Thomas Meade for their help with the Gaelic. Special thanks to Harlequin Mondadori in Milan for getting me a hotel reservation during the World Cup Quarter Finals!

Anne McAllister

Menu
For A Wedding

BOBBY
HUTCHINSON

A Note from Bobby Hutchinson

We have six kids, all grown now, and one of the wonderful benefits for me is that, sooner or later, they all get around to marrying a delightful someone. The weddings in our family are a bit unusual: half our kids are deaf, so the ceremonies are conducted in sign language and speech simultaneously.

My dearly beloved and I started the tradition fourteen years ago; it was a second marriage for us, and our children were our witnesses, so they all needed to understand what was being said. Since then, three of them have married, all in signed ceremonies.

There's a poignancy and richness to a wedding in sign language. The visual impact of seeing the traditional words of love in graceful, poetic gesture adds another dimension, a special and deeply touching beauty that reminds us love is truly a silent language, known only to the heart.

As a romance writer, I try to capture that essence, store it away so I can remember the feeling it evokes and, perhaps, reproduce the magic for you, my reader, through the imperfect medium of words instead of signs.

It's been such fun watching Frankie and Eric fall in love.

I hope you enjoy it as much as I have.

Warm regards,

Bobby

Chapter One

A GENTLE APRIL RAIN misted the downtown streets of St. Louis, and the warm breeze accompanying it trumpeted spring to the noon-hour crowds hurrying along the sidewalks.

Frankie Granatelli was impervious to the weather. Impatient and out of sorts, she dodged other pedestrians' umbrellas and hauled her plump and puffing mother along by the arm, furious at the time being wasted on this errand.

In the first place, the food at Nick's wedding should have been left to the bride's family, in the traditional fashion. But no, Mamma had to fret and pester and drive everybody half-crazy about it until at last the bride's mother, Cynthia Bauer, graciously turned most of the decisions about the menu over to the Granatellis.

Grudgingly, Frankie had to admit she half understood Mamma's concern. The food served at an Italian wedding, the type and especially the quantity, was a major issue to every relative attending, and every last relative they owned would be there, you could be sure of that.

Yes, she could see Mamma getting involved, all right. She just didn't see why she had to be dragged into the whole mess, just because her mother, Teresa Granatelli, thought her own English wasn't good enough.

Mamma's English was perfectly adequate. It certainly was good enough to deal with a lousy caterer over what to serve at her son's wedding, for mercy's sake.

But Mamma didn't think so, and all Frankie's fast-talking hadn't been able to convince her otherwise.

"Where is this darned restaurant, anyway?" She sounded short-tempered, and her mother assumed a martyred expression and sighed audibly.

"It has to be in this block. Isn't this the address you told me, Mamma?" Scowling out from under the tilted brim of her smart brown fedora, Frankie saw the sign at last, half a block ahead. "There it is. Finally."

The Fifth Quarter. Her stride lengthened in anticipation. Maybe they could get this whole menu thing settled before the entire afternoon was wasted, and she could get back to her shop. Her mind worried over the hat patterns she'd cut earlier that morning from the new shipment of raw Czechoslovakian felt. Right this moment she ought to be blocking, steaming, coaxing them into some semblance of the hats they would finally become. And instead . . .

"Francesca, a little slower, *per favore*, I'm all out of breath. I'm not a young woman anymore, you understand."

Teresa tugged at her tall daughter's arm, and Frankie sighed, but slowed. She forced herself to accommodate her steps to her mother's regal, sedate pace.

"I know this is a bother for you, Francesca," Teresa was saying, reverting to her native Italian and a particularly pathetic tone of voice guaranteed to make Frankie feel guilty. "I'm sorry to take you away from your work, but what can I do? It's your brother's wedding, after all, and the food has to be perfect. Nicky would say so himself if he were here."

Nicky would say nothing of the kind, Frankie knew that for sure. Her big brother wasn't exactly hung up on Italian tradition any more than she was. But neither was he around to help out with this chaos he'd created; he was safely back East in New York, getting his fledgling woodworking business off the ground, and he wouldn't arrive until just before the wedding.

Was that ingenious, or what? Avoid the hassle, but enjoy the party. Pretty clever of you, *fratello mio*.

Teresa was in fine form. "You know, Francesca, I never would ask this of you if Sophia was feeling well. Sophia is always happy to come with me and make sure things go right, no matter how busy she is."

Frankie clenched her teeth and rolled her eyes, almost trampling over a tiny old man in a black raincoat in the process.

She was twenty-six years old, and her older sister had been held up to her as the perfect Italian daughter for most of her life. Would it still be happening when she was thirty, forty . . . fifty, even?

"Poor Sophia," Teresa went on with another sigh. "This pregnancy of hers, it's not like the other three, you know. This *bambino*, he causes her much trouble. It was the same with me when I had Vinnie. Such pain in my back . . ."

Teresa continued in rapid-fire Italian, supplying lurid details Frankie didn't want to hear about the grosser problems of pregnancy.

At last, somewhere between chronic indigestion and false labor pains, they reached the doorway to the restaurant.

"Where did this Thorpe guy say he wanted to meet you, Mamma?" Frankie interrupted the litany, shoving open the heavy door and pausing for a moment in the foyer to get her bearings.

"I think upstairs in his office, but perhaps we can ask to be sure?"

The restaurant was busy. A steady buzz of conversation was interspersed with laughter, the clink of cutlery and rattle of dishes mingled with enticing smells of food. The Fifth Quarter had recently become one of St. Louis's hot spots for dining, and it was doing good business even on a quiet Monday noon.

Both Teresa and Frankie looked around with the assessing, critical glances of those who were involved in the restaurant business themselves and knew what to look for.

Framed photos of football stars lined the walls; attentive waiters hurried without seeming to; quiet, unobtrusive music played; tables with snowy covers were set far enough apart to allow for comfortable relaxation.

Not bad.

Not Granatelli's, you understand. Granatelli's was a St. Louis landmark, renowned far and wide for its authentic Italian food. But this was really not bad.

A tall, impeccably groomed waiter materialized, and Frankie snapped, "Where can we find Mr. Thorpe?"

"He'll be in his office, straight up those stairs and along the hall." He escorted them to the stairwell.

For Frankie, it was an effort not to take the steps two at a time. Teresa climbed at a pace that would put a snail to shame.

At the top, a short hallway led to an open door where a large male figure lounged behind a desk, chair tipped back and feet propped comfortably on its surface. He was talking on the phone, but he ended the conversation with abrupt good humor as soon as the two women appeared. He swung his legs to the floor and got to his feet, coming out from behind the desk.

"Mrs. Granatelli?" He extended a huge hand to Teresa, and his lopsided grin was engaging.

"I'm Eric Thorpe, delighted to meet you."

My God, he's a giant, Frankie thought.

He was big. He had dark brown hair, a little on the long side, tousled and inclined to curl. His nose was a trifle crooked, but his features were pleasing.

Very pleasing. He smiled easily, and there was a deep indentation in his strong chin.

His eyes were on Frankie now, clear green eyes that studied her with frank admiration.

"Here is my daughter Francesca, Mr. Thorpe," Teresa explained. "Sometimes I don't speak the English so well, and Frankie, she will translate for me."

Thorpe's gaze lingered on Frankie's face. "Of course. That's great, that's fine. Come in...." He backed up several paces and gestured toward two chairs.

"Sit down, Mrs. Granatelli." He again turned the full force of those clear green eyes on Frankie. "Nice to meet you, Ms. Granatelli?" One dark eyebrow rose in question, and his eyes flicked to her ringless finger and back up to her face again.

"Ms. Granatelli, yes," Frankie confirmed, then wondered why her voice sounded so choked.

"Can I take your coats? It's pretty warm in here."

Both women handed him their raincoats, and he hung them up on a coat tree behind the door. Frankie left her hat on, feeling that she needed all the confidence a marvelous hat could provide.

This Eric Thorpe wasn't exactly what she'd expected a caterer to look like, and it was throwing her a trifle off balance.

Which was silly, because what was a caterer supposed to look like, anyway?

Not like something from the centerfold of *Playgirl,* for sure.

When Thorpe's back was turned with the coats for a moment, she sneaked another quick and unbelieving look at his physique.

Wow. This dude was big. Shoulders out to there, a truly amazing taper down to that trim waist, nice tight buttocks, legs like long, strong tree trunks, but better shaped. *Magnifico.*

From under her hat brim, she studied his face again. He was rugged looking.

Nope, she amended as he moved past her and sat down on the chair behind the desk. Rugged didn't quite cover it, either.

It was the way he moved—fluid, athletic. Graceful in the way large, lean jungle animals were graceful. Larger than life, with a suggestion of power leashed just under the surface.

He caught her staring at him and for a moment her gaze was held fast by those intense green eyes. Embarrassed, she looked down at her lap and crossed and uncrossed her legs, giving her skirt a tug here and a pull there.

He fumbled around on the desk for a pen and opened a file folder. "Now, Mrs. Granatelli, this menu for the wedding. I've already spoken to the bride's mother, and we've tentatively settled some of the details, subject, of course, to your approval. This is what we've come up with so far. To start, hors d'oeuvres, then a light soup, salad, main course and dessert. With the wedding cake served later."

ERIC COULD ONLY HOPE that whatever he was saying wasn't total and absolute gibberish. He was doing his best not to stare at Frankie Granatelli, but the effort was killing him.

It was like trying not to watch a perfect field goal.

He was vaguely aware of Teresa asking, "These hors d'oeuvres, what kind exactly?"

"Marinated clams, lobster terrine..." He could hear himself rattling off a list of fancy-sounding names, but he had a feeling someone else was doing the talking. He felt as if he'd been winded.

The moment he'd laid eyes on this tall, leggy woman in the crazy brown hat, his heart had started hammering like a fullback lunging into the end zone for a touchdown. There was a heady surge of exhilaration, of recognition.

Eric was pretty sure he knew this woman with the dark, flashing eyes, even though he'd never actually met her till now. She wasn't the exact replica of the genteel creature he'd dreamed of most of his adult life, but he was willing to change the fantasy when the real thing walked in the door.

"...so we settled on a couple of hot hors d'oeuvres, and two cold..."

Was he making any sense at all? Maybe not, because Mrs. Granatelli began to shake her head, no, no, no. She held up an imperious hand, and he stopped, letting his eyes slide inquiringly past the mother to the daughter.

"Mamma says what about antipasto?"

She wasn't the most beautiful woman he'd ever seen. That wasn't it at all. She was tall, maybe five-ten or eleven, and her body was more supple than voluptuous. The face below the hat brim was a touch too angular for perfect beauty, the mouth a shade too large. Her lips were full, the bottom lip swollen as if she'd been kissed not long ago.

He hoped with his heart it wasn't true.

"Antipasto is great," he agreed with feigned enthusiasm. "But we did feel at a wedding, there's always the danger of someone spilling it on their clothing, and with all that oil..."

Her hair billowed out from under the hat, a scrambled mass of waves and curls the exact color of dark honey, and her expressive eyes and hands punctuated every word she said. A spate of rapid Italian was now zinging back and forth between mother and daughter.

With an impatient wave of her hand, Frankie said, "Mamma still likes the idea of antipasto. Also, she wants to know exactly what's in each of those other things, please."

Eric watched the provocative way her lips moved, and lost the sense of what she was saying. "You mean she . . . wants a list of the ingredients in the hors d'oeuvres?" he finally managed. Mother and daughter both nodded, and Eric began a lengthy rundown from memory, taking each item in turn.

"Clams, and then there's liver paste, and bacon, and cream cheese, and olives, and spinach wrapped in phyllo pastry . . ."

Teresa interrupted every other word or so, making suggestions about adding this or subtracting that, always in Italian, which Frankie relayed with obvious and growing impatience.

Eric politely jotted down the suggestions, delighted that this was going to take a long time but a trifle concerned that there were so many complications this early into the menu.

Half an hour went by in that fashion, and then Teresa inquired, through Frankie, about quantity.

"You understand, Mrs. Granatelli, that we don't want to fill people up on the hors d'oeuvres, because there's a substantial amount of food still to come at the dinner." He quoted the exact numbers of each item to be served, explaining how the amounts were arrived at, using the number of guests and the average amounts consumed and multiplying it out. "With four hundred guests, we estimate three per person."

Teresa became agitated at that, shaking her head and obviously objecting to something all over again.

Eric waited for the translation. He vaguely wished he'd had more experience at this catering thing. But a guy had to start somewhere, and after all, his chef, Gus Vilatszety, was a genius. A little temperamental, but Eric had found most chefs were.

Speaking of starting somewhere, what was the simplest, most effective way of getting to know this Frankie lady, he mused, as another long and voluble interchange occurred.

Eric passed the time by shooting quick glances at Frankie's legs, hidden between the top of her tall leather boots and the hem of her red-checked skirt. All he could tell was that they were extraordinarily long, and he fantasized for a few seconds about their shape.

"Mamma doesn't think that's going to be anywhere near enough hors d'oeuvres." There was an edge to her tone that indicated she was getting more than a little impatient with Mamma, and even Eric could detect a growing undertone of hysteria in the older woman's Italian.

"Well, no problem," he said with agreeable aplomb. "We can increase the numbers a bit, I guess. What quantities do you think would be generous?" he asked Teresa.

He was rewarded with a look from Frankie that spoke gratitude and made his blood pressure soar.

Another fifteen minutes went by as Teresa tried to figure out what Uncle Vito or someone called Luigi Depuouli might consume on a normal occasion.

Eric called down to the restaurant and had coffee and pastries sent up. He wasn't complaining, but it was beginning to dawn on him that this Granatelli wedding contract wasn't exactly going to be a snap. He'd been overly optimistic, probably because the bride's mother, Mrs. Bauer, had been delighted by his suggestions.

Mrs. Granatelli was a whole different ball game.

By now, Frankie was rolling her eyes, raising her voice and using her hands in a way that strongly suggested to Eric that her mother was making her more than a tiny bit crazy.

Eric wasn't sure whether the ripples in his own rock-steady nervous system were due to the menu upheaval or to this close proximity to an aroused—and arousing—woman. He could smell her light perfume in the warm room, a spicy, primitive blend that he imagined was a combination of her own particular scent mixed with something out of a bottle.

The coffee came, and Teresa nibbled at several pastries to regain her strength while she described three intricate Italian delicacies that Eric had never heard of, and which she insisted had to be included in the hors d'oeuvres.

Eric promised to speak to his chef.

"And the soup. Frankie, tell him what I just said about the soup."

Frankie gritted her teeth. "Mamma doesn't like the idea of cold avocado soup like you suggested. She thinks you should serve tortellini."

"I'm afraid it's a bit heavy as a starter, don't you think?"

Another long and heated conversation. Frankie seemed to have won this time, because no further mention was made of tortellini, for which Eric was humbly grateful.

Gus would have a stroke.

"Where is the ladies' room, please?" Frankie made the request for her mother, and Mrs. Granatelli got to her feet and sailed off down the corridor in the direction Eric indicated.

He and she were alone for the first time.

She slumped down in her chair, stretching her legs out and letting breath whistle through her clenched teeth.

"She's going to drive me over the brink with this menu thing," Frankie moaned. "We're going to be here all day and most of the night, I just know it. My God, we've barely made it as far as the soup." She balled her fists and waved them in front of her. "How could Sophia do this to me?"

She looked over at Eric and caught him staring at her.

"Sophia, my sister. She usually does all this stuff with Mamma. She's got more patience than me. I'm sorry, Mr. Thorpe. See, Mamma's not rational about this wedding. Nick's my oldest brother and he's marrying out of the Italian community and she's afraid the wedding won't be what her friends and relatives expect. I don't know what to do with her."

She glanced at the watch on her wrist and sat up fast. "Mother of God, it's after three. I've absolutely got to get back to work. Mamma will just have to leave this for now and finish it another day. The bloody wedding's not till June anyway. There's enough time."

She leaped to her feet and collected her raincoat before Eric could move, shoving her arms carelessly through the sleeves and shrugging it into place before he got close enough to hold it for her.

Was he going to lose her before he had a chance to really know what she was like? Desperate times called for desperate measures.

"Why don't you and I get together and try to come to some mutual agreement that would please your mother? It's obvious this is upsetting her, and maybe we could make it easier for her. You know what kind of thing she wants—I'm quite willing to compromise. Say, over dinner? Tonight?"

She hesitated a long time, her thick eyebrows pulled into a frown over her straight nose. Eric held his breath until his chest ached.

"I really ought to work late," she began. "I've got all these orders I haven't even started."

"Orders for what?" He needed to know more about her, like where to find her once she walked out the door.

"Hats. I'm a milliner. I opened a shop four months ago called The Mad Hatter."

"A milliner." The only kind of head covering he'd ever thought about were football helmets. He had a lot to learn about millinery.

"So you made this one you're wearing?" He reached out and touched the brim with one finger.

She nodded. Having him stand this close to her did weird things to her heart rate.

Their eyes met, and the sensual undercurrents running back and forth like mercury had nothing at all to do with hats or tortellini soup.

"All right, dinner it is," she finally agreed.

Eric felt as if he'd just won the football pool.

"And call me Eric, won't you?" Might as well make as much headway as possible. "Mr. Thorpe makes me feel like a maître d'."

She nodded again, and smiled a bit. She had the most enchanting smile.

"So where should I pick you up?"

"I can't get away until nine. Maybe you could come to my store?"

Eric would gladly have hired the spaceship *Enterprise* and collected her from another galaxy if necessary.

"No problem."

She gave him the address and he marked it down, even though it was imprinted in indelible ink on his brain.

"Nine it is."

They could hear Teresa's measured gait approaching down the hall.

"Think I could get permission to call you Frankie instead of Ms. Granatelli? Or do I have to ask your mother for that?"

This time she grinned at him, and a trace of mischief sparkled in her eyes.

"Oh, I think you could call me Frankie, and let's leave Mamma out of it, okay? She's liable to decide to change my name, the mood she's in today. Besides, only the IRS calls me Ms. Granatelli. It makes me nervous."

"Frankie it is, then." It was the most beautiful name he'd ever heard. "I'll be there at nine."

The hours between then and now seemed to stretch into infinity.

Chapter Two

THE MAD HATTER WAS a tiny shop situated just on the periphery of the prestigious Central West End shopping area. It was sandwiched between a used-clothing boutique and a health food store. There was an ornately carved wooden sign above the door featuring the profile of a Victorian lady wearing an immense, elaborate bonnet.

Eric stood on the sidewalk in front of the store for several moments, studying the chic display of hats in the softly lighted window. Then he knocked on the door. He felt a little shy now that the moment he'd anticipated all afternoon had finally arrived. Would he feel the same jolt of recognition when he saw her again? Would that feeling of rightness still be there in his gut?

It seemed to take a long time before he heard a lock turning, and then Frankie was silhouetted against a colorful background of hats of every description, ornate rose-patterned wallpaper, large and small mirrors and a small glass-fronted counter set along the back wall. A door behind the counter stood slightly ajar, and a bright beam of light leaked through it into the store.

"You're early," she said, but she smiled up at him when she said it. "That's okay, because I'm getting hungry anyway, and I don't work so well when my stomach's growling. C'mon in."

She'd changed her outfit. She wore slim black pants and a silky blouse the color of daffodils, and for the first time he saw her without a hat. Her luxurious hair was a glorious tumble of curls, part of it caught up in a silver clasp on the crown of her head, the rest spilling over her shoulders. He wanted to reach out and stroke it.

All the emotions he'd felt that afternoon rushed through him all over again. There'd been no mistake.

"My jacket's back here . . ." She led the way into the work-room behind the counter, hips swaying a little, drawing his gaze and raising his blood pressure.

In the store, order reigned.

In the workroom, controlled chaos was evident.

Carved wooden hat forms like so many bald heads sat in a crooked row on a shelf above a large, cluttered worktable, and scraps of felt and straw littered the floor. There was a strong smell of wet felt mingled with the sharp odor of glue. An efficient-looking sewing machine sat waiting under a bright lamp.

In a corner a cardboard carton overflowed with multicolored straw hats, devoid of any trim, bright as a summer sunset. Smaller boxes were strewn around containing chiffon scarves, huge silk cabbage roses, tiny sprays of artificial berries and fruits and ribbons. Everywhere were hats in varying stages of completion.

It was a fascinating, utterly feminine scene.

"How did you learn to do this, Frankie? Is there a college course you can take?"

She was unplugging the steam iron, and she flashed him a rueful smile over her shoulder. "Nope, I didn't go to college. I was stagestruck from the time I was a kid. I didn't want to act, but I was fascinated by the backstage scene, especially the costumes. As soon as I finished high school I got a job as wardrobe assistant for a touring company. We'd go from theater to theater—Seattle, Minneapolis, New York, back to St. Louis. Eventually I met this designer, Migs Crenshaw. She was about seventy then, brilliant, eccentric."

Frankie looked as if she were seeing the woman in her mind's eye, and she smiled a wistful smile. "She was my idol, Migs was. Anyhow, she took me on as an apprentice, taught me how to draft patterns, drape material, cut and sew. We were on the road a fair amount, and at night she showed me how to make hats. As a special treat, she used to say."

Frankie's hands were busy, tidying the table, giving a final pat and pull to a half-formed navy blue boater, but her eyes still had a faraway expression. "Well, the hat-making took over, as you can see. I quit the touring company last year and here I am.''

"Your teacher, this . . . Migs Crenshaw. She must be very proud of you," Eric said softly, watching the play of expressions on her mobile features.

Frankie flicked a quick glance at him, then turned abruptly and lifted a battered brown leather jacket from the back of a chair.

"Migs never saw The Mad Hatter. She died six months before I opened."

"I'm sorry. You must have been very fond of her."

He took the jacket from her and helped her into it, aware of the warmth of her body, the feel of her shoulders as he settled the worn leather in place.

"I loved Migs. She taught me a lot." Her voice was soft and full of regret.

With practiced ease, Frankie fitted a cap on her head, the color of her jacket but made in the style of a Greek sailor's hat. With automatic expertise, she tilted it at an angle that made her look chic and mischievous and slightly wicked.

She switched off lights, closed the workroom door, locked the front, and in minutes they were in Eric's low-slung sports car.

The restaurant he'd decided to take her to was new, small and quiet. The chef was a friend of Gus Vilatszety, and Gus had assured Eric the food was great.

As Gus had also suggested, Eric and Frankie agreed to leave the menu up to the chef. Eric ordered a bottle of wine, and they sipped it and chatted as they waited for the first course.

"So how did you get into the restaurant business?" Frankie finally asked. It was so easy, being with him, laughing over little inconsequential things. The wine was making her brave enough to ask the questions that had been in her mind all afternoon. She wanted to know about him, all about him. "You took me by surprise today, you know," she confessed with a smile. "I expected, well . . ." Frankie could feel her face turning pink as she struggled to explain without sounding dumb.

"I guess I just visualized a different sort of guy as a caterer, that's all."

He laughed, a nice, husky sound. "Wimpy, huh? Skinny and stoop-shouldered? Well, I wasn't always in the food business. This is my second career. I started off as a football player, middle linebacker for the St. Louis Cardinals, when they still played here. But after the fourth knee operation, the doctor said I'd better pack it in or accept being crippled for life."

Frankie knew less than nothing about football, except that the men who played it earned a great deal of money. But it made perfect sense, him being a professional athlete. When she thought about it, that's what he looked like.

"Was it hard, finding another profession? How old were you when you quit?"

"I'm thirty-five now, and that was five years ago. And yeah, it was rough for a while. I went through some major head trips, feeling as if there wasn't anything but football I was suited for. See, I was drafted by the Cardinals right out of college. Pro football was all I'd ever done, all I knew how to do. I loved it, and I felt as if my life was pretty much over." He shook his head and gave her his crooked smile. "Crazy, huh? At the ripe old age of twenty-nine? Then an old football buddy got himself into a tight spot financially and had to sell the restaurant he'd bought as an investment. Food and cooking had always been my hobby, so I bought it, renamed it The Fifth Quarter and learned the business the hard way. There were two rough years, but last year and this, things have been going pretty good. More luck than sense on my part, I'd say."

Frankie shook her head at that. "You're being modest. I know the restaurant business inside out—all the kids in our family do. We were brought up in the back of Granatelli's. And I happen to know The Fifth Quarter is a booming success story. That doesn't happen unless the person running things is good at his job."

He gave her a warm, grateful look. "Thanks, Frankie."

The waiter arrived with bowls of chilled soup, and after one taste, Frankie quickly spooned up every drop. "I don't know what's in this, it sure isn't tortellini, but it's wonderful all the same."

They laughed, and then it was his turn to ask questions. "How many kids in your family, Frankie?"

"Six. I'm third in the lineup. The oldest is Sophia, the one I told you about today. She's been married for years, she has three kids and is expecting her fourth soon. My folks think the mold got broken after Sophia, since she's the perfect daughter." She screwed up her nose and made a face, and he smiled.

"Then there's my brother Nick, the one who's getting married? He's twenty-nine. Nick's always been the model son in the family, just like Sophia's the model girl. Mamma and Papa should have quit while they were ahead, because then there's me. I'm twenty-six, and I'm nobody's role model, believe me. But then comes Carlo, who's twenty-four. Carlo is studying for the priesthood," she added with mingled pride and incomprehension in her voice. "I'll never understand how my bratty little brother could have decided to become a priest. You should have seen the things he and I got up to when we were little. Then there's Vinnie," she went on. "He's twenty-two. He plays in a rock band—talk about the opposite pole from Carlo. But Vinnie's okay, in spite of the headaches he causes my parents. He's actually got a great mind for business. And the baby of the family is Paula, who's nineteen. She's in college and she's driving everybody nuts, changing boyfriends every week, threatening to join the Peace Corps one week and the Young Communists the next. Even I have moments when I worry about Paula."

"They all sound great," Eric commented. He'd been paying close attention to her every word. These were people he hoped to get to know very well indeed, because of Frankie.

The soup bowls were removed just then and replaced with a spinach salad. The waiter refilled their wineglasses and left.

"Do you have a big family, Eric?"

He smiled at her again, a gentle, caressing smile, and shook his head. "I guess I grew up a lot different than you did. I was a foster child. I can't remember my mother. She gave me up when I was three—she was a single parent. I wasn't an easy kid, and I was moved to about seven different foster homes before I was a teenager. I got pretty wild by that time, out of control. Football probably kept me from being a delinquent. One of the social workers I had got me started on a junior team, and I won a football scholarship to college. From then on, football was my life, the other guys my family." He shrugged. "Probably kept me out of jail."

"Oh, Eric, that's awful. I'm sorry." She reached across and impetuously took his hand in hers and squeezed it before she let it go again. His skin was warm and slightly rough, and his hand felt strong enough to crush hers with ease. "I can't imagine what that would be like, growing up alone, not knowing and loving your parents...." She was shocked and horrified, but fascinated, as well.

He seemed to have turned out quite wonderful in spite of his disastrous beginnings. Respect mingled with the other emotions he was stirring in her.

After that the conversation turned to lighter things. Frankie related anecdotes from her days with acting troupes, and Eric told outrageous stories about his football buddies and the groupies who plagued them. By the time the exotic chocolate-and-cream dessert was devoured, Frankie was sure she'd never laughed as much with anyone before.

Over coffee it suddenly dawned on her that the original purpose of their meeting—trying to come up with a menu that Teresa might just approve—had been entirely forgotten. She considered bringing it up, then decided not to. There was a magic about the evening that she didn't want to endanger.

It was late by the time they left the restaurant. The rain had stopped and the stars were bright overhead. "Summer's almost here," Eric remarked as he handed her into the low-slung car as if she were precious china.

It pleased Frankie, this chivalrous side of him. So many men these days didn't bother with the little niceties anymore.

"How about going to a club now, maybe dancing a little?" Eric sounded eager as he slid in the driver's side.

Frankie was tempted. She wondered how it would feel, being in his arms. But she knew she'd have to get up especially early in the morning to go to the store and finish the work she hadn't done today.

She shook her head. "Can't, sorry. I've got a heavy day tomorrow. My business hasn't reached the point where I can hire anyone to work for me, so I have to be there before the store opens and after it closes if I'm going to get enough hats made to sell. And then there's the orders—I'm swamped because of the wedding."

He nodded and was quiet for a moment, allowing the powerful car engine to idle. "I used to feel I was married to my restaurant," he said at last. "But the time does arrive when it can get along without you. The trick is knowing when."

"Well, mine can't," she said shortly. "Not yet, anyway." Not for a very long time. Not until every red cent she'd had to borrow from her father was paid, with interest.

The exact amount she owed flashed like a neon light in her head, taking a little of the pleasure out of the evening. She found herself wanting to confide in Eric, without revealing the more hurtful parts of the whole transaction. What was it about him that made her instinctively trust him? She usually didn't confide in people this way.

"See, my dad, Dom Granatelli, was opposed to me starting a business," she began. "He couldn't understand why I didn't settle down and get married, like Sophia had. Or if I had to have a career, then why not his restaurant? There's lots of work there for the whole family, and he always tells us he started the restaurant in the first place as a family business. Now all of us are off doing something else, and it bothers him."

She didn't tell Eric about the loan. Borrowing the money from her father in order to set up The Mad Hatter had been awful. Frankie would never have asked him if any one of the numerous banks she'd approached had loaned her the money instead, at whatever exorbitant rate of interest they chose to charge. But none had. So Dom had been her last resort.

And although he'd finally loaned her what she needed, right away he'd done the very thing she'd been dreading most of all. He'd told Uncle Vito all about it, and Uncle Sal, and they had told her aunties, and they had told . . . absolutely everybody else. The entire Granatelli clan knew every detail of Frankie's business within a week, just the way they had always known what was going on in her life.

It drove her into frantic rages, this family habit of telling all. Why couldn't her family keep their mouths shut once in a while, she wondered for the three thousandth time. Why was nothing sacred?

Eric's voice interrupted her thoughts. "So now you want to prove to your father that your store can be a success?"

"Something like that," she agreed, and he let it go at that.

He was nice. He was easy to be with. Maybe this was the right time to emphasize what her goals were, the fact that there was no place in her dreams for marriage and three nice kids.

But she'd only just met him, for God's sake. Wouldn't he think she was reading more into one casual evening than he'd intended? Frankie let the moment pass, and the drive to her apartment seemed to take only seconds.

He stopped the car and turned towards her. Frankie's heart suddenly started hammering, and her nerves felt jangled. Was he going to kiss her? "Thank you for dinner. I really ought to go in. . . ."

He reached over with both hands and tugged at the collar of her jacket, pulling her with gentle ease toward him. "You're a fascinating woman, Frankie. I'm glad that I found you."

He paused for an instant just before he kissed her, his eyes searching every inch of her face, lingering on her lips.

"I've waited a long time," she thought she heard him murmur as he drew her against him and captured her lips with his. For the first second, she wondered what he meant. But then sensation took over, and thoughts became feelings, alarming messages of heat, of need.

There was no hesitancy in his embrace. He knew exactly how to angle his lips on hers, how to set flame to tinder.

She wanted his kisses. She was just unprepared for the response it roused in her. There was shock, and instant desire.

There was the burning need to press herself closer to him, to answer the question his tongue posed as it slid across her lips.

Between one moment and the next, she wanted him. God, how she wanted him. Her lips parted, and the world narrowed to this one moment in time.

Chapter Three

SHE STRAINED AGAINST HIM, pleasure filling every inch of her as the kiss deepened, changed, demanded. Yet there was no strangeness in the embrace. It felt as though they'd done this countless times before, anticipating each other's response, instinctively knowing how to inflame. The cramped space, with the intrusion of gear shift and bucket seats, made it impossible to get as close as they needed to be.

Eric's hands slid from her shoulders, down over her jacket, below it. He spread his fingers wide and slipped them under the leather to the warmth of her waist, feeling the shape of her narrow rib cage, thrilling to the heat of her skin through the layers of thin cloth. She was trembling in his arms.

She'd seemed so cool, so possessed, in that moment before he kissed her. Cool, and then instantly molten. Inflammatory. Dangerous.

He knew when the explosions that rocked both of them began to frighten her, when sensation was replaced by reason. This loss of control disturbed her, and he felt her struggling to regain it. He moved away, enough so she could feel free again.

"Eric, I..." She swallowed hard. "I have to go in now. It's, it must be getting late." Her voice was trembling just as her body had been.

"I'll walk you to the door." He touched her cheek with a fingertip and released her totally, opening the car door and stepping out, swiftly moving around to her side. His body was swollen and rock hard with wanting her, but there was time. There was going to be a future, he knew that for certain now. He drew in deep gulps of chilly night air and struggled for control.

It seemed to Frankie that he regained his composure a lot faster than she did. When he opened her door and helped her out, he was steady and relaxed. "Where'd you ever get this jacket of yours?" he teased, running a hand over the scarred leather sleeve.

"It was my brother Nick's. I kept borrowing it, and he finally gave it to me."

"I like it. It's got character. Like you, Frankie."

He made her feel special. He even made her feel tiny, he was so much taller and wider than she was. It was a unique thing, when you were a tall woman.

She liked it.

At the door he smiled his big, lazy smile down at her and said, "We never did talk about that menu, did we? I'll be in touch in the next couple of days, and we'll discuss it then. That sound okay to you?"

She gave a jerky, uncertain nod. Her lips were still burning from his kisses. They felt swollen and hot, and pulses inside were hammering. Right now she wasn't sure she wanted to risk one more single meeting with Eric Thorpe. He was dangerous to her health and welfare.

"I'm going to be pretty busy for the next few weeks," she managed, but it didn't come out as convincing as she'd wanted.

He shrugged. "I'll have to take my chances, won't I?"

There didn't seem to be much she could say to that. "Well, good night, then," she croaked. "Thank you, it was a wonderful dinner." And she all but bolted in the door before he got it in his head to kiss her again.

Once inside, she took her clothes off, had a hot bath and flopped straight into bed, telling herself the whole time that she wasn't thinking of him at all, she really wasn't. She forced her busy brain to review the past day's sales, mentally mapped out the work for the next day, reminding herself about which orders had to be finished when. She lay under the blue goose-down comforter her mother had given her last Christmas, waiting for sleep, determined not to think about Eric Thorpe at all.

DAMN. FRANKIE LIFTED her head one more time and squinted at the face of her bedside clock.

Three-thirty. Twelve whole minutes since she'd last checked.

She'd barely slept a wink yet, and she was getting desperate. At this rate, she might just as well have gone dancing. Or something.

Erotic images of that something floated unbidden into her brain. She groaned and flopped from her back to her side, pounded the pillows under her head with a vicious fist and tried to get comfortable. Her head was starting to ache, and she cursed the wine she'd consumed at dinner. Her body ached in a very different way, and she cursed the kisses she'd exchanged so eagerly with Eric.

At last she allowed the buried reactions of yesterday to come to the surface and be recognized. ERIC THORPE. The name appeared in capital letters in her mind.

He was a disturbing man. In one day he'd managed to disrupt her well-planned life. With a little help from her mother, of course.

Still, why should this particular man affect her in this particular way? Certainly she'd been kissed before—more times than she could count. But she'd never felt quite the way she'd felt last night when Eric kissed her, and that was a definite problem.

Because, Frankie reminded herself, serious romance or marriage was out of the question for her. At least for years and years, until The Mad Hatter was a success, its mortgage paid in full, employees at her beck and call. Right now the entire operation was up to her, sink or swim.

Not that one single evening with him meant that a marriage proposal was forthcoming, for heaven's sake. That was ridiculous. *But all the same*, she lectured herself, *better to nip this in the bud right now if he gets under your skin this way after one date.*

She was no Superwoman. She dreamed of love just the way every other woman did, and certain things never changed. Men didn't get pregnant, for one, despite all the hoopla about equality.

Frankie had watched her own sister almost kill herself just being a wife and mother, never mind trying to mix a demanding career in there, too.

Sophia, seven months pregnant, took care of three demonic—albeit lovable—little boys, kept her house spotless, was a gourmet cook, did tons of baking and would cluck in sympathy and bring her husband, Aldo, a drink when he came limping in at the end of the day complaining of how hard he'd worked. Even though her own ankles were swollen up like footballs.

Frankie would have handed him the laundry to fold, ordered in pizza, asked for hers on a plate and gone and had a nice hot bath. With the door locked. She didn't have it in her to cater to anybody the way her mother and sister catered to their men. So maybe men like Eric were different, a defensive voice protested. Maybe they took this equality thing more seriously than her father or Aldo did. Maybe a modern woman really could have it all, just the way the magazines promised—career, marriage, family. . . .

Forget it, said her practical, no-nonsense side. Migs had put it in context one day when a rising young actress, tremendously talented and recently married, had told them she was also pregnant. "But it's not a problem, my career comes first," she'd insisted. "Raymond and I are going to share absolutely everything about parenting, right down the middle. It's like a scale you have to keep evenly balanced."

"Ah, but the scale is already tipped," Migs had sighed when the woman left. "She's made a choice whether she realizes or not. Her career will have to be put on hold, perhaps forever. A woman can have a career, yes. She can have a career and a love life, certainly. But when marriage and children are added, the scale tips and something must go. And in most cases it's the woman's career, not the man's."

A younger Frankie had argued that the feminist movement had overcome such antiquated notions. Women were doing all sorts of things these days. Look at . . .

But time had proven Migs right, like it or not. The brilliant actress had suffered many complications of pregnancy and delivery, her child was sickly, and her career simply fizzled. Frankie had swallowed hard and filed the information away.

So two out of three really was the best a woman could hope for. Right now, at this point in her life, even one was too many.

So long, Eric Thorpe. It was short, but it was sweet all the same.

Maybe if she counted hats . . .

THE NEXT MORNING was gray and wintry, and Frankie's spirits matched the dull weather.

The flowers arrived fifteen minutes after she opened, a huge brown pottery jug spilling over with daffodils. The scent filled the shop with promises of spring, and Frankie couldn't help smiling when she looked at them.

The card just said, "'Morning, pretty lady. Eric."

He called that night and asked her if she'd like to have dinner again. She thanked him for the flowers and insisted she had to go to her parents' house. She did go, but she was in a foul mood the whole evening.

The bell over The Mad Hatter's door gave its musical tinkle at nine forty-five the next morning, and in the back room Frankie cursed under her breath. She was in the middle of threading fine wire through the brim of a swoopy pink number, and if that was Auntie Rosina to pick up her hat, Frankie was about to lose at least an hour and a half of good working time.

Her auntie's hat was ready, that wasn't the problem. Rosina was the stumbling block. She talked and talked and talked. She'd expect a cup of coffee; she'd want to see what Frankie was creating in the back room; she'd launch into a detailed account of what her four daughters were doing.

Maledizione! Nick's forthcoming wedding had brought all Frankie's legions of aunts and cousins rushing to buy a new hat from her, but the blessing was a mixed one.

Frankie came through the connecting door with a smile that showed a lot less enthusiasm than usual, but her first glimpse of the visitor turned the strained smile into an expression of openmouthed astonishment.

It was Eric. He wore faded blue jeans that fit like a second skin, and a white jersey under a worn old red jacket with a football emblazoned on the front. And he was holding a huge wicker picnic basket.

"'Morning, Frankie." His grin was wide and charming. "Have you had breakfast yet?"

"I . . . as a matter of fact . . ." She hadn't. "No."

For the second night in a row she'd finally fallen asleep somewhere near dawn and had slept straight through her alarm. Arriving at work late, she'd frenziedly set right in to finish two orders due that morning, without having so much as a cup of instant coffee.

"Exactly what I thought. Well, help has arrived, so stand aside. I had to be down at the docks myself before dawn, so I thought we might as well have breakfast together."

He strode across the store as he talked, angling his narrow hips past the counter, balancing the basket in front of him. He slid by a hypnotized Frankie and went straight on into the workroom.

She stared as he shook out a gleaming white linen cloth and spread it on an unused section of her table. With swift, practiced movements he brought out huge white napkins, two china plates, cutlery and two delicate stemmed glasses that he filled with chilled juice from one of the silver carafes he unpacked. There were two enormous coffee mugs and several steaming containers of food that gave off a mouth-watering aroma, as well as assorted small bags of pastries and bread.

"Grab a couple of chairs for us, woman, and come sit down," he ordered. "Everything's hot." Dazed, she obeyed.

"Now, we'll start with fruit. Berry salad with some of this creamy fruit dressing. And a croissant . . . good, they're still warm." He lavishly buttered two, handing her one and taking one himself.

He looked freshly scrubbed, incredibly handsome, wide-awake and inordinately pleased with his surprise.

She felt caught off guard, sluggish from lack of sleep, aware that her makeup this morning had been a poke with a lipstick and a fast pass with a mascara wand on eyes that wouldn't quite open enough. And she'd barely run a brush through her hair since it dried after her hasty shower.

She'd have worn her cream silk blouse if she'd known, damn it all, instead of this cotton T-shirt. And she had her oldest, most comfortable shoes on instead of her smart black flats. She felt irritated all of a sudden, annoyed that he'd obviously had a long and solid night's sleep while she tossed and turned and agonized.

Over him, if the truth were told.

It made her tone more than a little caustic. "Eric, is this some yuppie version of Meals on Wheels you're starting here?"

She was sorry right away, because a little of the shiny happiness faded from his face and he looked a bit uncertain. "I thought about you working so hard and probably not taking time for breakfast in the morning. This was totally spur-of-the-moment. I hope you don't mind?"

"No. I guess not." That sounded grudging, and she felt ashamed of herself. "Not at all. I was just . . . taken by surprise. I've never had a breakfast picnic before. It's very, very romantic."

She sipped the chilled juice and bit daintily into her croissant, getting used to the idea of having him across the table from her. This whole thing was quite nice, if she didn't think too much.

C'mon, Frankie. This whole thing was mind-boggling. No man had ever gone to this much trouble for her before.

"These taste wonderful." She smiled at him with her eyes as well as her lips. "Thanks, Eric. For doing this for me."

He winked at her, and she noticed how long his eyelashes were.

He was serving generous portions of a creamy egg dish, and Frankie forgot the eyelashes and realized she was good and hungry. She attacked the food with honest appetite and welcomed seconds, listening all the while she ate for the tinkling of the shop bell that would warn of Auntie Rosina's arrival. But by some miracle, it didn't come. Maybe Eric had woven a spell over the shop so time would stand still for a little while.

The coffee was hot and strong, and by the time she had her second cup, Frankie felt human again.

"Now, perhaps we should discuss this menu thing." He drew a paper from his pocket and unfolded it. "I've come up with another version. Perhaps you'd glance over it and see if you think it would please your mother?" One eyebrow tilted up in an endearing way.

Frankie took the paper, and their hands touched briefly. She felt the contact right down to the toes of her comfortable shoes, and she shivered.

"Because," he began, and now there wasn't a trace of humor in his voice, "I want to warn you that from now on I won't pretend to be seeing you over this catering job. I want us to get to know each other, man and woman, no hiding behind the wedding dinner as an excuse. You understand what I'm saying, Frankie?"

She understood all right. And right then, instinct told her that she ought to run as far from him as she could get, right now. She should resist him, avoid him, keep him at all costs out of her life. Otherwise . . .

Otherwise what? Her life might never be the same again? Her fledgling business would suffer? Her mortgage might never get paid?

All of the above. She had obligations, she had promises to keep. Panic filled her.

She wanted him to kiss her.

She scanned the detailed menu plan, wondering what in blazing hell he expected her to answer, then took refuge in the business end of it. "It looks great to me, but then, the other one did, too. I'll have to give it to Mamma and see what she thinks." She added in a deliberate way, "Then I'm going to tell her that she should deal directly with you, Eric. She doesn't need me along. Her English is fine, and she knows you now, so—"

"Are you telling me you don't want to see me again?"

He was straightforward, she'd give him that. Like a bulldozer.

And was that what she was saying?

God help her, it ought to be. But she heard her treacherous mouth giving a different message directly. "No, I don't mean that. Yes, I'd like to see you again."

Mother of God, was she possessed?

The smile he gave her was breathtaking. He moved with grace and speed around the table and had just taken her in his arms when the bell in the outer shop tinkled and a cheerful, high-pitched voice hollered, "Francesca, Frankie, *buon giorno.* It's Zia Rosina! Where is this marvelous hat of mine? I can't wait to try this *cappello* you make for me...."

Auntie Rosina had one hell of a sense of timing.

Chapter Four

"OH, MOTHER OF GOD, it's my aunt, here to pick up her hat." Frankie rolled her eyes heavenward in that typical exasperated gesture of hers that Eric found enchanting.

He held her for an instant longer, pressing a deliberate kiss on her full lips. The color rose in her cheeks, and her breath seemed to stop for an instant.

"Frankie? Francesca? Are you here, *cara?*"

"She'll be back here in a minute. Let me go...."

He did with reluctance.

Frankie snatched a hat form holding a dramatic, wide-brimmed, rose-colored straw hat off the far end of the table and dashed through the doorway into the shop.

"Frankie, aah, so beautiful..." A rapid explosion of Italian ensued, and with hardly a pause, another still longer and more emphatic exchange, little of it from Frankie.

Frankie's auntie sounded like a volatile and verbal lady, Eric thought with a grin. He poured himself another cup of coffee from the carafe. He'd have to go soon; he had to see the wholesaler and the greengrocer.

The kiss he'd stolen burned on his lips. This morning Frankie was like a volcano about to explode.

Those moments two nights before when he'd held her, kissed her, caressed her, had lingered in his thoughts, teasing him with the promise of what was hidden inside this responsive woman.

From the store came a series of oohs and aahs and a phrase, repeated often. "*Molto bene, magnifico,* Francesca."

Eric could only guess that meant Auntie liked her bonnet. He hoped she did, for Frankie's sake. Italian ladies could be difficult, he mused, thinking of Teresa and the wedding menu.

So could chefs. Gus had thrown a fit when Eric announced the changes he'd made to please Teresa. But he was eternally grateful to Teresa, regardless of how many problems she caused him, because she'd been the reason he met Frankie in the first place. And he planned, of course, to marry her daughter.

After a suitable courtship period. Frankie would need time to get used to the idea, he imagined.

Sounds from the other room floated in, Auntie's voice with an occasional short interjection from Frankie. He liked to listen to the husky richness of her voice speaking the dark, dramatic intonations of the Italian language.

He was going to have to learn to speak Italian.

Among a lot of other things. After he'd left her the other night, he'd spent a couple of hours planning how he was even going to find time to be with Frankie long enough to court her. He was a busy man, and she'd told him how frantic her own schedule was.

He was also a meticulous man when it came to planning strategy. His insistence on detail was, Eric felt, the secret of his business success. He had no doubts that the same methods would work in his campaign with Frankie.

He'd never seriously courted a woman before this, although more than a few had done their best at courting him. Football players got pretty used to being propositioned. He was a red-blooded male, and of course those efforts at seduction succeeded rather well at times.

But marriage? He'd been waiting a long time, because he wanted marriage, children, family life, more than anything else in the world. He'd planned for it most of his adult life, saving his money and investing it, buying a house and fixing it up.

But he was willing to wait until the right woman came along. He'd watched too many of his football buddies marry in haste and repent at leisure.

He'd always had a mental image of the perfect woman for him. He'd been certain he'd know her when he met her, and he had. The first moment he'd laid eyes on Frankie, he'd known she was the one. He'd fallen in love with her right there in his office.

Love at first sight.

Now he just had to make her fall in love with him, and that might take a bit of doing, but he'd damn well manage it. He knew he was attractive to women, but Frankie wasn't like most of the others he'd met. She was . . . unique.

What was she looking for in a man? He'd have to find that out, and soon. He'd have to learn everything he could about her.

And what about him? Was he what the society columns would label "an eminently eligible male"? Eric wasn't certain.

He was healthy, that was a good thing. A crooked grin came and went. His teeth were fine. That ought to count for something. He was pretty easygoing. He didn't consider himself brilliant, just a hard worker. Because of football, he had more money than most men his age, but that was more luck than anything. And a lot of prudent investing.

Well, maybe he had a lot of faults, but at least he recognized them. The major ones anyway. He admitted to being a little bit stubborn now and then, just a trifle single-minded, perhaps, especially when something he wanted was in question. He could be impatient, too.

Was he romantic? He'd always heard women wanted romance. Frankie had said the breakfast this morning was romantic.

The idea had popped into his mind when he was in the shower, and a quick call to his chef had set the plan in motion, but that was just practicality.

In order to court Frankie, he was going to have to steal moments like this, at odd times of the day, when his restaurant was quiet and her store was, as well.

The hat caper in the other room was still going on with no sign of an ending. He glanced at his watch and then quickly packed up the basket. There was a notepad by the phone. He thought a moment, frowning, then scribbled a few lines and folded the paper, putting it on the worktable where she'd be certain to find it.

FRANKIE'S BACK WAS toward him when he came through the doorway, and his eyes took in the lovely slim, sexy outline of her coltish hips and long legs. His body reacted, and he had to pause for a second before entering the store.

Frankie was leaning on the counter, suffering through an endless account of Rosina's hysterectomy and ensuing complications. She nodded at intervals and clucked her tongue while alternately thinking of Eric in the back room and mentally drawing the pattern for a special little hat she wanted to make for herself. When Rosina's mouth fell open in the middle of a sentence and her eyes grew round as marbles beneath the mad swoop of rosy hat brim, Frankie turned around.

Sure enough, Eric was standing in the doorway, an engaging grin aimed at her flustered aunt. "Hi, how's it going? Hey, that hat really does things for you, ma'am."

Frankie had to suppress an urge to giggle at the girlish blush that suffused her aunt's round face.

"Auntie Rosina, this is Eric Thorpe," she said.

Rosina inclined her head with a coquettish gesture and held out a plump hand. "*Ciao.* How do you do, Mr....um...Thorpe?"

The look she directed at Frankie contained at least forty urgent questions. Where had this fine-looking man sprung from? Why was Francesca hiding him in the back room? What relationship did he have to her niece? Why was he carrying a picnic basket when it wasn't even noon?

What exactly had been going on in that back room?

"I have to get back to work, Frankie. Ask your Mamma about that menu change we made and let me know, won't you?"

Eric understood Rosina's avid eye language, and he was providing Frankie with an alibi.

"I will. And tell your cook how much I enjoyed the breakfast he sent."

She waved a nonchalant hand as Eric said a casual goodbye to both of them, and when the door closed behind him and Rosina's mouth opened, Frankie said quickly, "Eric owns The Fifth Quarter, the restaurant that's doing the catering for Nick's wedding? Well, Mamma spent the day before yesterday changing her mind about the menu, so Eric came over here this morning to check out the new plan with me."

As she'd hoped it might, mention of Nick's wedding diverted Rosina for quite some time. Nick was marrying into St. Louis high society, and it was the talk of the family.

"How many bridesmaids? What colors have they chosen for the wedding? Have you seen the bride's gown? Such a beautiful girl, Teresa says. You're coming to the shower Bianca is having for her, no?"

Accustomed to Rosina's rapid-fire questions, Frankie dealt with them one at a time.

"Six bridesmaids, me included, and it's going to be in tones of dusty rose, peach and gray. And no, I haven't seen the gown yet. You should ask Diane about it at the shower. It's next weekend, right?"

"Saturday, at seven-thirty. You want I should pick you up?"

"No, Rosina, but thanks anyway. I'll probably be a little late. The shop's busy on weekends."

Frankie had forgotten all about the shower, probably because it was the third one she'd been invited to. And that was only on the Granatelli side; she knew from her mother that there'd been at least four others arranged by Bauer friends and relatives, plus numerous luncheons and several parties.

Poor Diane, having to live through all these social events. She must be showered to death by now, yet each time Frankie saw her, Nick's bride-to-be was more radiant than the last.

Better her than me, Frankie reflected grimly.

"She works in New York, this Diane?"

Rosina was determined to extract every last morsel.

"Yes, she has her own business. She conducts walking tours of the city for tourists, Rosina."

"So she'll fly up here for the shower, and then back to New York again? This doesn't give the family much chance to get to know her, Frankie, this fly in, fly out affair."

Infinitely weary of the inquisition, Frankie steeled herself to be polite. "She's busy, she's a businesswoman, like I am. There'll be years to get acquainted with the family. She's absolutely perfect for Nicky, and that's all that matters, isn't it?"

"Oh, to be sure." Rosina dropped that line of questioning and instantly found another. "And the bride's mother, what is she wearing?"

Frankie admitted ignorance to that and four more questions like it, and at last Rosina wore down about the bride and her family. She seemed about to return to the subject of Eric, so Frankie narrowed her eyes, stared hard at her aunt and frowned.

"What? What is it, Francesca?"

"You know, Auntie, that hat isn't quite right for some reason. I think the brim needs a touch more of a curve to it. Come on in the back and have a coffee while I fix it, okay?"

ROSINA HAD, after several aeons and four cups of coffee, finally paid for her hat and left. The owner of the second order came, paid and left right away, for which Frankie was eternally grateful. Two more customers came into the shop, and after an interminable time, one of them bought an Indian-print cloche.

When they left, too, Frankie made a trip to the bathroom, where she splashed cool water on her face, gave her tumbled hair a ruthless brushing and did a decent job of her makeup. As if it mattered what she looked like, now that Eric was gone.

She was back in the workroom, using the steamer on a stubborn hat crown, when the folded paper caught her attention. She read the large, clear scrawl.

This entitles the bearer to a moonlight stroll along
the river and a hamburger at a secret location.
Pick you up at seven tonight? E.

"Damn." Frankie crumpled the note and threw it as hard as she could at the wall, then followed with a few imaginative and descriptive Italian phrases.

Why did he have to be so sexy, so irresistible, so thoughtful, so persistent . . . so everything she didn't need in a man? Why couldn't he have come along when she was . . . oh, say forty-one? When her business was established; when she had some free time.

And why was she letting it upset her this way? Surely a liberated woman of the nineties could handle a little romance in her life. A liberated woman of any era, for that matter.

What would dear old Migs have said? What would she have done? Hadn't she said that a career and a love affair were possible? That it was marriage she balked at?

Migs would have suggested Frankie have an affair, no doubt about that. The woman had still been having discreet love affairs when she died, and she was well up in her seventies. Migs believed that men and women were put on this earth to give each other pleasure, and she often said she saw no reason to complicate things with legal contracts.

Thank you, Migs. Frankie blew a kiss into the air over the worktable, then went over and retrieved Eric's note. She used her hot iron to smooth out the creases.

There was not a thing wrong with just having a short-term affair with Eric, and the more she thought about it, the more appealing the idea became. In fact, she'd find a way to suggest it to him. The sooner the better.

Tonight, maybe?

Tonight, yes.

Chapter Five

"SO WHERE'S THIS secret hamburger place you're taking me for supper, sir?"

They were strolling along the banks of the Mississippi River near Laclede's Landing, and Frankie thought maybe he was planning on taking her to one of the funky little restaurants the Landing was famous for. They'd been walking for an hour, and he'd made her laugh so hard with tales of his football days, her stomach was sore.

"If I tell you where we're going, it won't be a surprise, right?"

The rain of the past few days was gone, and twilight lingered as if it were summer instead of early spring. There was a gentle mist on the water, and the paddle wheelers that were docked nearby rose out of it like eerie monoliths from the past. Frankie could hear a dixieland band tuning up on one of the vessels, preparing for the dinner cruise about to embark.

"Are you hungry?" Eric had her hand clasped firmly in his own.

Frankie nodded. "Starving." She gave a lighthearted little skip and laughed up at him with sparkling eyes.

"Let's head back to the car, then. It's only a short drive."

Ever since she'd made up her mind that afternoon about having an affair with Eric, she'd been in high spirits. She'd sold two more hats and taken orders for another three, which made the day a huge success as far as her business went, and she'd hurried home at closing time to have a hot bath and fix herself up for him.

Hamburgers meant casual, so she'd tugged on her favorite faded jeans over the skimpiest, sexiest coffee-colored lace teddy she owned. On top she wore an antique silk buccaneer's shirt she'd found in a theatrical costume shop, one shade darker than the teddy. She left the buttons undone enough so that the lace underneath showed, and slipped on a tapestry vest. Her brown leather boots were next. Then a pair of huge gold hoops in her ears completed the look, and she brushed her hair until it gleamed, pulling it up and tying it with a brown paisley scarf at the crown of her head so it spilled down over her back in tangled waves.

It was worth the fussing. Eric's eyes widened and swept over her when he arrived at her door promptly at seven.

"You're lovely, Funny Face," was all he'd said, but his gruff and urgent tone made gooseflesh run up her arms.

"How can I be lovely and have a funny face at the same time?" she teased, loving the label he'd given her.

"It I told you how beautiful you really are, you'd get a swollen head and none of your hats would fit."

"C'mon, you silver-tongued devil. Let's get out of here before the blarney gets unbearable."

Everything was going to be perfect tonight.

SHE GREW MORE AND MORE curious during the drive, but Eric still wouldn't tell her where they were going. He was heading toward the university, and she couldn't imagine where he was taking her. At last he turned into the circular drive of an old stone house in a residential area, stopped the car and came around and opened her door.

"Eric, we're not meeting people, are we? Whose house is this?"

She felt disappointed, apprehensive. She'd thought only of the two of them being alone together. She didn't want to have to make polite social noises tonight.

"It's my house, and I live here alone. C'mon in."

It hadn't crossed her mind that he might have a house like this. An apartment, certainly, or even a town house, with black satin sheets and a Jacuzzi. But for a bachelor to want to live in this family sort of place . . .

A disquieting thought struck her. "Were you married before, Eric? Is this where . . ."

He was leading the way up the front steps, unlocking the door, drawing her into a formal entrance hall, and his laugh echoed from the high ceilings. "Nope, never been married, honest. I bought this all on my own several years ago. Had to do a lot of fixing—these old places have awful wiring and plumbing—but it's nearly all working now. Give me your jacket and come in the kitchen, and I'll get our food started."

"Are you fixing it up to sell, then?" Maybe his hobby was renovation.

"God, no. I'd never do all this work just to sell to someone else. Nope, I always wanted roots, a home of my own, and when I first saw this place, I knew I'd found what I was looking for."

Mesmerized, she followed along behind him. There was lots of space all right. In several places the walls still showed signs of the work he'd done, plaster ripped out in jagged holes where wires or pipes showed through.

The furniture was nothing special, just well-worn and comfortable looking. The few pictures were all of football teams, and there were silver trophies on the mantelpiece in the living room.

Generally, the entire place was badly in need of paint, but when they reached the kitchen, Frankie could see where Eric had placed the most emphasis. Everything here was spanking clean, new and shiny, the walls sporting cheerful wallpaper with huge yellow sunflowers.

Copper-bottom pots hung from hooks above the efficient island work space, and ceramic crocks held every tool known to cookery. Frankie counted three different ovens, a dishwasher, professional juicers and choppers and beaters and an entire shelf of cookbooks. There was the most complete spice rack Frankie had seen outside of her mother's kitchen.

It threatened to make her break out in hives.

She'd watched female relatives cooking their brains out all of her life, and she'd vowed early on that she'd never learn more than the basics—like how to make tea. She hadn't, either, much to her mother's everlasting humiliation.

Eric was watching her, obviously waiting for a reaction. Well, no point in misleading him. She wrinkled her nose and shook her head, giving him a rueful grin. "I can see you've done a lot of work in here, but I have to tell you right up front that I hate and despise kitchens," she announced. "I also don't cook—I can barely make toast. I'm an unnatural Italian woman."

It didn't faze him at all. "Well, I'm good at it. It's my hobby, so there's no problem, is there?" He opened a cupboard, took out a bottle of red wine and poured some into a stemmed glass. "Why not take this and go wander through the rest of the house while I get our burgers under way?"

She took his advice.

The place was huge, and the more she saw of it, the more uncomfortable she became. Every room she peeked into, everywhere she turned, the silent message of Eric's house became clearer.

Family home, it trumpeted. Why else would a single man need five bedrooms, three full baths and two ensuite powder rooms, a huge activity room and a pool—empty now—in the spacious, fenced backyard? To say nothing of a full-sized deck and a barbecue big enough to roast half an elephant.

It was scary. He had no relatives, but she had the distinct feeling she'd been brought home to meet his house instead.

The only area she really liked was Eric's bedroom. It was a large, south-facing room at the top of the house. He'd paneled one long wall with rough-grained cedar, so it gave the feeling of a log cabin.

He had a king-size water bed and a goose-down comforter much like her own, except the cover on his was a masculine brown-and-black print. A stereo system was built into the headboard, and huge furry rugs were scattered over the brown woolly carpeting. His white terry bathrobe was slung carelessly over a chair, and a biography of some sports figure lay on the bedside table.

It didn't take much for her to imagine lying with him on that floating, undulating mattress, having him take her clothes off with slow, deliberate intent. Then she fantasized about taking off every stitch of her own clothes, wrapping herself in his robe and hiding in his bed until he came to find her, to heck with dinner.

Good idea, except that she couldn't bring herself to be that brazen.

She caught a glimpse of herself in the dresser mirror and pulled the corners of her lips down into a grimace of regret. She was still far too much the well-brought-up Italian daughter to do anything that wild, but the idea made her heart hammer.

Frankie still had to find a way to broach her idea of an affair, and even the thought of that made her lose her nerve. Then she had to grin at herself again. The men she'd known before Eric had been miles ahead of her at suggesting such things, and most of the time she'd had to figure out how to refuse without being cruel. She'd never dreamed a time would come when she'd be the one with the proposition.

The times, they were a-changing.

She was back downstairs, sipping her wine and staring out the wide bay windows in the living room, when Eric came up behind her.

"Food's ready," he said, putting an arm around her shoulders and guiding her into the dining room, where he'd laid a wooden table with mats and plates and cutlery. There was even a rose in a water glass.

And oh, how that man could cook.

THE FIRE ERIC HAD LIT in the living room fireplace, and one soft lamp in a corner provided all the light in the room. Frankie was intensely conscious of Eric, sprawled in an armchair a few feet away from the sofa where she'd been lounging since they finished dinner.

"That was incredible sauce on the burgers, Eric. I'm so full my stomach hurts," she groaned. "Where did you learn to make cheesecake like that?"

"A lady called Estelle taught me. She's my best friend's mother. His name's Danville Taylor—he's running back for the Falcons."

"Oh." Whatever a running back might be. Or a Falcon, for that matter.

"What you do is, you take a can of sweetened condensed milk and a package of cream cheese, and you mix it with lemon juice. And then..."

Frankie felt like shrieking at him. She didn't want the recipe for cheesecake, and she was getting more irritated by the moment. When was this man going to make a move on her, she'd like to know.

Here she was, aching to have him take her in his arms, kiss her, and there he sat, being the perfect gentleman and talking about somebody's mother's cheesecake recipe, for gosh sake. And every time their eyes made contact, it was like having him touch her. Intimately touch her.

IF HE TOUCHED HER AT ALL, things would be out of control within seconds, Eric knew. From the moment he'd picked her up tonight his desire had raged and flared, and been damped down so often and so ruthlessly that he felt as exhausted as if he'd played a full game against the Chicago Bears.

Hell. He didn't want her to think he'd brought her here, to his house, just to seduce her. But watching her in the flickering light from the fire, with that tantalizing bit of lacy cleavage showing, with those damn tight jeans outlining her hips and bottom like a second skin, he wanted her almost more than he could stand.

"How about some music?" He got to his feet in a desperate effort to distract himself.

"Eric." Her voice was husky and cajoling. "Turn on the music, sure, but then come over here and sit beside me. Please, Eric?"

Finally his arms were around her, and she sighed with pleasure as his lips came down on hers. The sigh became a gasp as he captured her mouth with a wild, urgent passion that brought her own need racing up from the depths of her being to meet the intensity of his kiss.

His huge muscles were quivering under her touch, and she slid her hands over his shoulders, down his chest, feeling the tumultuous pounding of his heart beneath her fingers. His hands, flat on her back, pulled her closer to him, and he put his feet up and stretched out on the sofa until she was cradled on top of him, her legs between his, bodies separated only by the roughness of jeans.

"Frankie..." He breathed her name in a voice half-choked with hunger. "If you want this to stop, you'd better say so now, because in another few minutes..."

His body was hard and pulsing beneath her thighs, and her own desire was a spiral of heat and need. She moved her pelvis against him, unable to control the instinctive gesture, and he cursed softly. "Frankie?" The query was rough and desperate. His breathing came in shallow gasps, but he retained control. "Is this what you want?"

He was letting her make the final decision, and now that the moment was here, she was filled with joy. Actions were so much more effective than words. She didn't have to struggle through a discussion about an affair after all. She could simply embark on one, right here and now.

She had one moment of awful hesitation, but she reminded herself of her decision. This was right, this was what she'd planned and wanted, wasn't it? Never before had anything felt as inevitable as this.

Being in his arms felt like coming home after a long and difficult journey. Beyond the passion there was also the strangest sense of safety.

Slowly she forced herself to relax. "Yes, Eric. Yes," she whispered close to his ear. "Love me, please."

Chapter Six

SHE FELT WARM AND SMOOTH, all curves and gentle planes and tantalizing hollows. He was rough and rock hard, with muscles that quivered beneath her exploring fingers.

"Let's get rid of these clothes...."

Despite the urgency they both felt, he undressed her slowly, with exquisite care, sitting up so he could unbutton the silky shirt and slide it off her shoulders.

"Damn, my fingers are too big for these buttons." His hands were shaking a bit, and he had to struggle with the tiny things. He followed the slowly opening pathway with his lips, making her gasp as his hot mouth trailed across her sensitive skin.

"This . . ." he breathed, running his fingers over the satiny texture of her camisole. "You wicked tease, you let this thing show just to drive me insane, didn't you?"

She nodded, and the green of his eyes deepened to emerald at the sexiness of her smile. His lips found the nipples barely covered now by silken lace, and he teased each swollen tip with his tongue until she writhed.

"I need you to want me, Frankie."

"I do. I do want you, more than I can say...."

At last the silky garment slid to her waist, and the breath in his lungs went with it as his eyes devoured her breasts, full and lush. "God, you're beautiful. I can't believe how lovely you are."

His words filled her with a special pleasure, because she'd always considered her baby sister the only beautiful one in the family.

With consummate gentleness he undid the scarf that held her hair back. He combed his fingers through the thick, golden mass and spread it over her naked shoulders. Then he took her aching breasts in his palms and cradled them, fondling her nipples with his thumbs, making them throb and pulse beneath his touch.

He was a wonderful lover, slow and gentle.

She was greedy. The wanting was a compelling ache, a need growing to insane proportions inside of her. "Eric, hurry...."

"Patience, love. Let's take it slow and easy. I want to enjoy every inch of you."

She couldn't be patient at all. Her breath was coming in short gasps, and her body was heated and moist, anticipating him. She grasped the bottom of his shirt and pulled it up and quickly over his head, needing to have him naked with her.

A mat of soft curls covered his broad chest, and she ran her hands over him, loving the feel of his heated flesh beneath the silky hair, feeling the powerful muscles flex beneath his skin. She found the hardened tips of his male nipples and teased them with her fingers, echoing what he was doing to her.

His sharp intake of breath told her how that affected him.

His hands dropped, found the snap of her jeans. He sat up, and in an instant he'd skinned them down and off, taking the scrap of lace pantie she wore with them. He stood up then and undid his own pants, his fiery gaze devouring her.

He was swollen and ready. His arousal sent a wave of awful wanting into her deepest parts.

"Come here, slide down beside me," he commanded, drawing her into his embrace, and then they were tangled in each other's arms on the soft rug in front of the fire, and there was no more gentleness in his touch.

All was urgency and fire and raw need. The feel of his huge, muscular body against her own made her dizzy with longing.

"Eric, *mio caro...*"

She opened every part of herself to him, welcoming the pressure of his clever fingers on tender, pulsing flesh, running her hands over his face and hair and body, murmuring lost phrases, unaware that she spoke in the soft and lilting language of her heritage, unaware, too, that her hands were shaking, her whole body trembling against his.

"Eric, please. I can't stand it unless you love me now...."

With the last shred of control, he drew away long enough to make certain she was protected, and then her long, restless legs wound around him, her slender arms imprisoned him, locking him to her in the dance of love.

Her body took him in, drew him deep into burning ecstasy. Her soul welcomed him.

Her need grew and grew with each long, shuddering entry, each pulsing withdrawal.

With fulfillment only a movement away, he paused, holding her quivering on the brink, nearly mad with wanting. "Frankie, be still. Don't move," he ordered with fierce insistence. "Do you—" His breath was harsh and shallow, his face starkly beautiful with the strain of holding back, the intensity of what he had to ask "—believe in love—" She groaned and moved just a little, and he shut his eyes tight and held his breath for a precarious instant before he could speak again, his voice hoarse "—at first sight?"

But she was beyond speech. She drew his head down and kissed him with frantic desperation, telling him with her mouth what was happening in her body, the glory that was beginning

It was too late for words.

He filled her one last time, and then they were lost together, spinning into the inferno.

"ERIC, THIS IS a disaster area. How many operations did you have on this knee, anyway?" Frankie touched his leg with gentle tenderness, loving the texture of hair-roughened skin, horrified at the crisscrossing of scars and the mass of damaged tissue that made up his right knee.

They were sprawled on the rug, and Eric had just put another log on the embers of the fire.

"Four. Knee problems are an occupational hazard in pro football. You're not getting cold, are you?" He reached up, took a soft plaid blanket off the end of the sofa and wrapped it around her, resting his back against the sofa and cradling her in his arms.

"Actually, the knee works pretty good, as long as I stay away from pro football or skiing. It won't make me a cripple or anything, when we get older."

She felt euphoric, filled with peace and happiness. She refused to be alarmed by his words. "It doesn't interfere with your lovemaking, that's for sure. It was glorious," she purred, and his arms tightened around her.

"It was better than that," he agreed with a total lack of modesty. She giggled and swatted him, but when he went on, she could tell that he'd become serious.

"I hadn't planned for this to happen quite yet. See, I wanted to be sure you knew that this is no casual affair with me, Frankie. You do know that, don't you?"

Warning bells sounded in her head, and she tried to laugh. "Hey, you don't have to reassure me, I'm a grown-up lady. And I was the one—" she began, but he interrupted.

"Don't make a joke of it, this is important. Do you remember what I asked you, when we were making love a few minutes ago?"

She'd shoved the words to the back of her mind, afraid to examine them. But she knew exactly what he was talking about, and it scared the hell out of her.

"I asked you if you believed in love at first sight," he reminded her with stubborn persistence. He took her chin in his palm and turned her face tenderly so that she had to look at him. His thumb rubbed across her swollen bottom lip with tender strokes.

"I fell in love with you the first moment I met you, don't you know that? Didn't you feel it? I want to spend my life with you, Frankie."

Horrified, she opened her mouth to say something, but he placed two fingers over her lips and shook his head. "Don't go making that funny face at me. I know, we have a lot of time to spend together before we discuss anything this serious," he said in a low, earnest tone. "We need to get to know each other in other ways. I'm aware of that. But because this happened tonight—and because it's going to go on happening, seeing

that I can't keep my hands off you—then I think you deserve
to know how I feel, right up front."

His beautiful eyes were filled with a soft light, and his honesty, his gallantry, pierced her heart with its sweetness. He was
unique, he was stating his intentions like a gentleman from
another era, he was ... Something snapped inside of her, and
she struggled to sit up straight, to think instead of feel. He was
telling her he wanted the whole catastrophe, wasn't he?

Marriage.

This house, those empty bedrooms upstairs—he'd want
babies, lots of them.

She'd never get her father paid off, pregnant all the time.

Get out of this now, Frankie, her rational brain counselled.
*He's sweet and funny and generous, and so damned honest, and
you're going to hurt him in the end.*

You're going to hurt yourself.

His arms came around her from the back, his lips nibbled
at her earlobe, and an involuntary shudder went through her.
This lovemaking between them. Addictive, explosive, un-
believably beautiful. She couldn't walk away from this, not
yet. Not quite yet. Not tonight, anyway.

But she couldn't mislead him, either. Could she?

"You're ... you're going way too fast for me," she managed to stammer. "I'm ... not ready to think about anything
serious. I told you how I felt about the store. Well, I've also
got a mortgage on it, with my father, and until I get that paid
off I have to put all my energies into the Hatter ..."

His lips were trailing kisses down her spine, and she couldn't
remember what she was trying to say. The blanket was slipping down and down.

"Of course you're not ready yet," he agreed in a hoarse
voice, nibbling at a vulnerable spot below her shoulder blades.
"We won't talk about it again until you're ready, I promise.
But I want to be a part of your life, Frankie. This is enough
for right now...." His hands crept around her front, settled
on her breasts, and she felt herself melting, her nipples growing hard at his touch. A spasm of awful wanting shook her to

the core of her being, and a low, tortured moan came from him.

"Frankie, why don't you turn around and kiss me?"

AFTERWARD, FRANKIE COULD remember little about the remaining days in that magic month of April. But the nights stayed etched in her memory—long nights wrapped in Eric's arms; nights perfumed with the heavy, intoxicating odor of their lovemaking, punctuated by the sound of their passion as well as their laughter, by confidences shared in the aftermath of ecstasy.

He was romantic, and caring, and passionate, and gentle.

He was thoughtful. When she insisted she couldn't see him for a while because the store accounts were in a miserable state and she had to do them even though she hated and despised bookkeeping, he came over and did them for her, working in the early morning hours after his restaurant was closed, and after they'd made love.

He was a whiz at bookkeeping, and he found two areas where she was being taxed for things she shouldn't have been. He saved her an appreciable amount of money.

And on top of all that, he really did love to cook. He even put her apartment kitchen in order and added spices and strange tins and boxes to her instant-soup supply.

That was the positive side of Eric Thorpe.

There was also a negative, and as the month of May blossomed and grew, the disturbing aspects began to bother Frankie more and more. For instance, Eric went right on talking about marriage and commitment every single time he found an opening. He went right on asking her what exactly it was she didn't like about his house, and what kind of house she did want, eventually. Because, he assured her, he'd buy her the one that pleased her. He went right on believing there was a forever after just ahead of them.

Frankie went right on sidestepping every reference he made to their future, but it was becoming more difficult all the time.

Eric, Frankie told herself irritably, was pigheaded, single-minded, stubborn and impossible to sidetrack for very long.

He was an infuriating, maddening man, and he was about as subtle as a Mack truck. He told her all the time, right out, that he loved her, for God's sake. Worst of all, on a gut level she refused to face outside of her troubled dreams, she also knew that she was falling in love with him.

She never told him, though.

In fact, if she were truthful with herself—and she made sure she never was, outside of those same dreams—she'd have had to admit that she'd been hopelessly in love for a very long time.

Probably since the first time she'd ever laid eyes on Eric Thorpe, on the tenth of April, in his office, with her mother beside her worrying about the damned menu for Nick's wedding.

It wasn't her mother on the phone that night in mid-May, however. It was her father, Dom Granatelli.

Eric had driven her home after the shop closed so she could change for dinner, but she hadn't managed to get dressed. In fact, she was totally undressed, as was Eric.

"Oh, hi, Papa." Frankie moved out of Eric's embrace so fast she almost knocked the phone off the bedside table.

"Yeah, Papa, I'm doing great. The store is doing fine— didn't you get the check I sent? Oh, good. No, no problems, I've just been awfully...busy." She tugged a sheet up over her breasts, as if Dom could see her scarlet face as well as hear her voice.

"Yeah, I know it's Mamma's birthday on Friday. Sophia called me about the party this morning. Of course I'm going to be there, Papa, what do you think?"

Familiar irritation filled her as her father reiterated just how long it had been since she'd come to the restaurant or the house, and how the family was worried about her, and how he understood what it was like when you were young, how time slipped past. But Mamma—Mamma wasn't like him. She needed to see her children now and then, no?

"But, Papa, I talk to Mamma a dozen times a day on the telephone."

Mostly over the dratted menu, which was threatening to put them all in the psych ward. She and Eric had just gone over the twenty-third revision, and still Mamma wasn't satisfied.

But the telephone, it just wasn't the same as having dinner together, Dom insisted. They missed Frankie. And then he added in a sly tone that he had heard there was a young man she was seeing. A cousin had just happened to glimpse them at the grocery store. Why not bring him along, the more the better?

So this was the whole point of the call. The family thought they were missing out on some juicy bit of gossip about her and Eric.

Frankie damped down her frustration and anger. She made noncommittal noises, trying not to let Eric know what was going on and seething inside at her father's nosiness.

At long last, Dom hung up. Frankie banged the receiver down and plopped back into bed, rolling her eyes and expelling a huge sigh.

"Your father?" Eric was propped on the pillows, hands behind his head, staring up at the ceiling.

"Yeah." She was on edge from the call, and she didn't notice the unusual tension in his voice at first.

"It's about your mother's birthday, I take it."

"Yeah."

There was a long moment of charged silence, and at last she turned and looked at him, frowning. He was so even-tempered, so good-natured, it took her a while to realize how angry he was. He was breathing hard, and his lips were compressed into a thin line.

"What's the matter, Eric?"

She knew, though, even before she asked.

"You're not going to invite me along to introduce me to the rest of your family, are you, Frankie? I'm right here in your apartment, in your bed with you, but you didn't mention to your father that anyone was here."

She bristled. "What do you expect, that I'll tell my father you're in bed with me right this minute? He'd be over here with a shotgun. Really, Eric, be reasonable."

But she knew he was right. She had avoided mentioning him or having him meet the rest of her family. She hadn't even realized how aware he was of her sidestepping or how much he cared.

Suddenly she felt hot and uncomfortable and guilty. She reached over to stroke his face, but he caught her hand and held it in a grip of steel, turning so she could see the fuming anger and the raw hurt on his face and in his eyes.

It startled and frightened her, and she stammered, "It's not—it's just this . . . this family of mine, Eric—you have to understand how it is with them. . . ."

"I'm trying to understand how it is with you, Frankie, and that's what bothers me." He swung his legs off the bed and started pulling on his underwear, his jeans.

"Where are you going?" She'd expected him to stay all night. She felt frightened, and deserted, and defensive.

"You make me feel like a gigolo—great in bed, but not important enough to include in the rest of your life. You talked to your sister the same way on the phone the other day, with me right beside you, and you never once mentioned my name. Last week I heard you turn down that invitation to your uncle's for dinner. We could have gone, but you made excuses. Why, Frankie? Have I got halitosis or warts or something? Are you ashamed of me?"

"No." She leaped off the bed, dragging a cotton robe around her naked body. "No, of course not. Eric, don't be ridiculous, it has nothing to do with you. For God's sake, you don't understand how it is with my family. They jump to conclusions, they gossip, they make demands, they assume—"

"So what's to assume?" His voice was dangerously quiet. He was fully dressed, and she didn't want him to leave. Not like this, angry and hurt. It frightened her, the thought of his leaving. It horrified her that he would think she could ever be ashamed of him.

Mother of God, she was in love with him. The conscious knowledge slammed into her awareness like a belly punch.

It was on the tip of her tongue to tell him, but he stood looking at her with such a stony, closed expression that she couldn't find her voice.

"I'm not playing any games with you, Frankie," he said at last in a soft, lethal voice. "Maybe you ought to figure out exactly what it is you want from me. God knows I've told you how I feel enough times."

He turned on his heel and grabbed his jacket from the chair. A heartbeat later, she heard the apartment door close, and he was gone.

Chapter Seven

ERIC CURSED HIMSELF all during the drive home. He'd meant what he said, but maybe he was pushing her too hard, too fast. Hadn't he promised her time? Sure, he'd got his feelings hurt. It was because he loved her, but he had no business making such an issue about meeting her family. There was a whole lifetime for that.

Why had he let his pride get the better of his good sense? Especially when he knew sweet nothing about how families operated anyhow.

His house felt bleak and utterly empty when he walked in, and he was heading for the phone to call Frankie when it rang.

"Eric?" Her voice, usually full of vibrancy, sounded small and insecure. "Eric, I'm really sorry. I never meant to hurt you. I just have this thing about my family knowing everything about me all the time. It makes me crazy. It has nothing to do with my feelings about you. I'm sorry I hurt you."

Every remnant of anger melted away. "Honey, I'm sorry, too. It wasn't fair of me to make an issue over your family." He glanced at his watch. "Look, it's only eleven-thirty. You want me to drive back over there?"

There was a tiny silence. "Yes, I do, please. I want you here. And, Eric?"

"What, Frankie?"

"Hurry, okay?"

IT WAS at the semiannual meeting of the St. Louis Association of Restaurateurs that Eric finally met Dom Granatelli.

The meeting was held on a Thursday afternoon, the third week in May. When the business portion of the meeting ended, old friends and business associates moved from their seats to meet and talk.

Eric knew Dom Granatelli by reputation. Everyone in the restaurant business respected the man who'd managed to retain the popularity and high standards of Granatelli's year after year.

Eric had noticed the dark, penetrating glances the patriarch had been shooting at him all during the lengthy meeting. He'd have had to be blind not to. Obviously Frankie's father had heard that his daughter was dating the caterer for his son's wedding, and to Eric, the glowering looks conveyed clearly that the older man wasn't too pleased about it.

At the first opportunity, Eric shouldered his way through the crowd, over to the jovial group surrounding Granatelli. Then he just stood there, using his size, his physical presence, to create awareness in the crowd.

Eric made deliberate eye contact. "How do you do, sir? I'm Eric Thorpe—I'm handling the catering for your son's wedding next month."

Physically Eric towered over the older man, but Dom Granatelli also had presence, a kind of massive dignity that made him seem larger than life. He had a florid complexion, handsome regular features and a swashbuckling mustache, as snow-white as the thick, wavy hair on his head.

"Dom Granatelli, pleased to meet you." He didn't sound it, although he shook the hand Eric proffered.

Dom's grip was strong and aggressive. At close range, Eric could see the resemblance between father and daughter, the same stubborn chin, the same deep-set, flashing brown eyes. Eric could feel those eyes assessing him, taking his measure. Dom Granatelli would be a formidable opponent, he decided.

"My wife, Teresa, she has mentioned you to me. The food for the wedding, it's all arranged now, yes?"

"Almost," Eric lied. Teresa had turned out to be a challenge, all right. She'd refused to go along with Frankie's suggestion that she deal directly with Eric, and Frankie had just as adamantly refused to waste more time on meetings. So Eric now made up endless lists and gave them to Frankie to give to Teresa.

Teresa had changed her mind again and again. Gus was threatening murder, and at times Eric was heartily sorry he'd ever gotten near the catering end of the food business.

"Good, good. So that's no problem, then." The older man's voice was cool, his manner remote.

The problem was obviously Eric's relationship with Dom's daughter. Eric was convinced that somehow Dom Granatelli knew all about the passionate nights the two had spent together. Maybe fathers had a sixth sense about these things.

It was also clear to Eric that Dom was very much an old-fashioned Italian papa. Without saying a word, he made Eric understand that if he, Eric Thorpe, was trifling with Francesca's affections, there would be hell to pay as far as Dom was concerned.

Somehow Eric had to set the record straight.

"Mr. Granatelli, would you have a drink with me?" Eric had decided there was only one play possible here—a direct run down the middle of the field. The game was far too important for fancy moves.

Dom looked as if he were about to refuse.

"Somewhere quiet, maybe. I'd like to have a private talk with you."

Dom hesitated. The group that had surrounded him was melting away, sensing there was serious business between these two. At last, after fixing Eric with a long, unsettling stare, Granatelli inclined his head, accepting the invitation with grudging impatience.

The hotel where the meeting was held had a small, intimate bar just off the lobby. At Eric's suggestion, they made their way there. Dom ordered beer, and Eric did, as well.

When it arrived, Eric took a long draw on his and said, "Mr. Granatelli, I've been dating your daughter Frankie for about six weeks now." He'd decided the best thing to do was take the ball and run it.

Dom inclined his head in a formal, regal gesture that didn't signal acceptance or agreement, only acknowledgment.

Eric took another long slug and consciously tried to relax his knotted muscles. He was gripping the beer mug so tightly he was afraid it might shatter. Damn, this was not the easiest man in the world to have a chat with.

"The thing is, I'm in love with your daughter, sir. And I want to marry her eventually, if she'll have me." There. It was said. Eric felt sweat trickle down his forehead and his armpits. His mug was empty and he signaled the waiter to bring them another round.

"You understand that nothing's settled between us yet. Frankie needs time...." Eric's voice trailed off.

Dom was staring at him, his half-empty glass poised on its way to his mouth. "You," he finally growled, frowning at Eric, "you are telling me you want to marry my Francesca?"

The fat was in the fire. Eric straightened his shoulders and stared the older man straight in the eye. "Yes, sir. I've told her what my plans are, and I wanted you to know, too. I'd like your blessing, Mr. Granatelli, that is if Frankie—"

That was as far as Eric got. Suddenly Granatelli reached across the table and seized Eric's hand in both of his, nearly upsetting the mugs of beer the waiter was placing between them. The formidable frown was magically being replaced with a beaming smile.

"So. This is how it is with you two. *Amore.* Ahh, *buono. Stupendo.* My Frankie, she's a fine girl, no? You call me Dom, yes? Waiter." He gave a peremptory snap of his fingers. "Bring us two doubles of your best Scotch."

When the whiskey arrived, he held his glass up in a formal toast. "*Salute!* To you, and to my Frankie. May you have happiness always."

He made it sound as if the whole thing were settled. Eric was a trifle uneasy for a moment, but he brushed the feeling aside. Surely Dom understood that Eric was only stating his own intentions, didn't he? Frankie could still refuse.

He was trying to figure out how to emphasize that point when Dom leaned forward comfortably on the table. "So, young man, I understand you played football. What a disgrace that they took away our major league franchise. What do you think our chances are of getting a football team again here in St. Louis?"

It was a subject close to Eric's heart, and in moments they were deep in discussion.

During the next two hours, they drank several more doubles each as they talked about football, baseball, then about the food business. As the afternoon progressed they grew more and more mellow, and more than a little drunk.

The two men were different in age, in background, even in language, yet both sensed they were also alike in many ways. Their attitude toward business was similar, a no-holds-barred personal involvement that included knowing every last detail about their restaurants. They favored the same sports, the same teams, and they were even critical of the same aspects of the sports industry.

By the time they rose to leave, they understood and respected each other.

They'd agreed it would be a wise idea to take taxis instead of driving, and they parted in the lobby with a warm handshake.

"*Arrivederci*, Eric. Tell Frankie to bring you to the house soon for a glass of my wine." Dom thumped Eric's shoulder in a comradely gesture.

Again Eric experienced that tiny sense of foreboding that had bothered him earlier. Since their quarrel, he and Frankie had carefully avoided discussing her family, and Eric sure as hell wasn't about to casually suggest they drop in at the Granatelli family home for a glass of Dom's wine. Not until he and Frankie had a rational discussion about this hang-up she had with her family.

But he felt good about being up front with her father, all the same.

DOM GRANATELLI and his brother Vito got together every Thursday night for a game of pinochle and a glass or two of wine. Naturally they talked about their children. What was a family if not to share joy and sadness, failure and success?

"This young man of Francesca's, this Eric Thorpe, he's a fine fellow," Dom bragged to Vito that Thursday evening. "Plenty of money put away—you know what these football players make. A good businessman and tough enough to handle that daughter of mine."

Dom emptied his glass and refilled both his and Vito's with his favorite Chianti. "My Frankie, she's a good girl, but she's always been obstinate and headstrong, you know that as well as I, Vito. But she's met her match, God be praised." He all but rubbed his hands with glee.

"And such a gentleman, Vito, you wouldn't believe. These days, how many young men come to the father and ask for the daughter's hand, like we did in the old days, I ask you? 'I'm gonna marry your daughter,' he tells me, straight out. Ah, he'll be a fine addition to the family, Vito. *Salute!*"

FRANKIE WAS WHISTLING a cheerful tune as she put the finishing touches to the six bridesmaids' hats. They were dusty rose straw with picture brims, dramatic, swoopy affairs with romantic wisps of peach and gray chiffon. One of them was her own. They'd turned out even better than she'd envisioned them, and she felt wonderful this morning.

Oh, a little sleepy, maybe. Color rose in her cheeks as she replayed details of last night's lovemaking.

Eric. Her heart overflowed with tenderness when she thought of him. She brushed a thread off the soft crimson shirt she was wearing, remembering how he'd burst through her door that evening before, arms laden with gaily wrapped packages and bags of food.

"What's the occasion?" She'd been full of curiosity as he handed her the parcels.

"It's our anniversary, lady. We've been together a whole six weeks today. Gus made me a double-layer chocolate cake so we could celebrate. It's in this carton."

"And what's in these other boxes?"

"Presents, of course. An anniversary is special."

The shirt had been in the first box. "Eric, it's fantastic," she cried. "It's the one we saw in that window. But why didn't you tell me we were going to have an anniversary? I'd have made you a hat or something."

"That's why I didn't tell you. Actually, this other present's for me anyway," he said with a wide, wicked grin.

"You bought yourself a present? That was smart thinking."

"You get to open it, though."

It was the frothiest, sexiest, most delectable peach-shaded lingerie she'd ever seen. She lifted it out of the tissue.

"You get to wear it, but I get to enjoy it," he whispered, nuzzling the sensitive spot on her neck.

The coolness of the night grew hot, and the cake was forgotten for a while.

Instead of diminishing, their need for each other seemed to escalate as time passed, and Frankie had to keep reminding herself that dreams of forever weren't in her game plan at all. This was an affair, a delightful short interlude that inevitably must come to an end. At times, though, she couldn't imagine life without Eric, and twice she actually caught herself fantasizing about a wedding.

Not Nick's wedding, either. Hers and Eric's.

When that happened, she panicked. She hauled up poor old Migs's ghost to give her a good down-to-earth talking-to about things like weddings and mortgages and career women.

The problem was, Migs's advice just didn't seem as effective as it once had.

The phone rang as Frankie was settling the bridesmaids' hats on their forms.

"The Mad Hatter...oh, hi, Zia Rosina..."

Frankie didn't get another word in for a while. Rosina was bubbling over with the wonderful news.

"I just had to call you first thing this morning and congratulate you—such a handsome man, and now another wedding! Teresa's going to be run off her feet with all the weddings in the family. And aren't you naughty, not telling your old auntie. When can you bring him over to dinner, Francesca?"

Frankie took the receiver away from her ear and frowned down at it. Rosina must have had too much caffeine this morning or something. She was sounding more confused than usual.

A fresh babble of words began pouring out. Rosina was suggesting an engagement shower now.

"Zia Rosina, wait . . . wait a minute. Whose wedding are we talking about here?"

"Why, yours of course, silly girl. Didn't your Zia Rosina smell a romance that morning when I came in to pick up my hat and he was there? Oh, Frankie, you're the sly one all right, trying to pretend nothing was going on. Uncle Vito told Salvatore that Eric Thorpe is quite a catch, too—lots of money from football, and that nice restaurant. Sal and I are going to go there for dinner, maybe next week. And have you set the date, or is that a secret still?"

Frankie was drowning in the rush of words, confused by the prattle and becoming frustrated and angered at being the subject of what was obviously the Granatelli family's latest gossip. Someone in the family must have seen her and Eric together and put one and one together to make fifteen, just as usual.

That had to explain it. Auntie Rosina always got things backwards anyway, the whole family said so. She decided to laugh it off as best she could.

"Hey, Auntie, I'm a confirmed bachelor girl, you know that. I've got my business, I'm already committed. Whatever made you think I was getting married, Rosina? Because you've got it all wrong. Eric and I are just good—"

Girlish giggles. "No, no, no, no. No more teasing now, *cara*. We got it straight from the horse's mouth. Your papa said this was so himself."

Rosina poured the whole story out. Dom had told Vito, who told Salvatore, that Eric Thorpe had come to him and asked for her hand in marriage. Frankie was speechless for several long moments.

"Such good manners from a boy not even raised on the Hill, Francesca. He's not Italian, is he?"

Frankie realized she was shaking her head. She managed at last to clear her throat and croak, "No, no, he's not."

"But he is Catholic, no?"

"I . . . you know, Zia Rosina, I don't really know. I'll find out for you, okay?" Frankie hung up the phone in Rosina's ear.

Her hands were shaking. Rosina had to have gotten it wrong, she had to have gotten it all wrong. Eric didn't even know her father, for heaven's sake. And anyway, Eric would never go and ask her father if he could marry her when he hadn't even asked her yet.

Would he? Could he do such a thing?

She'd been with him all last night and he hadn't breathed a single word about her family. Rosina was wrong, and that was that.

The phone rang again, and Frankie hesitated before she reluctantly picked it up.

It was her cousin Gina this time, and Frankie's stomach started to knot as she listened to the rapid patter. Gina, too, had just heard the news, via the family grapevine, about this hunk, this football player no less, Eric Thorpe, who'd asked Dom for Frankie's hand in marriage. Boy, the phones on the Hill were ringing off the hook this morning. He owned The Fifth Quarter, right? Wow, big potatoes.

Pretty quaint, pretty cute, sticking to the old traditions by having him ask Papa for her hand. Now the old folks were going to think everybody should do it that way. What was Frankie trying to do, start a rebellion here? Anyway, how about bringing him to the party Gina was giving next Saturday, so most of the younger Granatellis could meet him. . . .

This time Frankie crashed the receiver down without saying a word, the bile in her throat almost choking her. Disbelief had turned to rage, ice-cold fury that left no room for other emotions, like pain.

Betrayal. Eric had betrayed her. He'd proposed to her father, he'd declared himself to her entire meddling family, without even consulting her.

It was outrageous. It was unforgivable. It was the most humiliating thing that had ever happened to her.

Frankie grabbed her jacket and switched the sign of the door of The Mad Hatter from Open to Closed, oblivious of the two well-dressed women about to enter. "Emergency, sorry," she muttered, brushing past them.

It wasn't a lie. She was going to find Eric, and there was going to be an emergency, all right.

A major emergency.

Chapter Eight

THE FIFTH QUARTER was hosting its first luncheon for the downtown branch of the Rotary Club, and the speaker, an expert on tax laws, was halfway through his address. The club traditionally held its luncheons in the dining room of one of St. Louis's better hotels. However, the club president had contacted Eric and said that the members, wanting a change, had voted to try The Fifth Quarter.

Eric was keeping an astute and critical eye on his entire staff. Naturally he wanted everything to go well. Having fifty business people for lunch on a regular basis was a big financial plus, as well as great advertising if the Rotary members enjoyed their visit. Eric was determined they would.

He was staying in the background, making certain everything went like clockwork, when Frankie burst through the entrance door and began weaving her way among the tables toward him. He didn't see her until she was twenty yards away.

"...and thus take advantage of the government programs available..." the speaker was droning.

"Eric. How could you do this to me? How could you?" Frankie's furious voice cut through the subdued clatter like the warning notes of a bell.

She swept on through the restaurant, unable to stop herself now that she'd begun. "You went to my father behind my back! How could you do such a thing?" Her usually husky voice, raised now, was high and thin. She was beyond discretion, beyond knowing or caring that a roomful of conservatively dressed people were putting their coffee cups down, murmuring in amazement, turning around to stare at her as she advanced on Eric.

"You asked *him* if you could marry *me*—I've never been so humiliated in my entire life. The whole damn family knows all about it and you never mentioned a single word to me last night.''

Her voice had been steadily rising in volume, and the spectators were frozen in silence. Frankie saw only Eric, tall and elegant in his formal dark suit, a frown on his handsome face, approaching her, and her stomach filled with bile.

''Frankie, come upstairs to my office and I'll explain exactly what happened,'' he began.

She held out her hand like a traffic cop. ''Forget it. I'm not going anywhere with you, ever again.''

She'd fantasized about marrying him against every shred of good sense she possessed. She loved him. God, she loved him with all of her being. But at this particular moment, she hated him, as well.

He'd hurt her. The rage that concealed that awful hurt sustained her. ''Get away from me, Eric Thorpe. I'm not listening to any excuses. I never want to see you again. Our affair is over, do you hear me?''

Everyone in the entire restaurant heard.

Eric was beside her now, and he reached out to take her shoulders. Somehow he had to get her to simmer down enough to talk sensibly. Somehow he had to get her out of the center of the restaurant.

''Let go of me, Eric Thorpe.'' She wrenched away from him and whirled around, colliding with a waiter who was balancing a tray of stemmed glasses filled to the brim with red wine. Glasses and wine flew everywhere, splattering over Frankie and Eric as well as the customers seated nearby.

''Hey, my suit!''

''Waiter, a cloth....''

''There's glass all over the table!''

In the chaos, Frankie stormed out the door.

MUCH LATER that afternoon, Eric sat in his office with the door shut, slumped down in his chair, alternately cursing himself and wanting to murder Frankie.

After she made her dramatic exit, some comic had said in a loud voice, ''Hey, whatta floor show,'' and someone else had started to laugh. Soon the entire room was rocking with laughter.

Eric, wanting to slit his throat with the chef's carving knife, instead had to try to smile, shrug his shoulders, turn the whole thing into a joke even though he felt sick. It was the only way to even begin to salvage the disastrous scene.

And the spilled wine. He ought to just buy out a dry-cleaning establishment with the number of stained suits and dresses he'd promised to have cleaned.

She had one helluva temper, that woman of his.

She'd made him look like an ass in front of half of St. Louis, to say nothing of his entire staff. However, he was honest enough to admit his own fault in the whole debacle. He'd known last night he ought to tell Frankie right away about his conversation with her father. He'd had every intention of doing just that, but things had been so good between them he'd put it off.

Besides, he'd assumed that talk had been confidential. Dom must have assumed otherwise. Obviously, Eric had a lot to learn about the inner workings of a family. He'd just never had much firsthand experience with relatives. That was probably part of the problem here.

Which was at least partly why he'd let Frankie call the shots so far in this thing with her family. He'd tried to be easy-going, giving her time to get used to the idea of him being a permanent part of her life.

Well, easygoing was over as of right now. He was a patient man, but he wasn't a fool or a doormat. It was time to change his tactics.

Tactics, hell. He was out-and-out furious with her for the way she'd acted. If she were here right now, he'd turn her over his knee and paddle her.

His mouth twisted into a small and rueful grin at the idea of Frankie letting him get away with that. But damn it, if a football player ever mouthed off in front of the team the way Frankie had today, the coach would suspend him until he'd cooled down and come to his senses.

Maybe that's what he and Frankie needed—a cooling-off period, a sort of suspension. Time-out for each of them to think. Time and space.

The more he considered it, the more sense it made. Anger and hurt flared each time he thought of her screaming at him the way she had today.

No doubt about it, he needed to get away for a little while, until he was rational again. He'd been putting off a trip to Atlanta all year. He'd promised his buddies he'd visit them this spring, but there'd never seemed to be a right time.

Maybe this was it.

Without giving himself a chance to change his mind, Eric rummaged through his address book, picked up the phone and dialed a string of numbers. "Hey, Rambo, it's me, Eric. Yeah, I got your card. I just wondered if that spare bed you mentioned is still unoccupied...."

Within half an hour he had a reservation on a flight to Atlanta the next afternoon.

But instead of feeling excited and happy about seeing his old football buddies again, he felt sick at heart at the thought of being away from Frankie, whether they were fighting or not. He considered calling her, just to let her know that he'd be out of town for a few days, but he decided against it. Emotion between them was running far too high for polite conversation. Besides, his stubborn side insisted that maybe she needed to stew a little.

There wasn't much time for him to brood about it, either. If he was going away, there were a million details to settle before he left.

And the first and most important was final approval on the damned menu for the Granatelli wedding. There were less than three weeks left before the big event, and if he was going to be gone for one of them, things would have to be finalized right now.

He retrieved a thick file folder from a drawer, pulled out the last of the long series of menu plans and vowed that here, too, he was going to stand his ground. No more giving in to every whim of these volatile Granatelli females. He was going to be firm with Teresa, the way he should have been with Frankie. He was going to insist on meeting her one-on-one, no third person around, and then he would lay down the law about the food.

He found the Granatelli number and dialed it.

In the few seconds before the phone rang, he suddenly started to wonder how much Teresa really knew about him and Frankie. Was she liable to take a strip off him the way her daughter had? All at once the thought of meeting Teresa alone made his gut churn. Teresa Granatelli was a formidable woman.

Well, instead of meeting her alone here in his office, he'd suggest they have lunch downstairs. She was a dignified woman; she'd never cause a scene in the middle of a crowded restaurant.

Would she? Her daughter had.

"Hello, Mrs. Granatelli? Teresa, hello, it's Eric Thorpe. I've just learned I have to go out of town for a week or so, and I'd like to finalize the details about the menu."

To his amazement, she agreed right away to meet him the next day for an early lunch, and there was no mention of her bringing anybody to interpret for her.

That made him more than a little nervous. But, hell, if she got on the subject of him and Frankie, he'd just maintain a dignified silence.

For a guy who could face without flinching a horde of ugly giants on the football field, all bearing down on him with intent to kill, he wasn't doing so hot. Surely spending an hour in his own restaurant with a middle-aged lady couldn't be *that* traumatic.

AFTER HER DRAMATIC EXIT from The Fifth Quarter, Frankie went straight to the Hill, to the huge old stone house where she'd grown up. She needed to get things straight once and for all with this family of hers, she told herself, striding up the path and marching in the front door.

What she didn't acknowledge was that on a certain level she wanted her mother, the way she had when she was a little girl and something had hurt her.

She was hurting now. She was hurting badly, but she didn't dare allow herself to feel it quite yet.

Teresa came hurrying down the hall to greet her. "Francesca, how good to see you! But why aren't you at your store? It's not time for closing yet, is it?"

Frankie drew in a few deep breaths, trying to calm herself. It was important to be as reasonable as possible here. Mamma had a tendency to become very emotional, so Frankie was the one who must stay rational.

"I closed it for the afternoon, Mamma. I needed to get some things straight. Look, I'm sorry, but from here on in you're entirely on your own with that blasted caterer for Nick's wedding. I don't, as long as I live, ever want to hear Eric Thorpe's name again, you understand me, Mamma?" Her voice threatened to go out of control, and she paused and drew in another deep breath.

"You do understand?" This time a sob broke in her throat.

Teresa didn't understand at all, but she nodded soothingly. Putting an arm around Frankie, she drew her into the big old-fashioned kitchen and seated her at the long wooden table. Then she moved around quietly, starting to make cappuccino, giving Frankie time to recover.

"Also, Mamma, please make it crystal clear to Papa and to Zio Vito that I am never, never, ever getting married."

Teresa accepted this news with a nod and a word of agreement, getting two cups out of a cupboard and sitting them down on the table.

"Absolutely never, Mamma. I'm staying a *zitella*, a spinster, for the rest of my life, and if Papa and the rest of those...troublemakers...don't lay off me, I'll...I'll enter a convent, and then Papa won't even get the lousy interest on his damned loan. Tell him that from me, okay? Because if I try to tell him myself, so help me..."

At that point, Frankie wrecked the whole thing by bursting into tears. She knocked her chair over as she stumbled to her

feet, bumbled around looking for tissues and finally threw
herself into her mother's arms, resorting to her native Italian
as she babbled that in spite of it all, she loved him, she couldn't
live without him, and now Papa and Vito and Salvatore and
Eric—yes, him too; all the stupid men together—had wrecked
everything forever. Damn, damn men.

Finito.

How? Teresa begged. How did the men manage to do this
terrible thing?

But Frankie was sobbing too hard to talk anymore.

REMINDING HIMSELF with firm determination of the reso-
lutions he'd made the day before, Eric held Teresa's chair for
her when she arrived at the table he'd chosen.

After the waiter had taken their order and brought them
glasses of white wine, he held out the much-revised menu plan
and took a deep breath, steeling himself for the clash of wills
about to occur.

"This includes some of the dishes you asked for," he began, ready to argue and stand firm when she started her eter-
nal questioning and changing. "Not all, but most. My chef
insists that he'll talk to you in person if there's any further
problems. He feels this is the very best compromise we can
make."

Actually, Gus had said a damn sight more than that, but not
the sorts of things you could repeat to Teresa.

He waited for the explosion and almost fell off his chair when
she took a gold pen from her purse, scrawled her name across
the bottom of the sheet and said, "That will be fine, thank you
for your trouble," without giving the list more than a cursory
glance.

The waiter arrived with their salads. Dazed, Eric munched
his without tasting it. Something was going on here, and he
was apprehensive as hell.

Teresa took a few polite bites, then set down her fork and
allowed a long, dramatic pause to elapse while she looked
straight into Eric's eyes.

"My Francesca," she began, and Eric's heart started to pound. This was going to be worse than he'd feared.

"She's told me everything," Teresa announced ominously, shaking her head and pulling her mouth down into a doleful expression. "But I'm a fair woman. I came here today to hear from you, your side as well as hers. Now tell me, why you are breaking my little girl's heart?" She fixed him with a burning stare and waited.

Eric slumped back in his chair and gave a long, weary sigh. He'd vowed he wasn't going to get tricked into any more confidences with Frankie's parents, but there were a few things that needed to be said here. More than a few.

Before he knew it, he heard himself telling Teresa why he couldn't confide in her, which led to an explanation of his conversation with Dom, which of course led straight to the whole problem of Frankie not wanting him to meet any of her other relatives.

Teresa listened, nodding her head at intervals. By the time he'd finished talking, she knew a great deal about what was going on, and what she didn't know she could certainly guess.

"Ah, so my Frankie, she was not happy with you for talking with her father about marriage, yes?"

Eric had to admit that Frankie was not delighted, no.

Teresa nodded again. "And then Dominic, he told Vito. And Vito, he naturally told Salvatore." She nodded as it all began to make perfect sense.

"And my Frankie, she threw things, yes? Always, that girl had a bit of a temper."

"No, no, no," Eric defended. "Nothing like that."

Teresa raised disbelieving eyebrows.

Well, Eric conceded, a few wineglasses had gotten broken. But that was his fault as much as hers, really.

The waiter removed the salad plates, served the pasta with seafood sauce, refilled their wineglasses and left.

Teresa was still watching Eric with that disconcerting look that made him feel she could see through his skull, straight to the back of his head. "Tell me, you come from a big family, Eric?"

He shook his head. Explaining his childhood, he briefly described his trek from one foster home to another, making light of it the way he always did.

But to his amazement, Teresa's great dark eyes filled with tears during his explanation. She reached across and squeezed his arm, murmuring soft phrases in Italian and patting him. "*Povero bambino,* poor little boy."

It was embarrassing, but on some deep level he couldn't quite analyze, it was also comforting.

There was much more to it than that, although he wasn't aware of it yet. From that instant on, Eric had acquired, for better or worse, but definitely for always, an Italian mother.

Chapter Nine

"SO THE PROBLEM IS really the family," Teresa said at last. "And before you can marry my Frankie, *caro*, you must understand about her family, yes?"

Eric hoped to God that she could help him understand, because he sure hadn't done too well on his own up till now.

"This Granatelli family, they're always talking," Teresa began, using her hands and her eyes to punctuate her words. "It's very much like in Cuggiono, the little village where I grew up in Italy, near Milano. There, everyone was a part of everything that happened. Births, weddings, funerals, deaths, we all were in it together. There were few secrets. Everyone knew what was going on with everyone else, you understand?"

Eric nodded.

"Me," Teresa said with an expressive shrug, "always, I loved that closeness, the sense of safety it gave me." A touch of nostalgia crept into her voice, and she paused for a moment, sipping her wine.

"And then, when I married and came here, it's what I treasured about the Granatellis, that closeness even in America where so few of the old traditions still exist. I was so homesick, and being able to talk it out with Dom's family made it easier."

The waiter came with coffee, and Teresa was again silent until he left.

"But people are different—our own children are different than we were. My Frankie, now, she's always hated the way the Granatellis involve themselves in one another's affairs. From the time she was a child, she's very private. She's . . . *timida*. What's the English?" Teresa frowned.

"Shy?" Eric had never thought of Frankie as shy, yet when he thought about it, maybe Teresa was right. He remembered the way Frankie blushed at certain times.

"Yes, shy. You do understand. And so you can forgive her this little weakness, a man like you, so strong, so... *attraente*, handsome, and—" she waved an expressive hand around at the restaurant "—successful. Surely a man like you, with such a big heart, you can understand and excuse my Frankie?"

"Of course." Eric was trying not to grin at her extravagant flattery. But he also wanted her to understand how things were with him.

"Look," he said, wondering how to phrase it. "Teresa, I want you to know I love Frankie, and that's that. We're going to be married one day soon, it just might take a bit longer than I planned. I appreciate your telling me all this, but even if you hadn't, I'd never have let the little... argument we had yesterday come between us." He swallowed hard. Ever since yesterday, he'd been pushing away a thought too disturbing to contemplate. "That is, of course, as long as, umm, as long as Frankie is in love with me. Otherwise, there's no point, is there?"

Teresa slid forward on her chair, pinning him with those dark, liquid eyes of hers. "I tell you true, Eric," she said with slow and definite emphasis. "Frankie, she loves you. This I know for certain, because she told me so, not once, but many times. She loves you, be sure of that."

A huge weight seemed to lift from his chest.

"One more thing, though." Teresa was still giving him that penetrating look, and there was a worried frown on her face. "A very personal question, I'm sorry to have to ask."

Eric's eyebrows shot up and he got nervous all over again. What could be more personal than what they'd just been discussing? Safe sex? His less-than-puritan past?

"Eric, you are a Catholic?" she whispered.

Relief again spilled through him and he felt like laughing out loud. Technically he was indeed Catholic. He hadn't gone to confession for a long time, but he didn't have to tell her that.

When he nodded assurance, she rolled her eyes to heaven in that same way her daughter did. Then she leaped to her feet, bustled around the table and threw her arms around him. The other patrons of his restaurant smiled, and the staff tittered.

Eric sent them killing glances, but Teresa was blissfully unaware of any of it, talking a mile a minute and mopping tears from her eyes with a lace handkerchief she rescued from her sleeve.

This time, she assured him, for his and Frankie's wedding, they would have no problems with the food. For this wedding she would call on Costellini, the same Italian caterer who'd done Sophia's. Then Eric would see what a real Italian feast could be like.

And, oh, yes, speaking of that, Eric must come to dinner at the Granatelli home, to meet all the relatives. Maybe next Sunday?

Warning lights went off in his brain. "Hold it, Teresa. I'm going to have to spend a lot of time talking things over with Frankie before anything else, and I have to go out of town for about a week. In fact, my plane leaves—" He glanced at his watch. "Damn. It leaves in an hour and a half. I've got to get to the airport."

But Teresa was determined about dinner. She grabbed his sleeve and held on. What about the night before the wedding? A big family dinner party was planned for that evening. He could meet Nicky and his bride-to-be, and all the other Granatellis. Teresa wouldn't take no for an answer. Yes?

Eric agreed. He absolutely had to leave, but one more thing was still bothering him.

"Teresa, could we maybe keep this conversation just between you and me? Confidential, like? Because I won't be seeing Frankie for a few days, and last time she thought I'd been talking to her family behind her back, she got pretty upset with me."

Understatement of the century.

Teresa placed a finger on sealed lips and sent him a roguish wink. Not a word, not a syllable, would escape.

Knowing a bit about the Granatelli track record, Eric could only pray.

FRANKIE GAVE UP and ripped the huge silk rose from the brim of the navy boater, cursing under her breath. Nothing was going right today. It was all she could do to keep herself from throwing the cursed hat across the workroom and then running over and stamping on it.

The easy tears that had trickled and streamed and dripped down her face ever since her confrontation with Eric three days before now spilled over once again, spotting the cream felt she was supposed to cut out that afternoon.

Damn Eric Thorpe to hell. He was all she could think about, and he was the very subject she most wanted out of her mind. She put her palms flat on the worktable and closed her eyes, struggling for control.

She was a career woman, she reminded herself for the two hundredth time. Business came first in her life. She'd made a choice and she was going to live with it. Marriage was absolutely, positively, not for her.

Even her mother finally agreed.

Frankie had somehow managed to get through the weekend without Eric, but by Monday, time stretched out like an eternity. She'd avoided the phone until after lunch, but then she'd given up.

He was probably ready to apologize anyway, she rationalized. She dialed The Fifth Quarter and asked the receptionist for Eric.

"Oh, sorry, Ms. Granatelli, he's not here. He's out of town. I don't know for how long. I think he's gone to Atlanta, didn't you know? Armand's in charge here—do you want to speak to him?"

Frankie had hung up quickly. She felt cold and shriveled and sick. She could hardly believe it. He'd gone away without saying one single word to her. How could he do such a thing— just walk out on her like that? On top of everything else?

Atlanta. He'd mentioned two football friends who played for the Atlanta . . . whatever the team was called. Single men, she seemed to remember.

Divorced, he'd said. Probably playboys.

C'mon, Frankie. You teased him into telling you what it was like being a football player. Having women proposition him.

These two guys must have apartments outfitted with Jacuzzis, black satin sheets. Groupies everywhere. Nightmarish scenes sprang into her head, of Eric not resisting the slightest bit.

By the end of that long day Frankie had been certain she was developing an ulcer, besides coming down with something awful. But the last thing she wanted to do was go home to her empty apartment. Just when she was wondering whether the insurance policy on her store covered the mortgage in cases of suicide, her mother had phoned and invited her for supper.

"Papa and Vito have gone to watch the fights," Teresa explained. "I called Sophia to join us, but she's not feeling good tonight. So it will be just you and me and the minestrone."

"I'll be right over, Mamma." It was pathetic to be this grateful for an invitation home.

Her mother frowned at her and felt her forehead when she walked in the door. At first Frankie insisted nothing was wrong, but over the minestrone, she broke down and confided in Teresa. She told her everything about Eric, from the beginning.

Well, almost everything. She left out the parts her mother wouldn't want to hear anyway, the passionate, intimate stuff. That made the story a lot shorter, too.

"So, Mamma, I don't know what to do anymore," she concluded. "See, I was clear about my life and what I wanted out of it before Eric came along. But now . . ." She shrugged and buttered another piece of her mother's homemade bread. "I don't know anymore what I want."

She'd known in advance what Teresa was going to advise. Be like Sophia: choose marriage, children, home, church. Oh, well. There was a lot to be said for getting it off her chest anyway. Frankie listened with only half an ear when Teresa answered.

"*Cara*, sometimes in life you have to give up one thing to get another. We have to choose. No one has all."

Frankie sighed. Now came the lecture, and she'd asked for it, after all.

"You know," her mother went on, "I've come to understand that not every woman needs to marry, either. This is the nineties. Women can choose now, not like in my day. I hear them on *Donahue*, telling why they stay single, and in many cases I have to agree."

Frankie gaped. This was her mother talking? But Teresa was going on in a thoughtful tone Frankie had never heard before.

"Some women need a man's love, his support. Sophia does, I did. Others don't. They don't mind a cold and lonely bed. They live for other things besides a man's love, little babies, a family of their own. Like you, they value business success, money, fame. I admire such women, even though I couldn't have chosen that way for my own life. I fell in love with your father, and from there on . . ." Teresa turned her expressive eyes on her daughter and held up her hands in a gesture that said it all.

"But you, you are different from me, *cara*. You are the strong one among my girls, no question. Independent, that's you. It gives me great joy to have a daughter like you—tough, not afraid of growing old alone. So I say now, forget this man. You have your store to think about, your career as a milliner. Who knows what success you might attain?"

Frankie had been flabbergasted. She was also deeply touched by her mother's words. Teresa went on to tell her anecdotes about growing up in Italy, little stories about her life as a young bride in a new country, and Frankie felt as if they were friends as well as mother and daughter.

But later that night, alone in her empty apartment, she had wondered why Teresa's amazing show of support wasn't as reassuring as it should have been. She'd said all the things Frankie needed to hear, but somehow it didn't help one bit.

What was wrong with her?

Eric's spare socks and underwear were in a sports bag in her bedroom, his terry robe slung over a chair. Tender memories of their time together haunted her everywhere she looked.

Why did her head say one thing and her heart another? How had Migs ever managed to live her life the way she had, alone and self-sufficient to the end? And why did it keep coming back to her that when that end came, Migs had died alone, without any husband to mourn her, without grandchildren to remember what a unique old lady she'd been, without a family to grieve at her funeral?

THE MOST THAT COULD be said for the next eight days was that they passed somehow. Whoever had claimed that time made everything easier didn't know the first thing about loneliness, Frankie more than once raged.

She worked at the store to the point of exhaustion, and still sleep eluded her. She called The Fifth Quarter more times than she wanted to remember, and each time the answer was the same; Eric was still out of town and they didn't know when he'd be back.

Would he even come back for the wedding, or would he let his staff handle it? The big day was just over a week away. Where was that miserable man, anyway? What was he doing? Worst of all, who was he doing it with?

FIVE DAYS BEFORE the wedding, Frankie was in The Mad Hatter at the break of dawn. Four important orders were due to be picked up before noon, and one of the bridesmaids was causing untold misery, insisting she hated the fantastic hat Frankie had created.

Frankie had held on by the skin of her teeth and promised to alter it slightly, when what she really wanted to do was give the woman something serious to complain about.

She'd have to work on her bad temper. She was in danger of spoiling Nick's wedding if she didn't manage to improve her mood.

She was trying to figure out how to do that when a loud banging started on the front door. Frankie jumped and glanced at her watch. It was barely eight o'clock, two hours before her regular opening time.

She went to the door and undid the bolt. Eric stood there, leaning on the doorjamb with one arm. His eyes were bloodshot and there were faint lines around his mouth that hadn't been there before. But his crooked grin was the same, as was the intimate rasp of his deep voice. "Hello, Funny Face. You had breakfast yet?"

The nerve of him.

Her heart was hammering, and her emotions were in a turmoil. She was furious with him on one hand, and ridiculously relieved to see him on the other.

She didn't slam the door in his face. She managed not to fall into his arms, either. But her throat had closed up, and she couldn't say a darned word to him. She gulped hard, twice. She was trying not to cry, and she didn't want him to know.

His voice was so dear to her, so familiar. "We need to talk, honey. You gonna let me in?"

She tried to glare at him even as she nodded and held the door open, and he walked through to the workroom without touching her. She took a dozen deep breaths and followed him.

How was she going to deal with this? How was he? Nonchalantly, by the look of things.

Damn him, he was already setting a feast out on a snowy cloth he'd spread over the table. He glanced up at her as she came through the doorway. Their eyes met and held.

There was a world of love and appeal in that look, and she couldn't help herself. "Eric," she breathed. She moved toward him, aching to have his arms around her.

But just as she rounded the corner of the table, the phone on the wall beside her began to ring in long, urgent bursts. She considered not answering it, but the habits of good business were too ingrained. With a sigh, she picked up the receiver.

Chapter Ten

"MAMMA? MAMMA, is that you?" It took Frankie a moment to even recognize her mother's voice, it was so filled with tension and fear.

"Francesca, thank God you're there. It's your sister Sophia. She's hemorrhaging and her blood pressure has shot up. The baby..." Teresa's voice threatened to break, but she cleared her throat and went on. "Your father and I are at the hospital right now with her. The doctors are going to perform a cesarean, even though the baby isn't due for over a month." Teresa's voice trembled. "Your sister and the baby are both in terrible danger, *cara*."

"Aldo? Is he..." But Frankie already knew her brother-in-law was away on a business trip that week. "What about the kids?"

Eric, aware of the tension in her voice even though she and Teresa were speaking Italian, moved close to her without a word and put an arm around her shoulders, supporting her against the strong bulk of his body.

"Aldo's not back yet. We're trying to reach him. We left a message at his hotel," her mother confirmed. "A neighbor is at Sophia's with the boys. I've phoned Asunta—she'll be there by noon or shortly after to take over, you know how good she is with children. But in the meantime, Francesca, could you possibly go over and be with them? They're scared, they saw the ambulance take Sophia. They need family with them."

"I'm leaving right now, Mamma."

Frankie hung up the phone. In a few choked sentences she told Eric what was happening.

"Let's go," was all he said.

"You don't have to come with me," Frankie protested weakly, trying to find her jacket and the keys to the store as waves of shock and worry rushed through her.

She wanted him with her more than anything, but she was painfully aware that she'd been too stubborn to let him meet her family, her nephews, before this. Now it seemed unfair to catapult him into the midst of a family emergency.

"Don't be ridiculous, Funny Face. I'll take the food along, maybe the kids will like some of this stuff." He grabbed up the half-unpacked picnic basket and refilled it, rescued Frankie's keys for her from under a piece of fabric and hurried her out the door, locking it behind them. In a few moments they were in his car, and Frankie gave him directions to Sophia's house.

"How old are your nephews, Frankie?"

His question brought sudden tears to her eyes. Teresa had said that both Sophia and the unborn child were in danger. All of a sudden Frankie thought of how vulnerable her little nephews were. If anything should happen to her sister, their lives would be changed forever. She whispered a quick, desperate prayer under her breath before she answered Eric.

"Nick is seven, Ben five, and Eddie's two and a half. They're wonderful boys, but they're pretty rambunctious."

"I love kids." Eric reached over and took her trembling hand in his, holding it tight to his thigh for the whole ride. And in some crazy way, it soothed her.

The flustered neighbor met them at the door. "I've been trying to get the children dressed and fed, but I'm afraid I haven't managed quite yet."

She was obviously relieved that help had arrived. Frankie's nephews weren't easy little boys to control, and it was clear the woman had lost the contest sometime before.

The living room was a shambles. Toys, breakfast cereal and an assortment of minute jeans and T-shirts were scattered around, and there seemed to be small bodies everywhere. Her nephews were running wild, Frankie realized, and her heart sank. She wasn't much good at controlling them, either.

"Zia Frankie! Hey, you guys, it's our Zia Frankie." Three little boys, none clothed in more than underpants, flew at her, wrapping their arms around her legs and almost tripping her. Baby Eddie, almost trampled in the rush, plopped to the floor at Frankie's feet and started howling as loud as he could, clutching his favorite teddy bear to his chest. "Ma, Ma, Ma," he screamed.

"Our Mamma got sick. An am'blance came here," Nick was hollering, while Ben pounded Frankie's thigh, vying for attention and trying to tell his version.

Eric set the picnic basket down and squatted beside Eddie, murmuring to him in a soft tone. In moments the sturdy little boy was in Eric's arms, thumb in his mouth.

"This is Mr. Thorpe, guys," Frankie told the boys over the racket.

"Call me Eric, okay fellows?"

They liked him on sight. He talked to them quietly, and somehow that managed to calm them down. He listened to their gabble with patient attention, asking questions and reassuring them about Sophia. He explained just how the siren in an ambulance worked. They brought favorite trucks to show him, and Eddie gave him his teddy bear to hold.

Frankie wasn't certain how he managed it, but within a short time Eric had convinced Nick and Ben they should struggle into their clothes and pick up the mess on the floor.

While Frankie diapered and dressed Eddie, Eric spread a picnic out on the kitchen table, and the excited children helped him divide up fresh fruit and huge muffins among them. Soon they were devouring most of the food, chattering to Eric the whole time.

He even figured out how to run Sophia's state-of-the-art coffee maker, a feat Frankie had never mastered, and insisted she eat a muffin with the welcome cup of coffee he poured for her.

When the kitchen was tidy again and the boys settled in front of the TV, Eric suggested, "How about loading these guys in my car and going back to the store so you can open? You've probably got women coming for their wedding hats this morning, right?"

Worry about Sophia had driven all thought of her business out of Frankie's head, but now she remembered the hats to be picked up before noon. They left a note for Auntie Asunta, telling her where the boys were.

Back at The Mad Hatter, Eric took the three excited children into the workroom and somehow managed to keep them entertained as Frankie forced herself to smile at customers. Giggles and sounds of rowdy play escaped from the back room, and the phone rang constantly as more and more of the Granatelli relatives learned about the emergency, but today Frankie didn't feel the family grapevine was an invasion of privacy at all. Most of the calls were offers of practical help, and she found the warm and loving contact comforting.

At noon Eric took the boys out for a hamburger lunch, and shortly after they returned, Frankie's dynamic Auntie Asunta sailed into the shop to collect the children. Asunta also had her seventeen-year-old daughter, Maria, in tow.

"I think you should be at the hospital, Francesca," Asunta announced to Frankie in her usual bullying tone. "My Maria here worked last summer at a boutique, and she's been taking all these fancy design courses. She'll be able to run this place for the rest of the day for you, so you go. And these rascals..." She scooped Eddie to her hip and gave him a kiss, somehow managing to grab the other two by their hands at the same time.

"They're coming home with me. We're going to make gingerbread men and then we're going to the zoo, right, boys?" Out she went, and all of a sudden the shop was very quiet.

Frankie's head was aching, and all she could think of was the danger to Sophia and the baby. She wanted more than anything to be at the hospital with her family, but she was also reluctant to turn over her store to anyone else, especially such a young girl as Maria.

"She'll do fine, honey," Eric said in a low voice only Frankie could hear. "C'mon now, I'll drive you to the hospital."

Before they left, Maria asked intelligent questions about Frankie's sales system, where things were kept and what orders were ready, and Frankie felt a little reassured. It was obvious Maria was bright, and she was also smartly dressed and pretty.

She probably couldn't do that much harm in one afternoon. If The Mad Hatter had to be left with anyone, it might as well be Maria.

AT THE HOSPITAL, the waiting seemed endless. The long afternoon dragged on and on. Family members were allowed in to see Sophia for short periods, but her sister's pallor and obvious distress were almost more than Frankie could bear.

Sophia was terrified, not for herself but for her baby.

Eric, in spite of Frankie's halfhearted objections, stayed at the hospital all afternoon. He was a quiet source of support not only for Frankie but for Dom and Teresa, as well. He brought them endless cups of coffee, insisted they eat sandwiches, took Dom out for a walk in the fresh air and managed to affect them all with his own indomitable strength.

The doctors were doing what they could to slow the bleeding and lower Sophia's blood pressure before they attempted surgery, but they weren't succeeding. At last, Sophia's gynecologist hurried into the waiting room and announced that they couldn't delay any longer. They would perform the cesarean section immediately.

Sophia was taken to a nearby operating room, and now the tension was unbearable. Frankie's mother prayed, her lips moving silently as the minutes ticked away, and Dom sat close beside her.

Frankie couldn't sit still. Eric paced beside her, up and down the hallway, holding her hand. He understood when she didn't want to talk.

As they passed the waiting room for at least the tenth time, Frankie glanced in. And all at once she saw her mother and father as strangers—a handsome, worried-looking elderly couple sitting on plastic chairs, holding hands in stoic silence.

Frankie stopped and stared. For one extraordinary moment she saw them not just as her parents but also as a man and a woman. Still in love, after all these years. They didn't always need words to communicate their feelings for each other; they had a lifetime of trust and support and caring to fall back on.

Although it was invisible, that link between her parents seemed to fill the stark, neon-lit room with a kind of brilliance. It was a bond that only years could bring, a product of the kind of marriage they'd had. No matter what happened, they were united, sharing whatever life might hand them, whether it was joy or sorrow, victory or defeat. They'd made a lifelong commitment to each other, and they'd honored it. This unity, this palpable love between them, was there to sustain them at moments like this.

Frankie thought back over the past days, remembering the desolate sense of aloneness she'd experienced without Eric. Was that what she wanted? Eric had given her the choice, hadn't he? He'd made it plain that he wanted her forever.

And up till now she'd rejected his offer, treated it lightly.

"Mr. and Mrs. Granatelli?" Her thoughts were interrupted by the doctor, mask still hanging by a string, surgical suit rumpled and stained. A wide grin on his weary features, however, signaled his good news even before his announcement.

"Your daughter has a gorgeous baby girl, five pounds one ounce, healthy as can be even though she's tiny. She and her mother are doing great. Both of them are out of danger. Congratulations."

Chapter Eleven

IT WAS MUCH LATER that night. The bedside clock read eleven forty-five. The endless, stress-laden day was nearly over, and Eric's strong arms cradled Frankie's exhausted body, his huge bed an oasis of comfort now that the first of their passion was spent.

"You know, the wedding's only a few days away. Nick will be here tomorrow for the rehearsal." Frankie was floating in the aftermath of love, her mind touching on one thing and then another. "Did Mamma finally put the seal of approval on the menu, Eric?"

She felt him nod. "It's all under control," he rumbled. "Your brother's wedding's going to have the most eclectic, exotic mixture of food this town's ever seen." A lazy chuckle escaped him. "We compromised on the hors d'oeuvres, gave in on the salad, held fast against the pasta. Then, apparently your brother told Teresa he wanted your grandmother's *risotto milanese* or no wedding. So we added that and managed to avoid the zabaglione for dessert. Gus is creating a masterpiece instead, a three-foot-high swan made of puff pastry, decorated with pink cream, garnished with chocolate roses and fresh strawberries all around the base. Thank God your mamma finally gave up on the tortellini soup or we'd have ended up with a meal so heavy people would be falling asleep before the wedding cake is cut."

"Nick got in on the act? I can't believe it." She giggled at the idea of her brother meddling with the menu. After all the trouble her mother had been, the last thing Eric needed was Nick sticking his nose in.

Nonna's *risotto milanese*, huh? Mmm. She didn't blame Nick. She'd always loved it, too.

Her head was tucked in that wonderful place just below his chin, and their bodies were still intertwined in an intricate love knot. His arms held her locked against him, and she fitted perfectly just as if she were made to snuggle there.

"I'm glad you brought me here tonight, to your house, Eric."

"Yeah? I thought you didn't like my house much." It wasn't a complaint. He sounded as if he were smiling.

"I've changed my mind. All it needs is a woman's touch—some silk plants, a few pictures, some ornaments that aren't football trophies."

And a husband named Eric. She tried to say it and couldn't. Now that the moment was here, she was shy instead of bold, and he didn't pursue the subject, which worried her more than a little.

Wasn't he going to propose after all?

What if he'd changed his mind in Atlanta? What if his friends had convinced him that he should just have an affair with her? It would serve her right, in a way. She'd been a little stubborn when it came right down to it.

Please God, give me one more chance at this wedding thing, she begged silently. *I'm a fast learner. I'll make a good job of it this time.*

All day a part of her had watched him. Had marveled at his strength, at the endearing gentleness and understanding he showed for her nephews, at his willingness to be embroiled in a tense and difficult family scene like the one at the hospital. It made her realize that he was a man who would always give more than his share.

And at the end of the day, he'd driven her here, made her a scrumptious soufflé, insisted she take a long, hot bath in his massive tub while he cooked. After they'd eaten, he'd brought glasses of wine to the living room, and when she complained that her shoulders were aching, he'd given her a back rub. Then he'd moved down to her feet, kneeling on the rug and rubbing her arches, letting his hands slide up her calves in a sensual motion that set her insides throbbing.

Things had progressed rapidly from there. Her panty hose came off, and his hands slid higher still. With a groan he'd scooped her up and carried her to his bedroom.

The lovemaking was perfect, just as always. But neither had yet said a word about their quarrel, about his trip to Atlanta, about the scene she'd thrown in his restaurant.

Was it because Eric had changed his mind?

He went on in a lazy voice, discussing the events of the day, as Frankie became more and more anxious. "I never thought babies were that small when they first came out," he remarked. They'd stood in front of the window, both speechless with wonder, and stared at Sophia's tiny, exquisite new daughter. "She looks as if she'd fit in one of my hands," he'd whispered, his voice filled with wonder. Both of them had tears in their eyes before they turned away.

"I don't think they are that tiny, usually," Frankie remarked now. "The boys were lots bigger. Isn't it great, Sophia getting a girl after all those boys? She's adorable, her daddy's going to spoil her rotten. Aldo will have seen her by now—my cousin Louie went out to the airport to wait for the flight and take Aldo straight to the hospital. Poor guy, he must have been half-crazy all day with worry."

"Who were those elderly ladies dressed all in black who spent the afternoon popping in and out of the hospital chapel?" Eric sounded puzzled, and in spite of the anxiety building in her, Frankie had to giggle.

"Oh, that's Great-Aunt Fiorenza and her sister Camilla. They never married. They're up in their eighties now, and whenever there's an emergency, they hurry over and pray. One of their nephews is a priest, so they figure they've got a hot line to heaven. They drive Papa crazy, 'cause he always ends up having to make sure they're fed and their taxi fare is paid for."

The other Granatelli relatives had also outdone themselves today. Cookies, cakes, casseroles and pasta sauce had been delivered in a steady stream both to Sophia's house and to Teresa's, and cousins were still baking so that Teresa could have plenty on hand for the wedding.

Frankie knew that Sophia's house would be scrubbed from top to bottom before she came home, and the freezer filled with a month's worth of home-cooked meals so she'd have a chance to recuperate. Baby gifts would pour in, enough stuff to outfit quintuplets at least.

Her crazy family didn't do anything halfheartedly.

It had dawned on Frankie today that in their gossipy, big-hearted way, they maybe weren't so bad to have around after all. Which wasn't to say they didn't still drive her insane, but she could see the other side a bit better now.

Frankie's thoughts moved from her family to her business, and as if he were reading her mind, Eric said, "That pretty cousin of yours did a great job at the store, didn't she? She seemed to have made a lot of sales by closing time."

"She sure did. The Mad Hatter had one of its best days ever."

Frankie wasn't sure how she felt about that yet. A little tiny bit jealous, perhaps, that someone so inexperienced could come in and do so well? The store, after all, was her baby.

And if Eric didn't pop the question soon, maybe the store would be the only baby she would ever have.

But at least, Frankie reminded herself, she was a good enough business person to realize her young cousin's potential. "I've decided to hire Maria for Friday afternoons and Saturdays. If she goes on selling the way she did today, maybe I'll take her on full-time in the fall," Frankie announced hopefully.

After all, newlyweds needed to be together a lot, didn't they? Surely Eric would take it from there. He didn't, though. "That's a great idea. You'll have a lot more free time that way," was all he said.

Damn him. He was going to force her to bring up the subject of marriage all by herself. He really was an impossible man.

Where to begin? "Eric."

"Mmm?"

The whole thing had started with her family, so Frankie decided to start there, too. "You remember I told you how it made me nuts to have the family sticking their noses into everything all the time?''

"You did mention that once or twice, yes.''

He was being deliberately obtuse, and she was going to kill him for it. Later. "Well, today, I guess I changed my mind some about it. Not that I believe they should be so nosy, but I guess you take the good with the bad in a family like mine. Today they were a sort of... well, safety net, taking care of things, helping us out.''

She felt that she needed to see his face during this conversation, so she wriggled free and sat up, looking down at him. The brown-and-blue print sheet was twisted around his narrow hips. He was a beautiful man, no doubt about it.

He kept his eyes closed, so she couldn't tell what he was thinking, and she found herself hoping their daughters got his long, curly eyelashes. His hands was stroking her bare thigh in lazy circles she found distracting. She grabbed his hand and held it still. This was important, and she wasn't going to be seduced off the subject.

"I mean, the Granatellis... well, their mouths work overtime, but I guess their hearts do, too. Don't you think so, Eric?''

There was a plaintive note in her voice, but all he said was another "Mmm.'' He looked more than half-asleep.

She was going to punch him in a minute.

You still owe him an apology, some puritanical voice inside of her insisted. Hell. She might as well get it over with.

"I'm sorry for hollering and spilling all that wine at your restaurant, Eric. And...'' She swallowed hard. This was awful. "I feel rotten for not introducing you to my family. From now on, you'll get to meet every last great-uncle and third cousin, every dotty auntie and eccentric in-law. How's that?''

Finally, when she was almost out of her mind, he opened his eyes. The expression in them was tender, but it was serious, as well.

"That conversation with your father, Frankie. I didn't want him to think I was only interested in getting you to go to bed with me. I wanted him to know how I felt about you.'' He explained in detail how he'd come to talk with Dom in the first place, and exactly what was said. "I was declaring my intentions, that was all. I happen to love you, Funny Face."

At last she saw an opening, and she dived straight in. "I happen to love you, too. So what exactly are your intentions, Eric Thorpe?" Her voice wasn't quite steady. Her heart was hammering so hard she wondered if she was about to have some sort of attack. It was easily the most important question she'd ever asked in her entire life.

He kept her waiting. He looked up at her for ten long heartbeats. Then he pushed himself to a sitting position and bunched the pillows behind him, taking his lousy sweet time at it. In slow motion he reached out and brushed some of her hair out of her eyes, hooking it behind her ear. He moved the sheet so that intimate parts of her were decently covered.

At last, he took her hands in both of his and looked her straight in her eye. "Francesca Granatelli, will you do me the honor of becoming my wife?"

Every cell in her body filled with exultation, with love and joy and incredible happiness, and not a little relief. "I will, Eric Thorpe," she responded in a demure, dignified voice. But she couldn't restrain herself more than two seconds longer.

"Yes, yes, yes, yes," she hollered as loud as she could. And then she smashed him over his stubborn head with a pillow.

"Now," she said in a silky tone. "I want to know in exact detail what went on in Atlanta."

But he pulled her down on top of him and kissed her breathless, and soon Atlanta didn't seem very important at all.

Epilogue

"DEARLY BELOVED."

The intimacy of the two words lingered in Frankie's mind after the ceremony like an echo that symbolized for her the true meaning of the whole production.

And it had been a production, just as she'd known it would.

Since the ceremony at two, there'd been photographers, receiving lines, cocktails, speeches. Uncle Vito had outdone himself; Frankie honestly thought they'd all be pensioners before he finished talking. And now, finally, the wedding dinner, orchestrated by Eric and his staff like a meticulously planned ballet.

The weather was perfect. A light breeze wafted the heady odor of roses from the nearby gardens. The wedding guests were seated at tables surrounding the pool at the Bauers' lavish home, and a string quartet situated a discreet distance away softly played love ballads as the guests devoured the food.

Mamma was right after all about quantity, Frankie thought with amusement, watching as elegantly dressed Bauer guests ate their way through two and three servings, just as the Granatelli contingent always did.

Every now and then, someone began tapping a glass with a spoon, and when the entire company picked up the signal, Nick would kiss his bride.

It made Frankie shudder. In her opinion, it was a barbaric custom.

Frankie caught glimpses of Eric, circulating unobtrusively among the catering staff, making very certain everything was as near perfect as he could make it.

Eric. Her dearly beloved. Soon, very soon, they'd be married. But not this way. All these people, all this pomp and ceremony, to witness what was essentially the most private of moments between a man and a woman, the moment they pledged themselves, body and soul, to each other for all the days of their lives.

Nick and Diane were carrying it off with elegance, this public proclamation, but as Frankie savored each bite of Nonna's *risotto milanese*, she vowed that she and Eric would do it differently.

Private. Quiet. Without all this speech making and tapping of glasses.

A small, informal wedding. Or maybe they'd even elope....

She'd confided their engagement to Nick, but she was waiting until this was over before she told her parents and the rest of the family.

The glass tapping was beginning again, somewhere to Frankie's left this time.

Nick stood up, Diane beside him, but instead of embracing his bride he held out his hands, signaling for quiet.

"I want to thank Eric Thorpe, the man responsible for this wonderful meal we're having." Everyone applauded, and Frankie was aware that Eric was standing just behind her. She glowed with pleasure and glanced up over her shoulder at the man she loved, giving him a triumphant wink. He deserved every bit of the lavish praise he'd been receiving for the food and its presentation.

The applause died quickly as Nick again held up an imperious hand. "I'd also like to propose a toast. To my sister, Frankie, who's just become engaged to Eric. Seems we'll have another wedding soon. To Frankie, and to Eric. Congratulations." He lifted his stemmed glass in a salute.

There was a moment of stunned silence as everyone digested the news, and then came a deafening outbreak of applause and cheers and whistles.

Frankie was utterly dumbfounded. How could Nick do this to her? She shot him a killing scowl, but he was grinning at her and, of all things, tapping his glass with a spoon.

The rest of the party followed suit, demanding a response from her and Eric.

She couldn't move. Waves of embarrassment rolled over her. Then she felt Eric's powerful hands on her shoulders, half lifting her out of her seat. He moved the chair back out of the way and took her in his arms.

"Smile, Funny Face," he whispered. "All your relatives are watching." Then he slowly lowered his lips to hers.

Her hat fell off, and for the first few seconds she stood like a wooden statue, agonizingly aware of all the eyes on them.

But as the gentle kiss deepened, it became less important that all these people were watching, and finally, it mattered not at all.

She was, she would always be, his dearly beloved. There were the two of them, and then there was the rest of the world.

Her arms came up slowly and linked around his neck.

Father Of The Bride

BARBARA DELINSKY

A Note from Barbara Delinsky

There is nothing more exciting—or more frightening—than getting married. It is a ritual that channels the lives of two separate people, bound together from that point on, as no other event does. It is a decision made freely, a step taken willingly, a responsibility accepted for better or for worse. It is a highly emotional experience.

That's why I always cry at weddings. I cry at the weddings of friends and relatives; I cry over newspaper accounts of royal weddings. Actually, I didn't cry at my own wedding. I was too busy making sure that the florist had wrapped the Bible I was to carry with lily of the valley just as I'd asked; that the caterer knew to serve fish to my uncle who couldn't eat meat; that the limousine would be waiting to whisk Stephen and me to the airport in time to make our flight to Bermuda.

After twenty-three years of marriage, I have three gorgeous sons, two in their teens and one beyond. I can begin to envision their weddings on the horizon. I've already warned them that I'll cry.

So I *knew* I'd have trouble when Harlequin asked me to write a wedding story. Oh, it was wonderful, up to a point. The editorial team set the scene with the Bauers and the Granatellis; I created characters I loved, then coordinated my own story with those of three terrific writers. Then I reached the wedding scene and I sat in front of my computer unable to see the screen through my tears. I probably spent more time on that short scene than on any other scene in the book!

To this day, rereading the story, I shed those same tears of happiness. Cynthia and Russ loved so deeply and shared so much during their first marriage that it seems only right they should love still, yet and again. Forever is definitely a three-hankie affair!

Sincerely,

Barbara

Chapter One

TWENTY-FIVE YEARS was a long time not to have gone home. Russell Shaw thought about that on Monday afternoon as his plane winged south toward St. Louis. He had been eighteen when he left. He had lived more of his life away from St. Louis than in it. But he had left part of his heart there, which made twenty-five years a long time indeed.

The view out the plane window told him nothing. He might well have been on his way to Chicago or Denver or San Francisco, each of which he had visited professionally in the course of those twenty-five years. Despite the brilliance of the late afternoon sun to the west, the carpet of clouds beneath the aircraft hid the distinguishing features that would have branded the landscape home. But Russ didn't need the reminder. There was no possible way he could forget where he was headed and why. For one thing, there was a faint ache in the part of his heart that he thought had long since healed. For another, there was a vague knot in his stomach—excitement, nervousness, downright fear; he guessed a little of each. And finally, there was the letter in his hand.

He opened it along folds that had become soft with wear over the past few weeks. The paper was white, thick and rich-feeling in keeping with the embossed DIANE SARAH BAUER at its top. The ink was blue, again with a rich feel to it, and the script was confident and feminine—rightly so for a young woman who had been raised in high society, had a good job and a fledgling business of her own and was in love with a man she adored.

Love made people confident. Russ knew. He remembered those days so long ago when he himself had been on top of the world. Love could conquer all, he'd thought then. Love could hold people together regardless of how incongruous their upbringings, how disparate their bank balances or how angry their parents were about the union.

He had learned the hard way that love couldn't do all that, but he prayed to God that Diane would fare better than he had. She certainly had more going for her. She had maturity on her side, and she had the support of her family, if he had correctly read between the lines of her letter.

We're being married at Saint Benedict's, on Saturday afternoon at two. It's going to be a big wedding. Between my grandmother's friends and my mother's friends, and Nick and my friends and Nick's family, there may be four hundred people there. But they're all wonderful. You'll like them, I know you will.

He supposed he would, at least as far as Nick's people went. He had already met Nick—once, with Diane in New York—and liked him. Nick was from a large Italian family, and though the Granatellis weren't at all impoverished, the Hill, a historic ethnic neighborhood, was a far cry from Frontenac, the finely manicured, grandly built enclave of St. Louisians of the Bauer ilk. Russ could identify with the Granatellis. He had been from the wrong side of the tracks himself. He would be able to talk with them easily.

Actually, he would be able to talk with the rest of the guests easily, too. He had come a long way since leaving St. Louis. The Connecticut private school of which he was headmaster had, in addition to its many scholarship students, a healthy share of the upper crust's sons and daughters. Russ had learned how to deal with the wealthy, and how to do it with grace. In contrast to the eighteen-year-old boy who had left St. Louis with a broken heart and a single satchel containing all his belongings, he was a man of considerable social skills. He was counting on those skills to stand him in good stead over the next five days, through the inevitable confrontation with Gertrude Hoffmann—and the inevitable one with Cynthia.

The prospect of seeing Cynthia gnawed at him. Because of that, he had thought long and hard about the wisdom of returning to St. Louis. He had a satisfying life in Connecticut. He didn't need pain from the past. Nor did he want his presence to spark anything—tension, an argument, words of resentment, however brief—that would hurt Diane. This was her time. He wanted it to be perfect for her.

For that reason, he should have stayed away. But for the same reason, he was coming. Diane had asked him to, had handwritten her request. Russ read that part of her letter for the umpteenth time:

> Had Matthew been here, he would have given me away. But he died before Nick and I even reconciled. Mom has asked Matthew's brother to do the honors, and though Ray was always wonderful to me, it isn't the same. This is one of the most important days of my life. I want it to be perfect, which is why, more than anything, I want you to give me away. You're my father. I know that coming back may be difficult for you, but if you can possibly see your way clear to do it, I'd be so, so happy.

Russ believed her. In the dozen or so meetings that he'd had with Diane over the past six years—dinners, first in Boston, when she had been at Radcliffe, then in New York after her stint abroad—he had come to know her for her sincerity. While not the confrontational type, she let her feelings be known through the look in her eye, the set of her mouth, the tone of her voice. Her wariness at their first meeting had been obvious to him, as had her subsequent warming. The last few times they'd met, she had greeted him with a hug. A hug. A warm, genuine, happy-to-see-him hug.

Each time he thought of that, Russ choked up. He suspected he would walk barefoot over hot coals if Diane asked him to. Of course, she wouldn't. She had never asked a thing of him. Until now. So how could he possibly deny her this request?

The clouds had begun to thin out, breaking at spots as the plane began its descent. Russ folded the letter and replaced it in the breast pocket of his blazer, near his heart. He wasn't sure if he deserved the honor of walking Diane down the aisle; wasn't sure if he deserved Diane at all. The last time he had done anything of a practical nature for her had been when she was three months old, on a night he'd relived hundreds of times since. Having made his decision to leave St. Louis, he had bathed the baby and gotten her ready for bed. He remembered how small she was, how neatly, trustingly, she curled against him. He remembered her sweet smell, her smooth skin, the tiny noises she made as she sucked on her thumb in the crib. He remembered turning off the light and feeling himself thrust into the dark, then being caught up for a brief, bright time in Cynthia's arms, before slipping out into the deepest darkness he'd ever known.

"This is the captain again." A voice with a distinct Midwest twang filtered through the airplane. "At this time we are beginning our final descent into St. Louis. Weather conditions at Lambert Field are partly sunny, with the temperature a warm seventy-six degrees. Air traffic permitting, we should be on the ground in just about twelve minutes. I'd like to take this opportunity to thank you all for flying with us today and to wish you a pleasant stay in St. Louis."

The easygoing timbre of the man's voice snapped Russ from past to present, darkness to light, sorrow to joy—and he *was* here on a mission of joy. His daughter, his only child, was getting married. Sure, he was meeting with a former colleague, a man now teaching at Washington University. But that meeting was incidental to the occasion of Diane's wedding.

As the plane dropped lower, the knot in his stomach became more pronounced. His apprehension had nothing to do with flying, he knew, and everything to do with returning to St. Louis. He hadn't thought he would ever come back. His mother had died before he left, and his father, a wanderer in the best of circumstances, had set out for parts unknown soon after Russ joined the Army. Not that Russ would have come back to St. Louis after Vietnam even had his father remained. Memory would have made living there as much of a hell as the war had been.

So he had gone directly to Washington, D.C., where he had enrolled at Georgetown under the GI Bill. Four years later, with a history degree in his pocket, he had taken a teaching job in Connecticut and made a life for himself that was sufficiently far removed from St. Louis.

That didn't mean he hadn't thought about Cynthia, or Diane, or the life they might have had together. Particularly in those early days at Hollings, when he'd had a modest but reputable salary that would have supported them, he had thought of them often. But he had made a decision, and he couldn't go back. There was nothing to go back to. Cynthia had returned to the Hoffmann family fold and had their marriage annulled. Then she'd married Matthew Bauer, who had adopted Diane and proceeded to raise her as his own.

All that was what Russ had intended. As clearly as he knew the words on the letter in his breast pocket, he remembered the words in another letter, one he himself had written twenty-five years before. He had agonized over every sentence, every phrase, wanting to minimize Cynthia's hurt and make her understand why he was doing what he was.

This is the only way, Cyn. If I leave, they'll take you back, and if they take you back, you'll have all the things you and the baby should have. I can't give them to you. I thought I could, but I can't. I can take two jobs and work forever and still come up short. It's not fair that you should have to live this way.

"Excuse me, sir?" the flight attendant said. "We're preparing to land. Would you raise your seat back, please?"

With an apologetic smile, Russ pressed the button to return the seat to its upright position, then looked out the window again. At the sight of the skyline coming up on the right, his heart began to thud. The Gateway Arch identified the city— he remembered the excitement when its construction was complete—but otherwise he might well have been approaching a foreign land. He had never viewed St. Louis from the air before, true. But twenty-five years of growth had dramatically altered the city as he remembered it from the ground. Tall, gleaming buildings had sprouted where low ones had once been. Some shone with glass; others were more muted with stone. Some were square, some round, some terraced, some sleek.

Russ didn't know why he should be surprised. He had been in many a cosmopolitan area over the years, and he knew that St. Louis was as cosmopolitan as any. Having been a subscriber to the *Post Dispatch* for years, he also knew the specifics of what went on inside those new buildings. Somehow, though, seeing the city now, in contrast to the way it had stood for so long in his memory, served to emphasize just how much time had passed.

He had changed, too, he knew. He had grown taller and broader. He had also come by crow's-feet at the corners of his eyes and his once dark hair was shot with strands of silver, but he wasn't ashamed of either of those things. Given that he hadn't gained an ounce since graduation from high school— and that he ran upward of thirty miles a week—he thought he'd aged well.

He knew Cynthia had. The pictures that appeared in the paper from time to time told him so. She had grown into a beautiful woman whose clothes, hair, behavior were all eminently flattering and socially correct. No doubt Gertrude Hoffmann was pleased.

He wondered if the old lady knew he was coming. Surely Cynthia did, since he had received a formal wedding invitation from her with his name and address written in calligraphy on the front. He had no sooner returned the reply card with his acceptance than he had received Diane's personal note asking him to give her away. He wondered what Cynthia thought of that. He wondered what *Gertrude* thought of that, the old battle-ax.

The plane touched down with a small jolt. To gather his composure he closed his eyes for a minute and conjured up an image of his home in Connecticut and the life that he found so rewarding. When the plane finally pulled up to the gate, he rose with the other passengers, took his carryon from the overhead compartment and slowly made his way up the aisle.

The terminal was filled with welcoming committees. Families, friends, business associates, lovers—Russ's imagination touched on the possibilities as he passed by the expectant groups. Diane had offered to meet him, but he hadn't wanted her to fight through late afternoon traffic for him. Besides, he was renting a car.

Though both arguments were valid, there was another that he hadn't wanted to voice in his last letter to her. From the start he had known that returning to St. Louis would be an emotional experience for him. He wanted a little time alone to merge past with present, a little time to gather himself, because more than anything he wanted to come across as being self-assured and strong. He wanted Diane to be proud of who and what he was. He wanted Cynthia to be proud, too. He was the father of the bride—the father of a beautiful, personable, privileged bride—and it behooved him to fit the role. He had a point to prove. Based on little more than his home address, Gertrude Hoffmann had deemed him unworthy of her daughter's love years before. He was going to take pride in showing her how sadly she had underestimated his ability to rise in the world.

As had been true of the rest of the trip, his luggage came through without a hitch. So did the rental car his travel agent had reserved for him. With surprising speed he hit the interstate, intent on going straight to his hotel as he always did when he traveled, to shower away the fatigue of the flight. There wasn't any fatigue this time, though, or if there was, it was buried beneath excitement. Without quite making a conscious decision to do so, he found himself driving directly downtown, actually appreciating the traffic, which was slow enough to allow him to study his surroundings.

The Arch was as impressive as ever, as was the Old Cathedral, but those were mere jumping-off points for Market Street. He passed the Old Courthouse, which he remembered, and Kiener Mall, which he didn't. Farther on he passed the City Hall, but he didn't pull over until he reached Aloe

Plaza. He had always loved the sculpted fountain there, had spent hours as a boy studying the bronze figures that commemorated the joining of the Mississippi and Missouri rivers. Male and female, they had symbolized in his mind happiness, freedom and love. He remembered spending hours sitting in sight of that fountain with Cynthia, holding her hand, watching the play of the water. He remembered touching her stomach as they sat there, feeling the tightening of her muscles, the movement of the baby inside. Given what had happened to his marriage, he should have been disillusioned watching the water's spray now, but he wasn't. Good had come out of his marriage in the form of Diane. For the sake of her existence alone, the pain had been worthwhile.

With an odd mix of reluctance and curiosity, he looked across the street toward Union Station. He'd spent his last night there in St. Louis, slouched on a hard bench, waiting to take the dawn train out of town. At the time he was sure it would prove to be the most miserable night of his life, but that was before he had suffered through basic training without sight or sound of Cynthia. And before he'd been sent overseas.

Union Station was no longer a railroad station. Russ had kept abreast of its conversion into a complex of shops, restaurants and a hotel, and given his memories, he wasn't sorry for the change. The less there was to remind him of that sad and lonely night, the better.

Driving slowly on, he turned down one street and up another. None of the reading he'd done over the years had prepared him for so many alterations. What wasn't new was refurbished, and what wasn't refurbished had been carefully preserved. He was impressed. St. Louis had done well for itself.

He drove on a bit longer, gradually losing himself in his thoughts. He passed a restaurant that hadn't been there twenty-five years before, and one that had—not that he'd ever eaten in it. He hadn't been able to afford such places. Pizza and a movie had been his limit, but Cynthia had never minded. She'd been incredible that way. Raised with a silver spoon in her mouth, she had been willing to give it all up just to be with him. They'd be sitting in his secondhand Ford, sharing a pack of Lorna Doones and a milk shake, curled against each other in the dingy shadow of the soda shop because they couldn't go to her parents' estate or to his father's hovel, and she'd make him feel like a million bucks. He had loved her so much. *So much.*

The traffic eased. Though more than an hour remained before dusk, with the low slant of the sun and the exodus of the working set, it felt like evening. Turning west at last, Russ headed for Clayton. He had chosen to stay in the suburb for its proximity both to the university, where he would be visiting his colleague, and to Cynthia's home, where the wedding reception was being held. He had chosen the Seven Gables Inn not only for its New England connection but for its small size and its reputation for charm and warmth. He didn't think he could stand a large, impersonal hotel. Not this trip. Not when he was feeling more exposed than he had in years.

The inn proved to be brighter than the Nathaniel Hawthorne house Russ had visited in Salem. The personnel were upbeat, as well. His suite had a European flavor but was distinctly homey. A decorative headboard and footboard set off the large bed, which was covered by a quilt of a dusty blue design, picking up the color of the floral wallpaper and the café curtains. The artwork was gentle—dancers, a landscape. Cut flowers stood in a vase on a small round table, alongside a basket of fresh fruit.

After tossing his blazer on the bed, unbuttoning his shirt cuffs and turning them back, Russ picked up an apple and took a bite. Idly he ambled to the window, which overlooked the front of the inn, and opened it to let in the evening air.

Before he had taken more than a single short breath, he went very still. From behind the wheel of a pale gray Lincoln that had pulled up to the curb across the way, emerged a stunning woman. She was of average height—five foot six, Russ knew for a fact—and more slender than he remembered. What he didn't remember was the air she exuded. With the sleek linen suit she wore, the prim knot of her long, honeyed hair, the confidence of her carriage and the sober look on her face, she was all business.

Russ wished he could be, too, but the sight of Cynthia made his mouth go dry. She had been his whole world once. He had measured his days by the time he spent with her. She had been his warmth, his laughter, his hope. He had wanted nothing more in life than to take care of her and make her happy.

He hadn't done that.

Unable to move, he watched her cross the street and disappear under the awning of the inn. His heart beat loudly—the same way it had the very first time he'd set eyes on her in the soda shop twenty-six years before; the same way it had the very first time he'd taken her out, then kissed her, then touched her; the same way it had the very first time they'd made love. His heart always beat that way when he saw pictures of her in the paper, as though she were still his and simply on loan to another life for a time.

If that was so, their lives were about to collide. In a matter of minutes there was a knock on his door. Russ turned quickly and stared in its direction until the knock came again. Swallowing, he drew himself up to his full six-foot-three height, took a slow, deep, bolstering breath and went to open the door.

Chapter Two

CYN HOFFMANN and Rusty Shaw had been classmates for years, but it wasn't until late August, just prior to the start of their senior year in high school, that they looked at each other and were lost. For as long as she lived, Cynthia would remember the day she had gone into the soda shop with a group of her friends and seen him. He had been working behind the counter, fixing milk shakes and banana splits, when she ordered a lime rickey. His eyes had been brown and bottomless, his jaw straight and shadowed by the kind of beard that few of his classmates could boast. But his smile was what had done it, sending waves of awareness all the way to her toes.

She had returned to the soda shop the next afternoon, and the next. Each time she came with one less friend, until she was finally alone at the counter ordering the lime rickey she barely tasted for the excitement of being near Rusty.

He was tall and good-looking, a serious athlete, a fine student. Had he been part of her social set, she would have been drawn to him sooner. But he lived with his father in a part of town that Cyn had never stepped foot in, and he kept to himself.

That ended when he and Cyn started to talk. From the very first, they connected. If anything, their differences made the conversations they had more exciting. They became a party of two—Rusty and Cyn, Cyn and Rusty—letting other friends wander off while they talked and laughed, while they shared their thoughts, then their dreams.

The first time he kissed her, Cyn thought she would explode. She had been kissed before, but she'd never felt the heat. With Rusty, she felt it. She felt it ten times over. Simply looking at him stirred her, but when he touched his mouth to hers, everything inside her sizzled. And that was just the start.

When the soda shop proved limiting, they found different places to meet, different places to park his creaky old Ford. Kisses evolved into touches that grew bolder and more intimate. Then came the day when they needed to be closer still, when her skirt was pushed up and his jeans opened. Cyn was a virgin, and Russ not much more than that, but what they lacked in experience they more than made up for in love. She felt no pain that first time, she adored him so, and each time was better, then better, until they could no more have done without making love to each other than they could have gone without air.

By the time spring arrived, marriage seemed the only acceptable course of action. They had both been admitted to college, Rusty on a basketball scholarship, and they figured that with the scholarship and a little help from Cynthia's family, they could survive.

Gertrude Hoffmann didn't see things quite that way. She had envisioned Cynthia taking the year off to make her society debut. Everyone who was anyone in St. Louis society made her debut. But a married debutante was unacceptable. *Rusty Shaw* was unacceptable. He came from nowhere, was going nowhere. He was no proper match for her daughter.

But Cyn adored him. Everything about him excited her, from his intelligence to his liberalism to the way he turned her on with just a look. He worshiped her in ways the other boys she knew were too self-centered to do. She couldn't envision a life without him. So within days of their high school graduation, young and idealistic enough to believe that Cyn's parents would come around once their marriage was fact, they eloped.

Cyn's parents didn't come around. To the contrary, they cut her off without a cent, which meant there would be neither the grand coming-out parties nor college. Cyn was quite happy to do without the debut, and while she was sorry to be missing college, she would take Russ over college any day. What did bother her was that he had to put his own college plans on hold. He couldn't support a wife on his scholarship money, and his father couldn't help them at all.

Determined to make it, they came up with a plan whereby they would both work for several years and save every spare cent. Then Russ would reapply for his scholarship and return to school part-time. It would take him longer that way, they knew, but they could make it. And they might have, if Cyn hadn't become pregnant. The baby was born nine months after their marriage. They were both eighteen at the time.

Through the months leading up to Diane's birth, then the weeks following it, they struggled to make things work. But the cards were stacked against them. Not only were they not able to make much money, but what they did make they needed to live on, which left nothing to save. Shortly before Diane's birth, Cyn had to stop working, which meant less money to pay an increasing number of bills. Their dreams grew more and more distant.

But those dreams did remain, at least in Cynthia's mind. They helped carry her through the fatigue and the worry. She clung to them, convinced that if she and Russ loved each other enough, things would get better.

Then, when Diane was three months old, Russ left and took Cynthia's dreams with him. Her grief was unspeakable. Only Diane kept her going in those first lonely days. In time, there was her mother, and then Matthew Bauer, but it was ages before Cynthia could look back on those months with Russ without starting to cry.

Now he was back, and she thought she was prepared. She had been gearing herself up for seeing him ever since his name had appeared on Diane's wedding list, and she honestly thought she was ready. She was long over the anger and hurt of his leaving, long over mourning the dreams they had shared. She had assumed she would simply see him on Saturday, with hundreds of people around to remind her of who she was and where she belonged. She had hoped to say hello to him, shake hands, even smile. Then, without so much as a twinge, turn right back to the life that had been so good to her.

She hadn't counted on his looking so tall and broad-shouldered, and so strikingly handsome that her heart constricted. She hadn't counted on the years disappearing in the space of an instant—on being yanked back to the soda shop and the moment his deep, brown eyes first met hers, then being spun ahead to that awful, awful morning when she awoke to find her world had fallen apart. She hadn't counted on feeling bereft again.

For a minute she was unable to speak. In her shock, Russ found the wherewithal to rise above his own emotional tangle. Allowing himself a trace of the pleasure that he'd always felt looking at her, he smiled. "You're looking well, Cyn, really well."

She wanted to say the same to him, but words wouldn't come. His appearance stunned her. Oh, he had been handsome—gorgeous in that tall, dark, athletic way—when they'd been younger, and the physical details weren't so different. But he had something else now. He had confidence, poise. He had presence.

But then, so did she, she reminded herself. At least, she was supposed to. She was Mrs. Matthew Bauer, chairwoman of dozens of charity events over the years, and Gertrude Hoffmann's daughter. More immediately, she was the mother of the bride, on the verge of pulling off the most elegant wedding St. Louis had seen in years. It wouldn't do for her to fall apart—or freeze up—at the sight of the father of the bride, regardless of how long it had been since she'd seen him last.

"How are you, Russ?" she said in a voice that should have been stronger. But she wasn't about to quibble. She was grateful for any voice at all.

"I'm fine."

Because it was familiar and comfortable—and because St. Louis wasn't his home anymore—she lapsed into the role of hostess. "How was your flight?"

"Smooth."

"And the room here is all right?"

"Very nice."

She glanced at his hand. "Am I coming at a bad time?"

He lobbed the apple onto the plate by the fruit basket and wiped one palm on the other. "Nope." Then he dropped his hands and stood there, unsure of what she wanted, unsure of what *he* wanted. There was so much they could say, or so little. He didn't know which way it would go, but he did know that it wouldn't go anywhere if they stayed at the door. "Want to come in?"

What Cynthia wanted was to hightail it back to Frontenac, where the house and the gardens and the help made things safe and secure. But running wouldn't accomplish anything. She had come with a purpose. Stepping over the threshold, she let Russ close the door. When he gestured her toward a chair, though, she shook her head. She didn't think she could play at relaxing, not with Russ, not seeing him for the first time in so long.

Lips pressed together, she went to the window. Keeping her back to him, which made things easier, she said, "I feel badly about this, because I know you've come a long way, but Diane shouldn't have done what she did."

"Shouldn't have invited me to the wedding?" Russ asked.

"Shouldn't have asked you to give her away. I didn't know about it until earlier today. I told her she'd have to call you, but she said it was too late, that you were already on your way." She turned to face him. Her jaw was firm, and he caught a flare of defiance in her eyes. "If Matthew were alive, he would have walked her down the aisle. He raised her. He loved her. He was her father in all but the biological sense. Since he isn't here, his brother is filling in."

Russ didn't miss the criticism of him implicit in Cynthia's praise of Matthew. One part of him felt he deserved it; one part wanted to object. Both parts yielded to the more immediate concern. "That would be Ray. Diane mentioned you'd asked him. She didn't mention that there would be trouble if you told him I'd be here."

"Not trouble," Cynthia explained patiently. "It's a question of what's appropriate and what isn't. Matthew was here, you weren't. *Ray* was here, you weren't. For you to show up at this late date wanting to suddenly take over your fatherly duties is a little silly, don't you think?"

Once, Russ could overlook the criticism. Twice was harder. "Actually," he said, "I don't think it's silly at all. Given the circumstances, I think it makes a whole lot of sense."

"What circumstances?"

"My relationship with Diane. It's not a question of suddenly taking over my fatherly duties. We've been in touch for six years now."

"Yes," Cynthia acknowledged.

"Against your wishes?" he asked. He had often wondered about that, but he hadn't ever been able to ask. Diane made as much of a point not to discuss Cynthia as he did. It was hard enough forging a relationship between father and daughter without opening a Pandora's box of other issues.

"I knew Diane was seeing you. She's an adult. She can do what she wants."

"But you don't approve?"

"It's not my place to approve or disapprove."

"Come on, Cyn, that's a cop-out," Russ chided, but with a sad, gentle tone that took the sting from his words. "You're Diane's mother. Just because she's an adult doesn't mean you opt out of feeling where she's concerned. I'm asking whether you wanted her to see me. My guess is you didn't, since you'd already told her I was dead."

Cynthia quickly raised a hand. "I didn't tell her that. I never told her that."

"Someone did. She was sure it was true. After I contacted her the first time, she was so skeptical that before she would see me again, she flew down to Washington to look for my name on the Vietnam War Memorial. Did you know that?"

Cynthia dropped her gaze to the carpeted floor. She'd known it. She couldn't have *helped* but know it. Diane had been livid. It had taken hours of talking, hours of explaining thoughts and feelings, before her daughter had calmed down. "My mother was the one who said you were dead," she told Russ now.

"But you didn't deny it."

"No."

"That was wrong."

"So Diane told me in no uncertain terms."

"Did she tell her grandmother, too?"

"In gentler terms. Diane has always been more independent of Gertrude than I was. She isn't threatened by her. They're close in some ways, but in others Diane keeps her distance. Somehow she manages to find compassion for the woman."

"I never could," Russ scoffed, "and I'll be damned if I'll do it now. How could she tell my own daughter that I was dead?"

Cynthia wished she could sound as indignant as Russ. But since she hadn't refuted the story, she wasn't much better than her mother. "It was a comfortable scenario for her. Her friends all knew about our marriage. They all knew that I'd been estranged from the family. My mother had an easier time saying you went off to war than that you'd deserted me." More dryly, she added, "No one deserts a Hoffmann. We're too valuable."

If Russ hadn't been so embroiled in his own anger, he might have heard the self-effacing note. But he'd been stewing about his alleged death for years. "Your mother hated me. From the beginning, she thought I was good for nothing. All she had to do to prove her point was to say that I ran away."

"The war was more honorable." Cynthia frowned, running through the same arguments she had that night six years before with Diane. "My mother is a proud woman. What she did and said with regard to you was more by way of saving face than anything else. She had let it be known to her friends that I'd done a stupid thing in marrying you. Once she knew I was coming back home, she wanted to look a little less stupid. Mind you, she didn't broadcast your death around town. She didn't dare, lest she be caught in a lie by someone who knew you weren't dead at all. She just let it quietly slip when certain people asked."

"Like Diane," Russ said, tempering his anger. "Didn't she ask about me when she was little?"

Cynthia looked him in the eye. "She thought Matthew was her father. He had legally adopted her. She had his name. It wasn't until she was eight that I told her the truth."

"But what did you say, if not that I was dead?"

"I said you'd had to leave us. That was general enough."

But Russ knew children, particularly the intelligent kind, of which Diane had clearly been one. "Didn't she ask where I went?"

"I told her you went to war."

"But the war was over by the time she was eight."

"My mother told her you had died."

"Didn't she ask *you* about that? At her age, she'd have had all sorts of questions about death. What did you tell her?"

"I was vague. I never specifically said you were dead."

"But you didn't deny it."

With accusation in her eyes, she answered, "I wasn't in much of a position to be making denials, particularly about something coming from my mother. In case you've forgotten, I was destitute. I'd been kicked out of my house, totally disowned. The only money I had to my name was the little you'd earned. Do you know that I stayed in our apartment for a whole month after you left?" The memory brought tears to her eyes.

Russ's anger faded at the sight of those tears. "I told you to go home."

"I wanted *you*, not home!" she cried, uncaring of the emotion she displayed. Clearly he thought she had simply returned to the lap of luxury, with no harm done. He should know some of what she had suffered. "I kept hoping you'd change your mind and come back. I loved you. You loved me. I was sure we could make it if we just stuck things out long enough. Then my money ran out, and I had no choice but to crawl back to my mother."

"She didn't keep you crawling for long."

"And that's to her credit," Cynthia countered with renewed strength. "She accepted us back. She let bygones be bygones. She took care of everything at a time when I was totally shattered. If she had wanted to say you had drunk yourself to death in an alley, I'd probably have let her.''

''Would you have let her say that to Diane?''

Cynthia was slower in answering. She wanted to hurt Russ because he'd hurt her, but she had never been a vengeful person. With quiet resignation, she said, ''No. I wouldn't have let her say that. I couldn't have. It implied you were a bum. I wouldn't have let Diane think ill of you that way.''

Russ recognized the admission as the first hint that Cynthia didn't hate him completely. ''Thank you,'' he said, his voice as quiet as hers.

In the silence that followed, he found his eyes roaming her face, reacquainting themselves with the features he had once known so well. Her skin was smooth, as dewy as it had been when she was eighteen, and though he was sure she wore makeup, it was light and finely applied. Time hadn't changed the sculpted quality of her face. Nor had it changed the softness of her lips, the pale green of her eyes or the rich, honeyed sheen of her hair. He remembered when that hair had surrounded him, forming a veil around their kisses. Except for a few wispy bangs, it was anchored in a knot now. He wondered how long it was.

''I think—'' she began, then cleared her throat and began again. ''I think I'll sit down after all.'' Her knees weren't as steady as she wanted them to be—Russ's scrutiny had always done that to her—and there was still the matter of the wedding to decide. Slipping into the chair that he had offered her earlier, she crossed her legs, folded her hands in her lap and looked up with what she hoped was restored composure. ''About your relationship with Diane—''

''I'm not giving her up,'' Russ vowed. ''I'm not walking away. I did that once, because I felt I had no choice, but I can't do it again. She's my daughter. Anyone looking at the two of us together can see that.''

Cynthia would be the last one to argue. She remembered how painful it had been, particularly in those first hard years, to look at Diane and see the resemblance. In time that resemblance took a back seat to Diane's vibrant personality. Still, there were odd moments when a look or a gesture would conjure up Russ again.

"I've never denied that she was your daughter, and I'm not asking you to give her up. I'm simply asking that you let my brother-in-law walk her down the aisle."

"Why is that so important to you?"

"Diane has always been close to him—and to his daughter, Lisa, who's the maid of honor. Ray was good to us over the years, particularly after Matthew died. I felt it was an honor he should be given. Besides, I've already asked him. To take back the invitation would be a slap in the face."

"Not if you explained the situation."

"I'd rather not do that."

"Explain the situation? Or take back the invitation?"

"Either."

Russ sank into the chair opposite her. He sat forward with his elbows on his knees and laced his fingers in the gap between. "I can buy the problem about taking back the invitation. But I'm not sure I understand why explaining the situation is so difficult. If Ray is fond of Diane, he should want what she wants." An unpleasant idea intruded on that thought. "Are you dating him?"

"Of course not. He's my brother-in-law, and he's married."

"Are you dating someone else?"

"I don't think that's relevant here."

Russ knew it wasn't, but since he had broached the topic, he wasn't backing down. He wanted to know what to expect on Saturday. "I'm curious."

"You gave up your right to curiosity the night you walked out on me," Cynthia said more sharply than she'd planned. Seeing Russ had stirred up old feelings, the most immediate of which was anger at his desertion. She hadn't realized the feeling was still so strong.

He turned his hands over and studied them. In a grim voice, he said, "I didn't walk out on you. Not the way you make it sound."

"You left. I had a three-month-old baby, a one-room apartment with someone else's furnishings in it and two hundred dollars in my bag."

"That was more than I had." He had taken only the train fare, wanting to leave everything else for her.

"But I couldn't work. You could. You were supposed to take care of me."

"On *what?*" He raised his eyes. "I had a high school diploma and no skills. I was working two jobs, neither of which would get me to first base, and when I wasn't working, I was helping you with the baby. I was exhausted and scared and disgusted with myself that I couldn't do better. So I left. You can criticize me for that, but it wasn't a decision I made lightly. I agonized. I went through the alternatives again and again, trying to find a way to make it work. But it was a vicious circle. Without a college education, I couldn't earn good money, but I couldn't get the college education because I wasn't earning good enough money to stop working and study." He raked a hand through his hair. "Don't you think I wanted to stay? I adored the baby, and you—you were the light of my life! I wanted to give you so much, but I wasn't going to be able to give you a damn thing the way we were going. All I was doing was sentencing you to a life of hard labor. That tore me apart. So I sent you back home."

"Without asking whether I wanted to go," Cynthia challenged, but the challenge fizzled with Russ's immediate acknowledgment.

"Of course you didn't want to go. I knew that. I knew that as long as I hung around, you'd be right there with me. But your mother wouldn't accept me, and because of that, she wouldn't accept you or the baby. And because of that, you were suffering in ways you didn't deserve. We were living in poverty, for God's sake."

"I didn't think it was so bad."

"You would have after a year, or two or three. You would have thought back to what you'd grown up with and begun to wonder where you were going. You'd have hated me by then."

"No—"

"Yes." He was determined to make her understand why he had left her that fateful night. "I saw it happen with my parents. My mother kept thinking things would get better, but they never did. Poverty eats at relationships like nothing else can. By the time she died, she couldn't stand the sight of my father."

"But we loved each other!"

"So did my parents when they first married. I thought our situation was different because of your family. I thought that if I could support myself with my scholarship and they could support you until I graduated, we'd do fine. I assumed too much."

"We both assumed it," Cynthia argued. She didn't like Russ playing the martyr, when they had made their decisions together.

"Well, we assumed wrong. We were bucking the tide, Cyn. There was no way we were going to keep from drowning at the rate we were going. I was dragging you under. I had to leave."

"So you disappeared."

He let out a breath and sat back. "I joined the army. It was the only thing I could afford."

"You never wrote me."

"I figured you were back home and that there would only be trouble if mail arrived from me."

He was right, she knew, but she wasn't conceding the point aloud. For years she had been haunted by the fact that he had never tried to contact her after he'd gone. "You could have written to Diane."

"She was too young to read, and by the time she was old enough, you were married to Bauer."

"You could have written to her then. You could have contacted her. You could have let her know that her father cared."

"Would that have made life easier for her?"

"Yes!" Cynthia exclaimed, but the expression on her face that followed gave her away.

"It wouldn't have," Russ chided. "She had a wonderful life. She had you and Bauer. She had dancing lessons and private school and big birthday parties on the lawn of your home. She even had a horse of her own."

"You didn't know that then."

"I did. The Bauers were society. The *Post Dispatch* covered most everything you did."

"You read the *Post Dispatch?*" she asked in surprise. She knew he'd been living in Connecticut for years. She couldn't believe that the *Post Dispatch* was sold on newsstands there.

"I've subscribed to the thing since the day I was discharged from the army. It was the only way I could keep up with what you were doing."

Cynthia felt a small ache in the pit of her stomach. For years she'd assumed that Russ had pushed her into his past and gone on with his life. Believing that had made it easier for her to do the same. Now, knowing that he'd never forgotten her, she felt a rush of things that spelled trouble. To ward it off, she ignored his statement. Rather, out of sheer curiosity, she asked, "What made you finally contact Diane?"

"I read about her graduation from high school and knew she was going to Radcliffe. College seemed the right time to contact her."

"When she was away from me?"

Cynthia had always been quick. That was one of the things Russ had loved about her. She hadn't played sweet and dumb, like the other girls. She put two and two together, often guessing his thoughts before he expressed them. Apparently she hadn't changed.

"I didn't know what you'd told her," he explained. "I didn't know how you felt about me yourself. It seemed easier to wait until she was out of the house. That way I wouldn't have to deal with your feelings, too."

"But you waited until her sophomore year."

"Freshman year is tough for kids, with all that's new and different. I wanted to give her a chance to settle in and realize she wasn't going to flunk out before I threw her a major loop." He arched a brow. "Aside from not believing me, she wasn't terribly thrown."

"She has a level head on her shoulders." *She got that from you*, Cynthia wanted to say, but resisted.

"She's a great girl. You did a good job, Cyn."

The compliment was from the heart. Cynthia sensed that, and it touched her more than she wanted to be touched. Lowering her eyes, she twisted the ring on her finger. Actually, there were three rings, two simple gold bands flanking a central one studded with diamonds and sapphires—wedding bands and an engagement ring that Matthew had given her. Looking at them reminded her who had helped raise Diane into the great girl she was.

Eyes still lowered, she said, "I would really prefer to have Ray give her away."

Russ had felt she was beginning to soften and was immediately disappointed. "If you're ashamed of me," he burst out, leaning forward again, "there's no need. I have a Ph.D., a prestigious position and a fine reputation. I know how to talk, how to act, even how to waltz. I've already made arrangements with the shop Nick is using to be fitted for a morning coat, striped pants and the rest tomorrow, so I'll look as dignified as any man there, and if it's a matter of the amount of money in my bank account—"

"That's not it," she cut in.

"Then what is? Is Ray particularly fragile?"

"Not at all."

His eyes hardened. "Then it is me. My existence. That's it, isn't it? You have your place in society, and you don't want it threatened. You don't want people reminded that you married beneath yourself and that Diane's father deserted her. There'll be people there who don't know I ever existed, and you want to keep it that way."

"That's not it!" she cried. But her composure was starting to crumble—not so much because of what he was saying as because of the look in his eyes. The hardness was new. He had never looked at her that way before. In the past there had been nothing but gentleness, understanding and adoration. Irrational though it was, given that they were nothing to each other anymore, what she saw now hurt her nearly as much as his disappearance had twenty-five years before.

Rising to her feet with a surge of feeling, she cried, "It's me. *Me.* Seeing you hurts *me!* I've spent months planning every detail of this wedding because I want the day to be perfect, so I've been excited, but tense, too. When Diane put your name on her list, I knew I'd have trouble, but I told myself I could handle it. I'm grown-up. I'm rational. I'm past pettiness." She shook her head. "But your walking her down the aisle is too much."

"I'm her *father,* for God's sake, and a wedding is a milestone."

"So is going off to kindergarten, but were you there for that? Or for her first horse show? Or her first ballet recital?"

"I couldn't be there then," he said more quietly as he looked up at her. "I've already told you why."

But Cynthia wasn't thinking of his reasons. She was reliving the agony of losing him. "You weren't there when I ran out of money. You weren't there when I knew what I had to do but was terrified of doing it. You weren't there when I thought I was pregnant again."

The air was still. "Pregnant?"

"Yes, pregnant."

"With another baby of *ours?*"

"Who else's baby would I have had?" she cried. "All the signs were there. I was sure I was pregnant. I didn't know whether to be happy or sad, so all I was was scared to death!"

In hindsight, Russ felt all those things for her, plus a helplessness in the here and now. "I didn't know."

"Of course you didn't know. You were too busy playing soldier and convincing yourself that you'd done the honorable thing."

His eyes went wide in disbelief. "Playing soldier? I was *miserable.*"

"But you didn't come back!"

"I couldn't!"

"But I needed you!"

Hearing the words, seeing the look in her eyes that said she had felt betrayed, Russ understood that this airing of their emotions had been inevitable. But they were going in circles, and it was painful. He didn't know how much more he could take.

Cynthia was wondering the very same thing about herself. She hadn't planned to fall apart. It was fine to say that she'd been under pressure of late, but that didn't excuse what she was doing or saying. There was no point in lashing out about what was long since over and done.

"About the wedding," she began with a sigh, only to stop when he rose abruptly from his chair and crossed to the bed. The muscles of his shoulders flexed when he reached into the blazer that lay there. Her gaze fell to his pants, stylish twill ones that broadcast the tightness of his bottom and the length of his legs. She had always loved those legs—strong and well formed without being grossly muscular, and, though hairy, not so much a thick, wiry kind of hair as a wispier, smoother kind. She remembered sitting naked beside him, running her hands up and down those legs—

"Before you say anything else about the wedding, Cyn, I think you should read this."

Her eyes shot to the folded paper he held. She took it and lowered it to her lap, which gave her the excuse to drop her head, the only way she could hide the color she was sure stained her cheeks. The feel of the paper was familiar. Even before she opened it and saw the name embossed at the top, she knew it to be a piece of the stationery she had ordered for Diane six months before, at the same time she'd ordered the wedding invitations that had long since been mailed.

She read the entire letter. It was a chatty one, telling Russ in the lightest tone, almost tongue in cheek, about the parties and dinners of the past few months, then about plans for the wedding itself. The tone grew introspective when she related her feelings for Nick, her excitement about the marriage, her hopes for the future. The tone grew softer and more beseeching when she asked Russ to give her away.

Without raising her eyes, Cynthia held the letter for a minute longer before refolding it. She knew why Russ had let her read it. More than anything he might have said, it spoke of the relationship that had grown between Diane and him in the past six years. It made another point, too, one that was directly relevant to the issue of the wedding. Diane had asked Russ to walk her down the aisle. The idea had come from her. Clearly it was something Diane very much wanted.

The fact that Cynthia didn't want it was suddenly irrelevant. So much of what she had done in life—including returning to her mother's after Russ had left—had been done for Diane. Given her druthers, Cynthia would probably have gone off in search of him. But Diane had needed care and protection, and Cynthia had been determined to give her both. She loved her daughter. She wanted her to be happy. That would never change.

She passed the letter back to Russ, but for a moment she didn't let go. Quietly, thoughtfully, with her eyes focused on the spot where his large hand closed over the paper, she said, "When Diane was little, I spoiled her terribly. She was so undemanding, it was easy to do that. She rarely asked for anything she didn't really want, and when I gave her whatever it was, she thanked me forever. Despite all she had growing up, she never took things for granted. I know she couldn't possibly have remembered how strapped we were during the first three months of her life, but there were times when I wondered whether it somehow registered on her subconscious."

Dropping her hand from the letter, she dared raised her eyes for a final moment. "I'll talk with Ray," she said. Without another word, she left the room.

Chapter Three

BY THE TIME RUSS ARRIVED at the Bauer home at nine-thirty the next morning, he was already well into his day. He had awoken at six, taken a forty-minute run along a course that the hotel management had recommended, and returned to shower. After putting down a full breakfast at Bernard's, a restaurant at the inn, he set off in the car to see those things he hadn't seen the day before—namely, the neighborhood where he'd grown up.

He found a mixed bag. The schools he had gone to looked exactly as he remembered them, as did the library and the supermarket, but the soda shop had been converted into a video store, and the house he had called home had been razed.

Cruising down one street and up another, his eyes darting left to right in recognition of familiar landmarks, he gathered memories. Some were of the days before he had met Cyn; most were of the days after. They had had such good times together. The simple act of walking down a street with her had been a joy. He remembered the way she had leaned into him, wrapped her arm around his waist, matched her step to his. Mostly he remembered the way she had looked up at him with happy, trusting eyes. She had made him feel invincible, a grave error on his part. If he had been more realistic, he might have been able to prevent the pain.

Hundreds of times he had wondered what would have happened if he and Cynthia had known before they eloped what Cynthia's mother would do. He supposed they would have waited, gone to college, stolen time together. He supposed that when he finally got his degree and was gainfully employed, when he'd finally been able to support Cynthia without Gertrude's help, they would have married. Then again, in the ensuing years Cynthia might have been swept up into the whirl of society and left him behind. That thought had terrified him.

The irony of it, he realized as he headed for Frontenac, was that that early fear had come to pass with Cynthia's marriage to Matthew Bauer. In addition to being older, Bauer had been everything Russ wasn't. He'd been educated. Cultured. Wealthy. He'd been a perfect match for Cynthia, as society matches went. Had he made her happy?

If happiness was judged by the beauty of one's home, the answer had to be yes. Russ had known the Bauers lived in an elegant area, but he wasn't quite prepared for the extent of the elegance when he turned onto their street and found their drive. It was flanked by two brick gateposts covered with ivy, as was the gatekeeper's cottage just inside. Since the black wrought-iron gates were open, he passed through and proceeded slowly up the drive.

That slow procession was an education in and of itself. The drive was pebbled, perfectly edged and newly replenished, if the light gray of the stones was any indication. Lush green lawns rolled away from the drive on either side, ending in a stand of maples and birches on the left and an apple orchard on the right. Ahead was a collection of trees and shrubs that he was sure a landscape architect had been paid a bundle to create. Likewise, he was sure, the upkeep cost a bundle. Russ could see no fewer than three gardeners working—one mowing the lawn in the distance, two others trimming the greenery in front of the house.

The house itself was brick and ivy-covered, as the gatekeeper's had been, but that was where the similarity ended. This one was Georgian and large, with no fewer than twenty windows blinking back those rays of the sun that made it through the trees.

Russ lived in an area where ivy-covered brick was common. His own house had its share. But his own house was modest compared to this one—not that anything here was gaudy, he had to admit. It was impeccably kept, from the neatly painted black gutters to the shiny black shutters to the clean, bluestone walk and the polished brass numbers on one of the front columns. The house was clearly ready for a wedding. Russ felt good for Diane. And for Cynthia.

The drive branched to form a circle before the front door. Russ pulled to the right, parked halfway around and turned off the ignition. He had told Diane he would be there, so he was, though he had second thoughts about the visit. The words that had passed between Cynthia and him were still fresh and stinging. He wished he had had time to put them into perspective.

Diane. Think of Diane. She's all that matters this week, he told himself. Still, it was Cynthia he thought of as he climbed from the car and approached the house. He wondered whether Bauer had owned the place before she met him, whether she had lent a hand in shaping the landscaping, whether she remembered that she and Russ had always talked about owning a place in the woods.

The brass knocker was as polished as the numbers. He rapped twice, then waited. After a minute the door was opened by a young black woman, who, wearing a simple linen sheath, low heels and pearls, was as elegant as the house.

"Dr. Shaw?" she asked, then stood back with a smile to gesture him in. "Of course you're Dr. Shaw. The resemblance between you and Diane is marked." She extended her hand. "Diane told me you were coming. I'm Mandy Johnson, Mrs. Bauer's social secretary."

"Social secretary," Russ echoed, shaking the woman's hand. He had assumed a housekeeper, a cook and cleaning people, but not a social secretary.

"Actually," Mandy explained, "I'm here to help out with the wedding. Usually I work for Mrs. Hoffmann."

Russ found that even more surprising. His limited experience with Gertrude Hoffmann had taught him she was something of a bigot. If the young woman before him was for real, he was impressed. He was about to ask how long she had worked for Gertrude when a shout drew his attention to the top of the winding stairs.

"Russ!"

Diane came trotting down, ran to him and threw her arms around his neck. He hugged her tightly for a minute, then held her back for a speculative once-over. From the crown of her straight, dark blond hair to the tips of her white ballet flats, she was a beauty. His gaze lingered on her sundress. He recognized the pattern as a staple among girls at his school. "Laura Ashley?" he teased.

She laughed. "I know, I know. Totally out of character. If I were in New York, I'd be wearing either jeans or silk, but this is St. Louis, and St. Louis is Grandmother's turf. I'm going over to see her later."

"Ah," Russ said sagely. Mandy Johnson had quietly disappeared, leaving Diane and him alone. "You look great, Laura Ashley and all."

She grinned. "Thanks. You, too. I like the shirt. I've never seen you in anything but a tie and jacket before."

He was wearing a soft, oversize white jersey, tucked into a pair of snug-fitting chinos, and deck shoes without socks. "Even stuffy old professors have to relax sometimes."

"Stuffy?" she asked dubiously, and followed it up with a mocking "*Old?* If you looked any younger, they'd never believe you were my father."

"I was a child dad."

Chuckling, she gave him a final squeeze before releasing her hold on his neck. "Want some breakfast?"

"Already had some."

"How about coffee?"

"Yeah, that'd be nice—but only if it's made."

Slipping her arm through his, she guided him through the front hall and down a side corridor. "It's always made around here. Mrs. Fritz sees to that."

"Mrs. Fritz is the cook, I take it?"

"You take right." They entered the kitchen, where a small, round woman was kneading what Russ guessed to be bread dough. "Mrs. Fritz, say hello to Dr. Shaw."

The cook scowled. In a voice heavy with German intonation, she said, "How do you do, Dr. Shaw. I must make excuses for Miss Bauer once again. I have told her many, many times not to bring her guests through the kitchen. If you would like something to eat, I will be glad to serve you in the dining room.''

Undaunted by the woman's reprimand, Diane dropped Russ's arm and made for the coffee maker. "No need to wait on us. We're just having coffee. You make a great cup, Mrs. Fritz." She filled two mugs with the dark brew—remembering that Russ took his black—and motioned him toward a side, screened door. Moments later she was placing the mugs on the table and settling into a white, cushioned wicker chair.

"Beautiful setting," Russ observed. The patio was of flagstone and huge. In addition to the six chairs at the table, there were occasional wicker armchairs and lounges scattered among large potted plants. Beds of brightly colored flowers bordered the flagstone, broken only by broad stone steps that led to the lawn. Set into one side of that lawn was a gleaming turquoise pool. Balancing it on the other side was a rose garden in vivid red bloom. The remainder of the lawn was an expanse of lavish green, undulating gently into the distance, where a gazebo fronted a graceful grove of willows.

"Take a good look," Diane said with a sigh. "This is the last time you'll see it like this for a while. The tent people start bringing things tomorrow. By the time they've set up fifty-plus tables, four hundred chairs and a dance floor, the place won't look half as peaceful."

"It'll still be spectacular." He took his eyes from the view to study Diane. "How's Nick?"

She grinned. "Great."

"Are you excited?"

"Very. And nervous. There are so many things to think about. Mandy has been a godsend. So has Tammy—she's a party planner and, boy, she's earned her money with this one. If it isn't the caterer on the phone, it's the florist or the photographer or the videographer or the dressmaker or the jeweler or the stationer. I swear, if I'd realized what was involved with an extravaganza like this, I would have eloped. Up until the very day the invitations went out, I was considering it. If it hadn't been for my grandmother. . ." Her voice trailed off.

Russ raised the mug to his mouth and took a drink. The brew was satisfying—Diane had been right about that—but the true satisfaction came with the company. Having spent so many years alone and out of touch, he was stunned each time he saw her to realize Diane was his. "You're doing this for Gertrude, then?"

"In part. She loves productions." Diane sent him an apologetic look. "I know you never had cause to feel kindly toward her, but she's mellowed over the years. In some regards, she's a lonely old lady. She has lots of friends, but at the end of each day she has no one to go home to but the hired help. It's sad."

Russ couldn't feel too badly for the woman. "I'm surprised she doesn't live here with your mother and you."

Diane nearly choked on her coffee. With a hand on her chest, she said, "Are you kidding? I may have said she's mellowed, but that doesn't mean she's a peach. If she were here, she'd be driving everyone crazy. As it is, she's going to antagonize the photographer and the videographer when she insists they be hidden behind flowers and latticework at the wedding ceremony." She snorted. "I really *should* have eloped."

"No," Russ said. "That wouldn't have been right."

"You did."

"We had no other choice. If we'd told your grandmother what we wanted to do, she wouldn't have allowed us to get married at all. Then we wouldn't have had you, and that would have been awful."

Diane stared at him for a minute before breaking into the gentlest, sincerest of smiles. "I'm so glad you're here. I don't care if she's furious—"

"Your mother?"

"My grandmother."

"Is your mother angry?" Russ was anxious to know. He wondered how much of her feelings Cynthia shared with Diane.

"She was yesterday afternoon. She was quieter when she came in last night." Diane dropped her gaze to her coffee.

"I'm sorry about that. I didn't think she'd actually go over to see you. Was it very uncomfortable?"

"Not as bad as it might have been. Was *she* uncomfortable?"

"A little, I think." Her eyes returned to his. "That's why it's good you came on Monday. She has the whole week to get used to seeing you so she doesn't start to hyperventilate on the day of the wedding."

"Hyperventilate?" he quipped. "Your mother?" Cool, composed Cynthia Hoffmann? It was an intriguing thought. "Why in the world would she hyperventilate?"

"Because you're handsome enough in a shirt and chinos or a blazer and tie. In formal wear you'll be a killer."

Russ grinned. "Are all daughters good for their fathers' egos, or is mine just unusually biased?"

"Maybe I'm making up for lost time," she said with a softness that brought a lump to his throat.

He curved a hand around her neck. "You and me both." Leaning forward, he kissed her cheek. He barely had time to draw back when Diane's gaze shot past him. He caught looks of surprise, then pleasure, then unsureness on her face before he glanced around.

Cynthia had just come past the side of the house. The sight of her brought him to his feet and at the same time took his breath away. She had been running—at least that was what it looked like to Russ, who had run with enough people over the years to recognize the symptoms. Though she was standing stock-still now, she was breathing hard. She wore top-of-the-line running shoes that looked well used, a pair of brief, teal green nylon shorts and a matching singlet. Her hair cascaded from a high ponytail, from which had escaped loose, honey-colored wisps. Along with her bangs, they framed her face, several catching in the rivulets of sweat that trickled down her cheeks. Those cheeks were flushed with heat, but the eyes that were glued to Russ had a shocked look in them.

"Hey, Mom," Diane called, "perfect timing. We were just having coffee. Come join us."

Russ had begun to breathe again, but barely. Fully dressed, as she'd been last night, Cynthia had looked spectacular. She looked even more spectacular wearing so little. Her limbs were slim, well toned and lightly tanned, and if twenty-five years had added scars, liver spots or cellulite, he couldn't see any.

Aware of a quickening inside, he forced himself to inhale. The breath escaped in a shaky whoosh. "This woman can't be your mother, Diane. She's not old enough."

"She's my mom, all right, but she puts me to shame. She's so *fit* it's *disgusting*."

"Since when has she been running?"

"Since forever. I can't remember a time when she didn't. She says it clears her head."

Russ knew that for a fact, but any benefit he had derived from his own morning run was gone. His head was filled with images of the last time he'd seen Cynthia so undressed, and his body was responding accordingly. Unable to sit down while she was standing there, yet more fearful by the minute that his arousal would be noticed, he didn't know what to do. He was relieved when Mrs. Fritz created a distraction by barreling out of the kitchen with a slam of the screen door.

Every bit as relieved as Russ, Cynthia took the towel the woman handed her and covered her face. She hadn't been prepared to find Russ there. She wasn't ready to see him again so soon. She hadn't begun to analyze the feelings that had kept her awake for a good part of the night. But because she had been awake so late, she had slept later than usual, which was why she had gone running later than usual, which was why he had caught her in such a state. Not that he wasn't seeing anything he hadn't seen before. Russ had seen her naked and sweaty—just as she had seen him aroused. But neither condition was appropriate at the moment.

After mopping at her neck and arms, she took the glass of ice water from Mrs. Fritz and drained it before handing it back. "Coffee, ma'am?" the cook asked.

"No, thanks," Cynthia murmured. She waited until the woman had gone back into the kitchen before turning to Russ. The towel hung from her hands, the only shield she had against the exposure she felt. "I'm sorry," she said softly. Her breathing may have slowed, but her body still hummed. "If I'd known you were coming, I wouldn't have barged in this way."

"It's your house," Russ said as softly. He couldn't take his eyes from her, but that was nothing new. "You can barge in whenever you want. I'm the intruder. I just wanted to stop by and say hi to Diane. And make sure you're all right."

"I'm all right."

She didn't look it. She looked as paralyzed as he felt. No, he realized, *paralyzed* was the wrong word. *Mesmerized* was more like it. From day one in the soda shop, they had been captivated by each other to the extent that the rest of the world had fallen away, leaving only the two of them, drawn closer and closer. He decided now that the attraction was caused by something chemical, a magnetic response neither of them could control. He didn't imagine she wanted to be drawn to him any more than he did to her.

But Cynthia wasn't thinking about the soda shop or chemical attractions or magnetic responses just then. She had a more immediate quandary. She knew she should excuse herself and go inside, but she couldn't make herself leave. Nor could she continue to stand there. Needing more protection than the towel offered, she crossed the patio and slipped into a seat all the way across the table from Russ. With the towel draped around her neck so that its ends covered her breasts, she felt better.

Russ, too, sat. "Your house is wonderful, Cyn. Was it Matthew's before you married?"

"No. We bought it fresh. The woman who had owned it for years passed away right around the time we were looking. It needed a lot of work."

The little Russ had seen of the inside of the house was in wonderful condition, though he assumed it had been redecorated more than once since they'd bought it. "Did you have to do much with the grounds?"

"Uh-huh. Nearly everything had been neglected. Some things came back with just a little pruning. Others had to be replaced."

"Your landscape architect was brilliant."

"I didn't use a landscape architect. The ones I talked with wanted to do all kinds of lovely little things that would have given a prissy look to the place. I wanted the grounds to be lush, which, believe it or not, is easier to achieve. So I directed everything myself."

Russ was impressed, though not surprised. He had always known Cynthia could do whatever she set her mind to—and it had nothing to do with money or the confidence of the wealthy. She was a hard worker. Whether learning how to cook, keeping their tiny apartment neat and clean, caring for the baby or caring for him, what she did she did well.

"You must have designed everything with this occasion in mind," he commented. "It's a beautiful setting for a wedding. Now, if the sun cooperates—"

"It will," she said with a quick smile. "It always cooperates for weddings."

Russ's own smile was slower and filled with reflective amazement. "You were always so positive. I don't think I've ever met anyone as positive as you. When we were in school, you used to study your butt off for exams, but by the time you closed your books, you were sure you'd do well, and you always did. When we were looking for an apartment, you were sure we could find something we could afford, and we did. When we were looking for jobs, you were sure we could find ones close enough so we could meet every day for lunch, and we did." He remembered those lunches. From the affectionate look on Cynthia's face, he guessed she did, too.

"Brown paper sacks," she mused. "Peanut butter and jelly sandwiches, cream cheese and olive sandwiches or tuna sandwiches—two for you, one for me. Potato chips that were usually crushed in transit. An apple. And a thermos of chocolate milk."

"Bosco and milk," he added with a grin. "Remember that?"

She grinned back and nodded. "I always told you it would stay mixed, and it did."

"You also told me there was no rush to get to the hospital after your water broke. We were so damned laid-back that by the time we got there, you were fully dilated." He turned to Diane. "You were nearly born in the front seat—" He stopped at the sight of her eyes, which were bright with tears. "What's wrong?" he asked, instantly alarmed.

She smiled through the tears, which remained unshed. "Nothing. It's just so weird seeing you two together." Her gaze flipped to Cynthia, then back. "It kind of brings things full circle. On the eve of my wedding. That's poetic, don't you think?"

What Cynthia thought was that Diane was a gem. Some daughters might have been angry at their mothers for having made them wait so long for such an occasion. Diane merely seemed delighted that it had come, which went to prove what Cynthia had told Russ in his hotel room. Diane had never been a demanding child. Whatever she received she appreciated. She was so, so special that way.

Russ must have thought the same thing, because before Cynthia could brace herself, he hooked an elbow around Diane's neck and drew her face to his shoulder. Cynthia felt a sharp jolt inside, then a tilting sensation near her heart. This was a first for her, too—seeing father and daughter together as adults—and it affected her more deeply than she would have imagined. Russ's ease with Diane, his spontaneity, his obvious affection—he would have been a wonderful father if he had been around. She supposed the relationship was better late than never. Still, for her daughter, she felt a loss.

Marginally aware that the loss she felt was for herself, as well, she rose from her chair and started for the house.

"Cyn?"

"I have to shower," she called back. Ignoring the creak of wicker behind her, she continued on to the screen door, but before she could do more than draw it open, Russ was by her side.

"Wait." His voice was low and close. "There's something I have to ask you."

She kept her eyes on the floor, not that that helped. She didn't have to raise them to be aware of his height. It seemed he always towered over her. When they'd been eighteen, part of the towering had been in her mind. She had been in awe of him for the hardships of his upbringing and the person he was in spite of it, and she'd been in love. In theory, she was over both the awe and the love, but he was still tall. She wanted desperately to believe that it was nothing more than a physical fact.

"I'm really a mess," she told him. "I don't feel comfortable sitting out here like this."

"I've seen you looking worse."

"When we were kids. Things are different now."

"You don't have to stand on ceremony with me. I'm family."

She did raise her eyes then to meet his. "Not to me. Our marriage was annulled years ago."

Russ saw the hurt and sorrow on her face and was as surprised by their strength as he had been the night before. He would have expected her to have put the past behind her. After all, she'd gone on to marry well.

"That's . . . kind of what I wanted to ask you," he said quietly.

Her eyes widened. "About the annulment? Are you thinking of marrying again?"

"No, no. But one of the priests who'll be assisting at Diane's wedding is an old friend."

"Jackie Flynn," she breathed, then watched the corner of his mouth turn up.

"Better known on the basketball court as the Dunkin' Dubliner."

"I wouldn't try that one now, if I were you. He's Father John to his friends."

"Father John," Russ repeated in a properly subdued tone. "I wrote him that I was coming in for the wedding, and he suggested I call, which I did this morning. He's invited us to be his guests for dinner at the Ritz."

"Us?"

"That's what he said."

"*His* guests?"

"That's what he said."

"At the *Ritz?*"

Russ shrugged.

"That's *appalling*," she cried. "I can think of far more appropriate ways for the church to spend its money."

"That's what *I* said."

"What did he say then?"

"That we'd both made such generous contributions to the church in honor of Diane's wedding that it was the least he could do. And that the Ritz-Carlton is new in town and he wanted to eat there—and that, in fact, he wouldn't be paying a cent because he was making good on a bet he'd made with the manager."

"The rogue," Cynthia muttered, but fondly.

"That's just what I called him. So what do you say? Are you free tonight?"

"Yes, but—"

"He suggested we pick him up at the rectory at seven. Any problem?"

"No, but—"

"Good," Russ said with a sigh. "He really had his heart set on this. I wasn't looking forward to disappointing him."

"But you were the one who was his friend," Cynthia protested. She questioned the wisdom of spending any unnecessary time with Russ. Something told her that only heartache would come of it. "You'll want to talk over old times. Wouldn't it be better if the two of you went alone?"

"He said something about discussing the wedding."

"I've already discussed the wedding with him."

"He wants to discuss it with *us.*"

She squeezed her eyes shut. Russ was being persistent, and she didn't know how to handle it.

"I know what you're thinking," he said in a soft, private voice, "and believe me, there's a part of me that agrees."

"That we shouldn't go?" she asked without opening her eyes.

"That we shouldn't test fate by sharing the same table." As it was, he was testing fate by leaning close enough to discover that Cynthia's scent was as sweet and alluring as ever. In an attempt to lessen the torment, he straightened and took a small step back. "But he's a priest. What better buffer could we find?"

She thought about the word *buffer* as she opened her eyes to his. *Referee* might have been a more appropriate word, if being together was going to cause the kind of heated discussion they'd had the night before. Or *chaperon*, if she didn't get used to seeing him fast. She could understand that there would be an awareness of the time of their first reunion, since sexuality had played a major role in their relationship. But that first reunion was over. This was the second. Tonight would be the third. The awareness had to die down. It *had* to.

So she thought positively. "Okay. What time should I be ready?"

"Six forty-five?"

She nodded. "I'll see you then."

Chapter Four

CYNTHIA SPENT most of the day trying to find a way to get out of dinner. But though she had deliberately left her evenings early in the wedding week free for the inevitable flurry of last-minute arrangements, there were surprisingly few. She was in daily touch with the florist and the caterer, both of whom were skilled at their jobs and perfectly calm. Tammy Farentino had been in touch with the string quartet and the band to make sure they understood exactly when and what Cynthia wanted them to play; she had also touched base with the tablecloth person, the limousine service, the photographer and the videographer. Mandy Johnson had picked up the leather-bound book that Cynthia had ordered for guests to sign on entering the church, and she'd met with the calligrapher, who was busily writing table numbers on place cards as per the seating arrangement Cynthia and Diane had finalized the weekend before. Diane was in near-daily contact with each of her attendants and had been to the bridal shop for last-minute fittings. There was a small matter of picking up the gold rosebud earrings she would be giving to each of those attendants as a gift, but that was it.

So Tuesday evening found Cynthia sitting nervously on the Louis XVI-style settee at the far end of the living room. She was wearing a simple dress of apricot-colored silk and she clutched a patterned shawl, both drawn from her closet for their dignity. After the way Russ had seen her that morning, she felt compelled to repolish her image.

The bell rang at six-forty, which didn't surprise Cynthia a bit. Russ had always been prompt to the point of being early, which was why she had been on the settee since six-thirty. She rose so quickly her heart beat double time, so she forced herself to stand still for a good ten seconds, breathing slowly in and out. When she felt she had regained a modicum of composure, she started for the door.

Robert beat her to it. He was the butler, tall and lean, with those straight lines accentuated by perfect posture and the dark gray vest and trousers he wore.

"Mrs. Bauer, please?"

Cynthia arrived at the foyer. To the butler, in a soft murmur, she said, "Thank you, Robert." He nodded to her, then to Russ, before turning and, back straight, walking toward the kitchen.

"He's a dignified-looking man," Russ remarked.

"He's Mrs. Fritz's husband."

Russ would never have paired them. "You're kidding."

"No. They've been with us for years. Robert serves not only as butler but as chauffeur, courier and handyman. He's also the keeper of the rose garden."

Russ arched a brow. "A true master of versatility."

Cynthia arched a brow right back. "You could say that."

He smiled. "I'd rather say nice things about you. You look beautiful."

She said a soft thank-you, all the while reminding herself that compliments were a dime a dozen, that Russ's was nothing special and that the rapid thump-thump of her heart was left over from the anticipation that had built while she'd waited for him to arrive. Without quite planning it, though, she heard herself say, "You look terrific yourself." Her expression grew bemused as she took in his navy summer suit, crisp white shirt and paisley tie.

"What?"

"You look so—" she raised her eyes to his face "—so grown-up."

He grinned. "I am grown-up."

"I know, but the picture I carried in my mind all these years was of you at eighteen. To suddenly see you at forty-three is strange."

She gave a tiny frown, but it held the same bemusement of moments before. "I don't think I've ever seen you in a suit."

"I'd never owned one when we were together."

"It looks..." she struggled to find the right word, only to go with the simple and eloquent "...great."

His grin grew lopsided. "Thanks." He actually looked slightly embarrassed, but endearingly so. He had never been at all cocky. She remembered the way he used to blush when she said personal, intimate things, and the way she had loved it when he did. Though he wasn't quite blushing now, she loved the expression on his face nonetheless, particularly in light of the very sophisticated way the rest of him looked. She felt she had connected once again with the boy he had been—which was only right, since part of her felt like the girl she had been, young and starry-eyed and excited by the thought of being with Russ.

Memory. That was all it was, she told herself. Forcing her eyes from his, she glanced at the slim gold watch on her wrist. "Would you like a drink before we leave?"

"No, thanks. I have a feeling John will be offering us something at the rectory. Our reservations aren't until eight. Are you all set to go?"

Taking a small evening bag from the antique table by the door, she nodded. Moments later she was tucked into Russ's car and they were on their way.

The rectory was a modest stone house behind the church. John Flynn was waiting for them, but the look on his face wasn't as easygoing as Cynthia had come to expect from the man. He did produce a smile and a warm handclasp for her, and when he turned to Russ, there was mischief in his eyes and genuine affection in the bear hug he gave.

"Gee, Russ, it's good to see you!" he said, then repeated the words with several hearty shoulder slaps. But his smile faded soon afterward, and his gaze moved from Russ's face to Cynthia and back. "I was so looking forward to tonight, but it appears the Ritz will have to wait—for me, at least. I received a call twenty minutes ago from one of my parishioners. There's been a serious accident."

"Oh, dear," Cynthia said, wondering which of his parishioners it was and whether she knew the person. She knew many of the people who lived in the area. Father John was aware of that. She guessed that if he wanted her to know who'd been hurt, he would tell her. "An automobile accident?"

"No, it was a construction accident. A fluky thing, from the little I was told, but my source was quite upset. I promised I would be at the hospital as soon as possible. I tried calling the house to save you the trip here, but you had already left, and I didn't want to be on my way without speaking with you myself." He looked at Russ. "I'm sorry. I feel terrible standing you up."

Russ knew what it was to have emergencies. "Don't apologize, John. More than once in the past year I've been called from an evening engagement to see to an emergency at one of the dorms. Certain jobs demand that you be on call. Yours is one of those jobs. I'm only sorry we'll miss this chance to talk."

"We'll have to reschedule, that's all," John said. "And in the meanwhile, you two will go on to the Ritz tonight as my guests."

Cynthia came to attention. "Oh, no, Father John, we couldn't possibly do that."

"But it's all arranged," he insisted. "The manager owes me. I've already talked with him. He's expecting you."

Russ was feeling as uncomfortable as Cynthia. "Why don't we just rereserve. Are you free tomorrow night?"

The priest shook his head. "Not tomorrow or Thursday night, either, since I believe we all have a wedding rehearsal, then dinner at Granatelli's Restaurant." To Cynthia he said, "And you're not going to want to go out the night before the wedding."

"I don't dare," she said apologetically. "Annie D'Angelo will be at the house, along with who knows how many more of the bridesmaids. Diane may be nervous. I feel I should be available in case she needs me."

"So you'll go to the Ritz tonight," John instructed, "and you'll report back to me on how it is." He turned to Russ. "Can we talk at the rehearsal dinner?"

"Sure thing."

"I still don't think we should go without you," Cynthia said. The thought of being alone with Russ was making her stomach jump. "What good is a bet if you can't collect on it."

"I'm collecting," John told her.

"But for *you*."

"I'm a priest. Given the vows I took, the Ritz is a little too much, don't you think? Besides," he added with a mischievous gleam, "that bet had to do with the Blues. I've got another one going on the Cardinals that's a sure winner, too." He put an arm around each of them and, becoming more serious, turned them back toward the car. "My evening is apt to be difficult. It'll give me great pleasure thinking of you at dinner. Would you deny me that pleasure?"

"That's blackmail," Cynthia chided, but fondly.

As fondly, Russ added, "I can see that the old Jackie Flynn is alive and well behind that Roman collar of yours."

With an unrepentant grin, John dropped his arms to open the car door for Cynthia. "The good Lord understands that even the most pious of men aren't saints."

Cynthia slid into the passenger seat. "What fun will it be for us without you?"

John shut the door and leaned down to the open window. "You'll make your fun. I seem to recall a time when you guys didn't want *anyone* around."

"Those days are long gone," she said with a wisp of sadness, then, before he could add anything, covered his hand with hers. "We'll be thinking of you tonight. I hope everything turns out well."

"So do I," he said, and looked at Russ. "Thursday night?"

"You got it." Russ started the car and drove off. He hadn't gone more than a block when he realized what the Dunkin' Dubliner had done and what it meant. He'd passed Russ the ball and was expecting him to take it down the court. But damn, it was a long time since Russ had played the game, and the stakes were *so high*.

Silence reigned for another block, by which time he was desperate to know what Cynthia was thinking. So he said,

"That's too bad. I was looking forward to talking with John. I wonder who's been hurt."

Cynthia's thoughts had been on the so-grown-up man by her side and the evening ahead. At Russ's reminder, she felt instant guilt. Some poor soul was struggling for his life while she was debating the pros and cons of showing up at St. Louis's new Ritz-Carlton on the arm of her onetime husband. Turning her gaze to the window and away from Russ's too-imposing presence, she shrugged. "A fluky accident, he said. That's scary. I always used to worry that something fluky would happen to Diane." She reconsidered the words. "I used to worry that something *not fluky* would happen to her, too." Reconsidering yet again, she finally admitted, "I used to worry, period. There are times when I still do. She may be twenty-five and off on her own, but if I let myself think about her in New York City, I go a little nuts. I'm glad she'll have Nick with her from now on."

"Don't tell her that. She'll say she's perfectly capable of taking care of herself."

"Still, I worry. Not all the time. Only when I think."

Russ was about to say that was a mother's prerogative, when he shot her a glance. She was diligently keeping her head angled toward the window, but her profile was lovely enough to drive the words from his mind. Long after he returned his eyes to the road, he saw that profile, and felt increasingly confused. He was looking forward to the evening. He was looking forward to it too much.

"Cyn, if you'd rather not go to dinner . . . I mean, if being with me is going to make you uncomfortable, I can take you back home."

She lowered her eyes. Uncomfortable? Was that what she was feeling? She didn't think so. She didn't think it was possible for her to feel uncomfortable with Russ for long. He was too easy to be with, too accommodating, too interesting. When they'd been seniors in high school, she had wanted to know all about his life and his classes and his extracurricular activities. Twenty-five years later, she wanted to know the very same things.

There was danger, of course. He still turned her on. She could feel the pull even though—it stunned her to realize—he hadn't touched her once, not once, since that last night twenty-five years before when they'd made love. They hadn't shaken hands last night at his hotel. He hadn't so much as touched her arm to stop her from leaving the patio that morning or, when he'd picked her up tonight, laid a hand on her waist to guide her to the car.

"Cyn?"

The pull was still there. His voice touched all the places his hands hadn't, and his eyes touched more. But she could handle it. She was *determined* to handle it. With all that had been going on in preparation for the wedding, she deserved a quiet, private dinner, and who more appropriate to have that quiet, private dinner with than the father of the bride? Besides, she was curious. She had gotten glimpses of what Russ had done with his life. She wanted to hear more.

"I can handle it," she sighed, more to herself than to him.

The sigh hit him the wrong way. "Don't do me any favors," he muttered.

She shot him a surprised look. "Why do you say that?"

"Because I'm not so hard up for company that I can't eat alone."

"I said I'd come."

His eyes clung to the road and his hands to the wheel. "But you sound like it's the last thing you want, and if that's so, I'd *rather* eat alone."

"Maybe you'd rather eat alone, anyway. You sound like you're looking for an out."

"I'm not. I think you are."

She faced him more fully. "Why would I want an out?"

"Because you're uncomfortable with me."

"Did I say I was?"

"No, but you wouldn't. You're trained not to say things like that."

"Where you're concerned I'll say anything I want!"

He scowled. "Right, and maybe that's why we shouldn't go to dinner together. "You're angry at me for something that happened twenty-five years ago. You couldn't keep it in last night, and you probably won't be able to tonight."

"Because it still hurts!"

"Twenty-five years later?"

"Yes!"

"You should be over it."

"I thought I was, but seeing you brings it back."

"It shouldn't, damn it," he said, feeling angry. "Twenty-five years is too long a time for something like that to linger."

"Twenty-five years is *nothing* when people feel things like we did! Do you mean to tell me you didn't feel a thing after the night you left? That you didn't ever think of us over the years and feel a sense of loss? That you didn't ever wake up in the middle of the night with a longing so intense that you'd have turned a cold shower hot?" As soon as the words were out, Cynthia was appalled. But it was too late to take them back, and she wasn't sure she would have, anyway. She was being honest. No one could condemn her for that. "If you can truly say that you got over us—" she snapped her fingers "—like that, something was wrong, very wrong with the way we were then. Was it all a sham?"

Her words echoed in the car for the longest time before Russ could react. When he did, it was with carefully controlled movements, pulling the vehicle to the side of the road, letting the engine idle. He dropped his hands to his lap and stared at the center of the steering wheel. An air bag was packed there. In case of an accident, it would inflate and save his life—and he would want it to. But that hadn't always been so.

"It wasn't a sham," he said quietly. "What we had was the most beautiful thing I've ever known. There were times when the loss I felt was nearly unbearable. There were times during the war when I honestly didn't give a damn whether I made it home or not. Someone was watching out for me there, because I sure as hell wasn't. When I got back in one piece, I decided I owed that Someone for what He had done. So I worked harder in school, and after that at work, than I might have done otherwise. I had no one to do it for. You were lost to me—by my own hand—and if you think you were the only one lying awake at night, you're dead wrong. There were nights I wanted you so bad I swear I almost flew back here."

His lower lip came out to cover the upper one. Slowly it slipped down again. "You're right. Twenty-five years isn't long at all with feelings that strong. When I suggested it was, I was trying to deny things I've been feeling myself since I saw you last night." He hesitated, unsure of how much to say. But one of the most beautiful things about his relationship with Cynthia had been its openness. They had poured out their hearts and souls to each other. There was nothing they hadn't shared—except his decision to leave. In terms of forthrightness, he owed her one. So he confessed, "Everything's come back. I didn't plan on it happening. I didn't want it to. But it's there."

Cynthia sat much as he did, with her hands in her lap and her eyes straight ahead. She wanted to look at him but didn't dare. His words alone had a powerful effect on her. "Maybe it's memory. Maybe what we're feeling now is just the memory of what we felt then."

"Maybe."

"Maybe it's just a residual from things that went unresolved after you left."

"Maybe."

"Maybe it's not what we really feel—I mean, what you and I feel as the individuals we are today. Maybe it's all for old times' sake."

"Maybe." He raised his eyes to the windshield. "So how do we handle it?"

"I don't know." Still staring straight ahead, she threw the question back at him. "You were always the sensible one. How do we handle it?"

He thought hard, trying to separate what his mind recommended from what his heart did, only to realize there wasn't much difference between the two. "I think we have to talk. We have to get to know each other as we are now. We have to put reality between us and the past. Could be that once we get to know each other, we'll find a comfortable middle ground to stand on."

"Somewhere between attraction and antagonism?"

"Right."

"Do you think that's possible?"

"Yes. We're neither of us antagonistic people."

"About the other," she said in a smaller voice, because she could still feel it, could still feel the pull.

Russ didn't have to ask what she meant. He could feel it, too. Slowly he turned his head, and the sight of her heightened the feeling. He had dreamed about her over the years, and come morning had always pushed her image from his mind. But she was here. With him. After all those years of dreams.

"I think it still exists," he said in a voice so low she might not have heard if there had been any noise outside the car. But it was a lazy June evening. Traffic was light. The only noise was the whisper of cool air coming from the vents, and that coolness wasn't nearly enough to take the edge off his heat. "Look at me, Cyn."

After a moment's reluctance, she turned her head. What she saw in his eyes reflected what she was feeling inside, and it nearly broke her apart. She held her breath when he raised his hand. It hovered for a minute before ever so lightly touching her cheek, then curving around her neck. His thumb brushed her mouth.

"It still exists," he said, hoarsely this time.

"I know," she whispered.

"But we're adults now. We can resist it."

"We have to. I don't think I can bear the pain again."

"But what about the glory?" He was thinking about the way she had always taken him out of himself and elevated him to a plane where everything was breathtakingly beautiful. "Wouldn't you like a taste of that again?"

"Oh, God." She was being drawn in by his smoky eyes, his sandy voice, the spray of silver in his hair—and the silver hadn't been there before, which shot the theory of memory turning them on. She wanted him to kiss her, wanted it more than anything in the world at that moment.

It was her turn to raise a hand, then hesitate. Then she put her fingertips on his lips, moved them over his cheek to his temple, then back by his ear.

He drew in a shuddering breath and trapped her hand on his neck. "Don't tempt me, Cyn. Don't tell me it's okay. I haven't changed much where you're concerned. I never could resist when you touched me. Given the choice, I'd take you back to my hotel room right now and to hell with dinner. But I don't think that's wise."

One part of Cynthia wondered. That part would opt for the hotel room, too, on the premise that what was building between them simply had to be released to be gone. The other part was worried it wouldn't ever be gone, and she didn't know what she'd do then.

Retrieving her hand and anchoring it on her lap, she said, "You're right. Let's go to dinner." The words were rushed, she knew. Russ had to know she was torn. But he didn't say anything more. She was infinitely grateful when he put the car in gear and moved off.

"TELL ME ABOUT YOUR LIFE," Russ said. Having arrived at the Ritz in advance of their reservations, they were having drinks at the bar.

Cynthia took a slow sip of her martini. She felt much safer now that they were out of the confines of the car and surrounded by other people. "That's a tall order. Where should I start?"

"At the beginning." He wanted to know all the things the newspaper hadn't covered. "When I left."

She ran her thumb along the rim of the glass. "At the time I thought that was the end, not the beginning. I was so happy with you, then you were gone. I was sure life would go totally downhill from there."

Russ knew there would be pain in what she had to say, but he needed to know. What had happened after he left was all part of who she was now. "What did your mother say when you showed up at her door?"

"I called first. I didn't have the courage to show up without knowing whether she would let me in. If she rejected me after you had—"

"I didn't reject you."

"That's what it felt like to me at the time," Cynthia argued, then purposefully gentled her voice. She didn't want to be angry at Russ. All she wanted was to make him understand. "I was feeling very vulnerable. So I called her." She stopped then, remembering back to that sticky July day and the phone booth that had looked so dirty next to Diane's baby-soft skin.

"What did you say to her?" Russ asked quietly.

She sighed. "Actually nothing. I started to cry. She got the message. I managed to tell her where I was. She was there in ten minutes."

"You should have called her sooner."

Cynthia shook her head. "I couldn't. It took that month alone before I could face her."

Russ took a swallow of Scotch and jiggled the ice in his glass for a minute before he said, "I wanted you to go home, because I knew she would take care of you, but I was worried that she would make things impossible for you in the process."

"Like drilling my stupidity into me?"

"Yeah."

"She didn't. She didn't say a word about that. She really did play her cards perfectly. I was heartbroken that you'd left, and she could see that. She made things so easy for me at home that when I finally came out of my blue funk, I was ready to be the kind of daughter she wanted."

Russ wondered who had taken care of Diane while Cynthia had been in her "blue funk." She had been totally devoted to the baby when he'd been around. "I suppose you weaned Diane to a bottle pretty quickly, huh?"

"I nursed her until her first birthday."

He was inordinately pleased by that fact. As an afterthought, he grinned. "What did Gertrude think of that?"

Cynthia's mouth twitched. "What do you think she thought?"

"That it was a vulgar practice fitting only for peasants."

"That's pretty much it." Her eyes grew serious. "But what she thought didn't matter when it came to Diane. Diane was mine. I took care of her. She was the only peace of mind I had in those days."

The pain was there again. Russ wondered if they'd ever be able to escape it. "When did you meet Matthew?"

"When I was little, long before I met you. He was sixteen years older than me, but he moved in the same circles as my family. I was with Diane at the club one day—she was eighteen months old—and he and I started to talk. We were engaged two months later and married seven months after that."

"Why the seven-month wait? Was it so that Diane could get used to him?"

Cynthia shook her head. "They took to each other right from the start." She turned her glass on its cocktail napkin. "My mother wanted to do everything she had been denied the first time. There were engagement parties and postengagement parties and showers and prewedding dinners. She was in her glory."

"Were you?" he asked. He knew it was a loaded question, but the answer mattered.

She raised her eyes to his. "Was I in my glory? No. Did I enjoy myself? Yes. I never rejected my world when I married you. That world, thanks to my mother, rejected me. But I'd been raised with those people. I fitted back in. There were—are—many of them I really like. Sure, I had to deal with some shallow people, but there are shallow people at every level. I surrounded myself with the ones who weren't. They're the ones who work with me on fund-raisers for the art museum and the cancer society. They're the ones who helped me raise money for the homeless long before it became fashionable to do so." She gave a slow, sure shake of her head. "I make no apologies for what I did then or at any time since."

For a minute Russ couldn't think of a thing to say. He wanted to criticize her for taking the pleasure she had. After all, while she had been lifting canapés from silver trays, he had been slogging through rice paddies. But she was eloquent in her defense of the life she had lived. If she had made the best of the circumstances, using her position in society to benefit worthy causes, he couldn't find fault. He had to respect her for acting on her beliefs.

"Excuse me? Dr. Shaw?"

Russ swung his head around, and he found himself confronting a familiar-looking man. In a matter of seconds he placed him—the father of one of his students. With a smile, he rose from the bar stool and extended his hand. "It's odd seeing people out of context. I've only seen you in Connecticut, my own neck of the woods. But Chris is very definitely from St. Louis. How are you, Mr. Mason?"

"Very well, thanks, and the feeling's mutual. I've been sitting over there with my friends watching you, wondering if you were who I thought. I didn't expect to see you so far from home."

"I'm here for a wedding," Russ said. "Do you know Cynthia Bauer? Cyn, this is Phillip Mason. He's the father of one of my more promising sophomores."

Cynthia smiled and let the man take her hand. "We've been introduced before, I believe." She frowned, trying to remember exactly when and where. "Don't you sit with the Grahams at Powell Hall?"

"You have a good memory," Mason commented. "Powell Hall it was. And aren't you the one putting on the wedding?"

"That's right."

Releasing her hand, he pointed a thumb at Russ. "So what's his connection?"

With a serenity that stunned Russ, she said, "He's the father of the bride."

It wasn't a secret exactly. But someone like Phillip Mason, who had known Cynthia only as Mrs. Matthew Bauer and Diane as Diane Bauer, wouldn't necessarily know the truth. Indeed, the look on his face was priceless. His eyes lighted in surprise one minute, then grew perplexed the next, and when he opened his mouth to say something polite, nothing came out.

Russ, who was counting on the man to give a significant contribution to his school's Annual Fund that year, took pity on him. "Cynthia was my child bride. Diane was born shortly before we separated."

"I hadn't realized," Mason murmured. To Cynthia, he added, "I simply assumed Diane was Matthew's."

"Most people do," she said kindly.

Russ was reassured by her tone. So, apparently, was Phillip Mason, because he grew confident again. "She is one lucky young lady to have this man as her father. For years he's been one of Hollings's best teachers, and now he's proving to be a top-notch headmaster. You can tell her I said that." He turned to Russ. "Will you be in town long?"

"Only until Sunday."

"If you're free, we'd love to have you out at the house."

"That might be difficult. It's a short trip with a lot to do, but thanks for offering. Has Chris left for the Southwest yet?" He had been trying to remember what the younger Mason was doing for the summer. With more than three hundred students enrolled at the school, it was hard to know about each, but Russ did recall something about an archeological dig in Arizona.

"Next Tuesday. He's looking forward to it."

"Will you give him my best and wish him a wonderful trip for me?"

"I certainly will." Mason slapped him on the back. "You have a good summer, and congratulations to you both—" he broadened his gaze to include Cynthia "—on your daughter's wedding."

"Thank you," Cynthia said. As the man walked away, she couldn't help but consider the irony of being in one of St. Louis's newest and poshest hotels with Russell Shaw and having *him* be the one recognized. Not that it bothered her. To the contrary. She felt a glimmer of pride. Apparently he had made quite something of his life. She wanted to know more.

"TELL ME ABOUT *YOUR* LIFE," she said. They were seated at a pleasantly private table, but the privacy wasn't bothering

Cynthia. They had already been visited by the manager, the maître d', the wine steward, the waiter and the busboy. She was grateful for the momentary respite, during which she was hoping to learn something about the father of her daughter.

"That's a tall order," he drawled, echoing her earlier words. "Where should I start?"

"With your discharge from the army."

"What do you already know?" He wasn't the arrogant type. The last thing he wanted to do was to repeat old information.

"Only that you're Dr. Shaw and that you're headmaster at the Hollings Academy in Connecticut."

He would have thought she'd know more. Diane certainly did. He felt vaguely hurt that she hadn't been curious over the years. God knew he had been about her. "In a nutshell, I got my B.A. from Georgetown and went to teach history at Hollings. Over the years, I picked up an M.A., then a Ph.D. I was named headmaster last year."

She didn't seem at all daunted by his curtness. Her eyes were wide and expectant. "Go on."

"With what?"

"Why you chose teaching, why history, why Hollings, how you came to be headmaster, whether you like the job."

"I can't answer those in order."

"Why not?"

"Because they sound like they'd be a chronological succession, but they're not. I chose history because it fascinates me."

"It always did," she said, remembering. "You were good at it."

"Because it fascinated me. So I was getting ready to graduate with a degree in it, and the most obvious thing to do was to teach, but I was feeling unsettled. Homeless. Insecure. I had gone straight from the army to Georgetown, and for the first time in six years I didn't know where I was going. Then I heard about the opening at Hollings and went to visit the place. That was it. I was sold."

"What's it like?"

His mood softened as he thought of the school. "Green, very green. And warm. It's like a college campus in miniature, with tree-lined walks connecting one old stone building to the next. There's a feeling of history to it. And a sense of caring. When I first went there, it was all boys. More than half of them board, which means the school has to take the place of parents and family. And it does. More than anything, I think that was what appealed to me—the caring, the camaraderie between students and students, students and faculty. Hollings gave me a family. It also gave me a place to stay."

"You had an apartment on campus?"

"It was a two-room job in one of the dorms. It was furnished, so I didn't have to buy anything, and I got extra money by being a dorm parent."

"Was it hard work?"

"Not if you like kids, and I like kids."

"I never knew that," Cynthia said with a bemused look.

"Neither did I while I knew you. We were kids ourselves."

"When did you find out?"

"When I was at Georgetown. I took part in a volunteer project with inner-city kids. Those kids were tough, but they were great. Obviously the kids at Hollings were different, but they were great, too."

"So you stayed on. Did you take time off when you did your degree work?"

He shook his head. "I did it evenings and summers."

"That must have been hard."

He shrugged. "I didn't have anything else to do with my free time."

"Didn't you date?" she asked. He was such a strikingly handsome man. She couldn't believe that single women would come within range of him and not look twice.

"Some."

"Were there many female teachers?"

"Some. More now, since we've gone coed."

"When did that happen?"

Russ told her, then, when another question came, answered that, too. With the natural flow of her curiosity, he found himself relaxing. Their waiter brought rolls, then salads, and through it Cynthia was enrapt with piecing together a picture of his life. More than once, basking in her enthusiasm, he was taken back to their days together. Enthusiasm had been a mainstay of her personality then. He was relieved that that hadn't changed.

They were interrupted again, twice actually, when acquaintances of Cynthia's approached their table. Though Russ would have been happier without the intrusions, Cynthia was so apologetic each time that he couldn't be angry. Besides, she always picked up where they'd left off, letting him know that her interest was real, and in that, making him feel ten feet tall.

That was pretty much the way he ended the evening. By the time he returned Cynthia to her elegant, ivy-covered house, he felt just as high as he had after spending an hour with her at the soda shop—and as horny. Sitting across from her at an intimate table for two for the better part of three hours, watching the graceful shift of her hands, the gentle movement of her mouth, the curves of her shoulders and breasts, had taken its toll. His blood was hot and racing.

Cynthia was suffering a similar fate. As Russ walked her to her door, her heart was beating far faster than she wanted. After stepping inside, she turned back, hesitantly, to look up at him. "Thank you, Russ," she said softly. "It's been a really nice evening."

"I thought so, too." He wanted to kiss her but didn't dare. One kiss wouldn't be enough. It would never be enough when the lips involved were Cynthia's and his. But neither of them was ready for more. Too much shaky ground remained between them. Still, he couldn't bear the thought of waiting two days, until the wedding rehearsal on Thursday, to see her. It would be a waste of precious time. "I'm having breakfast with Diane and Nick tomorrow. Join us?"

Cynthia would have liked that if she trusted herself, but she didn't where Russ was concerned. She was feeling overwhelmed by things she hadn't felt in years. She needed time to think.

Doing her best not to drown in his gaze, she said, "I'd better not. I have an early meeting with Tammy, and besides, you haven't had much time with them. I don't want to take away from that.''

"You wouldn't be taking away. You'd be adding.''

"I'd better not.''

"I'd really like it if you came.''

But she shook her head. She had to be firm, had to act with her mind rather than her heart. She couldn't afford to be hurt the way she'd been hurt before. A second time she might not recover.

Chapter Five

RUSS KNEW ALL ABOUT ACTING from the mind rather than the heart. Over the years he had given lectures aplenty on the subject to his students and knew all the words to use. He had acted with his mind on the night he'd walked away from Cynthia—and when he'd joined the army, when he'd enrolled at Georgetown, when he'd taken a job at Hollings. Acting with one's mind meant considering every angle of a situation and making the most sensible decision. It meant acting deliberately rather than on impulse.

He thought he had done that when he refrained from kissing Cynthia good-night at her door. They weren't ready for a deeper involvement. The potential for warped judgment was too great. They were seeing each other for the first time in twenty-five years, a highly charged situation on its own. Add to that the emotion of their daughter's wedding and the highly charged situation increased in voltage. They were prime candidates for making a mistake.

So his mind said.

His heart said that it wouldn't be making a mistake at all but correcting one made long before.

His body pretty much echoed that conviction, with reverberations that lingered through the night and into the morning. When he arrived at the house to pick up Diane, he looked out for Cynthia, but she was nowhere in sight. She had a meeting with Tammy, she'd said. So he looked for her again when he brought Diane back after a thoroughly enjoyable breakfast with Nick.

"Think your mother's home yet?" he asked in a nonchalant way when he didn't see her wandering about.

"I doubt it," Diane said. "She had a list of things to do." She grew cautious. "Is everything all right?"

"Fine. I was going to offer to help, that's all."

"Aren't you spending the day with your professor friend?"

He nodded. "But I'll be free by four. I'm feeling a little fraudulent, accepting the title of father of the bride without doing any of the work. Haven't you got anything for me to do?"

"You're a guest. You don't have to work."

"I'm the father of the bride, and I *want* to work."

"Most everything's arranged for. Mom is good at that."

"Efficient."

"Very."

Frustrated by the fact, he frowned. "It's a bad habit to get into, Diane. Take my advice. When it comes to Nick, be helpless sometimes. Men like that."

She gave him a lopsided grin. "Modern women aren't helpless. For that matter, traditional women aren't helpless, either. They just pretend to be for the sake of their men. Nick isn't like that. He loves my independence."

"He loves everything about you," Russ corrected. Seeing them together over breakfast had reinforced his first impression of Nick. His daughter would be in kind, caring, capable hands—and he didn't give a damn about Diane's talk of independence. A man needed to be needed.

That thought stuck in his mind throughout the day, dallying there along with thoughts of Cynthia. He met with Evan Waldman, who had taught at Hollings before moving to St. Louis, but no matter how engrossing their talk, at the slightest break in the conversation Russ's mind wandered. On his drive back to the hotel later that day, he actually took a detour past Cynthia's. But he didn't stop. He hadn't been invited, didn't think he was needed, refused to make a fool of himself.

It was a matter of mind versus heart again. He stuck with his mind's decision through a dinner he barely ate, until loneliness eroded his resolve. This time, when he drove to Cynthia's, he pulled right up to the door and parked.

Robert answered with a genteel, "Good evening, sir."

"How are you tonight, Robert?"

"Just fine, thank you, sir."

"Is Mrs. Bauer in?"

"I believe so. If you'll come in and have a seat—" he showed him into the living room "—I'll let her know you're here."

"Thank you." Russ lowered himself to the settee but sat on its edge, his elbows on his knees. He shouldn't have come. She was going to be annoyed.

As it happened, Cynthia wasn't at all annoyed. To the contrary. If she had been able to wish for one thing, it would have been to see him just then. With a tired smile she leaned against the living room arch. "Hi."

He got quickly to his feet. "Hi." His eyes scanned her face. "What's wrong?"

She scrunched up her nose and took a deep breath. "Ooooh, it's been a bit of a rough day."

"Last-minute glitches?"

"In a way." She wrapped her arms around her waist. "You know the accident Father John mentioned last night?"

Russ nodded.

"The boy who was injured is the son of one of my friends."

He came closer. "I'm sorry, Cyn. I didn't know. Diane didn't say anything this morning."

"She didn't know. *We* didn't know. They kept things quiet until midday."

Tucking his hands in the pockets of his slacks, he came closer still. "What happened?"

"The boy's father—my friend's husband—is a developer. He got Jimmy a summer job working at one of his building sites. Scaffolding collapsed. Jimmy fell."

"How badly hurt is he?"

"They still don't know for sure. He's in a coma." Her eyes teared. "He's twenty years old with a whole life ahead of him if only he wakes up . . . and they were worrying about telling me, because they didn't want to put a damper on Diane's wedding week." She pressed a hand to her upper lip, which had begun to tremble.

Thinking only that he'd finally found a way to help, Russ reached out and drew her to him. "Good friends do things like that."

Against his shirt, she murmured, "I've been at the hospital for most of the afternoon. There isn't anything they can do but wait. They're positively distraught."

Russ knew that Cynthia was, too. He rubbed her back, willing her to relax against him. When she did, he rewarded her with a kiss by her ear. "I'm sure it meant a lot to them that you were there."

"I wouldn't have been anywhere else." She moaned. "They kept talking about having to miss the wedding and mess up the seating arrangement. Can you believe that? For God's sake, I'd redo the arrangement ten times over if it would make Jimmy better."

"I'm sure you would," he said, and continued to hold her. She felt so right in his arms. She always had, but now even more so. He had missed the way she nestled against him. He hadn't realized how much. Through a tight throat, he whispered, "Want to take a walk?"

She didn't lift her head. "Now?"

"Yes, now."

"It'll be getting dark soon."

"We still have an hour. Better still, how about a run?"

"A run?"

"Have you had one today?"

"Early this morning." She sighed. "Feels like an aeon ago."

"Then put on your gear, we'll go back to my hotel while I change, and I'll show you the route I've been taking."

She drew her head back. "You've been taking?"

"I run, too." He gave her a little nudge and stepped back. "Go on. It'll make you feel better."

What made Cynthia feel better was the realization that, on top of everything else that drew them together, they had this in common. She did feel like running, but she wouldn't have done it alone so late. Russ's company was a gift.

Less than thirty minutes later, they were running side by side. He tempered his pace to one he felt would be comfortable for her, then picked up a little when he saw that she could handle more. When he felt they'd hit stride, he asked, "How're you doin'?"

"Great," she said, breathing easily. "Feels good."

"It always does."

"Especially when you're down. That call shook me today."

"I could see that."

She ran on a bit before saying, "Life is so fragile. Things can be fine one day and shattered the next."

"Was that how it was with Matthew?"

"Uh-huh." Matthew's heart had been the culprit. It had ticked fine on Monday and stopped cold on Tuesday. "We weren't prepared."

"Is anyone ever prepared for death?" Russ gestured for her to turn right at the corner. "You had a good life with Matthew."

"He was a kind man."

"I'm surprised you didn't have more kids."

She was a minute in answering. "Me, too. I was so quick to get pregnant with Diane. I guess I wasn't meant to have more."

"Did you want more?"

"Uh-huh." But even as the word came out, she felt hesitant. Though she had never used birth control with Matthew, neither of them had been disturbed when she hadn't conceived. "With his being older, it was probably for the best."

"You could have more now."

Between strides, she shot him a doubtful look. "I'm forty-three."

"Easily done in this day and age."

She shot him another look, a chiding one this time. "Spoken like a man." Which he was. Quite definitely. She didn't have to shoot him another look to see the dark rumple of his hair, the lean strength of his shoulders, the muscular tone of his legs. "How about you? Didn't you want other children?"

"I've had hundreds over the years."

"Of your own."

He mulled over the question. "I wasn't sure I was worthy."

"Are you kidding?" She tried to make out his expression, but dusk shadowed his face.

His voice was sober, punctuated only by the rhythm of his pace. "I abandoned Diane. I wasn't sure I deserved another child. It's taken six years of building a relationship with her to give me back a little self-respect in that regard."

"So you want more kids now?"

He shrugged, shot a look behind him for traffic and gestured for her to make a left turn. "Got no wife."

"Which mystifies me. You should have married again."

"Didn't want to. No one would be good enough. You're a hard act to follow."

Her voice went breathless. "Don't say that."

"It's the truth."

"I have my faults."

"Like what?"

"Cowardice."

"When?"

"When you left." She didn't speak for several beats. "I should have stood up to my mother."

"You weren't in a position to do that. You said it yourself."

"I know. Still, I should have. Somehow."

As confessions went, it was filled with regret and, in that, was a world away from the anger he'd heard two nights before. Gone, too, was the bitterness he'd always felt when, in moments of self-pity, he allowed himself to think she could have done something to bring him back. They were moving on, past the pain, as they needed to do if they hoped to know each other in the here and now.

One shadow of the past, though, hadn't budged. "Cyn?"

"Hmm?"

"Does your mother know I'm here?"

"Not yet."

"But she knows I'm coming to the wedding."

"Yes."

"Does she know I'm walking Diane down the aisle?"

Cynthia ran on in silence.

"She doesn't," he said.

"See what a coward I am?"

He rallied to her defense. "You didn't know about it yourself until Monday."

"I should have called her then." The syncopated pat of their running shoes on the pavement was the only sound until she tacked on, "Then again, maybe it's best she not know. She can't make much of a fuss with everyone watching at the wedding." After another minute she darted Russ an uneasy look. "Can she?"

Russ didn't know, but the more he thought about it—which he did at some length after dropping Cynthia back home that night—the more he realized he didn't want to leave the matter to chance. Gertrude Hoffmann could be one unpleasant lady. Her narrow-mindedness had sabotaged his marriage. He wasn't letting it mar his daughter's wedding day.

To that end, he showed up at her house early the next morning. He remembered the way, having dropped Cynthia back there dozens of times. More often than not he had parked down the street and walked her to the house, so that Gertrude wouldn't hear the distinctly lower-class rumble of his car. Only once had he been inside.

He remembered being impressed by the size, the shine and the sophistication. But he'd been a boy then, and raw. Now he was a man with polish of his own, and while he could appreciate the stateliness of Gertrude Hoffmann's home, he wasn't terribly impressed. Cynthia's, which held an inherent warmth, was far more to his liking.

"My name is Russell Shaw," he told the uniformed maid who answered the door. "Mrs. Hoffmann isn't expecting me, but I'd like a word with her if she's home."

He was shown into the parlor, which amused him no end. The maid didn't know who he was, but making a judgment based on his clothing, his carriage and his confidence, had deemed him safe to let in. That was a switch from the judgment made twenty-six years before.

After no more than a minute, she returned. "If you'll come this way, Mr. Shaw." She led him across the hall and down a corridor into the dining room. There, at the far end of a huge table, at a place set with fine linen, bone china and sterling sil-

ver, sat Gertrude Hoffmann—and for a split second Russ
understood what Diane had said about the woman being alone.
There was no sadder image than that of a solitary figure amid
opulence.

Then the second passed, and he saw a woman in her mid-
sixties, well preserved and imperious-looking still. Her hair
was pure white and perfectly coiffed, her face neatly made up,
her blue blouse impeccably starched. She was in the middle
of a breakfast of eggs and toast that had come from a scrolled
chafing dish nearby. But her fork had been placed neatly across
her plate and she was sitting back in her chair, elbows on its
arms, fingers laced, staring at him.

"I was wondering whether you'd make it over here," she
announced boldly. "If I were a gambling woman, I'd have lost
money. I didn't think you'd have the courage to face me after
all these years."

Russ wasn't put off by her bluntness. It dispensed with polite greetings and told him just where he stood. "I have the
courage. I've always had it."

"Even when you deserted my daughter and granddaughter?" she asked archly.

With confidence, he said, "Mostly then. Leaving Cynthia
and Diane was the hardest thing I've ever had to do. They were
all I cared about in the world. More than anything I wanted to
stay with them, but that would have been the selfish thing—
the cowardly thing to do. I couldn't give them what they
needed or deserved, or what I wanted them to have. Not
without your help. So I sent them back to you. The way I see
it, that took courage. The way I see it, you should be thinking me."

Her chin lifted a notch. "For embarrassing me? For causing upheaval in my home?"

"For returning your daughter to you, and for giving you a
granddaughter who is better than either of us. She's the reason I'm here today. I love Diane. This is a special time for her.
If there is to be unpleasantness, I want it to stay between you
and me. She isn't to feel it."

Gertrude's gaze didn't waver, though her chin dropped slightly. "She was very angry with me for a while, all because of you."

"Justly so. You had no business telling her that I was dead. She had a right to know the truth."

"To what end? So she could chase after a man who had given every sign of not wanting her? You didn't contact my daughter after you ran out of here. Not once."

"Would you have wanted me to?"

"Heavens, no!"

"What would you have done if I had?"

"Gotten a court order to keep you away."

In a voice quiet with a common sense that chided, Russ said, "Do you have any idea what that would have done to Cynthia? Or to Diane?" When Gertrude didn't answer, he went on. "I left because I thought it was the best thing for both of them. I stayed away for the same reason. When I contacted Diane six years ago, it was because I felt she was old enough and because I couldn't stay away any longer. She's my daughter. There's no denying that fact."

Gertrude looked as if she did want to deny it but couldn't. Her frustration escaped in subtle ways—the faint compression of her lips, the shift of her fingers, her refusal to blink.

Russ refused to be intimidated by that unremitting stare. "I'm not sure how much she's told you about our relationship. We meet for lunch every few months. We've developed a mutual appreciation. I love hearing about what's going on in her life, she loves hearing about what's happening in mine. Do you know where I live?"

A muscle in her cheek moved. It could have been either a twitch or a gesture of dismissal. "She told me you lived at a school in Connecticut."

"Did she tell you that I'm the headmaster of that school? I was chosen last year from a pool of three hundred candidates. It's a position of responsibility and prestige."

Gertrude arched a pale brow. "Is there a point to this self-promotion, Mr. Shaw?"

He smiled with the sudden understanding that she was rather harmless—arched brow, starched blouse, thinned lips and all. In a softer voice he said, "It's Dr. Shaw, and indeed there is. I was up for a good part of last night thinking about this visit. I was prepared to spit in your eye—" he held up a hand "—not a terribly learned expression from a learned man, but apt. When I left here twenty-five years ago, I hated you. Since then I've come a long way in terms of who I am, what I do and how much money I make. I may not hate you now, but I'm not backing down. I'm here this week because Diane asked me to come. If she hadn't invited me to the wedding, I'd probably have come anyway and stood at the back of the church—just as I stood at the back during her graduation from Radcliffe, though she doesn't know that, and I wish you wouldn't tell her. She'd be upset, which would be pointless, since it's water under the bridge. I want her to be happy. That's all I've ever wanted."

He paused for the briefest of instants, then reached the point of his visit. "She's asked me to give her away at the wedding, and I've accepted. Cynthia just found out. She had already arranged for Ray Bauer to do it, and she wasn't thrilled at first, but she agrees that on Diane's day her wish should be respected. I'd like you to do the same."

The silence in the dining room was abrupt. Russ made no move to break it. He was waiting for Gertrude's consent, and the fact that she didn't instantly offer it neither surprised nor bothered him. Cynthia had mentioned the woman's pride. She would answer him in her own sweet time—which was fine, as long as she gave him the answer he wanted.

He didn't expect the subtle shift of her features, this time not in frustration but in what looked surprisingly like remorse.

"There are people," she began more quietly than before, "who take me to be arrogant and bossy and bigoted, and rightly they should. I can be all of those things when I'm crossed, and some of those things even when I'm not. But whatever I do, I do because I believe it's the best thing." She looked off to the side, keeping her jaw firm to show she wasn't apologizing for anything. "I'll admit that I was a bit cruel cutting Cynthia off without a cent when you two eloped, but I was angry and hurt that she hadn't taken my advice, and I truly believed that only drastic measures would bring her back to me."

"She had a *baby*. You didn't come to see Diane once in those three months."

"Four months," Gertrude corrected, looking him in the eye now. "Cynthia stayed in that apartment for a whole month after you left, waiting for you to return, and she mourned you in earnest for months after. I'd be less than honest if I said that didn't bother me."

"You hated me that much?"

"I loved Cynthia that much. She was my only child, and she was heartbroken."

"But you weren't ready to go out and bring me back."

"No. I didn't think that would be in her best interest. Matthew was a far better match for her. He gave her the stability you couldn't have provided. But that's not my point. My point is that I love my daughter and don't want to see her unhappy. The same applies to my granddaughter. So. If your giving Diane away at the wedding will make her happy, I won't fight it."

Russ couldn't quite bring himself to thank her, though he did feel immensely relieved. He also felt a glimmer of understanding for the woman. Lips pursed, he reflected on that for a minute before nodding and turning to leave. Beneath the archway, he turned back and in a tentative voice asked, "Just for the record, if Cynthia hadn't called you, would you have gone looking for her?"

Gertrude's chin tipped up again. "I already had, and I'd already seen the baby. I used to sit in a rented car on the edge of the park on weekends and watch while you two handed her back and forth."

Russ's throat tightened. He stared at her, thinking about stubbornness and pride and loss. Then, with another nod, he turned, only to stop again. He didn't look back this time. "One last question. If Cynthia and I were to start seeing each other again, if she were to visit me in Connecticut, would you give her trouble?''

After what seemed an eternity to Russ, Gertrude said, ''Cynthia is a grown woman. A widow. I no longer have any control over her.''

''She loves you and wants to please you. Would you give her trouble?''

The older woman's voice grew quiet. ''Now, that wouldn't be in my best interest, would it?''

He did look back at her then. ''What do you mean?''

''I have nothing to hold over Cynthia anymore. She is financially independent and socially secure. She doesn't need me the way she did twenty-five years ago. If she chooses to see you and I object, she's very well apt to defy me again, only this time she wouldn't have any reason to come back. Frankly, I don't care for the thought of being estranged from my only daughter at this point in my life.''

The implication of what she was saying boggled Russ's mind. He wanted to make sure he'd heard right. ''You wouldn't make life miserable for her?''

''Not on that score.'' One corner of her mouth moved in what Russ could have sworn was the germ of a smile. ''On others, of course, I would. I'm Gertrude Hoffmann. It's in my nature to be demanding and iron-willed, even overbearing at times. The day I can't cause a stir on one matter or another will be the day they put me in the ground. Have you any more questions?''

Russ thought about it, then shook his head. With a final nod and a small wave of farewell, he showed himself to the front door and went out to the car. The day seemed suddenly much brighter.

Chapter Six

THE WEDDING REHEARSAL went off without a hitch on Thursday evening, and Cynthia couldn't have been more delighted. She was pleased to begin with, having gotten word shortly beforehand that Jimmy Schuler had regained consciousness. Added to that, the bridesmaids and groomsmen—bar one Jared Flynn—had all arrived in St. Louis intact, neither of the flower girls had misbehaved, and her mother hadn't said boo when Russ went through the motions of walking Diane down the central aisle of the church, so Cynthia was feeling good all over.

The feeling got even better as they moved from the church to Granatelli's, Nick's family's restaurant on the Hill, where the rehearsal dinner was to be held. The restaurant was small, but upscale and classy in its way, with white tablecloths, white linen napkins and fresh flowers. Candles on each of the tables, as well as paintings and photographs on the walls, gave it the homey atmosphere that suited Nick's family so well.

Cynthia liked the Granatellis, many of whom she'd met before. She liked Teresa, who, plump but stately, had a natural dignity to rival Gertrude's. She liked Dom, with his white moustache and commanding nose, and Uncle Vito, with the ever-present cigar that smelled up the place but looked so much a part of the man that no one dreamed of complaining. She liked Nick's sisters, Paula, Frankie and Sophia, and his brothers, Carlo and Vinnie—all blond, as was Nick, whom she adored. Mostly she liked the fact that Nick and Diane were in love, and that their love surmounted the differences in background that a generation before had caused such heartache. If Gertrude had any objections to the match, she hadn't dared say so to Cynthia. She must have known Cynthia would fight tooth and nail for her daughter's right to happiness.

So Cynthia was feeling good about that, too. And then there was Russ, who had hardly left her side since they'd arrived at the restaurant. She enjoyed having him there. She enjoyed introducing him to Nick's family, enjoyed the way he fitted into the group, enjoyed the way he held his own in conversation. She enjoyed the way he stood with an arm or a shoulder brushing hers, the way he brought her a drink from the bar, put a hand at her waist to guide her to a table, pulled out her chair. He was a gentleman, and though she had never found him lacking in that respect years before, this was different. He was socially suave and urbane, more so than she ever could have wished. Twenty-six years before she'd been bowled over by the boy in the soda shop; now she was bowled over by the man that boy had become.

She was sorry when the evening ended. Too soon, Russ drove her home and walked her to her door. Though her senses were keyed up for something warm and exciting—and though the longing look he gave her suggested he wanted it, too—he didn't kiss her. Instead, he offered to come by the next day and give her a hand doing whatever last-minute things had to be done. If for no other reason than to keep him close, she accepted the offer.

The result was heaven and hell at the very same time. Russ was with her while she opened newly arrived gifts with Diane, oversaw the tent and table raising in the yard and made a final run-through of the wedding events with Tammy. He sat patiently while she made calls to various out-of-town guests who were starting to arrive. He drove her to the jeweler's to pick up the bridesmaids' gifts, to the dry cleaner's to pick up things Diane would be taking on her honeymoon, to the hospital to visit Jimmy. He even drove her to the manicurist's, then wandered around outside until she was done.

Though he was a joy to be with—calm, accommodating and patient—his presence was a torment. He touched her, but never for long enough. He looked at her with desire, but never acted it out. He spoke in the low, intimate tone lovers used, the kind that stroked her inside and out, then took a step back while she reeled. By late afternoon she wasn't sure whether the shakiness she felt inside was mother-of-the-bride jitters or pure lust.

Russ had barely brought her back to the house when the phone started ringing again. Whispering asides to him about who each of the calls was from, she talked with a cousin who had arrived with her family from Cleveland, a former business associate of Matthew's who was in with his wife from Denver, a friend of Gertrude's whom Cynthia had known forever. Then Diane called from Nick's, reporting that people were gathering at the Granatellis' and asking if they would be along soon. It was a perfect solution to Cynthia's problem. She could be with Russ, yet safe. The more people around, the more diffused her awareness of him would be.

That didn't turn out to be the case. The party at the Granatellis' was wonderful, but not once did Cynthia forget the man by her side. They talked together, moved together, laughed together every bit as naturally as when they'd been kids. Likewise, there were times when the party receded and they were alone, sharing a thought or a story or a reaction to something another person said as though they were the only ones in the room.

That happened increasingly as the evening went on. By eleven, Russ was feeling a distinct need to be alone with Cynthia, if only for a short time. Leaning close, he said, "Are you tired?"

She knew she should be. She knew she should go home to bed, given the eventful day that was ahead. But her senses were humming. She was more awake than she'd been in years. "I don't think I could sleep if I tried."

"Want to go for a ride?"

"I'd love to."

"Think anyone will miss us?"

She glanced around. The party was still in full swing. "Are you kidding?" Slipping a hand in his, she led him through the crowd to where Diane was laughing with a group of friends. "We're taking off, sweetheart. Shall I see you back home?"

"Sooner or later—probably later. Better still, don't wait up, Mom, okay? I'll be more relaxed that way. And I'll have everyone be quiet when we get back so we don't wake you up."

Cynthia touched her hair. She couldn't quite believe her baby was getting married in the morning. Then again, given the work she'd done planning the wedding, she could believe it quite well. "Don't forget, Franco and his crew are coming to do hair at ten. Pass the word."

Diane smiled. "I already have." She kissed Cynthia, then Russ. "See you tomorrow."

The air outside was hot and still. Russ didn't have to be told that a storm was coming on. Anyone could tell, what with the humidity and the dark, starless sky—even a person whose own senses had been storming for hours. His blood was hotter than the air, his arousal heavier than the humidity, and as for the darkness of the sky, that was the way he felt when he thought of leaving on Sunday. There was so much yet to be said, so much to be done. *So much.*

After tucking Cynthia into the car, he went to the driver's side and slid in behind the wheel, but he didn't turn on the ignition. Instead, he caught up her hand and brought it to his mouth.

"I don't want to go for a ride," he breathed against it. "Not really."

She was looking at him, sure that if she didn't kiss him soon she would die. "Me, neither. Russ?"

He rubbed her knuckles against his mouth. "I love you so much."

"Oh, God," she whispered, and opened her hand. She traced his lips for a minute, parted them and leaned over the gearshift to meet him halfway. Their mouths touched and fused, and it was as though twenty-five years of separation had never been. The fire, the balm, the bliss were so intense that by the time they parted for a breath, there were tears in her eyes.

"Can we go somewhere?" he whispered hoarsely.

"Please," she whispered back. "Quickly."

He drove one-handed. The other hand was wrapped in both of hers, anchored against her throat. Her eyes were on his face. He caught her gaze as often as he dared take his from the road. It was brilliant with excitement and need, both of which shone through the thick, dark night. Once, then a second time, he hastily pulled to the side of the road to kiss her again, and if his kisses held more raw need than finesse, he knew she understood. He could taste the hunger in her mouth, could feel the desire that set her slender body to shaking.

By the time they arrived at the inn, large drops of rain had begun to splatter the windshield. Leaving the doorman with a ten-dollar bill to park the car, Russ grabbed Cynthia's hand and ran inside. They took the stairs, moving as quickly as Cynthia's heels would allow, and when that wasn't fast enough, she slipped the shoes off and ran faster.

He fumbled with the door, finally unlocked it and pushed it open. The bed had been neatly turned back in his absence and a low light left on, but he barely noticed. As the door clicked shut behind them, he slid his fingers into her hair, covered her mouth with his and gave her a frantic kiss that spread to her cheeks, then her eyes.

"I can't believe you're here," he whispered.

"I'm here." She was unbuttoning his shirt, desperate to touch him. In a fluid motion that pushed the cotton fabric aside, she slid her palms over his chest and ribs to his waist. In the next breath, she put her mouth where her hands had touched.

Russ was in heaven. He braced shaky arms against the door on either side of her and bent his head over hers. "Sweetheart . . . sweetheart . . . what you do to me."

"I love you, Russ," she said, raising her face. Her mouth met his again, and this time, while their lips continued to nip and suck, they went at their clothes. Cynthia's halter dress fell to the floor not far from Russ's shirt and slacks. He released her bra and filled his hands with her breasts, while she pushed his shorts over his hips.

"Hurry," she cried, straining closer, frantic with need.

No less frantic himself, Russ kicked off his shorts, scooped her up and carried her to the bed. He set her down on her knees in the middle of it and, with time-out to touch all he bared, freed her of her silk panties. While they knelt facing each other, breathing harder than if they'd just come off a long run, he reached for the pins in her hair.

"I want this all over me. I've dreamed of it. It's so beautiful."

She helped him with the pins, helped him comb through her hair with his fingers until it flowed softly over her shoulders. Then, draping her elbows over his shoulders, she gave him her mouth. At the same time, he brought her body tightly against his, drew her thighs over his and entered her.

Her cry was muffled in his mouth. Seconds later, her back hit the bed and he began to love her inside with long, hot strokes. She wanted to savor them and everything else about his body, but the intensity was too great. Within minutes she erupted into a climax so powerful and prolonged that she was never to know where one orgasm ended and the next began.

For Russ, too, the pleasure went on and on. The memory of their lovemaking, which had kept him hard night after night for years, was nothing compared to the heat of the present. His body was slick with sweat by the time he finally let his weight go on her. He rolled to the side and drew her to him, tightening his arms when, still shaken by inner spasms, she began to cry.

"What, sweetheart? What is it?" But he knew even before she told him. He was feeling the same overwhelming emotion.

"I've missed you so much," she gulped through huge tears that wet his throat. "Part of me has been gone—"

"—gone all this time." His arms tightened until he feared he would crush her. His head was bent over hers, his breath was urgent against her temple. "There was always that empty spot. I kept thinking it would fill in—"

"—but it never did. I tried to put other things there, like Matthew and my friends and my causes—"

"—and my students and my courses, but it didn't work. There was always that void, and it hurt—"

"—*so much.*"

"Ahhh, sweetheart," he whispered, moving his head as he kissed her until he could reach her mouth again. "I love you, Cyn...love you, sweetheart." He rolled her over, then over again, kissing her all the while. Ending on top, he began to make love to her again, moving down her body, touching and tasting all the places he had missed for so long.

She writhed beneath him until she could take no more. "Now, Russ, *now.*"

Hard and heavy with need, he surged into her, then proceeded to make up for the time they had lost by loving her until she came again—only to realize that wasn't enough. He climaxed, but still he wanted her. The sounds she made, the touch of her hands and the motions of her body told him she felt the same.

They made love long into the night. Hours had passed before either of them was ready to settle onto the damp and rumpled sheets for long, and then it wasn't with exhaustion but with gales of breathless laughter that only two people who are pleased with themselves and in love with each other can produce.

"You haven't changed, Russell Shaw," she hummed against his shoulder. "You're as insatiable as ever."

He spread a hand over her backside to mold her closer. "Look who's talking. I haven't had a workout like this in years."

"How many years?"

"Twenty-five."

"Mmm. That's good."

"And you? Did you drive Matthew wild like you do me?"

"It was different with Matthew. Pleasant, but sedate. There were never grounds for comparison."

"Mmm. That's good."

"But he was a fine man, Russ. He was kind. He loved me, and he loved Diane. I tried to be a good wife to him."

"From everything I've read and heard, you were."

She sighed. "But did I love him? Ahhh, there's the question. I tried to, but it never came close to the kind of all-consuming love I had with you." She tipped her head back and looked over the plane of his lean cheek to his eyes. "I prayed I'd never see you. I went out of my way over the years not to know what you were doing with your life. I never quite trusted that I wouldn't want to run off to be with you—or that you wouldn't turn and walk away from me again." Her eyes misted and her voice fell to a plaintive whimper. "You won't do that, Russ, will you?"

He brought her over on top of him. "No, love." He kissed her eyes. "I couldn't."

"It would kill me."

"It would kill me, too."

"So what are we going to do? You're leaving Sunday."

"Only if you can't find room for me in your house."

Her heart soared. "You'll stay?"

"Why not?"

"What about school?"

"I'm on summer vacation."

"You have the whole summer off?" Her mind leaped at the possibilities.

"Yes and no."

"What does that mean?" She held her breath.

"I'm due in England on the fifth of July. I'm committed to spending the summer in Oxford collaborating with a don there on a book on education."

She continued to hold her breath.

"Want to come with me?" he asked, and started to smile just as she did because he knew very well what her answer would be.

"I'd love to."

"I'll be busy. Writing a book takes time and concentration."

"That's okay. I'll catch up on all the reading I haven't been able to do this spring, and write letters and take walks."

"I was planning to rent a house in the Cotswolds. Does that sound okay?"

She grinned. "I think I could live with it."

"Then, when I'm done, I thought I'd spend a few days in London, and maybe drive north to Scotland for a few more. Would that be a problem?"

"Are you kidding?"

"I have to be back before Labor Day," he cautioned. "School doesn't begin until a week later, but there'll be plenty to do before then."

She rested her chin on his chest. "What's it like, your place at Hollings?"

"It's a Tudor, wood and brick, with a grape arbor and an old-fashioned well and lots of trees." He ran his fingers through her hair, spreading it around her. "You'll like it, Cyn. It's on campus but set apart so that there's plenty of privacy. It's the kind of house we used to talk about having one day. I mean, it's not as grand as yours—"

She put her hand over his mouth. "I don't care about grand. I care about *you.* You could live in a shack on the tundra and I'd follow you there. That's what I was trying to tell you Monday night. It's one of the reasons I was so crushed when you left me. I've had wealth, and, yes, it makes life easier. But it isn't worth diddly if I can't have you. Don't put me through that misery again, Russ. Don't ever, ever, *ever* do it."

Grasping her waist, he raised her just enough for a kiss. He was about to tell her that he wouldn't ever, ever, *ever* leave her again, when the kiss heated and spread, and before he could contain the flame, she was beneath him and he was inside her again.

It was a while later before he said the words, and by that time they were both so drowsy that the words were slurred. But Cynthia heard them, and held them to her heart as she fell asleep in his arms. Just to make sure she knew he meant them, he repeated them several hours later, when, with dawn sending shards of pale color over the Frontenac treetops, he drove her home.

IT WAS A GEM OF A DAY, sunny and dry after the rain the night before. The rich alto of the organ filled the air. With rosebuds in soft shades of cream, pink and peach on the pews and on arbors framing the altar, the church looked beautiful, as did the guests, who filled row after row, waiting expectantly for the processional to begin.

Cynthia, too, waited, her heart beating fast beneath the corsage that had been carefully pinned to her dusty pink gown. She had just been escorted down the aisle and now stood beside Gertrude, who looked surprisingly soft in dove gray. At a change in the music, she turned to watch the groomsmen enter. They were a handsome group. She smiled at each one whose eye she caught, but her attention inevitably returned to the rear of the church. The bridesmaids appeared one by one, looking as exquisite as she had intended in shades of peach, dusty rose and gray. The maid of honor passed as planned, then the flower girls, leaving soft pink petals in their wake.

The music changed again, and this time when Cynthia looked back, her breath caught in her throat. The two people she loved most in the world were there—Diane, looking more stunning than any bride had ever been in her gown of satin and beaded lace, with her cascading bouquet and the headpiece of flowers and veiling, that barely hid the glittering tear-shaped diamond earrings her father had given her that morning; and Russ, looking more handsome than any father of the bride had ever been with his white standing collar, his pale gray cutaway coat and trousers, his cream-colored boutonniere.

Tears came to her eyes as she watched them slowly approach. When she brushed them away, new ones simply took their place. She smiled through them as she caught Diane's eye, and when she found Russ looking at her, her smile grew even softer. He was a beautiful man inside and out, with a beautiful daughter who had been the focus of her passion for the twenty-five years he'd been gone from her life. Now he was back, and the passion would broaden and shift. She felt she was the luckiest woman in the world.

Russ must have read that in her eyes, because his own spoke of sheer adoration in the brief minute before he passed. As she faced front, Nick was approaching the foot of the altar. Gently,

Russ lifted Diane's veil and kissed her cheek, then placed her hand in Nick's. By the time he had come to stand by Cynthia's side, the bride and groom were in the priest's care.

Cynthia felt Russ's fingers twine with hers. Looking up through her tears, she saw the sparkle of his own, and in that instant understood the precious second chance they'd been given. His fingers tightened possessively, and while Diane and Nick exchanged their vows, silently they did, too.

Their hearts heard every word.

Say It
With Flowers

BETHANY
CAMPBELL

A Note from Bethany Campbell

Weddings? Ah, yes. I had dozens.

When I was five years old, I had my first "boyfriend," Teddy, who was also five and lived a few houses away. We used to pretend to "get married."

I'd pin a doily on my head, pick dandelions, and we'd put one of my father's old ties on the handle of the back screen door and pretend the door was the minister.

Teddy was a treasured friend, but he had a problem: a serious stutter. Some people teased him cruelly about it. I hated this because he was my friend and I loved him.

When we were still young, we moved apart and, at last, lost touch completely. The last time I saw him, he was a tall young man—who'd conquered his stutter. I was not to forget him, though, for when I *really* married, I had a son who also had a speech impediment. So, twice I have seen young people who were dear to me struggle with this problem.

When it came time to write about a wedding, perhaps subconsciously, I recalled my many weddings to Teddy, and that reminded me of the sort of difficulty that Teddy—and many other people—have faced.

So, although this is a story about a wedding, it's also about stuttering and about a flower a bit more exotic than a dandelion, but mostly, I hope, it's a story about love.

Best wishes,

Bethany

Chapter One

LAURIE CHASE-SPENSER stood at the back of the empty church, looking down the long aisle with its rose-colored carpet. It was less than an hour before the wedding, and the place echoed with expectancy.

She sighed. Her emotions wanted to jig off in a dozen different directions, but pride in her work held her steady. The flowers looked beautiful, all of them.

The floral arrangements, as demanding as they had been, were not why her feelings danced so madly within her. Beneath her demure gray silk suit and grave manner, she was half-giddy with hope, nervousness and happiness.

Early this morning, this most hectic of mornings, she'd discovered that the rarest plant she owned, the fabled sorcerer's flower, had budded. For three years she'd been trying to coax the plant to bloom. She could hardly wait to get back to the greenhouse.

If this thing is ever over, she thought wryly. She remembered Diane fondly from high school and liked her, but for the last weeks she'd felt the wedding's demands taking over her life, devouring her every spare hour.

Laurie had risen at 5:00 a.m. to arrange the flowers. The fresh blooms—roses, sweet peas and lilies of the valley—were the most beautiful she could procure and the most delicate. They would not keep well in arrangements overnight, and to be at their best they had to be done just before the wedding.

But, she thought happily, they looked truly lovely; the effect was worth all the extra work. Each walnut pew bore a spray of cream, peach and pale pink rosebuds tied with a cascade of pearl-gray ribbon. French roses and sweet peas twined the walnut pillars behind the gray marble altar. More French roses heaped the antique flower holders that matched the pewter tabernacle.

She straightened her shoulders. She was almost through. She had delivered the bouquets, the corsages, the boutonnieres, the baskets of rose petals for the flower girls. Her assistant was in Frontenac right now setting out the flowers for the reception. Laurie's work and her worries were almost over. All she had to do was relax and enjoy her friend's wedding.

The only thorn among all her flowery labors had been the bride's grandmother, Gertrude Hoffmann. Mrs. Hoffmann had wanted floral arbors erected to camouflage both the photographer and the man videotaping the wedding. Laurie had resisted but finally given in.

Now on either side of the altar steps, toward the ends of the chancel rail, stood white latticework arches twined with roses and sweet peas. They had been an almost impossible piece of work, but Laurie felt a surge of satisfaction. Against all odds, she had made the arrangement look good.

She took a deep breath and surveyed it all again. The pale pinks, delicate pink-golds and creams of the flowers gleamed in contrast to the dark wood of the church. Everything looked so perfect it seemed enchanted, but she wanted nothing more than to get back to the greenhouse.

The sorcerer's flower, she thought, biting her lip. *If it finally blooms*... She remembered all the legends about the plant. How odd that it would bud on the dawn of a wedding....

Suddenly Laurie started, shivering at an unexpected touch. She'd been oblivious to the comings and goings of a few other people in the large church. But now a warm and mobile mouth pressed against the back of her neck, kissing her.

Two strong hands gripped her shoulders as the man behind her kissed her neck again. This time his lips were hotter and more lingering. Her nerves, already strained, shattered like the sparks of a Roman candle.

His mouth moved to her ear. A deep voice said softly, *"Da tempo ti desidero ardemente. Ti potrei dare un morsetto?"*

Laurie had spent a year in Italy, studying design. She understood Italian. What she didn't understand was how anyone could dare utter such a thing, for what he had said was, "Long have I hungered after you. May I bite you?"

She whirled and stared up at him in distress. Although she was tall, almost five foot ten in her heels, he towered over her. His unexpected height added to her shock. The man had to be six and a half feet tall, she thought in dismay. He made her feel dwarfed, almost tiny.

His tanned face was square jawed, with a straight nose, an irreverent mouth and thick straight brows. His dark hair was slightly curly, his eyes snapping black. He was handsome in a wide-shouldered, athletic way, and that, too, gave Laurie an unwarranted jolt. She was used to smaller men, with more civilized airs and softer faces.

Above all she was used to men with manners, not ones who crept up, kissed her neck and asked to bite her.

She stared up at him in disapproval. At first he'd had a smirky, half-seductive little smile on his lips, but it had begun dying the moment she'd whirled around. Now he looked at her with the same unhappy surprise with which she regarded him.

"Who are you?" he demanded, as if she'd sabotaged or insulted him. He looked as appalled as she felt.

Laurie's heart skittered from his touch, and confusion swarmed through her. She was basically shy, and at the best of times she had to watch her speech to keep from stammering. Startled as she was, she would have to monitor every word; otherwise she would stutter and sputter hopelessly.

She raised her chin and took a deep breath. "I'm Laurentia Chase-Spenser. I'm here to arrange the roses, et cetera."

Drat, Laurie thought. She'd spoken so carefully she'd sounded pompous. In times of stress, certain sounds gave her trouble, so she had to avoid them. Her answer might have sounded stilted, but at least she hadn't stumbled over the words *florist* or *flowers*.

"You mean you're the florist," he said, raising one dark brow.

She nodded, her face a mask of coolness. "Yes."

"Well, why don't you just say so?" he asked, mockery in his voice.

The question stung, but Laurie merely lifted her chin in disdain. Her neck still tingled from the warmth of his mouth, and her heart still tripped along at too swift a rate. "Who are you?" she asked, her voice more controlled and artificial than before.

"Jeff Remington," he said, eyeing her coolly. "I thought you were somebody else. The wedding adviser or whatever you call her. Tammy." He gave the barest shrug of one shoulder. "Sorry. Let's start over."

Sorry? A spark of anger flared through her. He didn't look sorry in the least. He looked frankly appreciative, even flirtatious. She was shaken by the look in his eyes, and she resented how badly off balance he had put her.

She wanted to tell him that his behavior was deplorable, that a church was a sacred place and this was a solemn occasion. But she knew her tongue would twist around the words. She simply stared at him for a long moment. Then she said, "Don't be ridiculous." The words sounded harsher than she'd intended, but she was too rattled to care.

His mouth thinned, but the mockery didn't die out of his dark eyes. "Are you really as proper as you sound?"

Laurie could stand it no longer. She marched a few paces down the aisle and straightened a spray of rosebuds that didn't need straightening.

He picked up an expensive video camera from one of the pews, set it on his shoulder and followed her. "Your hair's like Tammy's," he said, the dark eyes still assessing her. "That honey-colored hair pulled back. What do you call it? A bun, chignon, a French twist, a braid—what?"

Laurie didn't trust herself to answer. She usually wore her hair free, but for the wedding she'd woven it into a complex braid. She said nothing and concentrated on adjusting a pearl-gray ribbon that was already perfect.

"Look," he said, impatience in his deep voice, "I thought you were Tammy. I said I was sorry. Just laugh it off, okay? It was an accident."

His nearness affected her like some strange magnetic field, filling her with tickling nervousness. She gave him an icy glance, then moved on to the next pew and the next spray of flowers.

He followed her. "Are you always this haughty?"

She refused to look at him. "Would—you—just—go—away?" she asked.

Oh, really, she thought miserably, the words were sticking in her throat worse than they had in years. When life went smoothly, she controlled her stammer so well that few people noticed it. But somehow this man threatened to make her stutter as helplessly as she had when she was a child.

She pressed her lips together in angry determination. *Calm down*, she told herself. *Just calm down. You're tired and nervous about this wedding, you're excited about the bud on the sorcerer's flower, and this man caught you offguard....*

She heard a soft whirr and looked up in fresh dismay. He had the video camera on his shoulder and was looking through the eyepiece, taping her pale hands moving among the ribbons and roses.

"Stop that!" she ordered. She had no idea what he was trying to do.

"It's my job," he said laconically, and kept on taping.

A delayed realization hit her, so dreadful it actually made her head hurt. She stared at him with new consternation. "Oh, no," she said. "You're the—"

It happened. The word lodged in her throat, and she knew better than to try to force it out. "Oh, *no*," she said again, shaking her head.

He touched something on the camera and it went silent. The look he tossed her was electric with challenge. "I'm the cameraman. The videographer. Something wrong with that?"

Laurie turned toward the front of the church and gestured at the two dainty arbors flanking the foot of the altar steps. The videographer and the photographer were supposed to be camouflaged discreetly behind them, but Jeff Remington was so tall he'd have to bend double to fit behind the thing.

"That," she said, pointing at an arbor. "M-Mrs. Hoffmann wants you to hide in that. And you're too—too *tall*."

He followed her gaze and all amusement vanished from his face. His dark eyes flashed. "She wants me in *there*? No. I've got a wedding to shoot. And so's Spurgeon—the photographer. And neither of us works hiding in some...little lace outhouse."

"It does *not* look like a lace outhouse," Laurie said hotly, her feelings hurt. "It's what she—wants. She doesn't want—you—drawing attention away from the wedding—"

"Like I won't draw attention away from the wedding if I'm squatting in some elf bower, sticking my head out every now and then like a gopher?"

"It's what she—*wants*," Laurie said slowly and emphatically. Jeff Remington acted as if it were her fault he was expected to conceal himself. She'd thought the arbors a bad idea herself, and she didn't want to defend them. The last thing she wanted was a scene.

"What she—*wants*," Jeff said, mocking Laurie's careful pronunciation. "Well, I won't do it. Neither will Spurgeon. We've got to be free to move around."

Laurie bit her lip in frustration. "I think she was just worried that you'd be—" she took a deep breath "—conspicuous." She nearly sighed with relief. She'd gotten the word out—stiffly, it was true, but she'd said it.

"We know how to stay inconspicuous," he said between clenched teeth. "It's part of our job." He glanced at his watch. "I'm talking to Tammy about this. I want this cleared up now." He looked her up and down. "And I'll be back for *you* later."

Hoisting the heavy camera more securely on his shoulder, he wheeled and strode down the aisle toward the door. Laurie watched him go, her hands clasped nervously at her waist, her fingers twined together.

What did he mean, he'd be back for her? She didn't know if the words were a promise or a threat, and they filled her with apprehension.

Worse, she feared he was going to upset Mrs. Hoffmann. Would he insist Laurie take the arbors down?

She could envision everyone suddenly vexed and distressed: the formidable Mrs. Hoffmann, the nice Mrs. Bauer and poor Diane, who was good with people but who disliked confrontations. Tammy Farentino, the wedding adviser, would be caught in the center of the storm, as was Laurie herself.

Laurie bit her lip harder. She couldn't take the arbors down now. The first guests were already being escorted down the aisle.

She retreated to a back corner, faced the altar and squeezed her eyes shut. She kept her hands clasped tightly together.

Please, she prayed, *don't let there be trouble over this—please. Please, please, please, please. Just let Diane have a beautiful, orderly, perfect wedding.*

Then she added another request, slightly less selfless: *And please keep that man away from me. He makes me so nervous I can't talk.*

She opened her eyes. The loveliness of the flowers soothed her slightly. But more than anything, she wished she was back in the safety of her florist's shop. In the greenhouse, looking at the new bud on the sorcerer's flower. That, she told herself, was where she would be happiest.

Too restless to sit, she sighed and went out to the vestibule to recheck the floral arrangements by the guest book. Everything was fine, every bud, flower and ribbon in place.

She wondered, uneasily, what was taking place in the conflict over the camera arrangements. She had done flowers for Mrs. Hoffmann before and knew she was a stubborn and demanding woman. But even Mrs. Hoffmann might meet her match in the Remington man. Laurie winced when she imagined the confrontation.

She watched the growing crowd of arrivals and smiled as a harried-looking man herded three small, lively boys into church. She recognized him—Sophia Petrovelli's husband. She and Sophia had worked together on a children's project for the Crafts Alliance. But where was Sophia?

"Sophia's fine," she heard him tell someone. "She's happy she's finally got a girl."

So, Laurie thought with a smile, after three boys Sophia finally had a daughter. She must congratulate Mr. Petrovelli after the ceremony and send her best wishes to his wife.

One of the groomsmen, the young one with the long blond hair, asked her to adjust his boutonniere. She had felt him watching her before, but for some reason, younger men seldom made her nervous. She felt comfortable with this one; he had a twinkle in his blue eyes that was both kindly and mischievous.

"I'm Vinnie," he said. "And you're Laurie. You know my sister Sophia."

"I do indeed. And I just heard she had a little girl."

"Just this week. And I heard you had words with the cameraman," Vinnie said as she fiddled with the rosebud in his lapel. "That he mistook you for Tammy Farentino."

Her smile suddenly faded. "Nothing serious," she managed to say.

"Watch out for him," Vinnie warned with a grin. "Women aren't safe around him. I'd stay out of his way, if I were you."

She didn't reply to his statement. She merely brushed a speck of lint from his coat and said in a sisterly tone, "Aren't you supposed to be an usher, too? Go ush."

Suddenly she saw Tammy Farentino making her way through the crowd. Tammy's honey-blond hair was pulled back in a chignon, giving her appearance a coolness that belied her quick, warm manner and husky voice.

A pretty woman, almost stunning, Tammy was at least three inches shorter than Laurie and more voluptuous. Like Laurie, she wore a gray suit, but hers was formfitting and frilled rather than tailored. She had flashing brown eyes and a wide smile. Laurie's eyes were gray and often dreamy, her smile slow and shy.

How could he have mistaken me for her? Laurie wondered, thinking of Jeff Remington's lips warmly tickling the back of her neck. This was the type of woman he belonged with—glamorous and sure of herself.

Tammy rolled her dark eyes significantly and drew Laurie aside. "Listen, there was a little problem about the arbors. The photographer was giving me the very devil over them, and then that tall, dark videographer—Jeff—came storming up—"

Laurie gritted her teeth.

"Anyway, I took Jeff to talk to Mrs. Hoffmann, because he's the one with all the charm—"

Laurie looked at her in surprise. Charming was not how she would describe the man. Presumptuous, yes; mercurial of temper, yes; but she hardly thought him charming.

Tammy smiled. "Believe me. I met him earlier this morning. He can charm birds out of trees when he wants to." She rubbed the back of her neck meditatively, as if remembering Jeff's touch. Then she tugged her ear lightly, as if he had recently whispered in it, tickling her.

What's the man do? Laurie wondered irritably. *Go around kissing every female neck west of the Mississippi? Is that how he dealt with Gertrude Hoffmann? By nibbling on her nape and murmuring in her ear?*

"Anyway—" Tammy's smile of satisfaction was still in place "—he convinced her that cameramen, like creatures of the wild, have to roam free. She relented. Then *he* wanted the arbors taken down because he thought they set a bad precedent, so I had to turn on *my* charm until he relented. Anyway, it's settled. The arbors stay where they are, the cameramen roam where they will, and all we have to do is get these two people married. What could be simpler? And everyone—*everyone* is saying they've never seen lovelier flowers. Great job, just truly superior. Now—I want to check Diane's veil."

She gave Laurie's arm an encouraging squeeze, then swept off, leaving the scent of her expensive perfume behind her. Laurie looked after her and wondered why it rankled, ever so slightly, that Tammy and the Remington man found each other so charming.

Then Vinnie appeared at her side again, his youthful blond energy not quite matching his sedately formal clothes. "What are you thinking about so hard?'' he asked. ''This is a wedding. You're supposed to look happy.''

He offered her his arm. ''I'll take you in. Come on.''

She took his elbow gratefully and let him escort her inside.

''Really, what were you thinking about?'' Vinnie teased as he walked her down the aisle. ''About me, maybe?''

He was flirting with her, but she didn't mind. ''I was thinking about a plant,'' she said with her shy smile. ''I've got a rare one. This morning I saw a bud on it. I think it's going to bloom.''

''Ah, come on,'' Vinnie said, smiling back. ''Nobody thinks that hard about a plant. If it wasn't me, who was it?''

She looked him in the eye, for she was almost as tall as he. ''It was a plant,'' she said firmly, and started to take her seat.

But then out of the corner of her eye she saw a tall figure at the front of the church. Jeff stood at the base of the altar stairs, near the wall.

Across the broad expanse of the church, his eyes met hers. She felt a jolt of emotion she neither wanted nor understood.

Slowly, almost imperceptibly, he smiled at her. The back of her neck tingled. She looked away.

Think about the flowers, she told herself severely. *Think about the greenhouse. Think about the plant. That it's budding, at last.*

But the back of her neck kept tingling all through the ceremony, as if tickled by a flower petal or by a lingering, phantom kiss.

LATER, WHEN LAURIE WENT through the receiving line at the Bauer estate, Diane hugged her.

''The flowers are all beautiful,'' she said in Laurie's ear, holding her close. ''You're a genius.''

Laurie smiled. ''You're what's most beautiful today.''

She drew back and looked at Diane. Her gown was satin and lace, beaded with pearls, and delicate floral sprays held her veil in place.

''I've got rice in my hair,'' Diane said with a rueful smile. ''Nick's even got it in his pockets.''

Laurie laughed and moved on, shaking hands. She and her assistant had stayed up until almost midnight tying ribbons and tiny dried sprays of flowers on the net bags holding the rice. It was one of the thousand tasks she'd dealt with.

Now she sighed with relief that her concern with those details was over. Her assistant, Mavis Jefferson, had put the flowers in place at the reception, then vanished, like a good fairy whose work is done.

She made her way out of the marquee and toward the crowd of guests gathering around the swimming pool. A waiter carrying a silver tray of drinks held it toward her, and she took a glass of champagne.

She nodded greetings to a guest here and there. She knew only a few of the people, mostly long-ago acquaintances from high school. Diane's aunt came up to say that the flowers were the most beautiful she'd ever seen. So did Nick's ebullient Uncle Vito, who made her laugh in spite of her innate shyness among so many strangers.

"Such beautiful flowers," he raved. "Here—I buy you another drink to congratulate you."

He liberated another glass of champagne from a passing waiter, who took her nearly empty glass. "*Bellissimo!* The flowers are *bellissimo!*" Vito said, and kissed her gallantly on the hand. Then he saw someone he knew and bustled away.

"You're quite the hit." A deep voice behind her made her go cold to the bone. She turned, trying to maintain control of herself. She looked up.

There he stood, the intimidating height, the black eyebrows, the one-cornered smile.

She took a deep breath and willed her voice to behave. "I didn't—expect you here."

He nodded. "I didn't expect you. A friend of the bride?"

She too nodded, only more stiffly. He was not the sort of man she was used to, and he filled her with disturbing sensations. "And you?"

"Friend of the groom. From the good old days in second grade. When Sister Mary Columba kicked us both out of class for throwing spitballs." He smiled more intimately at her, but she felt too shy to smile back. He still carried the camera and gave it a fond pat, as if it were a faithful dog. "The video-tape's my wedding gift. The flowers, I take it, aren't yours. That'd be a bit extravagant."

Laurie's heart seemed lodged in her throat, trying to choke off her words.

"You and Diane close friends?" He had a low voice, a velvety baritone. "Acquaintances? What?"

She wished her pulses wouldn't leap so because he was there. She enunciated as carefully as possible. "We went to high school together . . . for two years."

The corner of his mouth curled a fraction of an inch more. "Ah. A fancy school, no doubt. Not like us lesser mortals."

She took another deep breath. Now he was assuming she was rich, simply because she knew Diane. In truth, her family was an old and respected one in St. Louis, but when it came to money, most of them were comfortable, nothing more.

"Well?" he prodded.

"It was just a school," she said, her voice clipped.

Her answer made something, perhaps dislike, flicker across his face. But his smile stayed in place. "You still act as if you don't want to talk to me. Did I really make you that mad?"

Laurie's heart hammered harder. She turned her gaze away and stared at the Bauers' rose garden, brilliant in the June sunlight.

"Look," he said, "I don't want you angry. For one thing, I respect your work too much. The flowers were . . . something. You're a sensation. Everybody's talking about two things—how beautiful the bride is and the job you did with the flowers."

She looked at him dubiously, unable to tell if his smile was sincere or merely part of the charm that Tammy Farentino had found so taking. She wondered why he was bothering to be charming to her.

"I mean it," he said. "I startled you when you had a lot on your mind. I was short-tempered because I had a lot on my own mind. When I'm shooting a wedding, I get one chance. If I lose it, it's gone forever. Not only for me, but for the bride and groom and everybody else. It's vanished like a snow-flake. So I get . . . temperamental."

She felt herself softening. She supposed they both had been on edge; the wedding was more job than social occasion for both of them. And both felt especially pressed to do good work because it was done for friends.

She found she was staring up with perhaps too much inter-est into his black eyes. Self-consciously she lowered her gaze and took a sip of champagne.

"And," he said, a new note coming into his voice, "if I made a mistake and kissed your neck, maybe it was because I wanted to make a mistake. Because it's such a lovely neck. And it felt so nice to kiss."

He paused. "So," he murmured, "if you'd tell me I'm for-given . . . and that we could be friends . . ."

Laurie raised her eyes to his again. She swallowed hard.

Then, suddenly, the most beautiful of the bridesmaids ap-peared at Jeff's side and took his elbow. Laurie remembered her well from high school—Suzanne Carrington had been a girl of enormous prettiness and almost overwhelming vivacity. Her pastel gown and dramatic, wide-brimmed hat set off her lav-shly coiffed auburn hair.

"I thought the reception line would never end." Suzanne laughed up at Jeff. "And you promised to make a long, long video tape of me in this dress so I can send it to my grand-mother in Cincinnati. Let's get a glass of champagne and then do it. Oh, hello, Laurie. You did a wonderful job on the flowers. Didn't she, Jeff? Don't you think she did a wonder-ful job?"

Jeff looked down at Suzanne's smiling face, then at Lau-rie's carefully blank one. "I was just telling her—"

"Oh, Jeff," Suzanne said, tugging on his elbow again, "there's the waiter. Please, I'm dying for a drink. And take me to the hors d'oeuvres table, please? I didn't have a bite for breakfast *or* lunch."

He smiled and absently patted the hand gripping his el-bow. He looked at Laurie again. "I'll talk to you later."

Laurie nodded with a mechanical smile. Suzanne, in a flutter of pale satin, swept him away. She was still holding one of the bouquets Laurie had risen at dawn to assemble.

Then Vinnie appeared at Laurie's side. "That guy," he said, looking after Jeff and Suzanne. "He never quits. I think I'll lock up my sisters."

Laurie pulled her distracted thoughts back to order and gave Vinnie a wry look. "You're certainly the pr-protective type," she said with a smile.

Vinnie's own smile faded. His blue eyes stared after Jeff, growing solemn. He turned to face Laurie. "I mean it," he said. "My brother's known him for years. He's a good enough guy with the guys, but . . ."

Laurie stared at him expectantly.

"But no woman should trust him," Vinnie finished, shaking his head.

He sounded so serious that Laurie didn't know what to say. Was there some scandal about Jeff Remington? Some secret too terrible to discuss in polite company?

Vinnie nodded, as if her worst suspicions weren't bad enough. "If you won't believe me, listen to somebody else." He stood on tiptoe, looking over the crowd. "Yo . . . Aldo!" he called. "Come here. Talk to the flower lady."

Laurie watched in puzzlement as Sophia's husband made his way toward them. He was a solid-looking brown-haired man of medium height, and she had met him once, briefly, at a Crafts Alliance picnic.

"This is Sophia's husband, Aldo Petrovelli. He's a brand-new father again. A family man. You'd believe such a good churchgoing family man, wouldn't you?"

Laurie nodded, feeling slightly bewildered.

"Aldo, my man," Vinnie said, gripping his brother-in-law by the shoulder. "This lady's name is Laurie. She did the flowers."

"I think we've met before. The flowers are lovely," Aldo said. He had a kindly, serious face.

"I heard the new baby's here," Laurie said, smiling. "A little girl this time."

Aldo nodded. "And everything's fine, thank God." He and Laurie shook hands.

Vinnie kept his hand on his brother-in-law's shoulder. "So listen. Jeff Remington's making up to this woman. Tell her not to trust him."

Aldo's face suddenly became guarded. He looked at Laurie, then at his young brother-in-law. "Vinnie, I'd just as soon keep out of this, okay?"

"Look into this woman's face, look into her *eyes*," Vinnie said, "then tell me you're going to keep out of it."

"Vinnie . . ." Aldo shook his head. But then he turned and looked into Laurie's eyes. He seemed to look a long time, and Laurie, perplexed, didn't know what he saw. *What's going on here? What's wrong with the Remington man?* she asked herself.

Complex emotions seemed to pass over Aldo's face, then they resolved into an expression of reluctance mingled with resignation. At last he nodded unhappily. "All I'll say is I'd be cautious about Remington," he said at last. "Maybe just a bit . . . cautious."

Laurie's heart took a dismal plunge. There must be some shadow of disgrace or dishonor tainting Jeff Remington, some danger she didn't understand.

Aldo dug into the breast pocket of his coat. "All right," he said, as if admitting to some unhappy truth. "I was at the hospital this morning. Sophia said to tell you hello . . . and she asked me to give you this."

He handed her a folded piece of notepaper. Perplexed, Laurie opened it. The message was brief: "Laurie— Watch out for the tall man with the video camera. Be *careful*. Love, Sophia."

"There," Vinnie said triumphantly, reading over her shoulder. "If you can't trust a new mother, what's the world coming to?"

"I don't know," Laurie said, deeply apprehensive. "What's all this about?"

But Vinnie, who looked well satisfied with himself, would tell her no more. And Aldo, who looked as unhappy as a man could look, refused to say another word.

Chapter Two

"I WISH YOU HADN'T dragged me into it," Aldo told Vinnie. "I like Jeff. I don't feel right about this. It's not honorable."

They stood together by the hors d'oeuvres table, where Vinnie was constructing a complicated stack of cocktail rye bread, cream cheese, pâté and olives.

"I told you," Vinnie said, "there's more than one kind of right. Life gets complicated."

Aldo shrugged. "I'm surprised Jeff got mixed up in something like this."

Vinnie shook his head. "Hey, it was a party. Everybody was getting very merry."

"That I understand. What I don't understand is why we had to get involved."

Vinnie took a bite of his sandwich. "Because Laurie's my sister's *friend*. She's your wife's *friend*."

"They're not lifelong friends," Aldo said, "they just know each other a little."

"Well, Sophia likes her. You were with Sophia when she phoned the house this morning. She hit the ceiling."

"I know, I know. You should have never told her." At least, Aldo consoled himself, Vinnie had had brains enough not to tell the rest of the family what was going on. They would have been as appalled as Sophia.

Vinnie gave a shrug of innocence. "At that point I still thought it was funny. She's in the hospital. I figured she could use a laugh."

"About twenty people in the house," Aldo said, shaking his head, "and you have to be the one to answer the phone. You— Motor Mouth."

"Well," Vinnie said righteously, "Sophia said somebody should stop it. Maybe she's right."

"She sent a note." Aldo looked miserable. "I delivered it. I wish I hadn't done that much." He gave Vinnie a suspicious glance. "This morning, after you blabbed, you kept telling Sophia to calm down, it was no big crisis. You said it was men's business. When did you all of a sudden decide to play hero?"

"When I met her," Vinnie answered, adjusting the layers of his sandwich. "Sophia says this Laurie's a very sensitive person. She's shy. Well, she comes across all cool and proper, but there's—I don't know—something when you look in her face. This girl shouldn't be part of anybody's joke. This girl is *real*. Her feelings are real."

"Wait a minute," Aldo said, eyeing his brother-in-law with fresh understanding. "You're too gallant all of a sudden. It's your older-woman fixation. I know it. It's struck. Have you fallen in love again?"

"A little bit," Vinnie said, for he fell in love almost hourly. "She's pretty and I like the way she talks. It's cute. I mean, there are a lot of beautiful women here, but she's...different." He demolished the rest of his sandwich with one bite.

Aldo looked away, wishing heaven had endowed Vinnie with greater restraint and fewer hormones. But the kid was right. There was something vulnerable deep in the woman's eyes.

When Vinnie had blurted out what he knew to Sophia over the phone, Sophia had read him the riot act. Then she'd hung up and read it to Aldo. Angrily, she had told them both about Laurie's stammering. Sophia said hotly that Laurie's speech made her sometimes seem distant, almost lofty, but that impression was wrong.

Furthermore, Laurie had confided about her problem only out of kindness, because Sophia had been concerned about her eldest son's stuttering. She certainly didn't want to see Laurie caught up and possibly hurt by a thoughtless joke.

Aldo hadn't wanted to get involved. He promised to take her note. He did not promise to deliver it.

Still, Sophia was his wife, the mother of his children. She was tired and emotional and he didn't want to upset her. And, like Vinnie, once he saw Laurie, he had an uncomfortable certainty that Sophia was right. Laurie was not the sort of woman whose emotions should be toyed with.

Aldo swore to himself, his hands jammed deeply in his pockets. Jeff Remington was a nice guy—who should have known better than to have gotten into this.

JEFF REMINGTON WISHED like hell he'd never gotten into this. It had been a bad idea when it hatched, and it seemed worse now. But it was too late to back out. His friend Gary Castiglione had a classic car engine, a 1968 Mustang in almost perfect shape, riding on this bet. As any man could tell you, *that* was a serious gambling stake.

It had started out the night before the wedding, at the party held at the Granatelli house. Drinks flowed, jokes were cracked, and then, somehow, the bet got made.

It began with one of the groomsmen, Steve Bostwick, giving Jeff a hard time about still being single. Jeff had laughed it off, saying there were too many good-looking women in the world to settle down. Steve, in the time-honored insulting manner of old college friends, had scoffed about Jeff's romantic prowess.

Gary, another groomsman, who'd been at St. Louis U. with both of them, jumped into the fray. Gary said Jeff could get a date with any woman at the wedding tomorrow.

Steve scoffed with greater derision still.

Jeff took another drink of wine and said that was right, he could. Name the woman.

But Gary Castiglione, who'd sampled a lot more of the wine than Jeff, said, "Listen, I have faith in my man here. He could get a date with any *three* women there tomorrow." Not only that, Gary said emphatically, he'd have each one in a clinch by the end of the date.

Jeff, who thought the whole thing was still a joke, said sure. No problem. Any three women.

And then all of a sudden, the betting started, and before Jeff knew what was happening, Gary had bet Steve his car engine. Both Gary and Steve were classic-car freaks, and Gary loved that engine the way some men loved a great work of art. It had taken him two years to find the thing, had cost him a small fortune. And, like a damned fool, he'd bet it.

Steve had grinned and said fine, he'd pick the women.

Now Jeff stood alone at the edge of the patio, twirling the stem of a wineglass between his fingers. He'd locked his camera in the trunk of his car after he'd taped Nick and Diane's first dance as man and wife. He wanted to enjoy a minute of solitude, have a moment to think.

Suzanne, the bridesmaid, had been surprisingly easy. He was taking her on a riverboat dinner cruise tomorrow night. He was not looking forward to it. She was beautiful, but she was also a woman of such excessive energy and nonstop conversation that she set his nerves on edge.

He thanked the fates she was pretty enough that plenty of other men kept asking her to dance. Right now she was whirling to the music in the arms of Vinnie Granatelli. Vinnie seemed seriously taken with half the women there. Let him have Suzanne, Jeff thought. They were about the right level of maturity for each other.

Tammy Farentino might have been more difficult, but by good fortune, Gary Castiglione knew a thing or two about her. He had taken Jeff aside and said she was picky about men, but that there were two things she couldn't resist: a bold approach and guys who whispered to her in Italian, the language of *amore*.

So every time he saw Tammy today, he'd nuzzled her neck and whispered sweet Italian nothings in her ear. And the night after tomorrow he was taking her to the Westport Playhouse. He wasn't looking forward to that, either. Beneath all that warm femininity, he sensed a certain ruthlessness and an eagerness to snag a man.

No, it was Miss Laurentia Chase-Spenser who was giving him trouble. He found it odd that he'd had no trouble getting a date with the gorgeous one, Suzanne, or the sexy one, Tammy. It was the one who was merely pretty who was turning out to be tough.

He strongly suspected that Steve had put her on the list precisely because she was so impossibly lofty. She had that

slow, deliberate way of talking, enunciating every word just
so, as if she were conducting an elocution lesson, not a conversation. She sounded as if she were imitating Katharine
Hepburn at her most patrician. He didn't like it.

True, she was pretty, and he had to admit the longer he
looked at her, the prettier she seemed. There was something
deep in her gray eyes that was dreamy, almost shy, and
strangely at odds with her haughtiness.

And she had talent, that was certain. He'd never seen flowers
as sumptuous before. She was practically a magician with
them.

He saw her again now, looking sedate in her tailored gray
suit. She was dancing with Nick's Uncle Salvatore and smiling at him. Funny, he mused, her smile was shy, too. She
didn't act snobbish in the least with Salvatore.

Well, Jeff thought, handing his wineglass to a passing waiter,
Salvatore was a member of Diane's family now. To relatives
of the Bauers she might condescend to be polite. She probably saw Jeff as a mere lackey and a rude one at that.

He had to admit he'd gotten off to a bad start with her. His
first effort at reconciliation had been sabotaged by Suzanne.
Since then, Her Majesty Laurentia had pointedly ignored him.
It was time to launch a second assault.

He sighed harshly, moved across the patio and tapped on
Salvatore's broad shoulder, cutting in. Ah, the sacrifices a man
makes for his friends.

But she was tall and fitted neatly into his arms, not like
Tammy, who was too short, or Suzanne, who was too wriggly.
And she smelled, he noted, like real flowers, fresh and cleanly
washed with rain.

"So," he said, smiling down at her, "we meet again."

She made no reply. She looked away from him. Her profile
was perfect, her hair in that complicated, elegant braid was
perfect, and he had a sudden irrational urge to take her down
a peg. He'd like to get her alone, loosen that smooth honey-
brown hair so it spilled down around her shoulders, and hold
her tightly just to see if her clothes might actually crumple like
those of an ordinary woman.

Instead he smiled. "Am I forgiven?"

She looked up at him, gray eyes cool as ice. She had an extremely lovely mouth, and the corners twitched almost as if she were nervous. Maybe they twitched in contempt for him; he couldn't tell.

"There's nothing . . . to forgive," she said in that tone that was so maddeningly deliberate.

"Then why do you act as if you don't even want to talk to me?" he asked. The music slowed. He pulled her a fraction of an inch closer, bent his face slightly nearer to hers.

She tried to draw farther away, but he didn't allow it. "There's nothing . . . to talk about," she said, and looked away from him again, too conscious of the strong body so close to hers.

Inwardly he swore, but he kept smiling. "Do I call you Miss Chase-Spenser? Or Laurentia?"

She sighed in apparent exasperation. "Laurie" was all she said. She acted as if it pained her to say that much.

He resisted gritting his teeth. He couldn't remember ever meeting a woman so hoity-toity. What did he have to do to get her to warm up? Was she capable of warmth? And what was the look forming deep within those cloud-gray eyes?

He racked his mind, trying to think of a way to appeal to her. In desperation he opted for a lie, even though he was normally an honest man.

"I told you how good you are with flowers." His voice was sincere so far, because at least that part was true. "I've got a shoot next week for the tourism bureau. I'm supposed to do five minutes on the Botanical Gardens. I don't know anything about flowers. If you'd go with me to tell me what's what, I'd be glad to buy you dinner."

In truth, he did have a shoot for the tourism bureau, and he was supposed to show the Botanical Gardens. But only for about thirty seconds, and he didn't need advice in the least. All he had to do was film the flowers, not know their names, pedigrees and astrological signs.

She raised her chin a little higher, looking more regal than before. "I'm certain . . . there are qualified experts there."

"No, listen," he said. *God will punish me for this*, he thought darkly, *even if it is a 1968 Mustang engine at stake*. "I've got to shoot footage of the Jewel Box, too. I'd really appreciate somebody who could go both places, tell me what's ordinary and what's unique."

Her face softened slightly. She probably loved the Jewel Box, a conservatory full of dazzling flowers and echoing with the soft chimes of its own carillon. That dreamy look he found so peculiarly disturbing came into her eyes again. He found that he was holding her closer.

"Look," he said, feeling worse every moment, "I should do Tower Grove Park, too, but what do I know about landscaping? It's some special kind of garden, right?"

She paused a long moment before she answered. "It was—patterned after an English walking garden. Victorian."

She pursed her lips so primly before she said "patterned" that he felt the conflicting desires to shake her and to kiss her, to see if he could make that perfectly controlled mouth soften in passion. She was impossible, the sort of cool, proper woman who drove men to hot, improper thoughts.

"That's what I mean," he went on, resisting the urge to hold her more tightly still. "I don't even know that much. I couldn't tell a tulip from a turnip. You could help me—and help the tourism bureau."

She opened her mouth as if she were going to make a long and careful speech. Then she raised those long-lashed gray eyes to his. All she said was one word: "No."

For a moment he could have sworn she saw into the very depths of his deceptive soul. It shook him more than he liked to admit. But the cold finality of the way she'd spoken annoyed him.

He tried to keep the irritation out of his face and his tone. "Just no? That's all you're going to say? You're not even going to bother to make up a good excuse?"

She had stopped dancing and so had he. He still held her in his arms, but she felt rigid as a statue. She gave him one of those looks that made his soul squirm and his body want to twitch. Her lips parted as if she had a lot to say, but once again, all she said was "No."

She stepped away from him, but he kept hold of her hand, and he stared down into her eyes. "And if I won't take no for an answer?"

She didn't so much as smile. She withdrew her hand from his and, without a word, walked away, never looking back.

He gazed after her, anger warring with determination. No wonder Steve had picked this one. She was colder than a midwestern winter.

Yet she was also desirable in a way that made his blood dance in frustration. Although she was no great beauty, she had that Princess Grace sort of perfection that could bring out the baying beast in a man. And in spite of her condescension, she had a mysterious air of vulnerability that he couldn't understand.

He stared after her. She was shaking hands, saying her goodbyes, getting ready to take her leave. He walked in the other direction, across the lawn, until he was among the willow trees that surrounded the gazebo.

Steve Bostwick, the author of Jeff's sorrows, followed him and came smirking to his side. Jeff looked away in disgust.

"She walked away from you," Steve said. Smugness vibrated in his voice. "You may have got the other two, but you didn't melt the ice queen."

Jeff stuck his hands in his pockets. He stared up at the silvery gray of the leaves against the sky. "Hey. I didn't say I'd get it all done in one day. There are logistics to these things."

"Did I tell you I've got a line on a beautiful '68 Mustang convertible body?" Steve said, gloating. "All it needs is an engine, and then, friend, I have a car worth dying for."

"I heard," Jeff said grimly. He'd heard it again and again last night. And if Steve won the engine from Gary Castiglione, Gary would be the one dying. He'd probably jump off the Eads Bridge in grief.

"I went to high school two years with Princess Laurie," Steve said with a knowing smile. "What we're talking here is *untouchable*. She'd hardly even talk to a guy. Just a few girlfriends, like Diane. She's still that way. You'll never get to her. You don't stand a chance."

Jeff set his jaw. "I'll get her yet," he said.

LAURIE STOOD in the greenhouse, staring at the sorcerer's flower. It was an unprepossessing plant, almost ugly, and well over five feet tall. Dusty green, its thick stem bore a sparse outcropping of swordlike leaves. Near its top jutted a new growth, a complicated little gray-green button.

The bud.

She wanted to touch it, to assure herself it was real, but she did not. She didn't want to disturb it in the slightest.

If the sorcerer's flower bloomed, it would make horticultural history in St. Louis. More than that, she would see one of the world's rarest and most beautiful blossoms, a cascade of scarlet and gold. The flower was unique, the stuff from which legends were made.

Was it a good omen for Nick and Diane, she wondered, that it had budded on the day of their wedding? No, she decided, she didn't believe in omens.

She glanced at her watch and gave a start of surprise. She had been in the greenhouse nearly an hour, just gazing at the plant. It was time to get home; she had indulged herself enough.

Still, she left the greenhouse with reluctance. She was half-afraid that if she took her eyes off the bud it would disappear. Besides, the humid scents, the warmth, the stirrings of life in the greenhouse always soothed her. After the jangling that Jeff Remington had given her nerves, she needed soothing. Why had Vinnie and Aldo—and Sophia—warned her about him? And why did he have to be a man she found so disturbing to both mind and body?

On top of that, Laurie had to cope with a houseguest, her cousin Shirley. Shirley, a music teacher from Paducah, was stopping for a few days on her way home to see her parents in St. Joseph. She was a take-charge woman, talkative and opinionated, not the easiest of visitors.

When Laurie arrived at her little house in the suburbs, Shirley was curled barefoot on the couch, wearing jeans and a sweatshirt and an orange towel around her freshly washed hair. She was a large woman of about thirty. She was painting her fingernails pink with a bottle of Laurie's polish.

"Hi," Shirley said. "It's about time you got home. I got so hungry I ate the pizza that was in the freezer. How was the wedding? Everything go all right?"

"Almost everything," Laurie said, undoing the top button of her suit jacket. She slipped off her shoes and padded into the kitchenette. She opened the refrigerator and poured herself a glass of orange juice.

"There was a call for you," Shirley said, lacquering a nail. "Somebody named Jeff. He sounded . . . interesting. He said he'd call back. Gee, I'm still hungry. Is there a Chinese restaurant or something around here that delivers?"

Laurie stared at Shirley, wide-eyed. She set the juice glass on the counter. "Jeff?"

"What's wrong with you?" Shirley asked, screwing the cap on the polish bottle.

"N-n-nothing," Laurie stammered, then cursed herself. How could Jeff Remington, even absent, confuse and disturb her? What did he want from her?

"Laurie?" Shirley asked, her voice stern. "You're stuttering. Something's upset you. What?"

Laurie didn't want to talk about it, but she knew Shirley would keep after her until she got an answer. "I met a m-man at the wedding." She tried to seem calm. "He b-bothered me. He got me . . . very upset. And people told me to . . . be careful of him. He wouldn't let me alone. That's all. I'm fine."

She sat down disconsolately at the bar that divided the kitchenette from the dining room.

Shirley stared at her. "Wow," she said at last. "That's the worst I've heard you in *years.*"

Laurie leaned her elbows on the counter and rubbed her forehead. She was in no mood for Shirley's bluntness. "It's been a long day."

Shirley rose from the sofa and crossed the room to stand behind Laurie. She reached down and started energetically massaging Laurie's shoulders. "Laurie, your muscles are hard as rocks. This guy really got you tensed up. Well, don't worry. If he calls again, *I'll* handle him."

"Ouf," said Laurie. She tried to change the subject. "Do you know how many roses Mavis and I arranged for this wedding?"

Shirley was not thrown off the track that easily. "How could I know that? So how did this man bother you? And who is he?" She energetically kneaded the tense muscles at the base of Laurie's neck.

Laurie sighed and closed her eyes. She supposed she might as well talk about it and get it out of her system. There was that to be said for Shirley: she was always eager to listen to someone's troubles. She loved being a confidante.

"First, he came up behind me and kissed me on the neck. Then at the reception, he just sort of b-bothered me. He got me so flustered I could hardly get a word out. That hasn't happened to me in years. In years—then *he* comes along."

"It's your own fault," Shirley said firmly. "You never relax. You were up late last night. You were up at dawn this morning. He caught you at a bad time. So who was he? A guest or what?"

"His name is Jeff Remington. He's a cameraman."

Shirley's hands suddenly went still on Laurie's shoulders. There was an ominous beat of silence.

"What?" she said, a strange note in her voice.

Laurie opened her eyes. Shirley was normally the most self-confident of people, but Laurie could sense a sudden wavering, a momentary loss of inner balance. "Remington. He had a video camera," Laurie said.

"Oh, no," Shirley groaned. She sat down heavily on the stool next to Laurie's. Her broad face was etched with distaste. "A tall—really tall—guy? Good-looking? Dark? Hair kind of curly?"

Laurie regarded her cousin with curiosity mixed with foreboding. "You know him?"

"I used to," Shirley said, shaking her head. "What did you say he's doing now?"

"He had a video camera. He taped the wedding."

Shirley nodded glumly. "That figures. I heard he went to film school in California after college. So is he back in town for good or what?"

"I have no idea," Laurie said. Her cousin's face was grim, her lips pressed together. "How do you know him?"

"I know him because he's a *rat*," Shirley said vehemently. Laurie stared at her in surprise. Shirley was bluff, bossy and dogmatic, but she seldom indulged in a show of temper.

"A rat?"

"As in Latin, *Rattus rattus*," Shirley said between her teeth, "as in English, rodent. He broke Mary Ellen Pfieffer's heart, the ratty rodent rat."

"Who's Mary Ellen Pfieffer?" Laurie asked, truly confused. Was this the scandal she'd suspected?

"Mary Ellen Pfieffer was one of the most promising music students in the history of St. Louis U.," Shirley said bitterly. "She was my 'little sister'—you know how they assign an older student to watch out for a new one? Well, she was mine. Until Jeff Remington destroyed her entire *life*."

"How'd he destroy her life?" Laurie asked, horrified. "What did he do?"

"Oh," Shirley said with an angry wave of the hand, "he did what he did with all the girls. He took her out, led her on, and then he dropped her. Only Mary Ellen was this very sweet, very innocent, very sensitive girl, and she really loved him with all her heart. She was so distraught, she flunked out of school. Flunked every single subject."

"How terrible," Laurie said.

"It was the worst semester of my *life*," Shirley said, shaking her head. "All Mary Ellen did was cry, cry, cry. She'd lie on her bed and cry, or sit at her desk and cry, or come down to my room and cry. And he got so he wouldn't talk to her at all. So then she'd send me to talk to him, and finally he wouldn't talk to me, either. What did he care?"

Laurie shook her head in sympathy.

"And then," said Shirley, her lip curling, "she flunked and went home, and *that* led to trouble with her parents, and then she went to Chicago and—because she was on the rebound from Jeff—she moved in with this really dreadful boy with tattoos and an earring and a motorcycle. She just didn't care what happened to her any more. She thought without Jeff Remington she was nothing. I mean, with him gone, she considered herself a dead person."

"Oh, no," Laurie said again. "How awful."

Shirley shook her own head angrily. The towel wrapped around her head made her look like some angry potentate in a huge turban. "Once when she had me call him up, he said to me, and this is an actual quote, 'Look, I'd like to talk to you, but I have a basketball game.' A basketball game! This woman's life has fallen completely apart because of him, and he can't talk because he has a *basketball* game."

"How insensitive."

"Exactly," Shirley said, acid in her voice.

They sat in silence for a few moments. Laurie was saddened by Shirley's story but perplexed, too. She had expected something a bit more dramatic on Jeff's part than indifference. Or was there more to the story, something Shirley didn't want to tell her? Something that had remained unspoken because it was, truly, unspeakable?

The phone rang. Laurie and Shirley stared at each other. Shirley's eyes narrowed.

"You'll have to answer it," she said. "If I'd known it was him before, I'd have told him off and hung up on him."

Laurie rose and went to the phone, her heart thudding. She picked up the receiver. She took a deep breath and willed her voice to behave. "Hello?"

"Hello, Laurie? This is Jeff." His voice was low, intense and intimate. "I don't feel right about what happened between us. I think I created the wrong impression. I'd like a chance to change your mind about me. I have tickets for the jazz concert at the Conservatory, and if you'd give me a chance—"

Laurie squared her shoulders angrily, Shirley's story still fresh in her mind. What did this man *want* from her?

"I'd appreciate it," she said, each word deliberate and carefully formed, "if you wouldn't call here anymore."

"But—" he said.

She hung up the phone.

Once more her eyes met Shirley's.

"Smartest thing in the world you could have done," Shirley said, nodding in satisfaction. She narrowed her eyes again. "And why's he chasing you? He was always one to let women chase *him*. I don't like the sound of this."

Laurie shook her head almost absently. She had no idea why Jeff Remington had pursued her. But he had been pursuing other women today with the same determination. What's more, he'd had no trouble catching them. Tammy Farentino, looking at him over her champagne, had almost purred like a cat as she'd basked in the warmth of his attention. When Suzanne danced with him, she'd snuggled as closely as she could and smiled up brilliantly at everything he said.

With a pang, Laurie remembered what it was like to be held in his arms, her body fitting against his muscled height. She remembered everything about him far too clearly—his tallness, his taunting smile, his dark good looks and searching black eyes.

She tried to shake the thoughts away. She had built a life that was safe, sensible and orderly. She intended to keep it that way.

Chapter Three

HE CALLED HER AGAIN the next day. She hung up on him. Shirley said that was exactly the right thing to do and celebrated by eating a wedge of chocolate cake.

Late that afternoon Shirley repacked her suitcases, climbed into her minivan and set off for St. Joseph and her parents. Laurie sighed with relief, glad to have a bit of solitude at last.

Just as she reentered the house after waving goodbye, the phone rang again. She stiffened with apprehension.

"Hello?" she said hesitantly.

"Don't hang up. It's Jeff. Laurie, all I ask is a chance. You've really gotten the wrong impression—"

His voice sent quivers coursing through her, and once again she remembered his height, his intent dark eyes.

Her temples pounded and the words tried to stick in her throat. She forced them out. "I—told—you—not—to—call."

"Laurie, just go out with me for a cup of coffee. Just talk to me. That's all."

She didn't want to go out with him, she didn't want to talk to him. Too many people had warned her against him too often. He was attractive, devilishly attractive in fact, but something was distinctly odd in the way he pursued her, and it made her nervous.

"No," she said flatly. This time when she hung up, she unplugged the phone so she wouldn't have to deal with him again. Sighing, she went into her bedroom to get ready to go to her shop and greenhouse. Nothing really needed tending today, but she wanted to see the sorcerer's flower again, to assure herself that the bud was really there.

She changed from her jeans and blue cotton shirt into a pair of navy slacks and a short-sleeved white sweater. She brushed her hair and stared at herself critically in the mirror. She'd often been told she was pretty, but if she was, it wasn't a flamboyant prettiness like Suzanne Carrington's or a lush one like Tammy Farentino's.

People had said that her eyes were lovely, even mysterious. To her they were simply two gray eyes staring out, somewhat uneasily, at the world around them. She looked away from her reflection. She could see the uncertainty in her eyes today and understood all too well that Jeff Remington had put it there.

As a child, she'd been extremely self-conscious about her stutter. Her father had been transferred often, she found herself in one new school after another, and she dealt with her problem simply: she didn't speak if she could help it.

Her parents divorced when she was sixteen and her mother moved back to St. Louis. It was the tenth time in Laurie's life she had changed schools. Although she'd worked successfully with speech therapists, she was still often afraid to talk for fear of suddenly starting to stutter. Even if she didn't, she had to speak so carefully and precisely that other people frequently thought she was affected. She stayed quiet and made only a few friends, like Diane.

It was not until she went to college that she began to come into her own. She learned to accept that if she was to talk without stuttering, her speech would be so deliberate it sounded artificial, almost stagy. If people chose to judge her by that, it was their problem, she told herself.

Still, deep within, she understood it was her problem, as well. Now only people who knew her intimately knew about her shyness or her stutter, and she'd let few people grow that close to her.

She was happy, she tried to convince herself, with her work, her family, her few really good friends. Work had always come first for her. In school she had escaped into her studies, and once out of school she escaped into her career. There had been little time for men.

Men, Laurie thought, picking up her purse and heading for her van. The men in her life all fitted a certain stereotype. They were bland, civilized, polite, artistic and boring. Everything about them seemed medium—their height, their weight, their looks, their intelligence, their personalities.

Or, she thought, thinking of Vinnie and shaking her head, they were *young*. She supposed it was because she felt at ease with younger men, although she wasn't attracted to them.

Jeff Remington was another story. He wasn't bland, he wasn't civilized, he wasn't polite, and while he might be artistic, he certainly wasn't boring. Nothing about him seemed moderate or average. He'd struck her as out-and-out dangerous, but in a fascinating way that made him more dangerous still.

She got in her van, put it in gear. She had to stop thinking about the man, she told herself. He had disturbed her safe and structured world, leaving her feeling as vulnerable as a teenager again. She hated it. She hated him for doing it to her. She hoped she never saw him again.

SHE SAW HIM the next day.

Monday was a typically hectic day at Laurie's shop. She stood at her worktable, arranging the primary flowers in florist's foam for a centerpiece of arum lilies. The door of the shop jingled and she turned, expecting it to be Rodney, her delivery man, back from his morning run.

With a shock she saw it was Jeff. All her senses prickled, and her blood quickened in alarmed excitement.

"I want to buy a flower," he said. He stood by the door, even taller than she remembered, one black eyebrow cocked. The long-sleeved white sweater he wore dramatized the width of his shoulders and the darkness of his hair.

She stared at him, her mouth slightly open, conscious that her apron had a smear of potting soil on it and that she had specks of sphagnum moss clinging to her fingers.

"You," she breathed, experiencing the familiar tightness in her chest. He was so tall that as he made his way to the counter he had to dodge a hanging basket of silk petunias. He barely glanced around the crowded little shop. He kept his gaze locked with Laurie's.

"Wh-what do you want?" she demanded, wiping a stray tendril of hair from her cheek.

He stopped and leaned his elbows on the counter so that his eyes were level with hers. She found herself suddenly lost in their darkness. "I told you. I want to buy a flower. What kind would you like?"

"What?" Laurie's heart was pounding in confusion. She held a perfect white arum lily, its stem taped, in her hand.

"Come closer," he said, beckoning her with his forefinger. He gave her a conspiratorial smile. It made butterflies and bumblebees do loop-the-loops in the pit of her stomach.

As calmly as she could, her chin held high, she stepped to the counter and laid down the lily. She gave him a sternly questioning look but refused to speak.

"Closer still," he ordered. He bent toward her so his face was only inches from hers. He was so close that his breath fanned her cheek, and in a stage whisper he asked, "What kind do you want?"

"I think," Laurie said with great primness, "the question is—what kind *you* want."

"No." He shook his head. "I want to make a peace offering. What's your heart's desire? A rose? An orchid?"

Laurie stared at him in exasperation. She wondered if he could tell how hard her heart was beating beneath her canvas apron. "My heart's desire—is for you to leave me alone."

"I don't seem to be able to," he said, shaking his head again. "They say there's a language of flowers. What would I bring you if I wanted to say, 'Give me a chance'? A bleeding heart?"

Laurie looked away. She felt as if his dark eyes had the power to scramble her common sense and drain away her willpower. "I don't—know. A—a jonquil."

"Fine," he said, "give me a jonquil. Give me a dozen. Two dozen."

Laurie stepped from behind the counter and toward the greenhouse door. "They're out of season. You're—out of luck. I'll send somebody to help you. Excuse me."

He caught her by the elbow, then stepped in front of her to bar the way. "Laurie..."

Although his hand on her arm was gentle, his touch stung her bare flesh like fire. She found herself trapped, staring at the broad expanse of his sweatered chest. She could feel the heat of his body and smell his clean scent, something that reminded her of prairie grasses stirred by summer wind. His face was no longer mocking. It was so intent that it half frightened her.

"P-please." She turned her face away.

"No," he said, taking her chin between his thumb and forefinger and forcing her to look up at him. The hand touching her face radiated power, but it was surprisingly light against her skin.

He bent his head slightly, staring into her eyes. His voice had that low intensity she found so disturbing. "I'm the one saying it—please. Please just talk to me. Please don't walk away from me. I never meant to make you feel this way...."

He seemed so sincere that Laurie felt shaken. He still gripped her elbow, and his other hand still touched her face, almost tenderly. He wiped the wayward strand of brown-gold hair away from her cheek, his touch so carefully controlled she barely felt it. Yet, paradoxically, it rippled through her body in waves so powerful she almost shuddered.

This time, although she wanted to turn her eyes from his, she couldn't. She stared up, feeling almost helpless. His eyes were brown like the earth, his skin golden like the sun, and the look he gave her was so elemental she fought back another shiver.

"Laurie," he said softly. "Please."

He was bending his face nearer to hers. The hand that had held her elbow slipped sinuously to her waist, resting warmly just above her hips as he drew her nearer.

He's going to kiss me, she thought in panic. *And I'm going to let him.*

She couldn't. She'd been warned about the man too often.

With startling quickness she broke away and darted to the door of the greenhouse. Only when she was safely inside did she whirl to face him for a final time. "Go—away!" she cried.

"Just—go away!" She slammed the door so hard the glass rattled.

Mavis, who was repotting an ailing staghorn fern, looked at her in alarm. "What's wrong?"

"N-nothing," said Laurie, her face hot. "There's a man out there. See what he wants. Then please get rid of him."

Mavis nodded. Tightening the strings of her apron, she stalked purposefully toward the shop. Laurie went to the corner of the greenhouse and leaned against its wall, her cheek against the warm glass. Her heart beat so hard it hurt.

She closed her eyes in consternation and breathed in the earthy scents. After a moment she opened them again. She found herself staring at the sorcerer's plant. The bud had grown. It was the size and shape of a small pinecone now.

Think about the flower, she told herself. *That's what's important in your life. Not that man.*

THAT AFTERNOON JEFF SAT in one of his editing suites. He stared at three different screens as he put together the footage for a new commercial spot for the racetrack.

The music, a theme he'd been told "pounded with excitement," echoed in his earphones. The music had long ago ceased to excite. Now it merely pounded. And pounded and pounded and pounded.

He had watched the same three horses thunder down their same separate stretches of track for the past half hour. All he had to do was piece these particular shots into four seconds of quickly edited action.

For some reason it wasn't working. He swore, took off his earphones and rubbed his eyes. It didn't help. He still saw horses galloping on the back of his eyelids. He still heard the thumpity-thump of their everlasting theme. But he couldn't concentrate. He kept thinking of the woman.

She was going to drive him crazy.

He had to get her to accept him or Gary would lose his engine. Laurentia Chase-Spenser was not worth an engine. She was so haughty she wasn't worth the price of a cheap spark plug. So why, he asked himself, had he begged her to listen to him and found himself meaning it? Why, when he asked her to go out with him, did he so deeply desire for her to say yes? And why, when he'd touched her, had he found himself wanting to touch her more, to feel her lips beneath his own?

He swore again, just as Alexander Nevins, his best cameraman, came in carrying a cardboard tray of coffee and doughnuts.

"Gee, having a bad time?" Alexander asked. He was a short, stocky, sandy-haired young man of twenty-seven whose blue eyes were as guileless as a child's. He never drank, smoked, swore or dropped expensive equipment. He was unfailingly polite with clients, and his calm and steady temperament was a necessary balance to Jeff's, which could be mercurial, even stormy.

Jeff glanced up at Alexander. He suddenly knew why the guy was so even tempered. Alexander seldom dated. There were no women in his life to make it complicated, senseless and miserable. Under those circumstances, what man wouldn't have the patience and demeanor of a saint?

"Here," Alexander said helpfully, offering him a plastic mug of coffee. "And I got your favorite kind of doughnuts—buttermilk."

Jeff switched the complex buttons on the console so that each horse froze in midgallop. "I don't want any doughnuts," Jeff muttered between his teeth. He spun his chair around to give Alexander an uncharitable stare. "Thanks anyway."

The younger man looked wounded. "I'm sorry—what about the coffee? Or do you want me to take everything away?"

Jeff relented and sighed. No matter how foul his mood was, he found it impossible to take it out on Alexander. The guy was too genuinely nice, too sincerely eager to please.

"Sit down, Alexander," he said. "I need a break, that's all. I worked late last night. It's catching up with me."

Alexander sat in one of the chairs in the editing bay. He nodded sympathetically. "I know. You were editing that tape for your friend. The wedding?"

"Right."

"Did everything go okay?"

Jeff shrugged. His company was the largest film and video production company in St. Louis. Normally he would never bother with a project so small as taping a wedding.

"I wouldn't want to shoot in that church," Alexander said. "The light's too tricky."

"It's tricky, all right," Jeff said, sinking into moodiness again. He remembered all those pale roses and shining ribbons. He remembered the gray-eyed woman in the gray suit, her hands moving like white butterflies among the satin and lace and buds. He frowned.

He turned and looked at Alexander, narrowing his eyes. "Didn't you go to one of those fancy schools? Didn't you say you knew Diane Bauer?"

"Ah," Alexander said, "it wasn't such a fancy school. And I didn't exactly know Diane. I mean, everybody liked her, but we moved in different circles."

Jeff gave him a wry look. Alexander looked both earnest and nostalgic. Diane Bauer seemed like the stuff of which high school popularity was made. Alexander did not, although he was as kind and sincere as a man might be.

"Just what circles did you travel in?" Jeff asked, raising one dark brow.

"Oh, you know," Alexander said, nodding over his coffee. "Math club."

Jeff waited. "And?"

Alexander looked surprised. "That's it. Math club. I was treasurer for three years in a row. That's very flattering, to be elected treasurer of the math club. It was kind of the high point of my high school career. Socially speaking, of course."

Jeff sank back more deeply into his chair, trying not to smile. Alexander was a good man, but he had somehow maintained a remarkable air of innocence.

Jeff tried to make his voice sound casual. "You don't happen to remember another girl from those days. Very snooty girl. Pretty, but stuck-up. She's even got a stuck-up name. Laurentia Chase-Spenser."

The change that came over Alexander startled Jeff. The round face lost all expression. It went pale. His hand jerked so hard that coffee splashed over the edge of the mug and onto the knee of his jeans.

But if the coffee was hot enough to burn, Alexander didn't seem to feel it. "Laurentia?" he said, disbelief in his voice. "Here? She's still in town?"

Jeff felt a sinister wave of foreboding. His long body tensed. "You knew her."

Alexander's face was solemn, almost reverent. He nodded. "I thought I was in love with her."

Jeff straightened in his chair. He put his coffee mug on the counter. "*What?*"

He couldn't think of a less likely combination than the cool Laurie and the ingenuous Alexander.

Alexander took a neatly folded handkerchief from his pocket and began scrubbing the coffee from the knee of his jeans. "It's the first time I ever thought I was in love," he said. "She was new in school. I thought she was beautiful—in a special way, not flashy. Just sort of elegant and . . . wonderful."

The words drove themselves into Jeff's brain like evil and poisonous tacks: *special . . . not flashy . . . elegant . . . wonderful.* Yeah. He supposed a man could see her like that at first.

"And she was quiet," Alexander went on, regret mingling with fondness in his voice. "I liked that. I thought maybe she was shy, too."

Yeah, Jeff thought again. He supposed a naive guy like Alexander could take the girl's haughtiness for shyness. He nodded, keeping his face blank.

"Well, it was my own fault," Alexander said with a philosophical air. "You see," he admitted unhappily, "I'd just been elected the treasurer of the math club again, and I was kind of . . . well, I guess it made me arrogant."

Jeff struggled even harder to keep his face an impassive mask. Alexander, arrogant? It was like imagining arrogance in a teddy bear. "I see," he said.

Alexander shrugged at his remembered folly. "And I had these friends in the math club—these kind of wild and crazy guys—who found out I liked her. And, well, Jeff, they talked me into doing something really insane. And I had no right to do it. And I'm not proud of it.''

Jeff raised an eyebrow in dubious curiosity. ''You did something insane? What?''

Alexander's shoulders sank. He sat with his elbows on his knees, staring at the floor in dejection. ''I asked her out.''

''What?'' Jeff almost barked. ''You asked her out? That was the terrible thing you did?''

Alexander nodded. He seemed too ashamed of his boldness to explain it any further.

''Well?'' Jeff demanded. ''What happened?'' He wasn't sure he wanted to know, but the thought of someone as vulnerable as Alexander at the mercy of someone as disdainful as Laurie Chase-Spenser held a fascination too horrible not to pursue.

Alexander kept his eyes on the floor. ''Well, of course, she didn't go out with me. She'd never go out with somebody like me. I was a fool to ask. I had no right.''

You had every right, Jeff wanted to yell. *She's not the blankety-blank queen of England.* Instead he stretched out, pretending to relax. ''So she said no?''

''Oh, gee,'' Alexander said, a slight tremor in his voice. ''She didn't say anything. She just looked at me a really long time. I felt like a worm. For a minute I thought she was going to say something. But she just turned her back on me and walked away. I . . . well, I asked for it, I guess.''

Jeff's skull suddenly ached. An evil feeling knotted in his stomach. He stood up. He paced the narrow aisle between the editing bay and the long counter behind it.

It made him sick, the thought of someone as gentle and artless as Alexander being snubbed so cruelly. Especially by Laurie Chase-Spenser, Miss Too-Good-for-Anybody.

''So what happened?'' he asked at last. Earlier that day he had found himself actually wanting her to talk to him, to be with him, to let him closer. He wondered why he'd wanted, almost against his will, to kiss her, to taste that beautiful, scornful mouth. He must have been crazy. He must be working too hard. Damn her, damn the bet, and damn Gary Castiglione and his stupid but beloved car engine.

"What do you mean, what happened?" Alexander asked, blinking wide blue eyes. "Nothing happened. I figured I'd put her in an embarrassing position and she didn't know what to say. I never asked her out again. I just admired her from afar."

"From afar," Jeff said in disgust. "Well, did you ever ask anybody else out? Somebody a little less untouchable?"

Alexander shook his head and looked at the floor again. "Not for a long time. I guess it showed me I'm not a ladies' man. You know. I just don't have it. Some guys do. Like you. Women always like you."

Jeff paced more angrily, his hands deep in his pockets. It was true women had always liked him. It was often flattering, frequently embarrassing and sometimes unpleasantly inconvenient. He remembered the terrible mess with Mary Ellen Pfieffer. She'd pursued him so relentlessly that he'd finally realized she needed psychological help. He'd done nothing to encourage her, nothing. But the experience had soured him on getting close to women. Until the untouchable Laurie had come along. He told himself again he was crazy to have felt a moment's attraction to her. Why wasn't she as easy to date— and forget—as Suzanne Carrington and Tammy Farentino had been? They were already past history to him.

He turned to Alexander again, his face grim. "I hope she didn't put you off women for life. Listen, I met her, and she isn't worth it."

"Oh, no," Alexander insisted, his face pained. "I mean, when the right time comes, I'll find someone. There's a girl at church I like a lot. I'm thinking about asking her out. I've given it a lot of thought."

Jeff reached down and gripped Alexander's shoulder. "So ask her, already. Ask her to the company picnic. Don't spend the rest of your life mourning for this stuck-up Chase-Spenser woman. She's not worth it, I mean it."

"Well, I'm older now," Alexander said, a serious line to his mouth. "I don't rush into things. And as for Laurie, I'm not bitter about her. She's very special."

Jeff gripped his friend's shoulder harder. "She's not special. And if it's any comfort, I asked her out and she wouldn't go with me, either."

Alexander looked up at him with genuine surprise. "You asked her out? And she wouldn't go? With *you?*"

"No. She wouldn't. But I might have to try again. It's more for a friend's sake than my own." He released Alexander's shoulder and paced to the other end of the room. He turned. "Would it bother you? If I asked her out again?"

Alexander's expression exuded sincerity. "Of course not. No matter what you say, there's something fascinating about her. Did you know a prince fell in love with her?"

"A prince?" Jeff asked in pained disbelief. "You mean a royal-type real prince?"

"A real prince." Alexander nodded. "I think in Italy. She studied design over there. And this prince—from someplace eastern—fell in love with her. He even wanted to marry her. But she wouldn't have anything to do with him, either. See, it's really not so bad being turned down by her—not if she's turned down a *prince.*"

Alexander glanced at his watch. "Oh, gosh! I'm almost late. I've got to go shoot that commercial using the marionettes— better run." He gathered up the cups, napkins and dough-nuts and bustled away, clucking about the time.

Jeff shook his head and sat down before the screens once more. He began pushing switches.

Laurie Chase-Spenser, he thought bitterly.

She had humiliated Alexander, she had spurned a prince, and now she was ignoring him.

He put on his headphones and glowered at the thumpity-thumps that echoed in his ears.

No matter what it took, he'd get to Laurie Chase-Spenser yet.

Chapter Four

ON WEDNESDAY, by messenger service, he sent her three dozen fresh yellow jonquils. The message, written in a bold hand, said, "In the language of flowers, these ask you to give me one brief chance."

They sat on her counter, a yellow profusion of blooms.

Jonquils, she thought, unconsciously biting her lower lip. Where and how had he gotten so many fresh jonquils? Jonquils meant "Return my affection." But how could he feel affection for her? He hardly knew her.

The phone rang. She usually let Mavis answer it, but Mavis was at lunch. Laurie picked up the receiver. "Ribbons and Roses," she said. She took a deep breath. "May we help you?"

There was a silence that lasted the length of a heartbeat. Then she heard the deep voice that she didn't want to hear. Its timbre sent conflicting emotions vibrating through her body.

"Laurie? It's Jeff. Did you get the flowers?"

She bit her lip again. She had to speak as deliberately as possible. "Yes. You made a mistake. You send flowers—from a florist. Not *to* one."

"It was no mistake."

Laurie stared at the jonquils. They were thrust artlessly into an expensive bowl of Irish crystal. Flowers and bowl, combined with the private messenger service, must have cost him a small fortune. And the jonquils were beautiful, almost dewy, as if they'd been picked that morning.

"Laurie?" he said, and the way he said it made her ear tickle and her nerves tingle.

"Why?" she asked in exasperation. "Why are you—doing this to me?"

"I'd like to know you better. Would you just go out for coffee with me some night after work?"

"No."

"Why do you always give me that flat no? Don't you know any other words?"

"No."

"Is there any way in the world I can get you to say yes?"

"No."

"Laurie, will you just *listen?*"

"*No,*" she said emphatically, and hung up the phone.

She had her delivery man take the flowers back to his studio. She'd put a snapdragon in the midst of the jonquils. In the language of flowers, a snapdragon said, "You're being presumptuous." It was her only message to him.

ON THURSDAY AFTERNOON, he appeared in her shop carrying a plant that looked as if it had been beaten, held prisoner and interrogated by torturers.

It was the saddest-looking aspidistra Laurie had ever seen. She glanced from it up into the eyes of Jeff Remington. She tried to ignore how dark and piercing those eyes were.

"I don't know what you've done to this—plant," she said between her teeth. "But you should—probably be—prosecuted for it in criminal court."

"It isn't well," Jeff replied in a masterpiece of understatement. "I brought it to you to cure."

He stood before the counter, commandingly tall. Laurie stood behind it, her arms crossed in stubbornness. The plant, its long leaves withered and mottled, sat between them.

"Look," Jeff said, pushing the plant toward her, "if you can't fix it, nobody can."

"Nobody can," Laurie said, and pushed it back. "It's dead. And you ought to be ashamed of yourself, neglecting it like this."

"I didn't neglect it," he said, pushing it toward her again. "I found it. I thought you could save it."

Laurie put her hands to her temples and shook her head again. "Nothing can save it. I didn't think it was—possible to kill an aspidistra, but somehow you've done it."

She turned away from him and ran her hand through her hair in exasperation. Once more he had succeeded in throwing her off balance. She had barely gotten out the word *possible* and was amazed she hadn't stumbled over *aspidistra*.

She wanted nothing more than to flee into the sanctuary of the greenhouse, but if she came from behind the counter, he would stop her. If he touched her again . . . She couldn't finish the thought. All she knew was that she didn't dare let him touch her again.

"Laurie," he said, his low voice sending tiny tremors through her, "Laurie, at least look at me."

She didn't dare look at him, either. She didn't know where he'd been—out in the country taping something, she guessed. He was dressed in faded jeans, slung low on his lean hips. The sleeves of his white shirt were rolled up, and their snowiness contrasted with the tan of his skin.

Today the line of his mouth had something grimly determined in it, and there was no longer mockery in his eyes. Even when his words were light, his eyes were serious, and she didn't want to look into them again. Such eyes could trap a woman's soul.

"Laurie? Just look at me. Please."

She kept her back to him. She stared down at her worktable, where she had been filling a basket with garnet roses and ferns.

"Laurie?" Once more his voice sent tingles surging through her. "I know there's not another man. I've asked around."

She crossed her arms. "Don't ask anybody about me," she said, almost savagely. "I'm none of your business."

"I've made you my business."

She shook her head, keeping her back to him.

The bell over the door jingled. Someone else had entered the shop. She whirled to face the sound.

A meek-looking man of about thirty approached the counter. Next to Jeff, he seemed pallid and dwarfed. He apparently saw the charged glances that crackled between Jeff and Laurie. Nervously he cleared his throat.

"Excuse me?" he said. "I'm not interrupting?"

Silence smoldered in the air a moment. Jeff shifted his shoulders in an impatient movement. "I'm just leaving."

Jeff's eyes settled on Laurie again. Their darkness filled her with stirrings of forbidden attraction. "I left the jonquils on your doorstep. They're yours. I don't know how to take care of them."

He turned, heading for the door. Once more he had to dodge the hanging basket of silk petunias. The bell jingled when he opened the door, then again when he closed it behind him.

"Jonquils?" asked the little man brightly.

Laurie shook her head. "Excuse me a minute." She went to the door.

The jonquils lay on the doorstep, damp and wrapped in cellophane. The snapdragon was gone. Laurie picked them up and carried them inside the shop, cradled in her arms. She couldn't stop staring down at them. For all their delicacy, they still looked remarkably fresh.

"Jonquils," the little man said again. "I came in for some carnations for my mother. But I like the looks of those—so sunny. I'll take half a dozen."

"I'm sorry." She tried to smile politely but wasn't sure she succeeded. "They're not for sale."

She put the flowers in the big glass-doored refrigerator. But their coolness lingered on her skin. The sensation reminded her, hauntingly, of how it had felt to be kissed by Jeff Remington.

THE NEXT EVENING Laurie didn't leave the shop until almost six-thirty, long after her employees had gone home. A fine rain, almost like a mist, was in the air. Her mood was pensive. Jeff hadn't phoned or showed up today, and she knew she should be grateful. Instead, she felt an odd emptiness.

She hurried to her van, trying to keep her mind on business. She had one more appointment this evening, for dinner with a Mr. Philipi. The man had called, wanting a special Fourth of July arrangement made for an ad for his lawn-supply shop.

The job would be expensive, and Mr. Philipi seemed to be one of those fussy, insecure customers who needed to talk at length about what he wanted. The only time he could take was at supper, he said. He had invited her to Granatelli's Restaurant at seven-thirty.

She did not look forward to spending the evening with a client. She'd already spent a long working day and she was concerned about the sorcerer's flower. The bud had shown no new growth for several days. She knew this was supposed to be normal, but she worried anyway.

She had to drive quickly and boldly to make it to the restaurant on time. She wished now that she hadn't lingered so long at the shop or wasted so many moments going into the greenhouse to check repeatedly on her precious plant.

Her greatest hope was it would finally blossom. So far, only one other sorcerer's flower had bloomed on the North American continent, at a university in Canada. The flower had been small and of poor quality.

What if the bud never matured, she wondered as she entered the candlelit restaurant. What if it withered and died, and all her hopes had been in vain? It would be years before the plant budded again. It would probably be decades.

She told the maître d' that she was with Mr. Philipi's party, and he led her into the smallest of the restaurant's private rooms. Granatelli's managed to combine luxury with homeyness, style with warmth. She sat, toying with the complex folds of the linen napkin and staring absently at the framed photographs of Milan on the wall.

It was useless to worry about the flower, she told herself. She had done everything in her power to nurture the plant. Either it bloomed or it didn't. It was up to nature now.

Then she heard a voice that jolted her to the marrow of her bones. "How deep in thought. I almost hate to interrupt you."

Her head snapped toward the doorway as her fingers tightened on the napkin. She drew in her breath sharply.

Jeff Remington stood there, in charcoal-colored slacks, a well-tailored navy blazer and a maroon tie. The lamplight gleamed on the waves of his dark hair.

He entered, pulled out a chair across from her and sat down. "So," he said, giving her a slightly crooked smile, "it looks like we'll be having dinner together after all."

"You," she said between her teeth. She was too paralyzed by surprise to move.

"Me," he agreed. "Except you make it sound like an accusation, not a pronoun."

He wore, she noticed distractedly, a slightly wilted snapdragon on his lapel.

"What are you doing here?" she demanded. Without noticing it, she had crumpled the napkin into a crushed ball.

"I came to meet Mr. Philipi, the same as you," he said with a shrug. He glanced at his watch. "He should be along any minute now."

Laurie released the napkin but nervously clenched her hand into a fist. "Why are you meeting Mr.—Philipi?"

"For the same reason as you. Business."

She winced slightly. She had almost stumbled badly over Mr. Philipi's name, and the near gaffe worsened the disturbance she already felt boiling within her.

"He asked me here to discuss—a flower arrangement."

Jeff nodded, then glanced at the waiter who appeared at the door. "Two glasses of your best Frascati, Alfredo."

He turned his attention back to Laurie. "I hope you don't mind if I order an aperitif for you. You look a little on edge. Listen, there's nothing mysterious about this. I always shoot Philipi's commercials. He's got this idea for a Fourth of July sale. He wants to have a flag made of flowers, a big one. He's good at selling garden supplies, but he can't arrange flowers. I recommended you."

Laurie stared at him in suspicion. He looked extremely handsome, and although mockery danced in his eyes, there was a grimness about his mouth that made her distrustful.

"Honest," he said, but somehow he didn't look honest to her.

"I find this hard to—believe."

"Why do you distrust me so much?"

"You're untrustworthy."

His dark brows rose in an expression of offended innocence. "Me?"

"You," she said firmly. She wished the light didn't fall on his face the way it did. It highlighted the strong curve of his cheekbones and the line of his jaw.

"Why?"

The waiter came in with two glasses of wine. She waited for him to leave. She stared across the table at Jeff.

He raised his glass as if in a toast. She refused to touch hers, so he clinked the rims of the wineglasses together. "Why?" he asked again. "Just why don't you trust me?"

"Because," she said as carefully as she could, "you chase women."

He took a sip of wine and shook his head. "You make me sound like the villain in a Victorian melodrama. 'What was his deep and deadly sin? He *chased women*.'"

To fortify herself, she took a drink of the wine. "It's true," she said, refusing to smile at his joke. "It's not—funny. At the wedding you chased Suzanne Carrington and Tammy Farentino. And you chased me. And you've—you've kept right on chasing me."

"You kept running," he said. "I had to."

"No," Laurie argued. Her nervousness had turned to passion, and the height of her emotion made the words come more easily. "You didn't have to. I don't think you even liked me when we met."

The line of his jaw went tense. He smiled, but the smile, charming as it was, looked forced. "Why don't we stop dwelling on my past sins? We have to work together, so let's try to get along, to get acquainted like normal people. Were you and Diane close friends?"

"No," Laurie answered. Her retort sounded sharper than she'd meant. "I told you, we were just—friends. I always thought she was very—nice."

He held his wineglass and stared into it moodily. "Nick and I were friends when we were kids. I practically lived at his house. The Granatellis are like that—they take in all the strays."

"That's nice," Laurie said, as if she didn't care a straw where or how he'd spent his childhood.

He finished his wine and set down the glass. He signaled the waiter for two more. He put his elbows on the table and laced his fingers together. The motion somehow emphasized the power of his shoulders. He had extraordinarily broad shoulders for a man so tall.

"So tell me about yourself," he said with the air of someone determined to be pleasant. "Like why do you have a hyphen in your name? To intimidate people? You can be intimidating, you know."

Laurie gave him a cold look. If she seemed intimidating, she thought, she was pulling off an illusion worthy of Houdini.

"My parents were divorced. My mother took her maiden name again. She wanted me to have both names."

He studied her so intently that she fought the desire to squirm. "Well," he said. There was irony in his voice. "We have something in common. My parents were divorced, too. I grew up with my Italian grandmother."

She picked up her wineglass and stared over its rim at him. She said nothing.

He lifted one shoulder in a careless shrug. "I'm only a quarter Italian. The rest is a little of everything. Melting-pot American. No blue blood. Is that what you've got against me?"

"I don't care what color your—blood is." She took another sip of her wine. She didn't want to look at him. He was too handsome, too masculine, too attractive, and she could not afford to be attracted to him.

The waiter silently entered with two more glasses of Frascati, setting them on the table. He whisked away Jeff's empty glass and disappeared.

"I didn't want another glass of wine," Laurie said. Her voice sounded overly prim, even to her own ears.

"Sorry." Bitterness edged his tone. "Listen, my blood isn't blue, my name isn't in the social register, and I didn't go to fancy schools. But I've built up a business and I've made it a good one. Would it be too much to ask you even to look at me?"

Laurie shook her head in agitation. She turned her eyes to his dark ones and once again was shaken by the impact he had on her. She clenched her teeth and said nothing.

"Apparently you don't think I'm worth your attention," he said, his upper lip curling slightly. "I keep trying to change your mind. And I keep failing." Once more he raised his wineglass to her. "Still, there's no reason we can't have a pleasant dinner. If, of course, you'd condescend to talk."

Laurie flushed. She pushed back her chair and tried to uncrumple the napkin she had crushed. "We have—nothing to say."

He flashed her a look that scalded. She tried to ignore it. She gave up on restoring the napkin's smoothness and, with a gesture of finality, pushed it away from her.

"I'm leaving," she said between her teeth.

"You can't leave," Jeff said, his face as stormy as hers. "Philipi isn't here yet."

She met his eyes, her own flashing. "And he won't—be here. Will he?"

"What do you mean?"

"You know exactly what I mean. Just about the time I'd get to the—bottom of that second glass of wine—" she pointed an accusing finger at the untouched glass "—a waiter will come and say to start dinner without him—that Mr. Philipi's detained. And later, after a few more glasses of wine, there'll—be a call that he won't—be coming at all."

She stood, snatching her purse.

He stood almost as quickly as she did.

She headed for the door. He blocked her way.

She found herself staring at his blazing white shirt and the muted paisley of his tie.

"Are you accusing me—" he began, bending down so he could look her in the eye.

"Yes," she said shortly, and pushed past him. She strode past the tables in the main dining room. He stayed right behind her, even as she made her way into the lobby.

"Laurie—"

"Look," she said tightly, fury in her voice. "I don't know what you want. I don't care."

She gave the front door a hearty push and tried to escape him. He was at her elbow. He touched her arm.

She drew away as if stung and marched purposefully toward the parking lot. Night had almost fallen and the air was misty with fine rain. "Don't touch me! We've had a drink together. We've talked. Isn't that enough for you?"

This time when he reached for her, she couldn't avoid him. An expression of angry determination darkened his face.

"Almost enough. Not quite."

He had forced her to stop. She wheeled, looking up at him. She had almost made it to her van, which was parked beneath a giant oak. Huge branches stretched above, the leaves providing patchy shelter from the damp.

Laurie studied the frowning face that loomed above her. Before, he had gripped her by the elbow, but now his hands grasped her shoulders, holding her prisoner. Her heartbeat increased to an almost frenzied pace.

"I can honestly say we've been out," he muttered. "We met. We had a drink. Half the staff at Granatelli's saw us. So that's that."

The misty rain had made his hair fall over his forehead, curling slightly. She was chilled through, but paradoxically filled with heat. "Wh-what do you mean?"

"I mean," he said, gripping her shoulders more tightly and bending nearer, "that it hasn't been fun. And it hasn't been pleasant. And I wouldn't have done it if I didn't have to."

"H-have to?"

"Have to. Somebody made a bet I couldn't go out with you—"

A wave of horrified anger surged through her. "A— *bet?* That's what all this idiocy has—"

He nodded curtly, his teeth clenched in anger. "That's what all the idiocy has been about. Because, believe me, I can't think of any other reason to want to be with you. You're cold, you're stuck-up, you're affected—"

"*Me?* Have you looked at yourself? This is—this is—" She was too angry to get out the word *despicable*, but she knew the message flashed in her eyes.

"I don't care what you think," he interrupted, his voice almost a growl. "I've just got one more thing to do before I'm through. And that's kiss you goodbye. And it's a pleasure, Miss Chase-Spenser, to say it. Goodbye."

He pulled her to him. All he'd meant to do was kiss her on the cheek, then let her go, let her exit his life for good. But somehow, in the darkness and the confusion and all the emotion leaping between them, his lips found her mouth instead of her cheek.

She gave a startled gasp, her lips soft and warm beneath his. "Oh," she breathed.

He should have pulled away from her immediately. But she had gone so still in his arms that he drew her nearer instead. And her mouth was so pliant, so silky and inviting, he found himself unable to keep from tasting it longer and more deeply.

At first he'd grasped her shoulders so she wouldn't run away. But something in the way he touched her changed. He held her now because he liked holding her, because he wanted her closer to him still. Wanted her as close as possible.

Her face was cool and damp from the rain. It reminded him of how flower petals felt early in the morning. Her body was warm beneath the rain-chilled fabric of her jacket. But she shivered. Suddenly she didn't seem haughty but only delicate and desirable and vulnerable. And he couldn't seem to be able to stop kissing her. The anger had died out of his touch. But something just as passionate had replaced it.

"Oh," she said again. She pushed hard against his chest, bolting backward with the suddenness of an animal fleeing for its life. Then she stared up at him, her face pale in the darkness. With dismay, he thought he saw tears glint in her eyes.

He didn't want her to run away. He no longer wished to make her angry. And he knew, with sickening certainty, that he didn't want to see her cry.

"Laurie—" he began.

"Lucky you," she said bitterly, in that maddeningly deliberate way she had. "It's all over now."

She turned from him and took the last few steps to her van. Hurriedly she got in, slamming the door.

Let her go, one part of his mind said cynically. *She got what she deserved. She's spent her life snubbing people. For a change, somebody walked on her feelings. So what?*

No, he told himself. She'd been nothing but trouble and she hadn't been worth it. She sure as hell wasn't worth a friend losing a '68 classic Mustang engine. She wasn't worth somebody as nice as Alexander being hurt.

He watched, his face emotionless, as she backed out of the parking space, then sped too quickly out of the lot and into the street.

She was gone. He stood in the misty rain, looking after her.

His work was done. He'd saved Gary's engine and his pride. He'd won the stupid bet. He was practically a hero. But he didn't feel like one.

He remembered her words in the restaurant, that Mr. Philipi would never have shown. She had seen right through him—there was no Mr. Philipi. It had been Gary on the phone to her, doing his best to imitate a querulous and exacting customer. She'd looked at him with those lovely gray eyes and seen through him as if he'd been made of glass.

She had every right to be angry. But she got under his skin so badly he'd gotten angry, too, and like a fool he'd blurted out the truth about the bet. Then he'd kissed her, and she tasted like wine and smelled like flowers and fitted into his arms as if she'd been born for him alone.

He'd made her cry.

He jammed his hands into his pockets and kicked savagely at the gravel of the parking lot. He swore. He told himself again that she was a cold snob and that she'd gotten only what she deserved.

The rain began to fall harder. Still, he stood in the darkness, staring toward the empty street.

Why should he feel this way? he wondered. He had nothing in common with the woman, he didn't like her, he never would have been involved with her at all if it hadn't been for the asinine bet.

Her words echoed in his memory— *It's all over now.*

So what? So what if it was over? What did he care?

He turned and walked back inside to pay the bill. He paused by the edge of the parking lot and unpinned the snapdragon from his lapel. Dropping it onto the gravel, he walked on.

It lay there, a small flower dying in the rain.

Chapter Five

LAURIE DROVE through the rain, as furious at herself as at Jeff Remington.

A bet, she thought wrathfully. *He's been pursing me because of a bet.*

Vinnie must have known. That was why he had warned her. And Aldo. And Sophia. They had all tried to protect her.

Tears stung her eyes, but she blinked them back, pretending it was only the rain on the windshield that blurred her vision.

He had treated her like an object, not a person. That hurt. He had said scathing things. That hurt, too, and she hated him.

And somebody had figured she'd be a challenge for him because she was aloof and untouchable. That thought hurt most of all—that someone believed it would be funny to set Jeff Remington on her trail, like a hunter after an elusive quarry.

And yet—her hands tightened on the wheel—when he had bent to kiss her, she'd found herself automatically raising her lips to his. She hadn't resisted, refused or run away. She'd stood there in the rain like a fool, letting him kiss her until his touch and closeness half dizzied her.

The man was no good, yet she was *attracted* to him. She had been all along, although she loathed admitting it. That's why he filled her with such uneasiness.

All right, she told herself, shaking her head in frustration. So she had found him physically attractive. What was strange about that? Nature had designed him to send female hormones dancing off in the giddiest way.

Unfortunately, for all his superficial charms, his arrogance was monumental. He had set out to use her, and he'd succeeded.

Laurie tightened her mouth in determination. No, he hadn't succeeded. Not really. She hadn't agreed to a date with him. And she didn't intend to let anyone believe she had.

He thought she was a toy, to be maneuvered, then cast aside. She would teach him otherwise. She would hit him where it would hurt him most: his insufferable pride.

And she knew exactly how to do it.

MORNING SUN POURED through the big windows of the shop, but the room seemed to have gone suddenly dark. The same messenger who had previously brought her the jonquils had reappeared. This time he bore an even larger bundle of blossoms.

"What's this?" Laurie protested as the man pressed a huge bouquet of white wildflowers and ferns into her arms. "What are these? I don't want them."

"I've got my orders, ma'am," the man said. "The message is on the card."

It was ten o'clock in the morning, and Laurie was preparing flowers for an afternoon wedding. Although she'd convinced herself she had recovered from the disaster with Jeff Remington, she was in no mood for new surprises from him.

Awkwardly she took the large bouquet and managed to open the card.

Laurie—I suppose I could feel worse about what happened last night, but I don't know how. Raspberry blossoms mean remorse. It's genuine.

For an instant her heart leaped up as if in hope. Then she forced it to harden. She thrust the card back into the envelope.

She stared down in distaste at the flowers. They actually were raspberry blossoms, long stems of them. They looked as if he'd picked them himself, then taken them somewhere to be arranged with the ferns, beribboned and wrapped in tissue.

She looked the messenger in his apprehensive eye. "How much do you charge to make a delivery?"

"Fifteen dollars in the city itself, ma'am. Twenty for the suburbs."

Laurie marched purposefully to the cash register and punched the button that sent it ringing open. She drew out a twenty-dollar bill and handed it to him. "Take this," she said. She pushed the white blossoms back into his arms. "And take these back to Mr. Remington."

"Yes, ma'am," he said, his eyes wary. "Any message?"

"Yes." Laurie turned her back and marched to her worktable. "Tell him to take his raspberries—and sit on them."

"Ma'am, he's not going to like that."

"Good," said Laurie, and she meant it.

She didn't know what Jeff Remington was up to this time, and she told herself she didn't care.

She'd already set her plan for revenge in motion. She'd called the classified ad department of the city paper that morning. She intended to announce to all of St. Louis that she hadn't gone out with Jeff Remington.

IT WAS LAURIE'S BIRTHDAY supper. Four days had passed since Jeff Remington had sent the wildflowers. She had not heard from him again.

But he and a large section of St. Louis had heard from her.

"So," her uncle said, "what's this about an ad in the paper? People keep asking me about it."

She was having dinner with her Great-uncle Merritt. On the weekend there would be a birthday picnic with her other aunts and uncles and cousins. But Merritt was somewhat deaf and didn't like crowds; he preferred his celebrations small.

Uncle Merritt was the only one of Laurie's relatives she considered truly rich. His walls were hung with oil paintings and his table gleamed with the finest silver and china. He was sometimes eccentric, but he had always treated Laurie with special kindness. He had no children of his own.

Laurie speared an oyster. "I put an ad in the personal column."

"Why?"

Laurie shrugged self-consciously. The ad she had taken out said, "To Whom It May Concern: I've never had a date with Jeff Remington. I never intend to." And she put her name on it.

"I needed to make it clear I'd never willingly been out with—with this man," she told her uncle.

"Who? Why?" Merritt frowned. "What's he done?"

Laurie cringed, glad they were dining in Uncle Merritt's home rather than a restaurant. Because of his deafness, Merritt often almost shouted when he talked.

"Just a man. He'd made a b-bet that he could get a date with me. He was going to say he had. So I took out the ad."

Uncle Merritt thought about this for a moment. He always claimed he liked talking with Laurie, that she spoke so deliberately he had little trouble understanding her. "Ha," he said loudly. He grinned in satisfaction. "Ha. Serves him right."

Laurie looked at him, unsure of herself. The ad had appeared in the city's largest paper two nights before. As much as she disliked the idea of making a scene, she refused to let Jeff Remington take advantage of her. Yet once she'd seen the ad, and her name there with his, it had given her a slightly sick feeling.

Merritt, however, seemed to have no doubts about her action. "Got what he deserved. Make bets about *my* great-niece. Ha. Show him the stuff you're made of."

Laurie said nothing. She really didn't want to talk about it. She had hoped that the ad would put an end to the whole humiliating affair.

Merritt seemed to sense her reluctance. "Try the French onion soup. Cook whipped it up especially for you. And I want to hear about your plant, the one you got from that fellow from Cambasia. The wizard flower."

"Sorcerer's flower," Laurie said, grateful for the change of subject.

"Really going to bloom, is it?" asked Uncle Merritt, raising a white eyebrow.

"Yes." Laurie nodded proudly. "I think it might." The bud had started growing again. In the past two days it had swelled to almost twice its previous size.

"So how soon will it happen?" Merritt asked.

"I'm not sure," Laurie said. "It may be another week, it may be longer."

"Then?" Uncle Merritt asked.

"Well," Laurie said. "Well, it's—a little unusual. It usually blooms at night. Or so they say. It begins about midnight, and it's usually completely open by dawn."

"Ha," he said gruffly. "Ha. Listen to you. 'A little unusual,' she says. Always the modest one. When this thing blooms, it'll be the first time it's ever happened in this country. Well, won't it?"

"*If* it blooms...."

"Listen to her. It'll bloom. And you're the one making it happen. This is going to be an *event*. You ought to be out shouting about it from the rooftops."

"I'm just—lucky," Laurie protested.

"Luck? Did you say luck?" Merritt asked, wriggling his white eyebrows in mock rebuke. "Luck had nothing to do with it. Ha. Pluck did. Pluck and knowledge. You're the best florist in St. Louis. Everybody says so. Do you know why that plant hasn't bloomed anywhere else in the country? Because nobody's *good* enough to make it bloom. You're the only one who's come close. You."

Laurie blushed. "If I hadn't been given the plant in the first place, I wouldn't have had a chance at it. And now Cambasia won't allow any more out of the country. So I really have been lucky."

"Do you suppose it was *luck* that made the prince like you that much? No. It was you. The kind of person you are. He had no choice but to adore you."

"The prince was just a—friend," Laurie said, embarrassed.

"*Quite* a friend." Uncle Merritt's white eyebrows were working again. "He wanted to marry you."

"We were students together for a while," Laurie insisted, shaking her head. "That was all."

"When the prince gave you a present, it wasn't luck," the old man said. "No! It's because he wanted to please you—and no wonder. You're young, you're beautiful, you're intelligent, you're talented, you're kind—"

"Uncle Merritt, *please,*" Laurie said.

"It's your birthday," he retorted, "so I'll compliment you all I want. Let me drink to you, Laurie." He raised his glass. "Do you realize how far you've come? I remember when you'd barely talk to people. When you barely *could* talk. But you worked at your problems, you overcame them, and you are, by the Great Lord Harry, *something.* I salute you."

Laurie hid her confusion by sipping her wine. Her uncle winked at her. "Blush all you want," he said. "I'm proud of what you're doing with this flower. This is botanical history you're making, my dear. I have every right to be proud."

Laurie couldn't help smiling at him. He was a dear man, even if he was prone to blustering. For a long time they had been the odd couple of the family—the shy girl who hadn't talked well and the opinionated old man who couldn't hear well. But he had understood her struggles, and he had encouraged her every step of her way. He had never let her give up.

"There are legends about this plant, too, aren't there?" asked Merritt. "Got a little bit of witchery in your shop?"

Laurie shook her head at his teasing. "No witchery. Just legends. Not a scrap of truth to them."

"No? Well then, what about your birthday present?" Merritt asked, teasing even more. "What do you suppose it is?"

Laurie laughed. "If I could guess, you'd consider yourself a terrible failure."

Merritt prided himself on giving unexpected gifts. They were always original, always thoughtful and always a surprise.

"Ha, I'll tell you this—it concerns that plant of yours," he told her. "When it's going to bloom, you call me—immediately. And then you'll get your present."

Laurie smiled, but inside a tremor of doubt shook her. She was afraid to be overly confident. "What if it doesn't bloom? I'm really not certain—"

"It will," Merritt assured her. "Because you're the one it's blooming for."

Laurie was warmed by his faith.

"Now, my dear," he said with a look that was part frown, part smile. "I'd like to get back to this business about the ad in the paper. Why, exactly, would this man *bet* he could get a date with you?"

Laurie's smile faded. She didn't want to remember Jeff Remington. When she thought of him, a strange and restless emptiness filled her. But she knew Merritt far too well to think he'd settle for no answer.

She took a deep breath. "Some people think I'm aloof. It's— the way I talk. I guess I was supposed to be—be a challenge to him—or something."

"Mmmph," Merritt said, a disapproving little noise. "Well. He got that right. You're a challenge—and he lost it. He met his match. An ad in the paper—ha. Nice touch. Good move. Grind the scoundrel into the dust. Don't get mad, get even. I *like* it."

He raised his wineglass to her again. His gray eyes twinkled.

But Laurie did not feel a sense of victory. She felt the same unhappy hollowness.

ONE WEEK TO THE DAY after her birthday, Laurie's plant gave signs of being ready to bloom.

She was almost afire with nervousness. Her fingers, usually sure, were awkward, jabbing flowers into their foam at the wrong angle, twisting tape when it shouldn't be twisted, squirting glue where it had no business being squirted.

By four o'clock in the afternoon, she was sure it was going to happen. The sepals of the calyx were parting, just barely, to show the first fine lines of pale yellow beneath the dusty green surface.

Even Laurie's normally unflappable assistant, Mavis, caught the excitement. "Why do I feel I should be rushing around yelling for hot water and clean towels? Like we're delivering a baby?" she asked.

"I don't know," Laurie said, shaking her head. She tried to stab a pushpin into a pert bow to keep it in place and almost stabbed herself instead. "Ouch," she muttered, throwing down the pin. "I can't take this any longer. Misery loves company. I'm calling my uncle."

With trembling hands, she dialed his number. Then she had to yell especially loudly to make Uncle Merritt understand her. She felt as if everything were going slightly insane.

"Going to bloom? Tonight, you think?" Merritt almost cackled with pleasure.

"Yes," Laurie shouted. "I'm sure. You said you wanted to know. Will you come watch with me? It's a rare occurrence, Uncle Merritt. They say it—blooms only once every century or so. Will you come? We may never get another chance to see something like this."

"You and your flower are young enough to stay up all night. I'm not. But don't worry. I'll see it all happen. Later."

"Well," Laurie said, "you can see the—flower itself, but—but wouldn't you like to see it open? I mean, nobody in the country's ever seen it happen before. Will I have to watch all alone? Mavis can't stay—she has children."

Merritt chuckled. "You don't understand. I'll see it bloom later. And you won't have to be alone. The Nature Channel is coming from Washington, D.C., to film it. Time-lapse photography. They're going to do a feature on it on their weekly news special."

"The Nature Channel!" Laurie was so excited she almost jumped up and down. "The Nature Channel? Really?"

"Really," Merritt assured her. The Nature Channel was a TV cable network specializing in programs about the natural world. It was young, thriving and in general, an example of high-quality television. To have her flower featured on the news special seemed as wonderful to her as winning an Oscar.

And to have the network make a time-lapse film, so the flower's opening would be preserved and shared—that gift was greater still. The flower would seem to open before the eyes of the viewer in the space of a minute, a magical act. She was so thrilled that tears sprang into her eyes.

"Oh, Uncle Merritt—"

"And," he said, obviously gleeful, "I've been in touch with the local television stations. They tell me the story may go national. You'll be famous. No, no, you won't like that—let me say it differently. Your flower's going to be famous. I'll also have a professional still photographer come by so we can get this thing's formal portrait done. *National Geographic* is interested. I've talked to them."

"Merritt, this is wonderful," she said, running her hand through her hair. "But it's too much. You're the most wonderful man in the—"

"What? What?" he demanded. "I can't hear you. This connection's gone bad. And why are you standing there talking to me? Go take care of your baby. I'll see the film when it's processed. Now go get ready—you're having company from Washington. Happy Birthday."

Laurie hung up the phone and wiped away a tear of happiness. "Did you hear?" she asked Mavis. "The Nature Channel is sending a crew—all the way from Washington—to film the flower opening."

"I heard, I heard," Mavis practically squealed, seizing Laurie by the shoulders.

"And he says all the television stations will send reporters—" She stopped, her smile suddenly dying. "Oh—Mavis. I can't talk to reporters—I'll freeze. You'll have to do it."

Mavis nodded reassuringly. She understood. "I'll do it. But you'll have to let them take *your* picture. I mean, you're the one who got it to bud."

"They can't take my p-picture," Laurie protested. "I'll have been up all night. I'll look terrible."

Mavis smiled and shook her head. "You just turn on a thousand-watt smile like you had a minute ago. You'll look fine."

She reached up and smoothed Laurie's rumpled hair. "You know, Laurie, I'm glad to see you happy again. I've been worried about you the past couple of weeks. Ever since that business with the Remington man."

Laurie's joy suddenly felt hollow. The Remington man. She looked away so that she wouldn't have to meet Mavis's sympathetic brown eyes.

"Laurie—" Mavis's hands tightened on her shoulders. "I didn't mean to bring him up if you don't want to talk about him. It's just that ever since he happened on the scene, you haven't been yourself. I'm worried."

Laurie shook her head. She took a few seconds to force her expression to be calm, even cheery.

She still felt saddened and humiliated by the bet. She had finally called Sophia to confirm it. Sophia had told her not to feel bad, the men were just being men. Laurie found cold comfort in that knowledge.

She forced herself back to the present. "I was worried about the flower. That was all." It was not the truth, but she made herself look Mavis in the eye again. She even managed to smile.

"Are you sure?" Mavis asked, searching her face.

"I'm sure," Laurie said. "He meant nothing to me. I thought the whole thing was actually very funny. Really."

He meant nothing to me, she told herself. *And I meant nothing to him.* Why did those statements fill her with such discontent?

LAURIE FELT as if she were twelve years old again and venturing on her first camping trip. She had changed into her jeans and an oversize gray mock-turtleneck shirt. She'd brought four lawn chairs, one for her and three for the film crew. She hoped there were no more than three of them, for the greenhouse would be far too crowded.

She had two huge thermoses of coffee and a box with a dozen doughnuts. She had a valise with her makeup, toothbrush and a change of clothes, in case she didn't have time to go home in the morning. She had her sketchbook, her colored pencils, her best thirty-five millimeter camera, her second-best camera, and half a dozen rolls of film.

There was a small cooler beside her chair. Mavis had insisted she bring two six-packs of cola, as well as bread, cheese and cold meats for sandwiches for the camera crew.

Mavis had read that making films was a tiresome business and people always had to kill a lot of time. She was worried about the crew wiling away a sleepless night and had even left a deck of cards and magazines so they might amuse themselves.

It was almost midnight. Laurie sat half-curled in the semi-darkness, her camera in her lap. The greenhouse lights were out. She kept the ones in the adjoining shop on but dimmed, so only a faint glow fell through the door. She wanted the plant to remain in natural darkness for as long as possible.

She glanced at her watch. It was almost midnight. The film crew from the Nature Channel should be arriving anytime now. She hoped they wouldn't resent her being there, that she wouldn't be in their way.

She thought she heard a car or truck in the parking lot. She jumped to her feet and looked out. In the shadows she could see a van. Her heart beat faster.

An insistent knock rattled the back door of the shop. She leaped to answer it. She made her way into the shop and unlocked the back door, swinging it open.

She looked, not into a face, but into a broad expanse of shadowy plaid shirt. She turned her gaze up to see the man's face. She had to look a long way up. The man was at least six and a half feet tall.

Hallucination, she told herself numbly, *a trick of light.*

But it was neither hallucination nor trick. The crazy, accelerated beat of her heart assured her of that. The last time she had seen the dark face now frowning above her was in the rain, in Granatelli's parking lot.

Jeff stood there, a large camera case balanced on his shoulder. She opened her mouth to say something but could not.

"Look," he said, his low voice without emotion. "I don't like this any better than you do. But a contract's a contract. This is business, not personal. I'm here to film your flower."

"You?" Laurie asked in horrified astonishment. "No. Not you. There's a crew coming from the Nature Channel."

He made his way past her. He was carrying a tripod and light case.

"Mind if I put some light on the subject?" he asked sardonically. "We'll need light, you know. It's one of the peculiarities of film."

She hurried to the switch and flicked on the greenhouse lights. They blazed into life. She and Jeff stood blinking at each other.

"Where are the—people from the Nature Channel?" she asked, staring up at him.

"I'm the people from the Nature Channel," he replied, bearing the camera into the greenhouse. "Is this your wonderful plant? It looks like a banana tree."

"That *is* a banana tree. *This* is the plant that's blooming." She pointed at the sorcerer's flower.

He gave a derisive snort. "Looks like a cactus with an identity crisis." With an expert movement, he set up the tripod.

She put her hands on her hips, watching his dark, impassive face. "Explain this. You can't be from the Nature Channel. They're in Washington. And they're sending a crew—"

"I'm the crew," he said shortly, locking the camera in place on the tripod. "You think they'd send somebody all the way from Washington for what's probably going to amount to twenty seconds of film? This is the kind of job they hire out. And in this area, I'm the man they hire."

"You?" she almost wailed. "You're the whole crew?"

He turned, glowering down at her. "I know my stuff. I can handle this. Who told you a *crew* was coming? This isn't the chariot race from *Ben Hur*. It's one flower—no big deal."

Laurie nibbled worriedly at the inside of her lower lip, trying to think. Had Uncle Merritt actually said a film *crew* was coming? She had been so excited she honestly could not remember.

"You mean," she said, "that they called you up from Washington and gave you this job?"

He put his hands on his hips, mirroring her unhappy stance. "Right."

"Did my uncle know you'd be involved in this?"

"I don't know who your uncle is or why he'd care."

Laurie passed her hand over her forehead in frustration. Uncle Merritt had made some kind of arrangement with the Nature Channel. He probably knew as little as she did about how a TV network operated. He would have no idea that it would hire local talent. Or that the local talent might be the man Laurie had clashed with so violently.

She looked up at him again, distrustful and displeased. "Well, you knew it was me you were getting involved with. Why didn't you refuse the job?"

He looked, if possible, less happy than she did. "I told you. I have a contract with these people. I do a lot of their work in this region. If you don't like it, maybe you should just go home and stay out of my way."

Laurie bristled. "It's my shop, my greenhouse and my plant. I've waited years for this. I'm staying."

"Suit yourself," he said, and gave her the briefest of glances. The ice in his look should have shriveled every plant in the greenhouse.

Chapter Six

"LIGHTS WON'T HURT this . . . thing, will they?" Jeff asked, setting up a light stand.

"They shouldn't." Laurie sat curled in her chair again, arms crossed. She struggled to keep her voice as businesslike as his.

She was certain that lights wouldn't throw the plant off schedule; it should respond to the deep-set natural rhythms of night and day. To be on the safe side, she had kept it in natural light until the last possible moment.

He made a final adjustment to the camera. He looked, obviously unimpressed, at the sorcerer's flower, now bathed in light.

He sat down in a lawn chair. He crossed his long legs and put his hands behind his head. He stifled a yawn, then glanced at Laurie's hoard of supplies.

"What were you expecting, an army?"

She snuggled more deeply into her chair, as if she could protect herself by doing so. She could think of nothing to say, so remained silent.

He stifled another yawn. "I see. Not talking, as usual. But I forgot, print is your chosen media. Taken out any good ads lately?"

Her body stiffened. "If you're talking about that ad saying I never agreed to go out with you—"

"I don't have to talk about it. All my friends are. You've given them hours of pleasure, at my expense. Congratulations."

She curled more tightly in her chair and raised her chin. "You got—what you deserved. I wasn't going to let you win your silly—bet."

He shrugged and stared up at the ceiling, bored. "You could have saved your money. The bet was called off."

She sat up straight. "What do you mean, off?"

He kept staring at the ceiling. "Off. As in canceled, withdrawn, kaput. Aldo started feeling guilty. He confessed that Vinnie blabbed to Sophia. That she told you. So the bet's void. You played me along the whole time. You knew what was happening."

"I did not," Laurie said indignantly. "People kept warning me about you—but I never knew why. I didn't know there was a—bet. I just knew that you were—were fishy."

"Fishy." Contempt vibrated in his voice. He cast her a black look. "Fishy."

"Yes," she countered, meeting his eyes. "You were. You were—chasing all the women there."

"I was not 'chasing all the women there,'" he said, imitating her prim tone. "Just the three most impossible ones."

"It was an insulting thing to do. It was—demeaning."

"Right," he said. He sat up straight in his chair, jabbing his thumb toward his chest. "And I'm the one who got demeaned most." He rolled his eyes heavenward. "I never spent three worse nights in my life."

"Ha," sneered Laurie.

"It's true," he answered, disgust in his voice. "I went out with Suzanne Carrington, who never shuts up. I went out with Tammy Farentino, who never lets up. She's always trying to smolder. It's like taking out a charcoal briquette, for God's sake. And then *you.*"

"You did not," Laurie said with great deliberation and disdain, "take me *out.*"

"Yes," he said, "I seem to have read that in the paper. Look, I didn't mean to hurt your feelings. And I did apologize. You, as I recall, told me to sit on it. Then to top it off, you took out that damned ad. Well, great. By that time the bet was already off, and I looked like the biggest fool in St. Louis. It made my day."

Laurie squirmed and turned her gaze from his. "I'm supposed to worry about—about *your* sensibilities? You lied to three women. You led them on. You deceived them, and I'm supposed—supposed to sympathize with you?"

"No. I didn't want to deceive anybody. I got hooked into this stupid bet, and I was trying to save my friend. He'd bet this 1968 Mustang engine—"

Laurie's head snapped back to face him again. She narrowed her eyes in disbelief. "You went through all that—for a car engine? You really are—despicable."

His eyes flashed. "I'm a man, damn it."

"It's the same thing," she said, and turned from him again.

"So that's your problem," he accused. "You hate men."

"I don't hate—men. I was just—warned about you. B-by my cousin, even. And she certainly didn't know anything about your—bet. So just leave me alone. Aren't you supposed to—be filming? Why don't you get to work?"

"I am working," he practically snarled. "The camera's automatic. Every ten minutes it takes a frame of film. I stay here to make sure *it* keeps working.... But why should anybody warn you about me? All I did was ask you out. That's all I did—I asked three women out. I didn't ask for anything else, except to buy them dinner. Okay, a friendly good-night kiss— that's all. The only reason I did it was to help my friend, because he made a bet he couldn't afford to lose. I suppose friendship's a sin in your book, too. And who's your cousin, anyway? I don't even know your cousin."

She gave him the coolest of her cool looks. "My cousin Shirley Spenser. She told me all—about you."

He rose from his chair as if too restless to stay in one place. "Shirley Spenser?" he asked, impatience in his face and his voice. He hooked his thumbs into the back pockets of his jeans and frowned. "Shirley Spenser?"

Laurie stared up at him in challenge. He was so tall and wide of shoulder that the little greenhouse seemed crowded by too much height, too much virility. The air almost vibrated with his presence.

"My cousin Shirley went to college with you," she said between her teeth. "She told me how you treated her friend, Mary Ellen Pfieffer. You were a—rat."

She thought he paled slightly. "Mary Ellen Pfieffer?" He shook his head in disbelief. "Oh, no. Your cousin's *that* Shirley?"

"Yes," Laurie said, and reached down to open the cooler. She needed action, any kind of action, to ease the tension she felt. "Why'd you ruin that poor Pfieffer girl's life? Did somebody—bet you a set of tires you could do it?"

Just as her fingers closed around a can of cola, his hand grasped her wrist. He knelt before her, his eyes suddenly level with hers.

His nearness, the feel of his hand against her bare flesh, stunned her. His dark gaze riveted her with its intensity. "Don't t-touch me," she stuttered.

"I didn't ruin Mary Ellen Pfieffer's life. She ruined it herself." His brows lowered in anger. "I remember your cousin. When Mary Ellen wasn't calling me up, *she* was. She was nosy, she was pushy, and she decided to make my life her business."

"Now listen here—" Laurie tried to draw her hand away.

He held it firmly, bringing his face closer to hers. "No. You listen. I don't know what your cousin told you, but Mary Ellen Pfieffer was an accident waiting to happen. She decided that she wanted to be tragically in love with somebody, and somehow I got elected. I took her out twice. *Twice.* I didn't have time to get involved with anybody. I was on a basketball scholarship. I never took anybody out more than twice—I told her that. Then she started hounding me. I didn't ruin her life, she was addicted to melodrama. So, unfortunately, was your cousin. Do you understand that?"

He grasped her wrist tightly, but Laurie was conscious that he wasn't trying to hurt her, only to make her listen. His indignation was so intent, his sincerity so obvious, that an unpleasant and sickening knot formed in her stomach.

She understood. Shirley was bossy and opinionated, and she did love to take charge of people's lives. She liked drama and fuss, and she hated being ignored. Yet it had hardly occurred to Laurie to question her version of the story about Mary Ellen Pfieffer. She hadn't questioned it because she wanted to believe the worst of Jeff Remington, and, unfairly, she had.

He seemed to become conscious that he was touching her and he released her hand. But he kept staring into her eyes. "Laurie, I mean it. There are people in the world like Mary Ellen. I never did anything to hurt her except tell her that I wasn't ready to get involved. I had grades to keep up and basketball, too. I was eighteen years old, for crying out loud. I never led her on, I swear. She practically drove me crazy."

She didn't know what to say. Concern mingled with resentment on his handsome face, and she noticed for the first time that sensitivity could mark the curve of his mouth.

She swallowed and looked away.

"Okay," he said, standing, "don't believe me. But it's not as if you're Miss Compassion yourself. You broke a few hearts. And not by accident. Do you remember what you did to Alexander Nevins?"

He turned his back to her and bent to check the camera. He squinted through the eyepiece. The bud had opened more widely; edges of crimson were starting to emerge.

"What?" Her voice sounded slightly strangled.

He turned to face her again. She was staring at him, the look on her face pained.

He leaned against the glass wall and crossed his arms, his straight brows lowered in a disapproving frown. "Alexander Nevins. He told me about your prince, too. Even royalty's not good enough for you. But I hear His Royal Highness sent you this plant."

He tilted his head toward the sorcerer's flower. "Is that why you cultivated the princely friendship? This thing is worth its weight in gold, I hear. You used your...attractions...wisely."

"The p-prince was a friend," Laurie sputtered. "I wasn't trying to get anything from him. We were in school together. In—Italy. We were both—foreigners, and he was very, very— shy. And I made—friends with him. That was—*all.*"

"He proposed." Jeff cocked an eyebrow, and his mouth took on a skeptical slant.

"He was seventeen—for heaven's sake," Laurie said. She rose and began to pace down the narrow aisle between the flats of houseplants. "I was older—I was American—I tried to be kind, and he got a crush on me. He was supposed to go home and get married—he had to marry somebody—and he asked me—b-because he liked me. B-because we could talk. B-because we were f-friends."

She turned to see if he believed her. People never understood about the prince. They thought it was some glamorous romance in which she had broken a noble heart. It was anything but that. His feelings for her were those of a lonely schoolboy and she had never exploited them. When he had sent the plant to her, she had been astounded and touched.

She looked across the little room at Jeff. His stare was almost burning, his frown more intent. She knew he didn't believe her.

She shrugged helplessly. "Oh, just f-f-forget it," she said in frustration. She was ashamed that she had let him make her stutter so badly, and she didn't want to look at him any longer.

She stared at the plant instead. A wealth of crimson petals was beginning to spill from the bud.

"Say that again," he ordered, his low voice lower than usual. "Say it again—'just forget it.'"

She refused to look at him. "No."

"Say it."

"No."

There was a long moment of silence. She thought she could almost hear her heart beating.

"That's why you'd never talk to me, isn't it?"

His question hung ominously in the air. She refused to answer. She stared harder at the plant. She thought she saw the tip of one of the golden petals among the scarlet ones.

"Laurie, look at me. Look at me and talk to me. You stutter, don't you?"

She licked her lips and didn't answer. She kept her attention focused on the bud. She was sure she could see a bit of gold. She stepped toward the lawn chair to get her camera.

"Laurie?" He blocked her way. He put his hands on her shoulders. She clenched her teeth and forced herself to look up at him. She had seen him angry, mocking, defensive, even guilty, but she had never seen his face so serious.

"That's it, isn't it?" he asked, looking into her eyes. "That's why you wouldn't talk. It's why you sound so prim and perfect when you do. My God. You cover it up so well I didn't realize you stutter."

The touch of his hands sent flames shooting through her. She moved away from him in confusion. She bent and picked up the camera. Once more she refused to meet his eyes. "All right. So I—stutter. Now you have—something else to laugh at."

She tried to adjust the light dial of the camera. Her hands shook.

He stepped to her. He took the camera from her and made the adjustment himself. When he handed it back, his fingers grazed hers. Even that slight a contact sent too much emotion coursing through her. He stared into her eyes, no trace of derision in his face. His voice was husky. "Look, it's easy to get the wrong impression about you."

She aimed at the bud and clicked the shutter. She knew the shot was a bad one, so she tried again. "Tell me something I don't know," she said bitterly.

"Laurie—I thought you were the biggest snob in St. Louis. Why didn't you tell me?"

"I don't tell—anybody," she said fiercely.

"Well, people are bound to misunderstand. Here you are, this beautiful girl, the society background—"

"I'm not—beautiful," she said, aiming the camera at the flower again. "And I'm not 'society.' I work for a living—just like you."

"Laurie, please. Look at me."

"No."

"Yes."

He moved between her and the bud. He took the camera from her and set it on one of the plant tables. He took her chin between his thumb and forefinger. "Yes," he said again.

She looked up at him, tears of anger and defeat blurring her vision. She blinked them back but one spilled over and began its slow descent down her cheek. He knew her secret, and it made her feel naked before him.

He wiped the tear away with his knuckles, a gentle movement. "I never would—I never could—I never meant to cause you pain. I always had this feeling that there was somebody behind that cool facade that I couldn't see. That you wouldn't let me see. Why be ashamed?"

She set her jaw. His touch was so tender that it filled her with more turmoil than she could bear. A man such as he—so handsome, so confident, so sure of his every word—could never understand.

She shook her head. "You don't know what it's like to—be different."

He surprised her with a half-bitter laugh. "Come here," he said, taking her hand. He led her back to the chairs, made her sit. He kept hold of her hand, taking it in both of his. His fingers were warm and powerful as he squeezed hers.

"Let me tell you about being different," he said, watching her face. "Different is being six foot six when you're fourteen years old. Different is being the only kid on the Hill with a non-Italian name and divorced parents. Different is spending your adult life hearing people ask, 'How's the weather up there?' I understand *different*. And what I came to understand is that that's all it is—just different. Nothing bad about it. Nothing wrong. Nothing shameful."

Kind, he seemed far more dangerous than he ever had cruel. She drew her hand away, her stomach feeling full of butterflies and bumblebees again. "Shouldn't you check that camera or something?" she asked, her voice shaky.

"The camera's fine." He leaned forward, his elbows on his knees. "And so are you. Trust me."

She shrugged, not knowing how to take his statement. Unconsciously she rubbed the hand that he had held. It tingled as if electricity had jolted through it. "Did you—did you really feel different when you were growing up?"

He shook his head ruefully. He gave her a smile that made her heart do a drunken little dance. "My grandmother started having terrible fights with bus drivers when I was about eight. They'd say, 'That kid's twelve years old. Pay adult fare for him.' And my grandmother'd say, 'Look at him! He's not old—he's just tall. *Volete l'indirizzo di un bravo oculista, lei?* You want directions to the eye doctor?' And believe me, she could *yell.*"

Laurie smiled.

"Once, in high school, I asked this girl out. I wanted to make a good impression on her, so when I went to meet her parents, I was on my best behavior. Except, right after I shook hands with her father, I turned around and walked smack into this bird cage hanging there. So hard I bloodied my nose. Do you know how to impress a girl? Step one—don't bleed on her parakeet."

"You didn't," Laurie said, smiling in spite of herself.

"I've still got the scar." He pointed to a small white mark on the bridge of his nose. "I was so embarrassed I could hardly talk to her for the rest of the night."

Laurie nodded. "I know what that's like."

His dark eyes became more intent still. "Good grief," he said softly. "That's what happened with Alexander, isn't it? You were too embarrassed to talk to him."

She bit her lip and nodded again. "Don't tell me he still remembers?" she said. "I couldn't stand that." She put her head in her hands, chagrined.

"He'd probably just like to know the reason," Jeff told her. "Hey, he doesn't hate you. He still thinks a lot of you."

Laurie shook her head miserably. "Oh, no. I'll write him a note or something. I never thought he'd remember. I guess I didn't want to think about it. I tried *not* to think of it. Oh, how awful."

Jeff looked at her, an odd pain cramping his chest. He had an inexplicable impulse to smooth her honey-brown hair. But he forced his hands to stay still. "I'd say you're taking this a lot harder than he is," he said gruffly. "It's not like he never recovered."

Laurie raised her face. Its paleness was etched with strain. "He was such a nice boy. But—but things like that happened when I was in school here. My parents had just divorced and my mother'd just moved us—back here. I don't think I'd ever been so unhappy. Then Alexander asked me out, and all of a sudden, I knew I couldn't talk. I couldn't stand it. So I just turned and ran away. I felt terrible for weeks. *Weeks.* I'm so sorry he still remembers. Maybe I'll send him a plant and an apology."

"I'm sure a note would be more than enough," said Jeff, his voice slightly harsh. He suddenly didn't like the idea of her sending presents to Alexander. Maybe she'd be attracted to someone like him—even tempered, unfailingly kind and too innocent to ever be dishonest. He didn't like that idea, either.

A silence fell between them. Laurie didn't know what to say. She looked at Jeff and then they both glanced away.

"So," he said, and shrugged nonchalantly. "So. But you must have outgrown some of the shyness. You went off to college and met the prince...."

"And you went off to college and—became a—basketball hero."

He shook his head. "Not a hero. I knew I'd never make the pros. I figured I'd teach. But then I fell into video, taping things for a class, and ended up doing this."

"I did the same thing," she said softly. "I majored in design. But I'd always loved—plants and—flowers, so decided to try to combine it all."

"So." He cleared his throat. "So here we are."

"Yes," she replied, lacing her fingers together in her lap and staring down at them. "Here we are."

This is getting awkward, Laurie thought. *I like him. But I can't like him. What if he's lying, or being nice, even now, for some reason?*

"So," he said. "Tell me about your plant. The news director from the Nature Channel told me a little. It's only supposed to bloom once every hundred years?"

She shook her head and rose, going to look at the bud. The flower was almost half-open now. She wanted to touch it but didn't want to take a chance of ruining a frame of Jeff's film. "They say every hundred years. That's just one of the legends. Really it's closer to seventy-five years. Once in a lifetime. And this—part" she gestured toward the heart-shaped red petals spilling from the bud "—this will be like a cascade. It'll be surrounded by more—petals, like a lion's mane, all yellow and gold. And then there'll be more still, like a wreath of—petals, red ones, around the whole thing. I've seen pictures. It's—beautiful. No wonder people say it's magic."

"I could get to like it," he said, looking up at her.

She smiled. "The flower?"

"No." His eyes moved up and down her body, resting again on her face. "The way you talk."

She shook her head. "Don't say things like—that."

"Why not?"

"You're just trying to make up for what happened—before."

A muscle worked in his jaw. "Won't you ever forgive me for that?" He kept his eyes fastened on hers.

Nervously she thrust her hands into the pockets of her jeans. "You seem like you might actually—be a nice man. But—but you agreed to do something to me that wasn't very nice."

"It makes no difference that I did it for a friend?"

"You did it for a car engine." She shook her head again.

"My friend Gary Castiglione *loves* that engine. I didn't want him to lose it. He's a good friend."

"He must be," she said.

"Look." His tone was grim. "When I was in California, going to film school, my grandmother got sick. Gary's the one who phoned and broke the news. He also wired me money to get home and met me at the airport. When they told me she was dying, he came to the hospital with me, just so I'd have somebody with me afterward. When she died he was a pallbearer. And after they buried her, he took me out and bought me just enough drinks to numb the pain. He never touched a drop himself, and then he drove me home."

He took a deep breath, laced his fingers together and cracked his knuckles. "He knew I didn't have any relatives left in St.

Louis. So before I went back to California, he said, 'From now on, when you come home, my house is your house.' When I did come back, to start my business, that's how it was. I lived with him for three months. He wouldn't take a dime. All right, so he made a stupid bet. But he's my friend. And if it helps, I can promise you I'd never do anything like it again. Not after this . . . mess.''

"All right," Laurie said, spreading her hands in a helpless gesture. "You make it sound almost—almost noble. But—but I suppose I'll always wonder if any of this is true. Or if it's just—more lies."

"Look," he said again, the muscle jumping in his jaw, "I'm not a good liar. You saw that the night at Granatelli's. I had the feeling all along that you could see through me. And if I'd wanted to get you, I'd have struck back after you put that ad in the paper."

"Struck back?" She didn't understand.

"Yes," he said, and bitterness resonated in his voice. "It was embarrassing, damn it. My first thought was get back at her. Take out an ad myself. 'To Whom It May Concern—I never *wanted* a date with Laurie Chase-Spenser. I do not desire dates with snobs.'"

Horrified, Laurie paled. "You would have done that?" It would have humiliated her so deeply she would have wanted to hide for months.

"No," he said, almost savagely. "That's the point. I wouldn't have. I didn't. It was too rotten. I'd put you through enough. You wouldn't accept my apology, so I figured the only decent thing I could do was leave you alone. I suppose it still is."

Once more Laurie didn't know what to say, so she said nothing. Moodily she moved to her chair and sat down. The awkward silence came over the room again, settling between them like a thick wall.

Jeff stood. He checked the movie camera. The flower had opened more widely. It was more exotic than any orchid he'd ever seen. A heady perfume was starting to fill the room. It was almost intoxicating and it made him restless.

He paced to the rear of the greenhouse, glancing back at Laurie. In her jeans and oversize shirt, she didn't look anything like the prim and perfect woman he'd met at the wedding. She looked like a flower herself, fresh faced and delicate.

He clamped his jaw shut, so tightly his teeth almost ground. He'd misjudged her badly. And he'd practically forced her to misjudge him. Under different circumstances, if he hadn't botched things so badly, who knew what might have happened between them?

Nothing, he told himself cynically. Nothing would have happened. They had nothing in common.

He'd do his job, he'd do it well, then he'd be on his way. He'd be out of her life and she'd be out of his. Just like he'd told her, he'd leave her alone. She hadn't objected to the idea.

He looked at his watch. It was almost three in the morning. Suddenly it seemed like several aeons until the sun would rise. And here he was, stuck alone with her until then.

He walked around the table, wishing he could escape the drugging perfume of the flower. The silence weighed down oppressively, and he began to whistle softly.

Laurie whirled in her chair to face him, her eyes wide.

He stopped whistling, stuck his hands in his pockets and shrugged. "What's the matter?" Irony edged his voice. "Is it bad luck to whistle in a greenhouse?"

Her gray eyes were still wide. "That song," she breathed. "That song—"

"What about it?"

"It's 'The Queen of Connemara.'"

He studied her and frowned slightly. She looked truly startled, almost frightened. Her beautiful lips were slightly parted.

He shrugged again. "It's my favorite song."

"Oh," Laurie said, and looked somehow embarrassed. "It's mine, too. What a—coincidence. Not many people know it."

He strolled toward her, trying to seem nonchalant, but he kept his gaze on those soft, parted lips. "It's off my favorite album," he said casually. "Makem and Clancy, *We've Come a Long Way.*"

Laurie's eyes grew rounder still. "That's *my* favorite album. Do you really like it?"

He sat down beside her, staring at her in disbelief. "I've got every album they ever made. Together and separately. Do you like Irish music? Scottish music?"

"Oh," Laurie said, nodding passionately, "I adore it."

"Me, too." He frowned in amazement. "Who are your favorite groups?"

"Well . . ." She sat straighter and started to count on her fingers. "There's Silly Wizard."

He nodded. "They're great."

"And Capercaillie."

"Of course."

"The Chieftains."

"Absolutely."

"And Steeleye Span."

"That's amazing," Jeff said, shaking his head. "I never find anybody who's even *heard* of these groups."

"I know," Laurie agreed softly.

Jeff realized he was looking into her eyes and she was looking into his. Her lips were trembling slightly, the way they did when she got excited or emotional over something. He glanced away.

"Are you telling the truth?" she asked softly. "This isn't some sort of trick?"

He turned back to her. Once more he damned the bet and everybody who had dragged him into it, even Gary. Would this woman never believe him? "I wouldn't kid about something like that. Try me. Name a song. By one of the groups you mentioned. Any song."

Laurie studied him. He looked sincere, even darkly indignant. She licked her lips. "All right." She thought a moment. "'The Loch Tay Boat Song.'"

The serious look was back on his face, and somehow it made him seem more handsome than ever. "All right," he said. "You asked for it." He kept his dark eyes fixed on her wary ones. Then he began to sing in a husky baritone:

"When I've done my work of day,
And I row my boat away
Cross the waters of Loch Tay,
And evening light is falling..."

Laurie listened, entranced. He had a fine voice, strong and expressive, and the song was one of her favorites.

"Come on," he said. "If you know so much, join in."

He gave her that sideways smile he had, and Laurie smiled back. Tentatively at first, then with more assurance, she joined her voice to his. Hers was a clear alto, glancing and bright.

"And I'd give the world to know
If she means to let me go
As I sing her praise beneath the stars."

They looked at each other. She smiled. They had sounded good together. "I don't—stutter when I sing. It's strange."

He smiled back. "Then it's obvious. You should sing more. Do you know 'Red-haired Mary'?"

She nodded and they began. It was a sassy, silly, fast-paced song. He followed it with a sassier, sillier, faster one, "Mary Mack." Laurie was almost breathless when they finished.

The flower was three-quarters open.

Its outer ring of scarlet petals was emerging, a bright corona like red flame. The flower was not a large one; it was, perhaps, no bigger than Laurie's hand. But its colors were as rich as jewels, its perfume so sweet it made her half-giddy with pleasure.

She stood and picked up her camera. She took a series of shots from different angles. Jeff had gotten to his feet, as well, and was double-checking the movie camera.

"It's working all right?" she asked, suddenly feeling self-conscious again. She believed him about the music. He loved the same songs as she did, loved them deeply.

"Seems to be." He straightened and stared down at her. "When I took this assignment, I thought it'd be a real yawn," he said. "Time-lapse isn't my favorite sort of shoot. Too long.

Too mechanical. But your flower—'' he nodded toward the blooming plant ''—is worth staying up all night for.''

She smiled shyly, pleased.

''What's it called? The sorcerer's plant?''

''The sorcerer's flower.''

She realized that she was gazing up at him a little too raptly. She moved back to her chair. To occupy herself, she poured them each a cup of coffee.

''Why?'' he asked, sitting beside her. Once more his hand grazed hers when he took the cup. Once more his touch sent a frisson of awareness through her. ''Is it supposed to be magic or something?''

''There are—stories,'' she said vaguely.

''What kind?'' He took a long drink of coffee, regarding her over the rim of his cup.

She made a dismissive gesture. ''Just—legends.''

''Hey, it's only three-thirty. We may have a couple more hours here. You might as well tell me.''

She shook her head. ''They're just folktales.'' She didn't want to discuss them with him.

''I like folktales,'' he said. He drained the last of his coffee and set down the cup. ''I minored in literature in college. Tell me some folktales.'' He crossed his legs and stretched out, obviously waiting for the story to begin.

She looked at him in new puzzlement. ''*You* minored in literature?''

He nodded. ''What's wrong with that?''

''Nothing,'' she said, feeling perplexed again. ''I did, too. I thought you'd study—sports or something.''

He smiled his crooked smile. ''I majored in art and minored in lit. Got introduced to video in a photography class.''

''That's—strange,'' Laurie said, shaking her head. ''I majored in art, too—design.''

An odd expression crossed his face. ''We had the same interests. Identical.''

''Mmm,'' said Laurie, musing on it. It did seem a bit eerie.

''So tell me the legends about your plant.''

She stared into her coffee cup. "Well, they say it has— powers."

"Powers?" he repeated, irony in his voice.

She nodded, staring into the black depths of her coffee. "The seeds are supposed to make you wise. But the seeds are so rare maybe that's a joke. You know, that's why there are so f-few wise people in the world—because there are so few seeds."

"That's why they call it the sorcerer's flower?"

She could feel the power of his eyes on her, almost as if his gaze were tugging the truth out of her. "No." She rose again, restless. She walked to the flower and stared at its red and gold petals.

"Once there was a—princess who swore she'd never marry. And there was a young knight—who loved her. So he went to a sorcerer. And the sorcerer gave him the—plant, and he said, 'Take it to her. Tell her it's about to bloom, but it won't bloom unless you're—by her side.' So he did."

Laurie hesitated, fearing she had sounded too caught up in this unlikely fairy tale.

The silence lasted only a moment. "And?" Jeff asked quietly. As always, his voice sent pleasurable shivers through her. "Did she let her guard down? Did she find she could care for him in spite of all her vows?"

She tried to keep her voice matter-of-fact, because she was sure that too much emotion trembled in it. "They stayed together that night, watching it open. And—they fell in love." She snapped a picture from another angle. "It's just a story. A silly story."

"So is the spell still supposed to work?" he asked. "Does it still bewitch reluctant maidens?"

Laurie shook her head, dismayed at her embarrassment. "They say—" She shrugged. "They say if two—people watch it—blossom, they're supposed to find true love. They'll never grow tired of each other—because they're so—right together. So perfect." Again she feared her voice told too much. It always did.

He said nothing. She moved and photographed the flower from still another angle. "Which is—probably a joke, too. Don't you think? I mean, people never find somebody—perfect for them. I guess that's how you think when your parents are divorced. You don't think about finding—perfect love."

She took a deep breath as she heard the chair scuff slightly against the floor and knew he had risen from it. She felt rather than heard him coming toward her, then sensed him standing behind her, looking at the plant over her shoulder.

"Well," she said, wishing she'd never told the stupid tale. "Don't you think so? That it's just—wishful thinking?"

"I wasn't thinking about the story," he said in a low voice. "I was thinking about something a poet said once." He put a hand on her shoulder. Its warmth and power radiated through her.

"A poet?" she said. Her own voice was almost a whisper.

"Yes," he murmured, so close that his breath fanned her neck. "You make me think of poetry. And stories of wonder, like the *Arabian Nights*."

Laurie couldn't help it. She quivered slightly. "I don't know what you mean," she said, almost afraid to breathe.

Jeff was toying with a tendril of her hair now, winding it slowly around his finger. "When you move among your flowers, you make me think of poetry."

Laurie didn't know how to change the subject. Everything was suddenly too intimate—his voice, his words, his touch. If things went any further, she sensed there would be no turning back.

"So—what do you think of the folktales?" she asked in a choked voice. "Don't you think they're jokes, in a way? I think they start out as jokes or explanations and then become tradition. What do you think?" By the time she finished her speech she had trouble catching her breath.

He bent down and kissed her neck, the way he had the first time she met him. "'I know how flowers think,'" he said softly.

"What?" Her knees trembled slightly.

"It's the line you made me think of," he said, and kissed her neck again. " 'I know how flowers think.' "

"What's that mean?" she asked, her heart trying to run away but finding it had no place to go. "I don't think I understand."

He turned her to face him. "That people can think too much. Question too much, fear too much. We both thought about each other, and we found out what other people thought. But all of it was wrong. We should have paid attention to what we felt. Flowers don't think. They just . . . flower."

"I—I don't think—I didn't mean to tell you that story so that you'd think—"

"I hardly heard the story, Laurie. Mostly I heard your voice. The wonder in it. Hardly anybody our age still has the gift of wonder. You do. Wonder and feeling, too. Maybe that's why you can create such beauty. And be so beautiful."

He bent and kissed her.

He kissed her a long time. She wound her arms around his neck. He wrapped around her like sunshine. He held her fast, like the earth. He fed something deep within her, as if he were the water of life.

He drew back. "Don't worry," he said. "This isn't happening because some flower is supposed to be magic. It's just happening. Magic doesn't scare me—what scares me is we almost lost this chance."

She looked up at him. And she knew she was falling in love with him, was already in love with him, more than a little. She supposed she had known it from the first time she'd wheeled around and seen him standing there, tall, with mockery in his eyes and a smile on his lips.

He looked down at her. He knew, too. Had half suspected it from the first. He'd begun to wonder from the instant those gray eyes had flashed up at him in church.

He knew, as well, that they were both rational people, and that no legend, no magic, no strange powers had brought them together, a chain of circumstances had. Circumstances had then almost torn them apart but had somehow given them one more chance. For this he was infinitely grateful. He believed he would be grateful the rest of his life.

The first pink rays of the sun were glowing over the tops of the buildings. They looked into each other's eyes again.

No, he told himself, it wasn't magic, it was luck. But what luck. What incredible luck. He bent and kissed her again.

"I don't think it's the flower that's magic," he said against her lips. "I think it's love itself."

And Laurie, who didn't believe in superstitions, thought the same thing: *How lucky we are. How wonderful that we've found each other, in spite of everything.*

The sun rose a little higher, sent its rosy beams a little farther. She kissed him back.

The scent of perfume surrounded them, dizzying and sweet as the flower opened to a new morning.

Marry-Go-Round

ANNE McALLISTER

A Note from Anne McAllister

Weddings are tricky propositions. Everyone involved seems to have an agenda. It's never just the decision of the bride and groom. You like daisies; your mother likes dahlias. You want to use your own car; your mother-in-law believes in chauffeured limousines. Long dress or short, morning suits or jeans, a sit-down dinner or canapés and cake. The list of potential disagreements goes on and on.

I'm happy to tell you that weddings in books aren't like that. When Bethany said, "How about this dress?", we all said, "Great." When Bobby suggested bridesmaids in floppy hats, no one demurred. When Barbara told us no matter what Grandmother Hoffmann thought, Russ was walking Diane down the aisle, we all agreed. When I said that Annie, my bridesmaid, had been married 119 times, no one uttered a word.

There are several morals that can be drawn from this stunning display of good-natured equanimity: (1) Don't get married, write books; (2) Marry into writers' families and hope they are as well behaved in real life as they are on paper; (3) Elope.

Seriously, I have enjoyed writing about Jared and Annie here, and about Nick and Diane in my American Romance, *I Thee Wed,* for the opportunity to look again at marriage. French theologian Pierre Teilhard de Chardin says that "union differentiates." In other words, by joining together, two beings do not lose their individuality, but become more themselves. A good marriage, I think, proves that axiom. It helps each person become more the person he or she is meant to be.

So I wish for Nick and Diane and for Jared and Annie, as well as for all of you who choose or who have already chosen to wed, just such a marriage—one filled with challenge and love.

All the best,

Anne

Chapter One

"ALWAYS A BRIDE, never a bridesmaid" had recently been the story of Annie D'Angelo's life. In the last four months she had got married one hundred and nineteen times. Six days a week. Twice on Saturdays.

She knew the wedding service backward and forward. She'd been through two mothers, three caterers, four dresses and five grooms. She could take vows in her sleep.

But her best friends, Diane Bauer and Nick Granatelli, were taking those vows for real in just two days—and *meaning* them.

It gave Annie, whose marriages had so far been off-off-Broadway productions, not real-life commitments, pause for thought.

Richer, poorer. Sickness, health. Till death did them part. Pretty awesome when you came right down to it, when the words weren't just lines in a play but actual honest-to-God promises.

Marriage—real marriage—despite how often one pretended to do it, was a daunting prospect. One that Annie had rejected early on for herself.

"Born to the stage," she'd told everyone from the time she had tap-danced her way across the stage at St. Catherine's grade school in suburban Chicago at the age of seven. And she'd meant it. Every word.

For Annie it was enough to do it seven times a week for laughs. She had better, more important things to do with her life.

Other people ought to, too, she thought. And most of her friends seemed to. In fact, until Nick had come home that morning in January and announced that he and Diane were taking the plunge, Annie had expected things would simply go on forever the way they were.

Then Nick had said, "We're getting married in June in St. Louis. We want you to be there. Diane wants you to be a bridesmaid."

Annie had laughed because until that point she'd always been the bride.

But regardless of what he'd said back in January it hadn't seemed real. Nothing had changed. Yet.

But now, getting off the plane, her bridesmaid dress folded into the garment bag slung over her arm, and being met by the normally quiet Diane chattering about how she and Nick could hardly wait for it all to be over so they could be "married at last," Annie felt it was becoming more real by the minute.

"I can't believe my mother," Diane was saying. "She's literally thrown herself into this as if it were her wedding, not mine. And my grandmother..." She shook her head, despairing.

"Maybe you should call the whole thing off," Annie suggested, only half-kidding.

Diane stared at her. "You're joking."

She wasn't, really. But obviously Diane thought she was, so Annie laughed. "Stop worrying. You'll survive. Two days more, that's all, and you'll have Nick to yourself. Piece of cake."

Diane's hands fluttered. "I hope. But it's turning into the wedding that ate St. Louis. You'd never believe all the rigmarole. Showers, parties, long-lost relatives. My dad is here, did I tell you?" Her voice was eager, but Annie saw the apprehension in her eyes.

She nodded, knowing the risk Diane had taken. "Pretty daring of you, wasn't it, asking him?"

"It's my wedding. I'll ask whoever I want." And the sudden steel in Diane's voice told Annie that, despite all the combined Bauer-Granatelli plots, plans and machinations, her friend would certainly survive.

She gave Diane a quick hug and grinned. "So, tell me, who else is coming?"

But she was only half attending as Diane chattered their way toward the baggage claim. She didn't know any of Diane's high school friends. She'd never met her cousin, Lisa. She'd met more Granatellis than the world had a right to, and she could never keep them straight.

" . . . and Jared, of course." Diane tossed the name casually over her shoulder as she walked, just as if she weren't lobbing a hand grenade at her dearest friend.

Annie stopped dead, smack in the middle of the B concourse in Lambert St. Louis International Airport.

Jared? *Jared Flynn*. The very sound of his name made her stomach clench, her palms sweat.

"What about Jared?" Her normally strong actress's voice was a mere echo of its normal self.

Diane turned, her smile self-conscious and fading now as she looked into Annie's suddenly pale face. She gave an awkward shrug and a small worried laugh. "Oh, Annie, Nick said I shouldn't even tell you. But I thought it wasn't fair. I thought . . ." She waved her hands ineffectually.

Annie still hadn't moved an inch. "Tell me what?" The look she gave Diane would, in the past, have reduced her friend to tears.

But this Diane didn't as much as whimper. Instead she took a deep breath and squared her shoulders. "Jared's coming, Annie. I just told you."

Around them passengers surged, bumping and jostling, shooting them irritated glances, muttering apologies. The heavy muted thrum of jet engines reverberated in their ears.

Annie stared, then slowly shook her head, unwilling, unable to believe it. "Don't make me laugh. Jared Flynn? The man staring out from the cover of *GQ* in every newsstand across the country at this very moment? The one who's made *People*'s sexiest man list for two years running? Ireland's contribution to prime-time TV?"

But all the while she was scoffing, Annie could see the truth in Diane's concerned hazel eyes. Annoyed, irritated, she pushed a hand through her long dark hair. "Oh, hell."

Diane took two quick steps and put her arms around her. "I'm sorry, Annie. I know you and Jared had a... disagreement."

Disagreement?

Was that what it had been? She supposed, to outsiders, it must have looked like no more than that. To Annie it had been more like the death of her soul.

"But you used to be friends," Diane went on, oblivious. "It's just that, well, he and Nick were always close. You know that. And Nick wanted him to come. He didn't actually think Jared would be able to. He is—" Diane grimaced "—everything you said. But, well, weddings are special, so you have to ask. You want the people you've been close to to be there." The look she gave Annie was beseeching. "To share your joy. For me and for Nick that means you. And for Nick, that means Jared, as well." She smiled ruefully. "But if it's any consolation, I know how you feel."

Annie doubted that. She couldn't imagine that anyone knew how she felt about Jared Flynn. She didn't know herself.

Diane had said they were friends. They had begun as friends, certainly. When Nick had introduced them over three years ago at a party, and they'd found out they were both actors, they'd decided to stick together. They had, in fact, become friends.

Then they had become more than friends.

They had moved to New York together. Worked together, played together, loved together.

For a year and a half Jared Flynn had been Annie's soul mate, the man she had trusted with her deepest secrets, her strongest yearnings. She'd thought he understood, had thought he'd shared them. And then he had betrayed her.

Betrayed himself.

And what was worse, Annie thought, her knuckles whitening as she clenched the handle of her bag, he didn't even seem to know it.

She stared unseeing out the large plate-glass window and tried to put Jared into the events of the next few days. The prospect didn't cheer her. She was having enough trouble coming to terms with the present. She certainly didn't want to have to deal with the past.

Still, what was she going to do? Stomp off in a tantrum? Say she'd changed her mind, wouldn't come?

How childish was that?

And childish was just what Jared had once called her. Even now the recollection could make her bristle. But not visibly. Never visibly. Mentally she gave herself a shake. She owed Diane and Nick more than that.

She took a deep breath; she sighed; she shrugged. "So Jared's coming to the wedding," she said finally, philosophically, making her voice flat and uncaring, pleased at how unconcerned she sounded. She wasn't an actress for nothing. "So what?"

Diane beamed and breathed again, obviously vastly relieved. "Thanks, Annie. I knew you'd understand."

"Mmm."

They started walking again, Diane almost on air, the way she had been since Nick had proposed. Annie watched, a wistful smile tugging at her mouth.

She took a deep breath and hurried to catch up. "Anyway, it's going to be a large wedding," she said, determined to be cheerful. "Hundreds at least."

Diane made a face. "All of St. Louis's best and brightest. And half of Italy, according to my future mother-in-law."

"Then I probably won't even have to deal with Jared."

There was a second's hesitation. "Well, he won't be here till the last minute because of his shooting schedule, but . . . I'm afraid you're walking out with him."

"What?"

"He's one of the groomsmen, Annie."

"But—"

"Nick picked the groomsmen. He picked Jared."

"He has brothers, cousins!"

"He asked Jared."

"In a wedding this size there must be half a dozen groomsmen!"

"There are."

"Then why—"

"It's your height."

Annie thought her hearing was going. She'd heard about the effect of airplane travel on ears, but— "My . . . height?"

Diane gave her a wry smile. "Grandmother paired everyone by height. You and Jared . . . match."

The hell we do, Annie thought.

But two days of protesting, of feeble and not so feeble excuses, got her nowhere.

She hinted, she suggested, she pretended inordinate fondness for Nick's cousin Joe, also a groomsman. She considered pleading, cajoling, and even, briefly, toyed with the tantrum she had earlier rejected.

Pride, fortunately, kept her from making an idiot of herself. But nothing kept her from being assigned a march up the aisle and a reception dance with Jared Flynn.

"WHAT IF THERE'S a traffic jam?" Diane said, plucking at the baby's breath in her bouquet. She paced the length of the room, peeking out the door anxiously, then retreating to fuss over her flowers some more. "What if Nick's late? What if his Uncle Sal has a heart attack or my mother and father fight? They're acting so strange, so . . . What if—"

"What if the sun goes into a totally unexpected eclipse, the entire assembled congregation breaks out in hives, and the priest forgets his lines? Hold still." Annie straightened Diane's veil for her, then smiled encouragement.

Diane gave her a weak smile in return. "You think I'm an idiot."

"I think you're nervous."

"Don't you ever get nervous? I mean, when you get married, don't you . . ."

Annie shook her head. "It's not the same." Not at all. And thank God for that.

Diane sighed and plucked some more baby's breath. "I suppose not." She looked at Annie, disgruntled. "But you wouldn't be, anyway, would you? It's that terrific self-possession you have."

Was that what it was? Annie wondered. It didn't feel like self-possession. Self-preservation, maybe. Inside she doubted she was any more put-together than Diane was today, and with more reason.

Diane might be getting married today, but she was plighting her troth with a man she dearly loved. She knew exactly what she was getting into in a few short minutes. And even if she was nervous, she could get through it just by saying her lines.

No one had written Annie's.

"Improvise, kiddo," she told herself. "That's what you're good at."

Onstage, maybe. But in real life it wasn't the same.

Jared was out there right now, smiling, nodding, making the day for scores of St. Louis matrons and teenyboppers who would be tittering for weeks about having seen or been winked at by TV's highly rated Reid McCullough, Interpol investigator.

Annie was willing to bet he wouldn't wink at her.

The last time she had seen Jared Flynn face-to-face he had told her she was a foolish, self-centered child. She had told him he was a stupid, insensitive clod. He had proposed marriage and she had thrown his proposal back in his face.

They had, in Diane's grandmother's politely euphemistic language, parted on "less than amicable terms," if flinging harsh words and coffee cups could be so described.

What would happen when she saw him today she didn't know. She trusted he wouldn't make a scene. Most probably he would be cool, curt even. He would acknowledge their prior acquaintance and no more.

He must know she was going to be there. A sudden panic seized her, and her fingers clenched on the stem of her own bouquet.

What if Nick hadn't told him? He hadn't been going to tell her about Jared coming.

Oh, God, surely Nick wouldn't be so foolish. Surely he wouldn't try to engineer a reconciliation at his wedding. He might not know all that had gone between them, but he did know enough.

She spun around, desperate. "Diane!"

Her sudden urgency made all the rest of the bridesmaids turn, too. Diane peered out from behind her veil. "What's wrong?"

"Jared..." Annie gabbled, "I just thought...I mean, he does know, doesn't he? About him and...and me. And today. That your grandmother...that we're...a couple. Just up the aisle, I mean. And for the dance." She felt like an idiot asking, as if it mattered. "Nick did tell him?"

Diane smiled behind her veil. Then she reached out and gave Annie's arm a squeeze. "Don't worry, Annie, he knows. He knows," she repeated more forcefully when Annie's expression didn't alter.

Somehow it wasn't the relief Annie had hoped it would be. All right, he knew. But what did he think about it? How did he feel? Did he care?

The Jared she knew would have cared desperately. But now she was beginning to wonder if she had really ever known Jared at all.

The Jared she thought she knew would never have given up his aspirations for a future on the dramatic stage to play some two-bit international cop. He would never have expected her to throw over her career and follow him to Tinseltown.

But that Jared had obviously been a figment of her imagination. The real one clearly hadn't known the real her.

So, she reassured herself, most probably he would look down his handsome nose at her, nod at her, give her the brief acknowledgment she planned to give him.

And all would be well.

The door suddenly swung open, the organist segued into *Ave Maria*, and Diane's father appeared, looking both distinguished and apprehensive in his formal attire. He surveyed the bridesmaids clustered together in their dusty rose, peach and silvery gowns and his only daughter in her embroidered gown of satin and beaded lace. He grinned. "Time to get married, ladies."

Diane made a soft little moan, and another piece of baby's breath bit the dust.

Annie shuddered, took a deep cleansing breath, reached out and gave Diane's cold, clammy hand a squeeze. "Be happy," she whispered.

"Tomorrow I'll be happy," Diane whispered back as she moved to join her father. "Today I just want to survive!"

Annie, trailing along after, knew exactly how she felt.

They lined up in the foyer as the ending notes of *Ave Maria* echoed throughout the cavernous church.

"Oh, help," Diane murmured behind her as the doors swung open revealing the long carpeted nave. Her father gave her shoulders a reassuring squeeze.

There was a concentrated hush, as if the assembled congregation were, as one, holding their collective breath. They turned to look expectantly toward the back of the church. Then the organ rumbled to life again, and the first strains of *The Wedding March* rang out.

At the far distant end of the nave Annie saw Nick, flanked by his brother Carlo, the best man, and a blurred line of other men. One of them Jared.

She chewed her lip, waiting as first Paula, then Frankie, then Diane's high school chums, Suzanne and Katherine, moved slowly and precisely forward. Then, at last, it was her turn, and she felt more nervous than when every eye was on her as a bride.

Whenever she was a bride, Annie practically raced down the aisle, her eager, flamboyant character champing at the matrimonial bit. And all the way along she would look side to side, catching this person's eye or that one's, winking, smirking, giggling, feeding the audience's enthusiasm with her own. That was the way weddings should be, Annie had always thought. Light and bright and sparkling, full of fun and fervor.

Now she could barely get her feet to work. And when, motivated at last by Lisa's hissed "Go on, for heaven's sake!" she finally launched herself with a—she hoped—inaudible "left, right, left," she ventured not a glance right or left, but instead stared straight ahead.

Calm, she told herself. *Cool.* And she fixed her eyes on the groom. It was a jolt to see Nick. She was used to actors. She'd gone through five, of course. Tall, short, suave, slick. All feigning stark terror, as if the bride approaching were a hunter with her sights trained on them.

Nick didn't look nervous. He looked stern and remote, but steady, not at all the laughing, gregarious man she was used to. And yet there was a sense of pure happiness about him. A sense of commitment. Serenity.

Annie wished he had a bit to spare for her because, as she approached the altar, the men beside Nick became clearer and, helplessly, inexorably, her gaze found Jared.

He stood next to Carlo, tall and straight, his dark craggy Irish good looks even more devastating than she remembered, his unruly black hair for once almost subdued, his green eyes hooded at first, then meeting hers.

Annie felt herself stiffen, expecting his silent recognition, then a polite but distant acknowledgment, and finally his cool dismissal.

He stuck his tongue out at her.

GOD, SHE WAS BEAUTIFUL. He'd been anticipating this moment for days, thinking about it for weeks. And now, the way she was walking down the aisle as if she were a queen, her head held high, her chin lifted, her sun-kissed complexion complemented by the dark pink roses that she held, made him catch his breath.

In his fantasies he couldn't count the number of times he'd pictured her walking down the aisle, coming to meet him, bringing with her her love and her life to share with him, her joy shining in her eyes. He'd always known she'd make a beautiful bride.

But, of course, she wasn't.

Not here, anyway, although he knew she did it for a living these days.

And there was irony for you, Jared thought savagely. She who'd said, "Get married? You must be joking!" did it daily now.

He wondered how she liked it. He wondered if she did it well and decided she must—when it came to acting Annie was determined to do everything well.

He certainly hoped she did it better than she was doing her bridesmaid role today, because whatever she was bringing up the aisle with her right now, it wasn't love and sweetness and light.

And it sure as hell wasn't joy that shone in the defiant brown eyes that met his.

Nor was there joy in his own. She'd put him through hell, had Annie D'Angelo.

Two years ago Jared Flynn had thought they shared everything—their lives, their hopes, their dreams, their love. And then Hollywood had called, he had answered, and he'd found out how wrong he was.

He'd wanted to share it with Annie. He'd said, "Marry me, Annie." And she had laughed in his face.

Not only laughed, but had got angry—so angry it amazed him still. He was copping out, she'd told him. Selling his soul to the great god Nielsen. And, she went on with bloody-minded fury, even if he was going to sacrifice himself, she was damned if he was also going to sacrifice her and her career!

What career? he'd asked with awful honesty.

That was when she'd thrown the coffee mug at him. He'd ducked.

But in the deadly silence that ensued there was nothing left to do save pack his bags and go.

And so he had.

To Hollywood. To fame and fortune, to opportunities unlimited. From the foothills of supporting roles in off-Broadway dramas he'd traveled to a considerably impressive pinnacle atop the Hollywood heap.

But if his career had risen rapidly in terms of actual time, two years in Tinseltown was a millennium in terms of the experience it had given a naive country boy from County Cork.

He was a man of the world now. A man who commanded a
high salary, who was offered steadily improving roles, and who
increasingly had some of the world's most gorgeous women
throwing themselves at his feet.

But in the back of his mind there was always Annie.

He hoped he'd outgrown his feelings for her. He had prayed
that when he saw her again she'd mean no more to him than
any of the women who simpered and flirted with him day in
and day out.

He had agreed to come because he truly liked Nick and Diane and wanted to be a part of their wedding—a wedding that
still astonished him. But it was knowing Annie would be there,
too, that had decided it.

Was he over her? He'd come to see.

It had taken only a look.

ANNIE THOUGHT she must be hallucinating. Too many late
nights, too few hours of sleep. Too much stress, too little fresh
air. It happened sometimes. She was sure of it.

What she was equally certain of was that Jared Flynn, fore-
most example of talent and self-possession among actors, Ireland's gift to the women of America, couldn't possibly have
stuck his tongue out at her!

Could he?

The mind reeled. She positively goggled at him, stunned.
His face was perfectly composed now, not a trace of a smile,
certainly no tongue. But his eyes met hers defiantly, and there
was a wicked glint in their sea-green depths that made her
wonder. And worry. A lot.

She hadn't let herself think about what she would do if he
decided to do more than acknowledge her. It was a mistake.
She should have been prepared. She could hardly think ra-
tionally about it now.

She took her place next to Katherine and tried desperately
to compose herself. It was difficult. For one thing, though now
she couldn't see him, only a sea of suits and stylish hats, she
knew he was there. She'd had a sense of awareness where Jared

Flynn was concerned from the moment she'd met him three years before.

For another, above the sounds of the priest's welcoming words, above the whispers and giggles of Nick's wide-eyed nephews and his brother-in-law Aldo's futile attempts to shush them, above the sniffles of Nick's mother and the audible swallows of Diane's mother, not to mention the stern throat clearings of her martinet Grandmother Hoffmann, Annie was sure she could hear Jared breathing.

Logic told her that wasn't possible. Common sense told her that it was Nick she heard, or Carlo, or one of the altar boys. If in fact she heard anyone at all.

But it sounded just like Jared did. Deep, even breathing the way she remembered it when she awoke in the middle of the night to the soft sounds of him next to her in the bed.

God in heaven, she couldn't start thinking about Jared in bed! Not now! Not in the middle of Nick and Diane's wedding. Not when the very notion made her face flush, her own breathing quicken, her palms sweat.

She forced herself to focus on Diane and Nick, to watch, to listen. It was harder, she decided, being a bridesmaid than being a bride. You couldn't *do* anything, you could only stand there letting the experience wash over you, bringing with it the "what ifs," the "if onlys," the "might have beens."

Don't be an idiot, Annie told herself sharply as Nick slipped the ring on Diane's finger and Diane placed a matching gold band on his. *That isn't what you want. Not at all.*

If it had been, she could have had it two years ago.

The very thought made her shudder. That would have been it—the end. Everything she'd worked for all her life—her drive, her goals, her sacrifices—would have all been smothered in wedded bliss.

No way, she'd thought then. And she thought it again now. Marriage was fine for some people. People like Diane, who looked starry-eyed in Nick's presence, who glowed whenever he touched her, who became even more vibrantly Diane whenever he was near. And people like Nick, who married for love, not convenience, who had exuded more of a sense of purpose and of self since his commitment to Diane than he had in the entire three years Annie had known him. They were both warm, steady, loving people, not mercurial, temperamental, stubborn people.

They were the sort of people who should be married. Not people like Jared and herself.

"I now pronounce you husband and wife," the priest said, beaming on the newly wedded couple. He looked at Nick. "You may kiss the bride."

Annie watched with interest and increasing admiration as Nick did just that. This was no stage kiss, no studied smolder. This was Nick Granatelli telling the world in no uncertain terms that he was the happiest man on earth since Diane Bauer had finally become his wife.

Annie had been kissed under similar circumstances one hundred and nineteen times. But never like that. Never had her many grooms kissed her with the hunger and need that Nick so obviously felt.

She felt a faintly hollow aching deep inside and promptly squelched it. There was far more to marriage than kissing, she reminded herself.

But it occurred to her, as the organist began to play the first bars of the recessional, that as far as weddings went, life certainly had more going for it than art.

Chapter Two

"SMILE," HE SAID IN HER EAR as he hooked her arm through his for the recessional. "You're on Family Camera."

And as the flashbulbs popped and Annie's expression went from gape to glare, Jared bent his head and soundly kissed her.

It was like stepping into a mine field. One moment careful containment, the next an explosive conflagration. From somewhere in the assembly there came a titter and a few assorted gasps.

One of them, Annie thought, could have been her own. For whatever mischief Jared had hoped to accomplish, Annie was sure he'd succeeded.

The sheer unexpectedness of his kiss stunned her, and there was simply no help for it. Mind reeling, lips burning, unable to squelch the traitorous memories that swamped her, that undid her, Annie kissed him back.

And then, just as if it had meant no more to him than the one hundred and nineteen wedding kisses had meant to her, Jared pulled back and gave her a wink. "Good show," he said.

And with that he moved purposefully up the aisle, sweeping Annie, furious and fuming, alongside him.

PRUDENCE DICTATED that he bide his time, be a proper groomsman, behave like a gentleman, cool his heels. Wait.

Good thing he'd never been a gentleman, Jared thought.

He could still taste her on his lips, could still feel the soft yielding of hers, still smell the hint of spice that had always meant Annie to him. And if his memories of her had driven him to distraction over the past two years, they were nothing compared to the reality of her.

He'd heard the flashbulbs popping, and he cared damn all if they did. Let them take a million. He'd needed just once to kiss Annie.

Just once? Ah well, once for starters, he thought, smiling. There would be more, he thought, pleased, because however stiffly she held herself, however distant she seemed, for a split second she had responded.

"Jar-*ed*," she said now between her teeth, but he ignored her, savoring his discovery, smiling at the picture-snappers, winking at the girls who ogled him as they walked sedately up the aisle.

Let her fuss. Let her fume. If she hadn't forgotten him in two years, she would come around. He had been foolish to let two years go by. He should have come back and made her see sense before this.

Well, now he would. By tonight, he was confident, he'd have his heart's desire.

They reached the vestibule and the moment they did, Annie pulled her arm away.

Jared caught her hand and smiled at her. "I've got to go wrestle some old aunties back up the aisle."

"By all means," Annie said coolly.

"Don't you be moving. I'll be back. We've things to discuss."

"We have nothing to discuss," Annie said flatly.

But Jared knew better.

How dare he? He was even worse than she'd thought.

Annie supposed she should have expected it. One did not survive Hollywood if one's finer sensitivities remained intact. Still, somehow it hurt to be proved right, to know that exactly what she'd feared had happened to Jared had really come to pass.

"Over here! Annie, over here!"

She looked up to see Frankie beckoning her. The videographer, Jeff Somebody-or-Other, a gorgeous tower of a man with a glint in more than his camera lens, was standing behind Frankie, also beckoning.

She remembered Jared's imperative: Don't be moving.

"I'll move when I damn well please," Annie muttered and promptly headed toward Frankie.

Outside the church now that the guests were pouring out, pandemonium reigned. More than four hundred of St. Louis's finest milled around, beaming and smiling. Scores of Granatellis large and small swarmed about, hugging and kissing one another as well as Nick and his bride.

Annie watched, overwhelmed. "What are we supposed to do now?"

Frankie laughed. "How many times did you say you'd been married?"

Annie shook her head. "Not the same thing. This is mind-boggling."

Frankie squeezed her hand. "Never mind. I think you're just supposed to look happy."

Frankie herself looked radiant. Not surprising, Annie thought glumly. Impending marriage seemed to do that to people. Still, the fact that it was Frankie who was actually engaged to be married surprised Annie a good deal.

Of all the Granatellis, Frankie had always struck Annie as the least likely to marry, the most independent and self-determined. Not for her the traditional home and family that had satisfied her sister Sophia. Not for her the conventional route to Italian womanhood that the Granatellis had always expected. Annie had always considered Frankie a kindred spirit.

To find that, despite her independence, despite her self-determination, Frankie, too, was about to succumb to matrimony was a decided shock.

"It must be catching," Nick had said with a grin when he'd told Annie just yesterday morning of Frankie and Eric's engagement.

Annie had looked at Nick, baffled. "What's that?"

"Love."

"Lord, I hope not."

It wouldn't catch her. The only man who had ever come close to making her reconsider her single-mindedness had been Jared. And she had been right to resist. Unwittingly her fingers crept up to touch her lips. They still tingled from his touch.

"Don't let him," she murmured to herself. "Oh, Annie, don't let him."

She wouldn't. She made up her mind to that.

SHE WASN'T WHERE he'd left her. Not surprising. If Annie D'Angelo had ever done anything she was told in her entire life, Jared didn't know when it had been. The only good thing was that, decked out in one of the bridesmaids' gowns, she wouldn't be hard to find.

He caught sight of one bridesmaid, saw that it was Paula, and looked beyond. He spotted Lisa heading toward one of the cars, then spied two more gowns moving that way—Katherine and Suzanne. That only left Frankie and Annie unaccounted for. Damn it, where was she?

Elbowing his way past Nick's Uncle Vito and assorted nameless cousins, he made his way toward Lisa.

"Have you seen Annie?"

But he had scarcely got the words out of his mouth when Nick's youngest brother, Vinnie, bounded up and thrust a set of car keys in his hand.

"They're in the Chevy parked over there." Vinnie jerked his head in the direction of the rectory. "You're supposed to drive Auntie Asunta and Auntie Tina and Uncle Sal's mother-in-law. They're waiting."

"I—"

But Vinnie was already gone.

And anyway, what was Jared going to do, argue? It was part of his duty as an usher. Besides, he told himself, there'd be time later for him and Annie. He'd make time. That was all there was to it.

IT WAS THE RECEPTION to end all receptions. Annie's one hundred and nineteen combined didn't come close to equaling the Bauer-Granatelli bash.

There was wine, music, fabulous food and a spirit of love that wouldn't quit. Annie thought she would have enjoyed it enormously if she hadn't spent the whole of it glancing over her shoulder.

"Where's Jared?" Diane asked her once the almost endless receiving line was over and the waiters were slipping through the crowd with trays of champagne.

"There." Annie nodded across the pool where he stood surrounded by a battalion of teenyboppers.

It was the great advantage of swimming pools, she'd discovered. Like moats, they could be used for protection. She'd spent the last hour keeping this one between herself and Jared.

He knew it. The glint in his eyes told her so. He'd seen her the moment he'd arrived, a trio of Granatellis in tow. And she'd watched as, deft as a sheepdog, he'd steered the Granatelli ladies in the direction of the receiving line, dumped them, and headed straight for her.

Annie, equally deft, had eased her way around to the far side of the pool.

She didn't understand what he was up to. Coolness she could have comprehended. Indifference wouldn't have been suspect. After all, he had it made now—he was a star—and she was just what she'd always been—no more, no less.

Maybe, she thought grimly, he wanted to rub her nose in his success. Probably. He who didn't think she had a career.

She could think of no other earthly reason he would be pursuing her this way. Surely he wasn't going to renew his illadvised offer of marriage.

But whatever he had in mind, one thing was certain: he was coming her way. He had just slipped around a cluster of society matrons, his gaze on her.

Annie kept on talking to Diane's Auntie Flo, steering her right around the pool as she did so.

Jared followed, moving along the shallow end. She and Auntie Flo, still talking gamely about Diane's burgeoning tour business, backed steadily toward the deep one.

Then all at once Flo paused midsentence and regarded her archly over the top of an empty champagne glass. "Tell me, dear, are we doing laps? Or are you avoiding that handsome young man?''

Annie started, then sighed and gave her companion a brittle smile. ''I am avoiding that handsome young man.''

Auntie Flo made a tsking sound and filched another glass of champagne as the waiter moved past, sipping at length as she considered Jared.

''I don't know what the younger generation is coming to,'' she complained. ''He's quite gorgeous, you know. In my day we'd have plotted his seduction. Have you no taste?''

Annie grimaced. ''I have. That's the trouble.''

''Ah.'' Auntie Flo beamed. ''You've already seduced him.''

Annie felt her cheeks burning. What was the younger generation coming to, she wondered, that she could allow Auntie Flo to embarrass her like this? Determinedly she edged away.

Undeterred, Flo crab-walked alongside her, bemused, still watching as Jared doggedly followed in pursuit.

She tsked again. ''Pity. I'd have said he'd have been a treat. But you can't tell from looking at them, can you?'' she added brightly.

''Let me get you a canapé,'' Annie offered hastily. ''A stuffed mushroom, perhaps?''

Auntie Flo laughed. ''So tactful. My mother just used to say, 'Florrie, let's see you get this whole apple in your mouth all at once.' '' She patted Annie's cheek. ''Just tell an old woman to shut up, my dear.''

''Er,'' Annie began, and found herself vastly relieved by the announcement of dinner.

She gave Jared one last apprehensive glance, saw that with the dinner announcement, he was no longer after her, and led Auntie Flo toward the table set aside for Diane's immediate family.

Then, having settled Auntie Flo next to Gertrude, she went to find her own place at the head table.

Jared was waiting, holding her chair for her. He smiled his wolf-at-the-door smile. ''Nice try.''

Annie stifled a groan. She shot a desperate glance around, but there was no help for it. Protocol prevailed. A placard with her name sat right next to Jared's.

Grimly she took her seat, careful not to let even the sleeve of his coat touch her arm.

"Can't avoid me forever, Annie."

She stared straight ahead. "I don't know what you mean."

Jared's brows lifted as he slid into the seat beside hers. "The hell you don't," he said, then smiled blandly at Katherine and Nick's cousin Joe, who sat down next to them. "Grand wedding, isn't it?"

Annie, smarting, glowered at him.

Oblivious to anyone but Jared, Katherine sighed. "It's beautiful."

"The family will be talking about it for years," Joe said.

"Inspirational, don't you think?" Jared settled back in his chair, smiling.

Katherine's eyes were like saucers. "Oh, yes?"

He smiled at her, a cat-who-got-the-cream smile this time. "Indeed."

Annie felt her irritation grow. Damn Jared Flynn and his wicked Irish charm. And what did he mean, inspirational? Was he contemplating marriage, too?

She supposed he might be.

A man like Jared wanted a woman in his life. Someone to trail along after him, picking up his socks and fixing his meals, the way Annie's mother did for her father, the way Jared had expected her to do for him. She gritted her teeth.

Who would the lucky lady be? Heaven knew the gossip columnists had been only too willing to match him up with a score of potential candidates over the last two years. And although Annie knew that ninety percent of everything they wrote was hype, some of it might be true.

Had Jared found someone for real?

The question stuck in her throat. She couldn't—wouldn't—ask.

Katherine did. "Are you...thinking about getting married?" There was a breathy hesitancy in her voice, as if the hopes of a million women hung in the balance.

Jared tapped his fork on the table as if considering her question. Expressive dark brows lifted quizzically as if he were contemplating a secret no one else knew.

"I'm...thinking," he agreed in a musing tone. He gave Katherine a conspiratorial wink that almost made her swoon. Then he turned his gaze on Annie. "You're a source of inspiration, too."

"Me?"

"Her?" Katherine sounded miffed.

Annie, still recovering from his acknowledgment that he was thinking about marriage, tensed. "What do you mean?"

"You're getting married every day, I hear." There was an ironic twist to his mouth, a sardonic look in his eyes. "Agrees with you now, does it?"

"In its proper form, as a part in a play, yes, it does," Annie said stiffly. How the hell did he know what she was doing?

Her career was generally a well-kept secret. Outside of a few critics, her parents and her best friends, her daily march down the aisle was not common knowledge.

A moment's rational thought, however, told her that his knowledge meant nothing. He'd spent last night at Nick's. Undoubtedly Nick would have said.

"It's a challenge," she added.

"Which? The marriage or the acting?"

She gave him a frosty glance. "Which do you think?"

"I haven't a doubt in the world," he said silkily. "Annie's a Serious Actress," he told Katherine and Joe, his tone capitalizing the words. "Not like some of us," he added mockingly.

"Oh, what nonsense!" Katherine sprang to his defense at once. She glared at Annie. "He's wonderful." Then she turned back to Jared. "You do a marvelous job week after week. I stay home on Fridays just to watch. You are a fantastic actor!"

"Were," Annie corrected quietly.

"Thank you very much," Jared said, and whether he was speaking to her or Katherine she had no idea. His smile, directed at Katherine, was mild, but his gaze was sharp when his eyes met Annie's.

She looked away quickly, relieved a moment later to have a salad set in front of her. Saved by the endive, she thought, and dug in.

Katherine, delighted that Annie seemed uninterested in the celebrity in their midst, rabbited on. Annie never thought she'd appreciate hearing someone gush over Jared's mindless performance as Reid McCullough, but she was grateful now. As long as the other woman kept talking, there was no way Jared could talk to her.

Obviously he wasn't ready to forget their differences. But he seemed to have the good sense not to launch attacks in front of spectators.

If all went well, Annie thought as he fobbed off another of Katherine's silly questions, it would never occur. They were hardly likely to have time alone in the midst of a wedding reception. If she could make it to the end without being alone with him, she'd be home free.

She felt rather like a horse halfway through a steeplechase. Having hurdled the ceremony itself, the cocktails and now dinner, she had only dancing, the cake cutting and the farewells left to go until she'd run the race.

"It's all reruns now," Katherine was complaining. "Not that I mind, of course. But I am looking forward to the new season just the same. I love anything you do."

Annie fully expected Jared to pounce on a suggestive remark like that. But he only gave the other woman a bland smile. "You're very kind to say so."

"And your last movie—" Katherine gave a little groan of ecstasy "—it was so . . . so . . . steamy."

Annie gagged quietly, and was surprised when Jared flushed. Why should he? It was no more of an artistic comedown than doing Reid McCullough every week was.

She hadn't wanted to see the movie at all, but Diane and Nick had dragged her. And she'd had to go or admit more than she wanted to admit to her friends.

So she'd sat there alternately entranced and mortified by displays of Jared's remarkable talent and his equally remarkable body.

They were both wasted, she thought.

And afterward she hadn't got a good night's sleep for a week.

Seeing Jared's heightened color now made her wonder what he thought about the film. Was it the story or the love scenes that he found embarrassing? She ventured a sidelong glance at him. His eyes skated away at once.

Katherine pressed on. "Are you working on any other new projects now? Besides Reid McCullough, I mean."

"I'm supposed to be starting a new movie. Shot in Mexico." He named a couple of high-powered co-stars.

"Really?" Katherine was all ears. "What's it about?"

Jared smiled ruefully. "I'm not at liberty to discuss it right now."

Annie wondered if he was saying that for dramatic effect, expecting to be coaxed, but she couldn't tell. She could see Katherine fighting both her dismay and her curiosity before she apparently decided not to pursue it and said brightly. "Oh, well, of course. We understand, don't we, Annie? Joe?"

"Sure," Joe said, ever helpful.

Annie, ever skeptical, didn't say anything at all.

HE'D THOUGHT she might ask a question or two. Show a little interest.

She didn't. She sat there like a lump, eating her salad as if it were the most important thing in the world, leaving him to make conversation with the insipid Kathleen or whatever her name was. He'd hoped to pique her interest, wanted to tell her about the movie deal he was within inches of signing. She'd be impressed; he knew she would.

But she asked nothing, and the only remarks she did make were pithy little one-liners designed either to wound or, at the very least, to put him off.

It was a good thing he'd kissed her, Jared thought, or he might've decided she really didn't like him anymore.

He wished he could kiss her again right now. He wouldn't because surprise was no longer on his side. She was wary now, skittish. She'd probably claw his eyes out if he so much as moved in her direction. At the very least she'd say something scathing and embarrassing, making them the focus of all eyes.

As much as Jared liked being the center of attention in his acting, he wasn't fond of scenes in his private life. And a scene was exactly what Annie would provide.

So he waited, smiling, biding his time. Wedding protocol would take care of his problem. He'd have her in his arms soon enough.

THE REST OF THE MEAL passed in relative calm and before long a waiter whisked away her plate and the dancing began.

That would be, most likely, the biggest hurdle of all. She had contrived to think of a way out of it, but Diane's grandmother would not be moved.

"All the bridesmaids will dance with their respective escorts," she had decreed. And the Pope sounded less authoritative than Gertrude Hoffmann did when she was handing down wedding edicts.

Annie sat back and mentally geared herself up for the coming event.

Despite her own apprehension, she couldn't help smiling as Nick led Diane out onto the patio and took her into his arms.

For the first time today it was just the two of them, focusing wholly on each other. No attendants. No relatives. No business associates of Nick's family or Diane's. No demands. No obligations. No one—nothing—but the two of them. At last.

Annie felt her throat tighten. Her eyes stung. The love between them was so obvious now. It was also new and fragile, yet growing deeper and stronger day by day. Annie thought back, remembering all the pain they'd gone through to get to this moment. The years, the hopes, the battles.

Who would ever have thought . . . ?

The music penetrated slowly, the clarinet solo weaving its way into her consciousness. "Stranger on the Shore." The song that had been playing the night Diane had first danced with Nick.

The night that Annie had first found herself in Jared's arms.

It had been so simple, so unexpected, their original meeting. In the larger course of events, Annie would have called it "insignificant." An engagement party. An arranged date. With Nick.

Her mother's godmother's aunt's nephew or some damned thing. Even now Annie couldn't remember. All she remembered was her mother's "She told him you're going to be there. He's expecting you. You go."

Annie's mother had a habit of giving royal commands. She despaired of her daughter ever finding a suitable man, and she wouldn't accept that Annie wasn't even looking.

It was easier to humor Lucia D'Angelo than it was to fight her. So Annie went, dragging Diane along for moral support. Exactly, she discovered that evening, as Nick had dragged Jared.

"This is my friend Jared," Nick had said almost at once.

"My friend Diane," Annie had replied in turn.

That was all it had taken for Lucia D'Angelo's matchmaking efforts to bear fruit. Only the two who fell in love that night weren't Annie and Nick, but Nick and Diane.

Annie and Jared had smiled at each other, had shrugged philosophically. They had danced, talked, discovered common ground.

They had seen no fireworks. Had felt no earthquakes. Not then.

But in retrospect Annie knew that with "Stranger on the Shore" it had begun.

She blinked now, fighting back tears she abhorred. She hadn't cried when he'd slammed out, why in God's name should she cry now? She sneaked a glance at Jared. She found his eyes, dark and unreadable, on hers.

She pressed her lips together, swallowed and quickly looked away.

Diane's father was cutting in on the bridal couple now, and Annie saw Nick stand back and watch them for a moment, a tender smile on his face. Then he crossed the patio and drew Diane's mother to her feet.

He said something to Cynthia that made her smile and blush as she looked over at her ex-husband and her daughter. Then she looked back at Nick and gave him a squeeze. Nick hugged her, too.

Then Nick's father cut in to dance with his new daughter-in-law, and Diane's father claimed her mother. Nick went to get his own mother, smiling at her as he drew her into the dance.

"Our turn," Joe said, and he and Katherine got up and moved to join them. So did Vinnie and Suzanne, Lisa and Carlo.

Annie held her breath. Next to her, she felt Jared stir. "Shall we?"

Dare she? Annie thought, was a better question.

But the one that mattered, of course, was dare she not? And the answer to that was no.

If there was a confrontation, so be it. However much Jared still appealed to her on a physical level, however much he had mattered to her once on an emotional one, their differences were irreconcilable.

Any hollow feelings she had, any misgivings she now felt, were simply products of the moment, brought to light because of the wedding and her unusual proximity to Jared once again.

In the clear light of day they would be gone.

She had simply to see this through. To be polite. To be pleasant. To dance with him now because it was expected. To smile at him and make small talk because that was expected, too.

Then she could hop in Vinnie's truck tomorrow with a clear conscience, pleased with herself for having played another tough part.

She turned and gave Jared a stunning smile. "Why not?" she said brightly and held out her hand.

"Stranger on the Shore" had, happily, ended. But a moment's reflection told Annie that the opening bars of "Hello, Again" didn't promise much better.

Still, she steeled herself less against the words and music than against the effect of Jared's hand in hers, his arm drawing her near.

She would have been fine, she thought, if he had just danced with her, made small talk with her the way Lisa and Carlo were doing, or even ogled her the way Vinnie was ogling Suzanne. She would have been better even if the confrontation she expected had occurred.

But it didn't. There was nothing confrontational about Jared as he drew her close, molding her body against his, laying his cheek against her hair.

Annie stiffened, trying to hold out, but he simply held her closer, whispering in her ear.

Words soft and Gaelic, words she couldn't translate but which needed no translation, words she remembered all too well from the times he'd whispered them before—the times when they'd made love.

Her face flamed, her body smoldered. "Jared!" she bit out and trod hard on his foot.

He pulled back and blinked down into her face, his own a mask of perplexed innocence. "Mmm. What's that?"

"Stop it!"

"Stop what?"

Annie pinched the back of his neck. "Stop whispering! Stop *what* you were whispering!"

His eyes widened. "Was I whispering?"

"Damn you, Jared!" But she couldn't help it; his feigned innocence mocked her outrage. She started to smile.

Jared grinned, too, and said aloud whatever it was he'd been whispering in her ear, though still in a voice that only she could hear. *"A chroí a ghrá, a stór. . ."*

"What's it mean?" Annie demanded.

He stopped dancing and just stood there watching her. "You sure you really want to know?"

She wasn't, no. But how outrageous could it be, really? "Yes."

He continued looking at her for a long moment as if seeking something, assessing. He wasn't smiling now, and the look in his eyes made her heart pound and her palms sweat. She lifted her chin and met his gaze defiantly.

There was another moment's pause and then, "Milk," Jared said, his voice just slightly rough. "Milk and butter. Eggs, oatmeal, bacon..."

"A shopping list! You were reciting a shopping list?"

Jared shrugged and began to move with the music again, taking her with him, his steps as light as his words. "Why not?" he said lightly. "It's a grand distraction. Keeps me from doing what I want to do." He winked.

Annie stiffened. She'd heard of men reciting timetables, state capitals and—in the case of a medical student her friend Ellie was engaged to—the names of all the bones in the hand when the sensations of the moment were overwhelming them. But to hold a woman close and whisper words like "oatmeal" and "bacon" and heaven knew what else just to keep from...! Annie's face flamed.

"You don't want to do that," she said flatly.

"Don't I now? Shows what you know." And the rough, hungry edge to his voice sent a shiver down her spine, bringing with it a host of memories Annie would rather have forgotten.

She sighed with relief at the tap on Jared's shoulder and Vinnie saying, "May I?"

Jared scowled blackly. "May you what?"

Taken aback, Vinnie stammered, "C-cut in, of course."

"Why?"

For heaven's sake, Annie thought. *You don't give a man the third degree when he cuts in for a dance.*

But Jared was. "Why?" he persisted when Vinnie didn't answer at once.

"I... need to talk to her about tomorrow," he said finally, then grinned and rubbed his hands together. "We got plans, man."

"Yes," Annie said quickly, gathering her wits at last. "We do. Thank you for the dance, Jared." And she spun away into Vinnie's arms, smiling up at him.

Vinnie, all too aware of his own considerable, albeit youthful, charm, grinned back. "He didn't much want to let you go."

"He only wants to fight with me," Annie said, catching a glimpse of Jared's grim face over Vinnie's shoulder. He was standing, arms folded across his chest, glaring at them.

"Yeah?" Vinnie sounded doubtful.

"Yes," Annie said forcefully. "Thanks for the rescue."

Vinnie shrugged, then grinned. "My pleasure. So, what time you want to split tomorrow, sweetheart?"

"The sooner the better. The crack of dawn if you will."

Vinnie groaned. "Have a heart. This bash won't be over till then."

"Nonsense. Another hour and they'll cut the cake, toss the bouquet and be off. You don't suppose Nick and Diane want to hang around forever, do you?"

"'Course not." Vinnie laughed. "But there's no reason the rest of us can't. Did you see all the food? Hell, Frankie an' Eric oughta tie the knot tonight, eat up the leftovers and save everybody the trouble of having to do it again."

"I think Frankie and Eric will want their own wedding in their own fashion," Annie said gently.

"Maybe. Weird about them getting married, too, isn't it? Frankie, of all people! Next thing it'll be you."

Annie blanched. "Oh, no."

Vinnie looked surprised at her vehemence. He looked from her to where Jared stood scowling at them from the sidelines, then back at Annie. A brow lifted skeptically. "Mmm."

Annie scowled. "Don't get any ideas."

"Nicky says he used to be your man."

"Nick talks too much."

"You don't want him back?"

"No!"

Vinnie eyed her carefully, then shrugged, and as the combo neared the end, he executed a particularly snazzy step, spinning Annie out and back so fast that when she flew against his arm, the momentum bent her over so far that her head flopped back. She had a brief glimpse of Jared upside down glowering at her.

Then, as the music ended, Vinnie hauled her up again and pulled her directly into his embrace and a Vinnie Granatelli lip-smacking kiss.

"How 'bout that?" He beamed down at her.

Annie gave him a slightly dazed smile. "How about that?" Her head was still whirling.

He gave her another peck on the cheek, then glanced over her shoulder. "Oops, gotta run. Suzanne's free. Pick you up at ten, okay? Have a blast." And as quickly as he'd come, he was gone.

The combo started to play again, and she moved to take a seat near the shrubbery. She was looking forward to a stint as a wallflower. But no sooner had she sat down than Jared materialized at her side.

"My turn." He held out his hand to her.

Annie stared at him wordless.

"My turn," he repeated.

"We've danced, Jared."

"We didn't finish."

"I don't—"

"I do."

The look on his face was implacable. He would stand there forever with his hand out, expectant, waiting. And it wouldn't be long before someone noticed, someone else commented, and it would be all over some god-awful tabloid. If she ever made the tabloids, Annie was damned if she wanted it to be because she was in a battle of wills with Jared Flynn!

Endure, she told herself.

What was it her mother used to tell her when she went to the dentist? Ah yes, "This, too, shall pass."

Well, so would Jared.

In an hour or two the wedding would be over, Nick and Diane would be on their way and she would be safe in bed asleep.

Given that, what difference did a few dance steps make in the course of the universe?

Jared still waited, hand out. She sighed and stood.

"What plans?" he said the moment she was in his arms.

She frowned and looked up at him, bewildered.

"You and Vinnie and your—" his mouth twisted. "—'plans' for tomorrow. What plans?"

"We're driving to New York together."

Jared's surprise was obvious. He scowled. "What for?"

"Vinnie's taking all their grandfather's woodworking tools to New York for Nick."

"And you?"

She laughed. "I'm keeping an eye on Vinnie."

"Just the two of you?"

"Yes, just the two of us." Annie laughed. "What difference does that make?"

He didn't answer. He was still frowning. "Is your bride stint over, then?"

She shook her head. "No. I'm just taking a break. It's my vacation. It's the first I've had since I got to the city."

"The hell it is! What about Vermont?"

Damn him. Damn him for bringing up Vermont. Annie didn't want to think about Vermont.

Of *all* the things she didn't want to think about tonight, Vermont was very close to the top of the list.

"Don't!"

The sheer desperate force of her voice stopped Jared dead. They weren't dancing anymore. They stood staring at each other, a million memories pouring in on them.

She'd been crazy to agree to this, crazy to think she could spend even one day with Jared. There was too much between them. There was no way to talk about the future without it containing the past. Every conversation was a mine field, each sentence ready to explode with memories better left untouched.

Like that trip to Vermont.

Damn Jared—damn him—for bringing it up!

It was the best—and the worst—memory of her life. It had been for her equal parts tenderness and excitement, joy and love. It had been perfection.

And it had been interrupted by a phone message from producer Abe Duncan offering Jared the chance to be Reid McCullough, and Jared offering her the chance to become his wife.

"Forget Vermont," Annie said tersely.

Jared eyed her narrowly. "Have you forgotten it?"

She looked past him toward the swimming pool. "I'm doing my best."

"Fighting reality, are you?"

"Accepting it," she said with a calm she was far from feeling. "And moving on. Keeping my mind on what's important."

Jared's mouth twisted. "Ah, yes. The world according to Annie D'Angelo. Annie Knows Best."

They stood close together, their words coming in undertones, harsh and angry in each other's ears.

Annie stiffened in his arms. "I know best when it concerns me."

"And if I disagree?"

"Then you'd be wrong."

A dark brow lifted. "I'd be wrong?"

"Yes."

"Never you'd be wrong?"

Annie steeled herself against the hint of mockery in his tone. "Not about this," she said through tight lips.

He pulled back and looked at her from beneath hooded lids. "We'll see about that, Annie D'Angelo," he said. "We'll just wait and see."

But Annie just shook her head. There would be no time to wait and see. Soon they would be cutting the cake, then she would be helping Diane change out of her bridal gown, then the wedding would be over.

And when—thank God—the wedding was over, Jared Flynn would be finally and irrevocably out of her life.

IT WAS, SHE SUPPOSED, a wonderful wedding. Nick and Diane certainly seemed to have thought so. As did the million or so Granatellis and the few of Diane's relatives Annie talked to for the rest of the night.

The best that Annie could say for it, from her own standpoint, was that it was over. And if she hadn't actually vanquished Jared, she had at least survived.

She hadn't had to talk to him after their ill-fated dance. She had kept to the far side of the pool. And Jared seemed to have got the message, for he spent the rest of the evening dancing and flirting with every female there from the flower girls to the grandmother of the bride.

Unless Nick and Diane had the ill judgment to ask them both to stand as godparents at some unforeseen future date, Annie went to bed confident that, though she might see him in films, on TV and in magazines, she would never have to come face-to-face with Jared Flynn again.

All things considered she slept well. And the thought that her ordeal was over and that a relaxing trip with Vinnie lay ahead of her made her bounce out of bed with considerable enthusiasm.

She had jumped at Nick's hesitant suggestion that she ride back with his brother instead of flying.

"It sounds wonderful," she'd said. "Just the break I've been looking for."

"I'm not doing you any favors," Nick cautioned. "You'll have to keep an eye on him, make him keep going. I want those tools to get there, and I'm not sure Vinnie will."

Nick's youngest brother was, at twenty-two, the free spirit Nick had never been. A drummer for a perpetually out-of-work band, Vinnie was funny, irreverent, relaxing. Exactly the sort of nondemanding companion Annie was sure she would need after confronting Jared Flynn.

"I like Vinnie," Annie protested.

"We all like Vinnie," Nick replied darkly. "But he's so unreliable. Send him out for a loaf of bread and he comes home—*if* he comes home—with a kite. He goes north instead of south if the wind shifts. Takes off if he gets a better offer. If a pretty girl crossed in front of the truck, he might end up following her to Acapulco. You can't trust him.''

"No problem," Annie had said. She trusted him.

And, she thought as she heard the doorbell ring even as she pulled on a pair of shorts and a T-shirt, he was even on time.

She stuck her head out the door of her room and hollered, "Be right down. Sorry I'm late." Then she tossed her clothes into her bag and began tugging a brush through her long dark hair.

"See, Nick," she said aloud to a man already on his way to Italy, "you can trust him. I knew you could."

But when she came down the steps five minutes later, bag in hand, it wasn't Vinnie sitting in the living room talking to Cynthia and Russ.

It was Jared.

Chapter Three

"DON'T TRY TO TELL ME," Annie said in a deadly tone, "that Vinnie got a job."

They were on the on-ramp to Interstate 64, the truck wheezing and banging as Jared urged it up to freeway speed.

"He did."

"Oh, right." Annie was flatly disbelieving.

Jared might be a world-class actor, but nobody could make her believe that.

She glanced over at him. He looked strong and determined and tough. A man out to get his own way. Reid McCullough in the flesh. She stifled a groan and bent her head. The morning sun glinted off the face of his watch, making her blink.

She blinked again, hoping against hope that she'd roll over and find she was still in bed at Cynthia's and that the realistic views of the St. Louis suburbs slipping past the window were part of a megabucks nightmare and not the story of her life.

No such luck.

"The whole band got a job," Jared went on. He'd been talking almost nonstop since he'd stuffed her and her bag into the truck. He seemed to think that Annie would use any available silence to protest. He wasn't far from wrong.

She'd opened her mouth to object the moment she'd seen him, but he'd whipped her bag out of her hand, grabbed her elbow and steered her right out the door while she was still trying to find the words.

"It was grand having met you," he'd said to Cynthia and Russ. "We wish you all the best."

"We wish *you* all the best, too," Russ had replied, giving them both a grin and a wink.

Annie gaped. Jared bent his head and kissed her soundly, then stowed her in the truck while she was still catching her breath.

"Have a wonderful time," Cynthia said.

"We will," Jared had assured them. And he put the truck in gear and shot down the driveway so fast that Annie felt she'd left her stomach on the porch.

And ever since, he'd been explaining how it had happened that he'd been the one to drive to New York, not Vinnie.

"In Kansas City," Jared continued now. "Terrific opportunity, he said."

Annie rolled her eyes. "I'll bet."

"He'll be making a fair bit of cash," Jared said defensively.

"Nick was paying him," Annie said sweetly. "How much more did you give?"

There was a long moment's silence. Annie imagined he'd deny it. He'd denied everything else. But to her amazement he grinned lazily. "Wouldn't you like to know?" he teased.

"If this is your idea of a joke—"

"No joke, love."

"Don't call me 'love,'" Annie snapped.

He grinned. "I do love you."

Annie snorted.

"You don't believe me?"

"You lie like a rug, Jared Flynn!"

"Do I now?" He was laughing at her now. "Want to lie with me?"

"Oh, shut up!"

She didn't want to talk to him, didn't want to look at him, most certainly didn't want to drive to New York with him. She couldn't believe this was happening.

Twenty minutes ago she'd been certain she'd never see him again, had been congratulating herself on having survived their encounter unscathed.

Now he was not only back, he seemed to think he was running her life. She flung herself back against the seat and glared at him.

He gave her an impudent smile.

"Drop me off at the airport," she said. "I'll fly."

"I thought you wanted a vacation."

"Not with you."

"I make you that nervous?"

"You do not make me nervous!"

"No?" His green eyes mocked her.

"No!"

"You're giving a grand imitation of it, then."

Annie turned her head and seethed.

Jared looked back at the road, whistling softly as they passed the turnoff that led north to the airport and instead headed straight through riverfront St. Louis and onto the bridge spanning the Mississippi.

It wasn't until they were past the sprawl of East St. Louis and heading out into rolling Illinois farmland that he spoke again.

Then he looked over at her, that teasing smile that made her want to smack him still on his face. "If I don't make you nervous, just exactly what is it that you're afraid will happen, Annie, my love?"

"Nothing's going to happen," Annie said. She was certain of that.

He laughed. "You're sure?"

"Quite."

He grinned. "Don't be." And he began that damned whistling again.

She would kill him, Annie thought. She would reach right over and strangle him, dump his body in the nearest ditch, and head straight on for New York without looking back. No one could blame her. God knew she had the provocation.

Count to ten, Annie, she counseled herself. *Count to a hundred.*

"This, too, shall pass," she muttered and invoked the determined, enduring spirit of Lucia D'Angelo.

Jared laughed, and Annie knew it wouldn't matter if she counted to a hundred or to seventy-five thousand. When she quit she would still be heading east with Jared Flynn, a thousand miles of highway ahead of her, and no use looking back.

IT HAD BEEN EASIER than he'd thought. Vinnie'd had none of the rigid Granatelli scruples Nick so often seemed plagued by.

"You wanta drive to New York with Annie?" he'd said when Jared had approached him after the wedding. Vinnie had been lying on the couch in the Granatelli living room, a beatific smile on his face. He'd had plenty to drink and was feeling no pain.

Jared had felt a moment's guilt about approaching a less-than-rational being, but promptly squelched it. He needed to do this and it wasn't his fault Vinnie was soused.

"Yes."

Vinnie shook his head slowly. "I don't think she wants to drive to New York with you."

Jared clenched his teeth. "Annie doesn't know what she wants."

Vinnie looked doubtful. He closed his eyes and hummed a little, then he stopped and lay perfectly still. Jared was afraid he'd gone to sleep.

"You're too tired to go," Jared said.

"Not too tired," Vinnie protested sleepily. "Gotta go. Everybody else works."

Ah. Jared considered that. He smiled. "You couldn't go, either, could you," he asked after a moment, "if you had a job?"

"A job?" Vinnie sounded as if it were a foreign expression. He opened one eye and looked at Jared.

"What do you do? When you work, I mean."

"Drum."

"What?"

"I play drums for the Outrageous Raiders," Vinnie enunciated carefully.

"Oh, right." Jared remembered now. "What if your band got a job then?"

Vinnie laughed. "By tomorrow?"

"If one turns up, will you take it?"

Vinnie grinned. "Hell, yes."

It had taken fewer phone calls than Jared had imagined to accomplish it.

"Kansas City?" Vinnie had sounded doubtful when Jared woke him to tell him. "That's like hours from here."

"Best I could do," he said. "Big city. Lots of people will hear you." And it meant Annie couldn't go over to the Granatelli house and haul Vinnie off by the ear. "You have to leave right now."

"Now?"

But in the end money had talked—as had Vinnie's fellow band members. It was a terrific opportunity, they said.

Vinnie left before dawn. It only remained for Jared to finish packing the tools around the workbench he and Nick had already put in the camper portion of the truck the morning before.

It was a crazy thing to be doing, taking off for New York, and he knew it.

He was supposed to fly to Acapulco on Tuesday for a script consultation. His agent, awakened at four in the morning to hear the news, had been less than thrilled.

"You're doin' what?" Larry had demanded, his voice croaking with indignation and broken sleep.

"Driving to New York for a friend."

"Why in hell can't you fly to New York for a friend? You could be back in L.A. the next day. You got commitments, responsibilities."

"I can't," Jared said.

"Mmmph." Larry's doubt was clear. "What'm I gonna tell 'em, for God's sake?"

"Tell them I have commitments, responsibilities."

"Very funny."

"I'll call you tomorrow. We should be halfway there."

"You better be. You sure you know what you're doin'?"

"I'm sure."

But now, glancing over at Annie, sitting like a statue next to him, he wondered.

Annie always talked. He couldn't remember a time when she wasn't spouting out something or other. Now she sat as silent as a stone for mile after mile.

It unnerved him.

"Smile," he said to her as they trundled on over hill after rolling hill.

"Why should I?"

"It makes you beautiful."

She rolled her eyes. "I am not beautiful."

"In the eye of the beholder, you are."

"Flattery will get you nowhere, Jared."

He cocked his head. "What will?"

She gave an impatient snort and drummed her fingers on her thigh. "Why are you doing this?" she demanded.

"Friendship?"

"Oh, right."

"Nick *is* my friend."

She glared. "But Vinnie's his brother. Vinnie could have done it."

"What do you want to hear? I'm doing it because of you? Fine," Jared said. "I'm doing it because of you."

"But why?"

"Why do you think?"

"How should I know? Your mind is a mystery to me. Always has been. Probably you want to rub my nose in your success."

Was that what she thought? Given her perversity, probably it was. Damn but sometimes she could be an idiot. And what was he supposed to do to convince her otherwise? Grovel?

He grinned at her instead. "There's an idea."

"I'm not impressed," she informed him primly and looked away out the window.

"No?"

"No."

"What would it take to impress you?" he asked, curious.

She turned to face him, her brown eyes challenging. "Seeing you in a good role. A demanding one."

"You don't think Reid McCullough is demanding?"

"I think Reid McCullough is a waste."

Jared disagreed. "He's taught me a hell of a lot."

"He's a two-bit he-man cop who has the emotional depth of a slice of bread. To misquote Dorothy Parker, his feelings run the gamut from A to B."

Stung, but unwilling to show it, Jared laughed. "Sure you're not exaggerating a bit?"

"Oh, I'll give him A and B," Annie said magnanimously. "But I won't go beyond it."

Jared just shook his head, unsure whether to laugh or cry. The only thing he was beginning to be sure of was that getting through to Annie was going to be tougher than he'd thought.

"It's true," Annie insisted. She was warming to the topic, he could tell. "Doing him week after week you sell yourself short. You had enormous talent. *Have* enormous talent. You could be Hamlet, Prince Hal, Romeo, for heaven's sakes!"

"And so many people knew that," Jared said mockingly. "Besieged with offers, I was. Casting directors lining up around the block."

"You could've waited."

"For what?"

Annie's fingers strangled each other. "You don't see it, do you?"

Jared just looked at her, thinking how much he'd loved her, how happy he'd been to get the offer—any offer—so that finally he had something to offer her. "I thought I did," he said quietly.

Annie frowned. "What's that mean?"

"Think about it."

SHE DID, TO NO AVAIL. She couldn't see the point of selling out, of becoming less than the best you could be. Not when you had a talent like Jared's.

And to expect her to sell out her talent and go with him!

But then, he didn't think she had talent, did he?

What career? he'd asked her.

The words were burned on her brain. And even now, two years later, the pain of them was still sharp.

But there was no point in talking about it. No point in arguing. He couldn't see—or wouldn't. And she ought to know by now that she couldn't make him.

What difference did it make, anyway? Jared was a part of her past. They weren't living together anymore. They weren't lovers. He lived in Malibu, she in New York. He had his life; she had hers.

In the meantime, however, she reminded herself, they had to get to New York. For whatever perverse reason Jared had connived it, for a thousand miles they were stuck with each other. To bring up painful topics would not be the best way to go on.

"Let's agree to disagree and forget it," she said.

"Then what would you be wanting to talk about?"

Annie sighed and stared out the window. "Nothing."

"Nothing? Annie D'Angelo? Ms. The-World-Needs-My-Opinion Personified?"

Endure, Annie told herself. *Just endure. This, too shall pass.*

But a thousand miles was a lot longer than a wedding.

THEY COULD HAVE DONE IT, she told herself, if only Jared had cooperated. He didn't. And the close confines of Vinnie's rattletrap truck undermined her resolve, as well.

It was virtually impossible to sit side by side with Jared, listen to him hum the same soft Irish tunes she used to hear while he was shaving each morning, smell the same subtle hint of Patrick's soap that she remembered so well, and not remember other things, too.

It didn't help that Jared seemed to have no qualms—in fact took considerable pleasure—in reminding her.

"Do you remember the day you got the part in *Vampire Lesbians*?" he asked her while she tried to ignore him over a lunch of hamburgers in Effingham.

"Mmm," she muttered discouragingly, crunching down on a pickle and staring past his left ear.

"We took a picnic to Central Park."

"Mmm."

"Salami and cheese, I think. And beer. Some kind of beer."

Ale, Annie thought, but didn't say. It was Murphy's Ale.

"We went down near the boathouse and lay in the sun. God, it was hot that day."

It had been beastly, but they hadn't cared. They had spread out a blanket near the boathouse, then had lain down in the sun, basking in its warmth and Annie's great good fortune.

They had smiled at each other, nibbled their sandwiches—and each other—tasted the ale—and each other. . . .

"And that rainstorm . . ." Jared said.

It had come out of nowhere, drenching them. And Jared had finally pulled her to her feet and hurried her home. The rain might have dampened their bodies, but it didn't touch their ardor. They barely made it up the long flights of stairs to their apartment before they were making love.

"Remember that day, Annie?" Jared asked her softly now.

And Annie shut her eyes and pretended she didn't hear.

"How about the night we were supposed to go with Diane to South Street after we wallpapered the bathroom?" It was midafternoon now, and they were approaching Terre Haute.

Annie's fists clenched against her thighs. *No, Jared,* she pleaded silently. *Please, don't.*

"And we almost wallpapered each other instead?"

You started it, Annie thought. He had dabbed a bit of paste on her nose when she stepped in front of him. She'd retaliated with a swipe across his cheek. And what had started as a simple paste fight escalated until they were both covered. They stood there, faced off, breathing hard. Then Jared tossed aside his brush and, with smoldering eyes, came toward her, reached for her shirt and pulled it off her. Annie tugged his over his head. Her jeans followed his to the floor.

Between kisses they called Diane to beg off, then climbed into the shower together.

Annie had never made love in the shower before. Jared hadn't either. For novices they felt quite pleased with themselves.

"But I'm thinking we could do with a bit more practice," Jared had said the next morning, and within minutes they were starting all over.

"Remember that?" Jared asked her now.

It was psychological warfare, what Jared was doing to her. Annie prayed for earplugs, for mind plugs. Mostly for memory plugs.

But God wasn't listening. At least not to her.

"WHAT ABOUT THE NIGHT we got locked in the library," Jared said, slanting her a sidelong glance as they approached Indianapolis. "What was the play I was working on?"

Desire under the Elms, Annie answered silently.

Jared snapped his fingers. "*Desire under the Elms*. How could I forget? And you said you were sure they'd have a copy."

They had, but neither Jared nor Annie had a library card, so they couldn't check it out.

Instead they had sat huddled in the back reading it to each other in whispers, while the librarian shushed them. Finally, realizing she wasn't going to get rid of them, she had sent them into a storeroom to practice.

In the throes of rehearsing, neither of them had noticed the time. The librarian, apparently in the throes of eagerness to leave at quitting time, didn't remember them.

It was nearly eleven when Annie discovered they were locked in.

There was no way to get out without setting off the alarm system, no way to do that without getting themselves and the librarian into more trouble than it was worth. So they had spent hours prowling the stacks, reading aloud to each other from their favorite plays, acting and arguing, exchanging interpretations, staging, directorial approach.

At last, shortly before dawn, Jared had settled in one of the lumpy old armchairs and held out his arms to her. And Annie, sleepy and smiling, had curled up to sleep in the secure, loving warmth of those arms.

Oh, yes, she remembered, God help her. She burrowed more deeply into the lumpy seat, remembering all too well.

HE WASN'T MAKING A DENT. It was like talking to the woman who wasn't there.

Mile after mile now, hour after hour, Jared reminisced, determinedly dredged up every damn thing he could think of, every single warm, glorious moment of the time they'd shared.

And all he had to show for it was an ache deep inside, two hundred and forty six miles on the odometer and tired vocal chords.

She was so different to the Annie he remembered. Quiet. Contained. No, not contained; vacuum-sealed. There was no touching her. No reaching her.

The Annie Jared remembered had worn her emotions on her sleeve, her thoughts in her mouth.

Sometimes, in their communal past, he had even wished for a bit of peace and quiet, a few moments of serenity.

But he would have rather had her flinging coffee mugs at his head than sitting in tomblike silence mile after mile.

It wasn't like Annie.

It made him nervous.

Was it possible she really didn't care?

No, he thought frantically. She cared. She had to! She'd kissed him, hadn't she?

But what if it had simply been because she'd been caught unawares? What if she had merely been reacting because of some past shared memory?

What if, here and now, she really didn't give a damn?

Damn it, it wasn't fair! If he had tumbled again at a simple glance, the least she could do was care!

There had to be a way, he told himself, to jar her out of her apathy, to make her look at him again, smile at him again, love him again.

THEY WERE in the middle of nowhere.

Fields of corn stretched off in all directions. There wasn't a car, a house, even a cow to be seen. Annie jerked up and stared.

"Where the hell are we?"

As she spoke Jared pulled over onto the narrow shoulder of the barely graveled road. "Here."

He waved an expansive arm to include mile upon mile of undulating uninhabited countryside and seemed perfectly satisfied with that less-than-enlightening response.

"And where is here?" Annie asked tightly.

She was hot and sticky and growing more irritable by the minute. The humidity was oppressive, there was clearly a storm brewing, and Vinnie's truck didn't run to such amenities as air-conditioning. The open windows had turned her hair into an ebony haystack. She raked her fingers through the snarls.

"I think," Jared said, consulting the map and then jabbing it with his finger, "we're somewhere about here."

Annie moved closer and looked. "That's somewhere between Akron, Ohio, and the Mississippi."

Jared shrugged equably. "More or less."

Annie glowered at him. "Why are we here?"

"Shortcut."

"*Shortcut?*" The road seemed scarcely more than a cow path meandering through the corn.

"And I saw that." He turned his head and Annie followed his gaze.

What she saw made her stomach feel hollow and her throat tight. Out in the middle of one of the fields stood a barn, windburned and decaying, its roof crumbling, its doors gone.

She sat very still, swallowed carefully. "So what?" Her tone was level.

He looked at her, surprised. "You're saying you don't remember?"

If she was really an actress, she could do this, Annie told herself, and managed an indifferent shrug.

Jared's eyes darkened. He looked almost angry now. Annie saw his fingers clench against his jeans.

"I'm going to look at the barn," he said, his tone controlled.

Annie allowed him a polite, distant smile. "Go ahead. I'll wait here."

The storm clouds coming were nothing compared to what she saw in his eyes as he spun away from her and strode off through the corn. She watched him go, chewed her lip, and only when he'd disappeared inside did she breathe again.

. . ."I'M GOING TO LOOK at the barn," Jared had said. It had begun just that way.

They were in Vermont. A week's holiday. A magical time. Just the two of them, with no auditions, no curtain times, no lines to learn. Nothing but time for each other.

One afternoon they'd rented bicycles and had ridden for miles seeking the proper picnic spot. Annie had in mind a verdant brookside, a smooth stone outcropping on which to spread a blanket and lay out their repast.

Jared had found them a moldering old barn, half falling down, certainly unused in the last fifty years, and declared it perfect. "Let's eat here."

Annie still remembered her astonishment.

"Here?" she'd demanded.

"Sure. And why not?"

"It's full of—" Annie had swallowed and made a face.

Jared had laughed, held out his hand to her, and smiled his beguiling smile. "It's full of dreams," he'd said.

And Annie, perplexed, but besotted, had given in.

It was musty and smelled of long-forgotten livestock, but it took only a few moments for Jared to convince her that he was right.

He led her into the barn's murky darkness, leaving the half-hung door ajar. Annie stood staring in mute amazement while he prowled about.

He touched the supports, ran his fingers along the rough-hewn wood, then smiled and beckoned to her. "Look at this."

Annie came over to see what he was pointing at. In one of the uprights she saw faint initials carved.

"R.B. 1832," Jared said. "I wonder who he was. The farmer, do you suppose?"

Annie shook her head. "His son."

Even as she said it, she'd had a sudden vision of a young boy, bored with chores that would have to be done again tomorrow and yet again the day after, seeking to leave his mark in some more permanent way.

She saw him, dark-haired and lanky, his young face intent as he carved out his initials in the wood, then smiling as he traced them with his finger when he was done. She blinked, astonished at the clarity of her vision.

Jared nodded, his own finger tracing the initials. "Could be," he said.

"No could about it," Annie replied. She was sure.

Jared touched her cheek with his hand. Then, just when she thought he might kiss her, he smiled and slung the bag with their food in it over his shoulder, then tested the strength of the beam-and-peg ladder to the loft.

Finding it stable enough, he climbed up and cajoled Annie up after him.

"Here?" she'd said again, but this time her voice was merely doubtful, not disbelieving.

"Here." Jared took the blanket from her and spread it on what was left of the hay. Then he sat down. "R.B. would have been coming here, too. Bringing his lady love."

"He was ten," Annie argued, smiling.

Jared grinned. "A boy's not ten forever, *a stór*. He brought her here." He sounded positive.

"Ah, you think so, do you?" Annie had teased.

Jared nodded, his expression turning serious. "Can you not see?"

He drew her down onto the blanket beside him, and with words and imagination he showed her what he meant. In the shadowy depths of the loft, Jared's soft Irish voice created the scene for her. He rebuilt the barn, recreated the life of the family who owned it. The boy and his family came alive.

Jared made her feel the stubborn determination of the man who'd lugged the stones for the foundation, who'd sawed the lumber for the walls and pegged the joists and beams. He made her see a boy pitching hay, mucking out stalls and, in the darkness, stealing a few heady moments with the girl he loved.

And there were those words again, as the boy might have whispered them, as Jared whispered them to her. *Aine, tá mo chrói istigh agat.*

And through Jared's words, in the sound of his voice when she didn't even know what the words meant, Annie saw it all.

She lay back against the blanket and envisioned that long-ago family—their pride of accomplishment, their joys and sorrows, their loves and hopes and dreams.

"They're here, you see," he'd said to her. "Those dreams. Floating around, waiting. Do you feel them now?"

"Oh, yes."

Then he took her in his arms and whispered, "You are my dream."

And Annie went to him willingly.

Food forgotten, picnic postponed, she lost herself in Jared's arms, dreamed as he did, secure in the warmth of the blanket and their love.

Love. She loved him.

It was the first time Annie had realized it, and she wanted . . . *wanted* . . .

"Hey, up there!" a man had hollered while they were still trembling in the aftermath. He rattled their bicycles down below. "'Tain't safe! Best come down."

And Annie, jerked back to reality, had sat up and wrapped her shirt close around her.

"He's right," she'd said, afraid of her dreams, knowing they were too much to ask for, unwilling to face the implications of her love. A tremor ran through her. She fumbled with her buttons.

Jared reached for her, but she shook him off.

"Come on," she'd urged. "Get up. Let's go."

But he had lain there a moment longer, his green eyes almost black in the filtered light. His gaze roved the leaky roof, the rotting timbers. His eyes lit on Annie, lingered, moving over her in visual caress as loving as the physical ones they just shared. She bit her lip, still wanting.

Jared smiled. A gentle smile, a wistful smile. "And what are you thinking, Annie, *a stór?*"

"I think," Annie said shakily, torn between an impossible dream and an even more impossible one, "that we'd better go."

"WE'D BETTER GO," she said when he got back.

She'd watched him coming, her head averted, but her eyes keeping track of his every move. He'd taken forever. She'd thought she might have to go after him.

She didn't know if she could have borne it. The memories hurt too much.

"Hurry up! It's going to rain."

The storm clouds were building behind them quickly now, dark thunderheads moving in, filling the horizon to the west, blotting out the sun. But it wasn't the storm that was making Annie feel strung out, tense. It was the look on Jared's face.

The impatience was gone, as was the eagerness. Even the anger had fled.

He seemed remote now. As if the whole man, body and soul, had gone to the barn, but only the body had come back.

Chapter Four

SHE DIDN'T CARE.

He couldn't believe it, but it had to be true.

While he'd stood there staring at that barn, reliving every bittersweet moment of their lovemaking in Vermont, remembering every sweet sigh and tender touch, Annie had stayed in the truck.

While he had been waiting, hoping, praying that she was experiencing the same memories that had compelled him to stop the minute he'd spied the ramshackle building, Annie had been sitting, consummately bored.

She really didn't care.

Because if the dreams they'd shared that day in Vermont didn't reach her, nothing would.

So be it.

Maybe it was the heat of the moment, envy of Nick, the phase of the moon . . . but whatever it was that had compelled him to pursue Annie again, it was obviously a mistake.

He'd done his best, but there was damn all left he could do.

He got into the truck without sparing her a glance. Flicking the key, he gunned the engine.

They hit the road just as the first rain began to fall.

Not that this was your gentle Irish drizzle. Within moments the sky had opened up and a sudden lashing gale, with hailstones the size of mothballs, pelted down.

Jared rolled his window up with one hand while he gripped the wheel tighter with the other and struggled to keep the truck on the road.

Maybe the storm would be a blessing, he told himself. Maybe Annie would have developed an aversion to thunder, a fear of lightning. Maybe she'd throw herself into his arms and beg him to protect her.

And maybe the snakes would come back and drive St. Patrick out of Ireland.

Enough of your foolishness, he chided himself. *Enough of your hope. What's over is over.*

What mattered now was getting them to New York as quickly as possible, thus putting his mistake behind him.

Doggedly Jared drove.

The roof leaked. So did the seal around the windshield. The rain obscured his vision. The windshield wipers did no good at all.

An hour ago, Jared thought, he'd have rejoiced at the storm. An hour ago he'd have considered it a blessing from God, a chance to get through to Annie.

But there was no getting through to Annie, and now all he wanted was to be gone.

Lightning crackled around them, and the thunder rocked the truck. At least Jared hoped that was thunder causing the truck to shake.

But when the jarring thuds became suddenly more intense, faster, rhythmic, he knew there was more to it than the weather and the bad road. He cursed under his breath as he pulled over onto the narrow shoulder next to the drainage ditch.

"What is it?"

"We've got a puncture."

"A flat tire? You're joking."

He wished he were. Rain and hail were bad enough. He sighed and shut off the engine, then started to open the door.

"Where are you going?"

"To change the tire."

"In this?" Annie's disbelieving gaze went from him to the downpour. Hail still rattled against the roof.

"Have you a better idea, then?" he asked politely.

There was a pause. A gust of wind shook the cab. Annie looked away. "No."

Not, stay here and enjoy the pleasure of each other's company? Jared thought mockingly.

"Right, then," he said and plunged out into the storm.

AND JUST LIKE that he was gone.

Annie supposed she should be glad. It meant that many fewer minutes of being together, after all.

But, she reminded herself, they weren't getting any closer to New York as they sat here, so it didn't make a lot of difference.

She rubbed the tip of her nose where a raindrop hit, then squinted out the fogged-up windows to see if perhaps there was a break in the clouds.

She saw no break. She saw no Jared, either.

She'd heard him get into the camper. She'd heard fumblings and mutterings. Then nothing. A minute passed. Two. Then four. Another bump. Another mutter. Perhaps he couldn't find a spare.

Perhaps Vinnie didn't have a spare.

An ungodly awful thought.

An extremely likely possibility. Annie groaned.

She heard another bump. Another thump. A muffled exclamation. Then nothing again except a fresh spatter of hail against the roof.

Jared was an idiot to go out in this.

The fact was that he had surprised her. It seemed so contrary to his purpose, which appeared to have something to do with spending as much time tormenting her as possible.

She would have thought that being trapped inside the cab together would've been a golden opportunity for him.

Why hadn't he taken it?

She tried peering out the windows again, but there was so little visibility due to the condensation that she had to open the door a crack instead.

Jared still wasn't there. The drainage ditch was, however, and it seemed uncomfortably closer. Even as she watched, the rain washed another inch away.

"Jared, where are you?" she muttered.

More bumps and thuds gave her an answer. Maybe she ought to go help him.

Nothing in her wanted to do it.

Every single molecule of her being cried out for her to stay as far away from Jared Flynn as possible. But emotional self-preservation gave way to the need for physical self-preservation. If she didn't help him, chances were they'd end up in the ditch.

Without giving herself time to reconsider, she wrenched open the door and plunged out into the deluge. Torrents of rain plastered her shirt to her skin before she'd taken five steps. The water washed up over the tops of her sandals. She hoped to God Jared had found a spare.

But when she opened the door, Jared was, to her astonishment, spread-eagled across the top of the workbench, facing her, while he struggled to get a tarp in place.

"What in heaven's name are you doing?"

"Just help me and shut up," Jared bit out.

And Annie, seeing now just exactly what he was doing, scrambled in and began to help. The water was leaking in through the seams in the roof, soaking the surface of the workbench, drenching the tools. Jared had apparently used every available rag to wrap as many as he could. Apparently he'd just started using his clothes.

"Did you find the spare?" Annie asked him.

"I'll find the bloody spare when I've got this done," Jared snapped. "If you're in so much of a damned hurry to get away from me, maybe you'd have a shirt or two to donate to the cause!'

Taken aback, Annie grabbed her garment bag and flung it at him. "Use anything you want, just let's get this show on the road because we'll damn well wash away if we don't!"

Jared stopped his frantic wrapping, pushed past her and poked his head out the door. A string of Gaelic curses followed. He thrust the garment bag at Annie and scrabbled under the bench to wiggle the jack loose, then pulled out the lug wrench, as well.

"I see the tire," Annie said and pointed silently toward the front of the camper when he looked up.

Jared groaned. It meant moving a box of files and chisels, a set of clamps, boxes of unidentified woodworking gizmos and several saws. But there was no choice, so he did it.

He gritted his teeth and wrestled the tire past the boxes of Nick's tools, then crawled back out after it. When he raised his head again, Annie was staring out the back toward the rapidly widening ditch.

She looked at him doubtfully, but she didn't say a word.

She didn't have to. He knew what she was thinking—that she could hardly wait to get rid of him and that they'd be that much closer to their destination if he hadn't taken them off the main road.

"Get out of my way," he said and shouldered past, then splashed out after the tire onto the soggy ground.

Lightning split the sky behind him even as he landed. The reverberations from the thunder were almost instantaneous. He ignored them and strode around to crouch by the right rear tire. There was barely room to work. The shoulder of the road was slipping away behind him as he hunkered down.

There was no hubcap. Just as well. He doubted he'd have got enough purchase to pry it off if there had been. And any exertion of force might have flung him right into the ditch if the screwdriver had slipped. Thank heaven for small favors, he thought. They were doubtless the only sort he was going to get.

Taking the lug wrench, he began to loosen the nuts. Water streamed down his back, trickled beneath the waistband of his jeans. He muttered curses under his breath. There weren't enough of them in Gaelic and English combined to say what he was feeling at the moment.

At last, the nuts loosened, he turned away from the truck, made his way along the shoulder, bent down and picked up a good-sized rock, which he carried back and lodged against one of the front wheels. When he turned around to look for a second one, it appeared in Annie's outstretched hands.

She stood, silently holding it out, rain sluicing down her face.

He looked for bitterness and didn't see any. He looked for impatience and didn't find that, either.

He took the rock and bent to secure the other wheel. "Thanks."

He felt her eyes on him as he moved past her to set the jack beneath the bumper and to begin to pump it. Please God it would hold.

The shoulder of this less-than-wonderful gravel road was uneven, causing the base of the jack to dig in at an angle. Jared righted it, continued to pump. It slipped. He swore, then wedged it more firmly into the earth.

More of the shoulder slipped away, the weight of the truck and the force of the water causing it to crumble. He wondered how much longer it would last.

He pumped harder, faster. At last he had the back bumper raised. Not much, but enough. He hoped.

It was hailing again. The stones battered him, stinging as they hit his head, his ears, his back. He wiped the water from his face and bent again beside the flat, working the wrench on each nut in turn, spinning it as fast as he could. Every time he got a nut off, a hand reached out and took it from him.

He pulled the flat tire off and rested it against the side of the truck, then dragged the spare around and shouldered it into place. Mud was everywhere—on the tire, on the truck, on the wrench, on him. His hair hung in his eyes and he swiped at it with a muddy hand, succeeding only in blurring his vision.

A clean hand reached out and brushed his hair away. He grunted his thanks. The hand gave him a lug nut. He put it on and spun it around with his fingers, then took the next one offered, and the next.

When all the nuts were back in place he lowered the bumper and eased the jack out.

Wordlessly Annie took it from him and stowed it in the back while he used the wrench to tighten the lug nuts. The wind was picking up, flinging rain and hailstones at his back again. He winced and grabbed the flat tire, horsing it around to the back of the camper and flinging it in.

Annie handed him a rag. He wiped his face on it, then his hands, then looked for the first time into her eyes.

She smiled at him.

And Jared, thanking God for what was, in his eyes, the biggest miracle of the day, smiled back.

THEY HADN'T FINISHED any too soon. As he edged his way alongside the truck, another chunk of earth slipped and fell away into the ditch. Another three inches and the truck would go with it.

"I'll drive," Annie said and held out her hand for the key.

"I'm fine," he protested through chattering teeth.

"You're a great actor, Jared," she said. "But not that great." The fingers beckoned. "Give me the key."

He couldn't help it—he was a man, God help him. He grinned and said, "They're in my front pocket if you're wanting to get them."

And damned if she didn't.

She stuffed her hand right down into his pocket, thrusting around inside his soaking jeans, finding the keys—and him. Jared's whole body jerked in response.

Triumphant, keys in hand, Annie got into the cab.

Jared, still reeling from her touch, from a sense of things not being what he expected, from a feeling of the world slipping out of control, slid carefully in next to her and sat there shivering.

Annie started the engine. "You need a shower and dry clothes."

His teeth were chattering now. "So do you."

She was every bit as wet as he was, just not as muddy. She squinted through the windshield and slowly, carefully, edged the truck out onto the road and headed back toward the Interstate.

Jared watched her, trying to figure her out.

He had expected her to stay in the truck where it was safe and at least somewhat dry. He had expected her to let him get soaked and then tell him it was his own fault.

He hadn't expected her to volunteer her clothes to wrap up Nick's tools. He hadn't expected her to stand by, to hold the nuts, and wipe the rain off his face.

And he certainly hadn't expected his invitation to get the keys to be acted upon!

Even now in the most intimate part of his body, he still had the sensation of her touch.

Did she care?

Or didn't she?

She might have touched him for either reason: because it didn't matter, or because it did.

He shook his head, confused, shivering. He'd figure it out later. He only knew there was one thing he had to say before his teeth were chattering too much to get the word out. "Thanks."

Annie was silent for a long moment—long enough for him to wonder if she was becoming the woman of stone again. Then she said, "You're welcome." She turned her head and gave him a gentle smile. "Thank *you*."

ANNIE SUPPOSED THEY'D reached a truce.

At least Jared seemed to have subsided into relative silence, punctuated by periodic sneezes. And she herself felt disinclined to pick a fight. It was enough, at the moment, to fight the rain still buffeting the truck.

It was getting dark, the rain clouds making night come more rapidly than usual. The going was slow even when they got back on the Interstate. Part of it was due to the rain and part to a long repaving project. But finally a sign loomed on the right announcing mileage to the next town, a metropolis of eleven hundred people.

"I'm stopping," Annie said.

"Fine," Jared said, and sneezed. Twice.

Annie stomped down harder on the gas. In her mind's eye she could still see those few inches of crumbling mud, could still see the truck teetering almost on the edge, could still see Jared crouched there between the truck and the ditch, his dark hair plastered to his head as his hands moved swiftly to change the truck's tire.

And in her imagination she could see all too well the truck slipping and crushing him.

The very thought made her shiver with horror.

She didn't want to argue with Jared right now; she was too busy rejoicing that he was still alive.

And she had no intention of jeopardizing that fact by allowing him to get pneumonia. There was one motel sign for the small Ohio town they were coming to. Annie turned off.

Long and low and less than luxurious, the one-story sagging structure wasn't exactly beckoning. But Annie pulled in anyway.

"Any port in a storm," she said only half facetiously.

Jared smiled, but didn't reply.

"Are you all right?" His silence was beginning to concern her. It was so wholly out of character.

He sneezed.

Annie muttered an expletive. "Stay here," she commanded and headed for the office.

"I need two rooms for the night," she told her clerk, a spotty teenager who looked up from her movie magazine to give Annie the once-over.

"Don't got two," she said. "Only one left."

One room? In a town the size of this one?

Annie looked at her doubtfully. "Big convention in town?" she asked, trying for a light tone, one that wasn't directly challenging but that said she wasn't taking any nonsense.

The girl snapped her gum. "Highway department's got 'em."

"I beg your pardon?"

The girl let out a long-suffering sigh. "Down the road, y'know, where they're workin' on it. They all stay here during the week, see?"

Unhappily Annie did.

"What's wrong with the room?" she asked.

"'Sa nice room," the girl said. "Got mirrors on the ceiling an' everything." She smirked and snapped her gum again. "You want it for an hour or all night?"

Annie didn't want it at all. But given the circumstances, she decided, one room in the vicinity was worth two twenty miles away. "We'll take it for the night."

"Sixty dollars."

"*Sixty—*"

"It's a popular room."

"I'll bet," Annie muttered, foraging in her bag and handing over the money.

"Room eight." The girl lodged her gum in her cheek and handed Annie the key, then jerked her head in the direction of the long covered couch. "Down that way. Ice machine's broke, but th'air conditioner works."

Swell, Annie thought. The storm had brought the temperature down twenty degrees by itself. At the rate things were going, they'd need blankets by morning. She sighed and went back to the truck, climbed in and handed Jared a key.

He raised his eyebrows.

She ignored him, driving the truck down to the stall in front of the room. "This is it," she said and plunged once more into the deluge.

Jared hesitated a moment, then fetched their bags and followed.

It was not the Motel 6. The room was small, shabby and poorly lit. It also had only one double bed, which would no doubt complicate her life later on.

But it was clean and, more importantly, the mirrors didn't leak. A quick check of the bathroom showed it also had plenty of hot running water.

At the moment, Annie was content.

She dropped her bag on the bedside table. "Home sweet home."

Jared still stood mud-caked and dripping in the doorway. He looked at the double bed, at the mirrors, at Annie. His eyebrows hiked even further. He grinned, then sneezed.

"It was the only room left. The highway crew has all the others," Annie replied defensively, wrapping her arms across her chest. "You might've got pneumonia before we found another motel."

A corner of Jared's mouth lifted. "Objecting was I?"

She made a face at him. "Just don't get any ideas."

Jared paused, considering.

She waited, expecting the worst, but he didn't say anything; he just looked at her oddly for a moment, then nodded. "Right," he said and began unbuttoning his shirt. His chest was tanned with swirls of dark hair matted damply. Annie remembered how she used to trace with her fingertips along the lines of his muscles, making him shiver and arch and—

"Take the bathroom," she said quickly. "You can shower first."

She jerked open the door to the bathroom for him, waiting pointedly, heat suffusing her face.

She expected the inevitable suggestive remark. But he didn't make one.

He just said, "Thanks, I will," and scavenged through his duffel bag for dry clothes. There was one crumpled pair of jeans he hadn't used to wrap Nick's tools and a T-shirt. He looked doubtful, but tucked them under his arm and strode past her into the tiny bathroom.

It wasn't until the door shut firmly behind him and the shower began to run that Annie realized she'd been holding her breath.

THE MIRRORS WERE AMAZING. Jared had never been in a bed roofed by mirrors before. He'd heard about them, read about them, joked about them, but even in his wildest Hollywood escapade, he'd never experienced them.

"Welcome to the heartland of America," he intoned solemnly.

He lay back on the bed and stared up at his own amazed expression and started to laugh.

Fate, he told himself, was an amazing thing. An hour ago the last thing he would have expected was to be spending the night in a motel room with Annie in a bed beneath a ceiling full of mirrors.

An hour ago he would've expected her to push him in the ditch.

That she hadn't, that she'd helped him, that she even seemed concerned about him, that she hadn't balked at spending the night with him—well, hell, it gave a guy cause for hope!

He folded his arms beneath his head and waited, wondering what else fate might have in store.

The door to the bathroom opened and Annie emerged.

She was wearing a clean pair of white shorts and a scoop-neck shirt with the name of some New York eatery on it. Her long dark hair was wrapped up in a towel. She was barefoot, and her toes curled now against the threadbare carpet.

"What's funny?" she asked when she saw his smile.

"The mirrors," he said. But as he rose up on his elbows and looked at her—his eyes skating slowly over the lissome curves of her body, his mind remembering what that body looked like naked, his body reacting to that memory—the mirrors suddenly didn't seem so funny anymore.

Involuntarily he glanced upward and sucked in his breath.

Annie, following his gaze, grimaced. "It doesn't mean anything."

"Of course not," he agreed, folding his arms beneath his head, looking up at her.

Annie's eyes narrowed. She looked at him suspiciously. "Behave yourself, Jared Flynn, or you'll be sleeping in the truck."

Jared sneezed.

The immediate consternation on Annie's face made him smile. She took two steps in his direction, then stopped abruptly, stuffed her hands into the pockets of her shorts and glared at him. "You were an idiot to do that, you know."

"Do what?"

"Change that tire. You could've been killed." She looked almost angry.

He shrugged. "Would you rather the truck and Nick's workbench and tools were at the bottom of a ditch?"

She paused, as if weighing the choices, as she unwrapped the towel and began brushing through her tangled hair.

This morning Jared knew there would have been no hesitation. That she was considering it seemed hopeful as hell.

"It was still a stupid thing to do." Her voice was gruff.

He smiled. "It was," he said meekly.

She turned and glared at him. "Stop that!"

"Stop what?" He was all innocence.

"Stop agreeing with me. It means you're up to something."

He wiped the smile off his face. "Of course," he said. "I mean, of course not."

He grinned again as Annie threw her hairbrush at him.

At last! A sign of Annie, at last!

He sat up and stretched, retrieving the brush.

"Give me that." She held out her hand for it.

He shook his head. "Come then and get it."

Their eyes met, green challenging brown, brown defying the challenge.

"We're not playing games, Jared."

He swung his legs over the side of the bed, stood up, and began to walk toward her.

"Jar-ed." It was as much plea as warning. She took a step backward.

He moved closer, tapping the brush against his palm. "What?"

She moved away, but her hand came out again. "Give me my brush."

He shook his head no.

She was practically in the bathroom now. "Jared! Stop it!"

"Is it running away from me you are?" His voice teased her.

She stopped stock-still and lifted her chin. Annie D'Angelo's chin. Always ready to take whatever anyone dished out. He wanted to kiss it. Didn't. He wasn't pressing his luck.

"Jared—"

"Turn around."

She blinked. "Why?"

He scowled at her. "Were I going to beat you, you'd know it by now, Annie D'Angelo."

She flushed. "I know you won't beat me."

"Then turn around."

Their eyes locked. There was less challenge between them now, more patience, more wary curiosity. Slowly Annie turned.

Jared lifted the brush and began brushing her long dark hair.

He saw her shiver as the bristles slid gently down her scalp, heard her suck in her breath as he raised the brush and brought it down to stroke through her hair again.

"Jared." It was a protest. Not angry. Plaintive. Her fingers twisted in the towel.

His own tightened against the handle of the brush. His hand crept up and stroked the hair back away from her ears, threading through the heavy dark strands, weighing the cool silky feel against his fingers.

"Come here," he said, took her arm, and towed her over to the bed. His voice was rough with need. He sat down and drew her down to sit between his legs on the floor.

"Jared, I can—"

"I know you can," he said, brushing rhythmically, smoothly. "I'm wanting to."

He had always loved Annie's hair. It was so soft, so long, so luxuriously thick. He had loved to bury his face in it, had loved to thread his fingers through it, had loved to sit her down after she had washed it and brush it dry as they sat in the firelight and listened to Bach in their warm, cozy apartment.

There was no Bach here. No firelight, either. Certainly no warm, cozy apartment.

But there was Annie.

And Annie was what Jared needed more than anything on earth.

SHE SHOULDN'T LET HIM. She should get up and grab the hairbrush. She should walk—no, *run*—as far away from Jared Flynn as she could.

It was folly to let him close, disaster to let him touch.

But even knowing that, Annie sat, mesmerized, luxuriating in the feel of Jared's fingers in her hair, in the gentle tug of the brush against the tangles.

The shower had mellowed her. The hot water had revived her, at the same time making her feel warm and sleepy. She should never have taken one. She should have gritted her teeth and opted for cold.

Instead she had foolishly gone ahead and pampered herself. Then she had come out to find Jared lying there bare-chested on the bed, a pair of faded jeans low on his hips, a smile on his face.

It was like being hit by a truck.

She'd tried to sound indifferent, cheerful. Her eyes had kept straying to the mirrors. Jared's eyes had done the same. And his smile had mocked her, had said he knew she would be putty in his hands.

And she, fool that she was, had challenged him, trying to deny it.

Silence had definitely been the safer route. She tried to think how she could retreat to it now.

Her mind wasn't cooperating, nor was her body. No one had ever brushed her hair the way Jared did. No one else had ever taken the time. She was always impatient with it herself.

It was Jared who had taught her to love the soft curls of her hair. It was Jared who had made her glad she so rarely got it cut.

After Jared left her, she had cut it. Spite, perhaps. Revenge? That, too.

But, of course, Jared had never known. And all of her other friends had stared at her close-cropped curls with dismay.

"What have you done to your hair?" they'd demanded. "It was so beautiful long. Grow it back, Annie! Grow it back!"

She had. Because they all wanted her to, she told herself. But deep down she knew that wasn't the whole reason.

She grew it back because she didn't feel like Annie without it.

And sometimes, when it finally got long again, she found herself washing it, then brushing and brushing it until it was dry, and remembering Jared.

Remembering what a scoundrel he was, she reminded herself now. Remembering how unscrupulous, how manipulative, how selfish.

Keep on remembering, she urged herself and stiffened under the steady rhythm of the brush.

FOOD WAS THE LAST THING on Jared Flynn's mind, but he had to do something before he went berserk.

He could, of course, try pulling her back on the bed, ripping off her clothes and making love to her. God knew it was what he wanted to do.

Annie was skittish, like an unbroken filly. It would take time. But Jared Flynn knew how to wait.

So when he said, "I'm starving," he hoped she'd misunderstand, because it certainly wasn't steak and potatoes or even mulligan stew he craved.

Annie appeared startled by his suggestion to have supper. She had been sitting cross-legged, slumped forward as he stroked the brush through her hair, her body swaying gently with each long stroke.

At his words she jerked upright, then scrambled to her feet, snatching the hairbrush away from him, the color high in her face.

"Of—" she cleared her throat "—of course. Good idea. I'll just get my shoes." She headed for the bathroom, tugging the brush through her hair as she went.

Jared, watching her go, lay back on the bed, looked up at his reflection. And winked.

THE MEAL WAS A QUIET ONE, the silences that grew between them papered over by the bustling bonhomie of their waitress.

As they were, for part of the evening, the only patrons in the tiny café that advertised "24 Hour Breakfast, Videos and

Night Crawlers," she took it upon herself to attend to their every need.

"You're not from these parts," she said right off as she pointed them toward a table. But then she looked more closely at Jared. Annie, who had seen the fluttering interest of the women at the wedding, waited expectantly for him to be recognized, curious as to how he would handle his fame.

"You been in here before?" the waitress asked him. "You look familiar."

He shook his head. "Lots of people think that," he said, his usual Irish accent carefully masked. "I've got a common face."

The waitress laughed and patted his cheek. "Not hardly, sweetheart. Sure do look familiar, though."

It was on the tip of Annie's tongue to enlighten the woman, but she didn't. It was simply interesting that Jared didn't enlighten her, either. Perhaps Hollywood hadn't entirely gone to his head.

Jared ordered the trout and Annie the meat loaf. The waitress praised their choices, then squinted once more at Jared. "You related to the Burnses? Cal's brother?"

"No, sorry."

The waitress sighed, took their menus and headed back to the kitchen.

"The price of fame," Annie said.

Jared laughed. "Everyone thinks you're somebody's brother."

In her fantasies—those designed to assure her she was quite well off without him—she imagined Jared basking in the adulation of fans across the continent, lapping up the notoriety, the praise, the fawning looks.

In fact he seemed indifferent. She looked at him closely, trying to decide how he really felt, where the actor left off and the real Jared Flynn took over.

He looked up and caught her eye. A brow lifted. "Well?"

She lifted her chin. "Well, what?"

"Are you only looking or do you want to buy?"

Annie could feel the blood burn in her cheeks. She pressed her lips together, halfway between fury and laughter. But now, with a soup and salad in her and the promise of a good meal to come, it was easier to laugh than to get angry, easier to ignore the teasing than to fight it.

"You're incorrigible," she told him.

"I try."

Annie, unnerved by the warmth of his smile and by her instantaneous reaction to it, glanced away out the window. "The rain is slowing down," she said, more to fill the silence than because it was true.

But Jared gravely agreed, "Yes, it is," as the waitress came and set their plates in front of them. She offered Annie ketchup for her meat loaf, brought Jared more lemon for the fish, refilled their coffee cups, told Jared he really looked remarkably like Cal Burns. When she had left, the silence stretched on and on.

"I wonder if we'll get much more rain," Annie ventured.

"The weather report said so," Jared replied.

"It did?"

He nodded. "Until morning at least. Low pressure area all across the Ohio Valley, the forecaster said. One to two inches more possible. Look for rain until midmorning. Pollen count's down. Good news for allergy sufferers."

Annie looked at him suspiciously.

Jared laid his fork down. "Molds are up, though," he added solemnly. "Bad news for other allergy sufferers." He cut another piece of fish, then looked up in the face of her complete silence. "What?"

Annie's mouth twitched. "You didn't hear any of that," she accused, a grin tugging at the corners of her mouth.

He was all blank-faced innocence. "I did. Swear on my Uncle Paddy's casket."

"Your Uncle Paddy's alive and well in County Cork." Her gaze narrowed. "Isn't he?"

Jared grinned, sunshine breaking through. "That he is."

"Definitely incorrigible." Annie gave him a dirty look.

But the warmth and the meal seemed to have mellowed Jared, as well. He might tease, but he didn't push. Instead he seemed content to eat his trout and baked potato, to nod at the easy chatter of the waitress, to smile at Annie.

And for the first time Annie dared to smile back.

THE RAIN HAD IN FACT slowed considerably by the time they finished their supper. Annie didn't know about Jared, but she felt warm and well fed and sleepier by the minute. She pushed away her plate, yawned and stretched.

"Ready to leave?" Jared asked her.

She nodded and stood up, fumbling for money in her bag.

Jared put a hand on her arm. "My treat."

Annie opened her mouth to protest, but Jared had already handed the waitress a bill. He winked at her. "Keep the change."

She looked at the money in her hand, her eyes widening. Her gaze went back to Jared and she beamed. "You sure as hell ain't a Burns, sweetheart. They're skinflints."

No, Jared wasn't a skinflint. Never had been. He'd rarely had much, but he'd always been generous with what he had. Annie slanted him a glance as they walked along the road.

"That was nice of you," she ventured.

Jared shrugged. "She works hard. Besides—" his grin flashed in the darkness "—I'm a nice guy."

"Yes," Annie agreed slowly, "I suppose you are."

"Let's hear it for enthusiasm," Jared said wryly.

Annie shrugged. "You did force your way along on this trip, you know," she reminded.

"I got Vinnie a job, though."

"Yes, but—"

"And I fixed the puncture."

"Which it was your fault we got."

"Perhaps. But at great peril, I saved us, the truck and all Nick's tools."

"And you're modest, too."

Jared grinned. "I never claimed to be perfect."

"It's about the only thing you haven't claimed," Annie said tartly as they stepped up onto the walkway in front of their room and Jared slipped the key into the lock.

"I haven't yet claimed to be a great lover." He pushed open the door and flicked on the light, illuminating the bed and the mirrors above it. "I thought I'd let you make your own judgment on that."

Chapter Five

ANNIE STARED AT HIM, shocked, her cheeks flaming. "If you think for one minute—"

Jared spread his hands, palms up. "I had to say it."

Her mouth went slack.

"I did."

"Why?"

"Because it was there. Deny you were thinking it. Tell me it never crossed your mind."

"I never wanted you to make love to me!"

"Liar."

"Never!"

"Ah, Annie." And before she could stop him, he reached for her, hauling her into his arms, holding her close, his lips against her ear, his cheek resting on her hair.

She stiffened, pulled back, resisted, and found herself held fast. She could feel the solid warmth of Jared's chest against hers, the soft denim of his jeans brushing her bare legs. She could hear the uneven rasp of his breath and the steady beat of his heart. And against his neck she could smell soap—not the subtle spice of the Irish Patrick's this time, but the strong institutional brand she'd used only hours ago herself.

She steeled herself against him, waiting. It had to happen, she'd told herself.

Ever since Jared had appeared at Cynthia's this morning, she'd known it was only a matter of time before he tried to assert his power over her.

All day long she'd been expecting it, anticipating it, waiting for it.

She waited for the nibble on her ear, the soft persuasive kisses and even softer persuasive words that Jared was so good at. She waited for his hands to leave her arms, to slide around beneath her shirt, slipping up to caress the smooth expanse of her back. She waited for the questing fingers to inch beneath the waistband of her shorts, to seek the heat growing even now within her.

She waited in vain.

He simply stood there, holding her, rocking her against him. And then, when she relaxed almost imperceptibly, he loosened his grip and stepped back, though he still held her in the circle of his arms.

And when Annie looked up into his eyes, bewildered, his expression was rueful. "Can you deny it, Annie?" he asked softly.

She couldn't.

Not when he asked like that. Not when he didn't push, demand, exhort. Not when he respected her right to make a choice.

Her resistance faded. The steel within, the resolve that would have made her fight his demands slowly melted. She shook her head.

His hands fell to his sides, and he nodded. He drew a deep and, it seemed to Annie, somewhat shaky breath. She thought she saw a tremor run through him.

But then he was smiling at her, giving her hair a playful tug. "So, we've got that settled. Now let's go to bed."

SHE WASN'T SURE whether it was the blatant come-on followed by the hands-off behavior or whether it was the fact that he'd said, "Let's go to bed," and sneezed right after, but, whatever it was, all Annie's fears fled.

This was Jared, the man whom she had once loved.

And even though they no longer meant to each other what she'd thought they once had, there was no reason to fear him. If Jared were really out to seduce her again, she told herself, to try to manipulate her into doing what he wanted, he wouldn't be backing off now. Not Jared.

So he just wanted to be friends again. Well, so did Annie. But to be friends, she began to realize, it was necessary to acknowledge what they'd once felt for each other.

"You're right," she said and reached up to kiss his cheek. "Come on." And she took his hand and drew him down onto the bed.

It felt so warm, so right to snuggle up next to him, to feel the knob of his knee with her knee, to nestle into the curve of his arm.

She felt warm, safe, comfortable.

Which just goes to show how far you've come in a day, she chided herself.

And, of course, that was true. She wasn't denying it. Far be it from Annie to deny such a wholesale shift in her consciousness. But even though she wouldn't have believed it this morning, now she felt glad that it had happened.

For too long she'd had a huge gaping hole in her life where Jared had been before he walked out. No one else had ever filled it.

No one else, she began to realize now, ever could.

So it was good he had come back, good that he had, in inimitably arrogant Jared Flynn fashion, pushed his way back into her life again.

Because now they would have each other again. He would have his career—she wrinkled her nose, still uncomfortable with the Reid McCullough part of his life—and she would have hers. But once more they could also be friends.

The way they should be.

IT WAS AMAZING what a well-placed sneeze could do, Jared thought. Without that sneeze, he'd have been spending the night in the armchair. He would certainly never have had Annie lying right next to him, her arms around him to keep him warm.

But here she was, her knee touching his knee, her head resting in the curve of his shoulder, her breath fanning the hair on his chest.

It was torture, but it was sweet torture, and he loved every painful minute of it, because he knew where it would lead.

"You know, you were right, Jared," she murmured sleepily.

"Mmm?"

"It was foolish to worry. I don't know why I did. There's no reason why, even though you go your way and I go mine, that we can't be friends."

"Friends?" Jared muttered hoarsely.

Her hand splayed across his stomach. Fire licked through him. "Mmm-hmm." She sighed and patted him.

"Go sábhála Dia sinn."

She stirred and lifted her head to look at him. "Wha'?"

Jared shook his head. "God save us," he translated under his breath.

Or rather, God save *him*.

THE MORNING brought with it sunshine streaming through the curtains and masculine mutterings reverberating through paper-thin walls as the highway workers prepared for the day.

Jared opened one eye blearily, grumbled, then shut it again.

Annie tousled his hair, smiling, then bounced out of bed. "Come on, sleepyhead. Let's move it."

Jared groaned. "Come back here."

Annie shook her head. The temptation was very real. But she wasn't going to let herself. She had to maintain balance.

She had found the place for Jared in her life. He was her friend again, and she was determined to keep it that way.

Staying in bed with him wasn't the way to do it.

Jared gave her one more hopeful look, but when she just grinned and headed for the bathroom, he sighed and got up, as well.

He even smiled once before he had downed his requisite two cups of coffee. And by the time they hit the road, he was actually whistling.

"You're in a good mood," Annie commented as they rattled along the Interstate toward Columbus.

"It's a beautiful morning and I spent the night with a beautiful woman."

Annie flushed but didn't contradict him. She even began to hum along with his whistling.

Even Vinnie's truck seemed to sense their good humor and complemented it with a benevolence of its own. The rattles and pings were almost rhythmically enthusiastic as they bounced along.

Just like old times, Annie thought as morning gave way to lunchtime and lunchtime to afternoon.

Dayton and Columbus, Zanesville and Pittsburgh all slipped past them in a haze of conversation so reminiscent of days past. And Annie was aware of how much she'd missed him.

No one else had the patience to discuss the virtues of Shakespeare in the Park or to argue about the adaptation of *Driving Miss Daisy* to film. No one else was willing to dissect the costuming in *Henry V* or had even read David Mamet's new play, let alone had an opinion of it.

She smiled, feeling alive, expansive, as if she'd regained life in a dead limb, as if she were whole again instead of merely a part of herself.

And because this relationship was so new and so fragile, they were careful with it. Annie did not bring up Reid Mc-Cullough or her opinions of prime-time TV. She didn't mention her family, whom they'd rarely seen, or his family, whom they all too often had.

Jared didn't bring up any touchy topics, either. He didn't mention Hollywood or Malibu or the movie he was making next. He certainly didn't mention marriage.

Instead they talked about the Middle East, *glasnost*, capital punishment, life in New York.

They chugged across Pennsylvania, putting through Harrisburg, heading north on 78 toward the New Jersey border.

Jared asked about Annie's neighbors in the brownstone they'd shared.

"They're fine. Malcolm and Julie just celebrated their last mortgage payment. Jack got married."

"*Jack* got married?"

Annie laughed. "To a romance writer, would you believe? He was on her cover. Her perfect hero."

Jared grinned. "That's great."

And Annie nodded because, amazingly enough, so far it seemed that it was. They divided their time between Frances's place in Vermont and Jack's in New York, juggling two careers, a herd of sheep, four goats, and now a baby, as well.

She didn't see how they did it. Once she had said so to Jack.

"Have to," he'd replied simply. "I can't imagine life without Frances. She makes me real."

Annie had looked at him doubtfully, then had given him a weak smile and walked away. Now she had a vague idea what he meant.

But it didn't have to mean marriage. That intense a commitment to another person wasn't a notion she was comfortable with at all. It was, in fact, the very notion she'd been fighting her entire life.

She was damned if she was going to be the sort of woman her mother was, living constantly in her father's shadow, a helpmate without a life of her own.

She couldn't believe it when Jared had asked that of her. It meant he hadn't understood her at all. But now he was back. Now he was her friend again. Now she was hoping he might.

She slanted a quick glance at him. And when she caught his eye, he grinned at her.

Relieved, comfortable with the way things were going, Annie grinned back.

THE SUN SET BEHIND THEM, the hills of eastern Pennsylvania loomed before them, and they clattered into the darkness toward the New Jersey border.

Jared drove steadily while Annie dozed, first against the window and then against his shoulder.

He marveled at how right it felt to have her there. Sometimes he'd thought his memories were idealizations, that she wasn't as special as he remembered her. But it wasn't true.

He had tried feeling this way about other women over the past two years. He'd never ever come close.

He shifted slightly and slipped his arm around her, pulling her close. She sighed and snuggled against him, her arm falling across her body to rest lightly on his thigh, then sliding between his legs.

His breath caught in his throat. He shifted again and her fingers curled against him, touching him intimately. Her head slid down his chest and came to rest against his thigh. His gaze dropped, and he looked wryly at her innocent profile.

"Ah, Annie, what you're doing to me," he muttered, sighed and drove on.

"WE'RE HERE."

The voice was soft, almost reluctant, in her ear. Annie shifted, felt her body protest, her neck cramp. Reality was a far cry from the most delicious dream.

Then she opened her eyes and saw Jared's green ones, almost black in the dim city light, peering down into hers. Reality suddenly didn't seem so bad, after all.

She groaned, lifted her head from his thigh and sat up, flexing her shoulders, trying to work the kinks out. "Here where?" she mumbled.

"New York."

She jerked, startled. *New York? Already?* She blinked, looking around, trying to get her bearings. It was the middle of the night, but she could still see the skyscrapers, hear the sirens, smell the exhaust fumes. She was home.

"What time is it?"

"Just past three."

It had to be, because for the first time in Annie's memory she could look five blocks up Tenth Avenue and not spot a single moving car.

The reason for this became apparent when Jared turned onto Diane's street; they were all parked.

"Now I remember what I forgot to miss about New York," Jared said as they drove the cross streets, back and forth, looking for that one elusive parking spot.

"It's not always this bad," Annie replied defensively. And anyway, she thought, it prolonged their time together.

Now that they were actually in the city, she was loath to let him go. Now that she'd found him again, she wanted to hang on. She wondered for the first time what his plans were. They'd unload Nick's gear, of course. But then what? Was he leaving right away, heading off to Mexico or wherever?

"You don't...intend to move the tools in tonight, do you?" she asked him. "Or should I say, this morning?"

"I thought you'd want to." He gave her a searching look.

She shook her head. "Not really. I'm sort of beat."

"That wasn't you, sleeping from Allentown on?"

"Well, yes, but your thigh was a little hard." As soon as she said it, she felt her cheeks burn.

Jared just grinned wickedly. "Was it now?"

Annie chose to ignore him. "We can move Nick's stuff tomorrow," she said.

Jared hesitated a moment, then said, "I'll take you home."

Annie lived less than ten blocks north of Diane, a drive of a minute or two. And then...and then Jared would be gone.

She felt a sudden sharp pang. A need. She didn't understand it at first. It wasn't as if she hadn't known he was going. She'd always known. Had *wanted* it, in fact. But now...now she wanted more.

She wanted to share the closeness they had once felt. She remembered the hard warmth of Jared's arms around her the night before, remembered the feel of his unshaven cheek against her shoulder.

She'd never had that with anyone after Jared left. Had never wanted to. She was far too busy with her career, she'd told herself. It had nothing to do with Jared himself.

But now that he was back, she knew it did.

So, she told herself firmly, there was no reason they shouldn't share that closeness again. Even if it was only for one night. Especially if it was only for one night.

Maybe, she thought hopefully, loving him again would finish it. Maybe reality wouldn't hold a candle to her memories.

And if it was better? she dared to ask herself.

Well, if it was better, he'd be back in New York again. Maybe someday—God help her—she would even visit him in L.A. They could be friends. They could be lovers. Lots of people were.

She slanted a glance at Jared now. Her fingers tightened into fists against her thighs, and she knew what she would do. "Why don't you . . . stay?"

The smile Jared turned on her was pure heaven. "And here was I, thinking you'd never ask!"

There weren't any parking places close to Annie's, either, and she could tell that Jared was fast losing patience.

"I'll be damned if I'll drive around for the rest of the night," he said. And the look in his eyes spoke eloquently of the reason he had no intention of doing so.

Annie knew what he meant. She felt that way, too.

Finally they found a spot five blocks away, near the New-York Historical Society.

"We'll have to move the truck before seven-thirty."

Jared shrugged. "I reckon we'll still be awake."

And Annie, face-to-face now with just exactly what her invitation had implied, took a deep, steadying breath, then leaned over to kiss him. "Yes," she said, "I expect we will."

Jared parked the truck and they walked quickly back up Columbus and turned onto Annie's street. He was walking fast and Annie had to hurry to keep up. It was no problem. There was an urgency in her now, a need blossoming that had been growing hour by hour.

It had been there, Annie realized, since the moment she'd seen Jared in the church two days before.

She'd denied it then, had ignored it, pretending that it wasn't there.

There was no denying it now. She had been foolish to try.

It didn't have to change things, she thought.

It would simply enhance them, the way having Jared in her life had always enhanced it.

What happened tonight—or rather, this morning—wouldn't alter her priorities. Rather, it would confirm them.

She would be in the happy position of having her cake and eating it, too. And instead of nagging at the back of her mind, a speck of unsettled business, her relationship with Jared would be in its proper place.

He followed her up the steps and waited, not speaking, while she unlocked the door.

It was the first time they'd been back to the apartment together since they'd left it to go to Vermont.

After Jared had sprung the news of his TV offer—and his proposal—on her, and after she'd rejected them both, he had slammed out of their room, never to return.

Annie had remained, ignoring the pain in her heart, the numbness in her soul, all the while telling herself she was right and he was wrong and sooner or later he'd see it.

When she'd come back to the city, Jared—and all his things—were gone.

Now as she opened the door, the memories crowded in on her. Ruthlessly she pushed them away.

Memories weren't the point now, she reminded herself. What remained was to put things right.

Jared still didn't speak when she flicked on the light.

"Are you hungry?" she said, suddenly nervous. "Do you want something to eat?"

Jared pushed the door shut behind them and locked it. Then he shook his head. His eyes were like dark pools of jade. "It isn't food I'm wanting now, Annie D'Angelo," he said gruffly, holding her mesmerized. "It's you."

And there it was—bold and plain and honest, stretched out in front of them, spoken aloud—the truth.

Her nervousness vanished. Her hunger fled. Annie smiled and lifted her arms, putting them around Jared's neck.

His hands came up and framed her face, his thumbs stroking across her cheekbones, his fingers threading her hair. He bent his head, resting his forehead against hers. His eyes shut.

Annie stepped back, drawing him with her into the bedroom, not bothering to turn on the lamp. There was moonlight enough splashing across the wide white spread.

Jared paused now, his gaze moving slowly around the room. Remembering? Annie wondered. And then, because memories were dangerous, she reached for him again.

"No going back," she said softly as she sank down on the bed and kicked off her shoes. She hooked a finger through his belt loop and pulled him down with her.

He came unresisting, smiling, to sit beside her, to slide his hands up under the cotton top she wore. His fingers were warm and strong and slightly rough against the smoothness of her back. He had workingman's hands. Carpenter's hands, he'd told her the first time she'd danced with him and she'd felt the calluses on his palms, had seen the split fingernails, the roughened pads of his fingertips. He'd been working in construction then. Acting had been only a moonlighting occupation then, a pipe dream.

She'd imagined that his hands would have changed, softened over the ensuing two years. She'd been wrong, and she was glad. Jared polished and manicured would not have been Jared at all.

He skimmed the shirt over her head, tossing it aside. Then he pulled back, resting his hands on her shoulders as he looked into her eyes.

"Annie, *a ghrá*," he whispered.

"Oatmeal?" she asked with a nervous giggle. "Or does that mean bacon in Gaelic?"

Jared smiled at her, but the expression in his eyes was grave, not humorous. "What do you think?" he asked softly.

Annie, suddenly embarrassed, looked down. "Oatmeal, then, I would think," she said and darted him a look. "Sounds like mush to me."

Jared's white teeth flashed in the moonlight. "Does it now? We shall see about that." He rolled her backward onto the bed and slipped the straps of her bra down, undoing the clasp and sliding it off.

Then he knelt next to her and bent his head, and Annie felt his hair soft against her breasts. Then his lips caressed her, too, sending a curl of longing down through her, making her shiver and moan and twist her fingers in the thickness of his hair.

Desperately she tugged him up so that his lips met hers. She felt the need in him and knew it was matched by her own. "Jared."

She reached for him, drawing him close so that he lay down next to her, still kissing her, pulling back only to ask her, "What do you want?"

And all she could answer was "You."

He sat up, yanked his shirt over his head, then began fumbling with the snap of his jeans. Annie smiled and batted his hands away. "Let me."

Jared made a strangled sound deep in his throat, but his hands stilled, even as his body tensed at the feel of her fingers on him. She moved slowly, deliberately, making the moment last—needing the moment to last. She was no fool; she knew all too well she'd be living on this moment for years to come.

She unfastened the snap, then eased down the zipper. Her fingers brushed his hard flesh and she felt him tremble. She smiled and slid his jeans over his hips, then down hair-roughened thighs. Her fingers grazed his skin, paused at his knees, then moved on down, until, impatient, he kicked the jeans away and reached for her.

"My turn," he muttered. He pressed her back into the bedspread, then let his fingers trail across her rib-cage, then walk slowly down to her belly and hook inside the waistband of her shorts. Spreading her legs, he knelt between them and, as she watched, he unfastened the buttons and slipped his fingers inside, tugging slightly. Annie lifted her hips and Jared slid both the shorts and her panties down in one swift movement, shifting aside only long enough to pull them off. Then he was back, still kneeling, his fingers doing a slow walk up the insides of her thighs.

His eyes were dark, his face taut, the skin tight across his cheekbones. Annie watched him, memorizing every flickering expression. She lifted her hands and ran them from his shoulders down across his chest, her fingernails raking his nipples, making him shudder. She shuddered, too, for at that moment his fingers found the center of her, touched, teased, tantalized her, making her ache with her need of him.

"Jared." She said his name through her teeth, then bit down on her lip as his fingers moved further. He smiled at her reaction. She caught the elastic of his briefs and peeled them down over his hips, then drew him down to her, welcoming him.

And Jared, welcomed, forgot to measure his movements, forgot to hold back, to maintain control. Drawn down, he was lost, surging with a force he couldn't rein in, compelled by a desire he couldn't master.

And Annie, though she tried, couldn't master it, either. She couldn't step back and analyze, couldn't hold herself apart. She could only move with him, absorbing and being absorbed by the sensations Jared evoked in her.

And when at last the blessed release broke over them, first Annie, then seconds later, Jared, she didn't immediately pull herself together, tie up the memory in a neat little package and file it away in the back compartment of her life. She lay spent, exhausted, yet sublimely sated, holding his sweat-slick body in her arms, enjoying the moment, the peace, the man.

She even, after a time, fell asleep. She didn't know how long she dozed. Not long, probably, since it was still dark when she opened her eyes again.

Jared was no longer lying on top of her. But he hadn't moved far. His legs were tangled with hers as he lay on his side, his head propped on his elbow as he looked at her.

Annie smiled at him. She ran her hand down the length of his arm, pleased, settled, glad when he smiled back. *The way it should be,* she told herself.

"It was perfect," she told him. "You were perfect."

He grinned. "As were you." He touched her cheek, his beautiful dark eyes looked straight into hers. *"An phósaidh tú mé?"* he whispered.

And Annie thought that for a shopping list it sounded perfectly marvelous. She smiled. "I agree."

Jared wrapped his arms around her and hugged her tight. *"Buíochas le Dia.* Thank God," he murmured and kissed her. "We've only one thing left to settle."

A frown creased Annie's brow. "What's that?"

"Shall we get married here or in Ireland?"

Chapter Six

SHE FELT as if he'd punched her in the gut.

"Married?" she croaked. She scrambled up, dragging the bedspread around her, groping for her clothes.

Jared sat up, too, reaching for her, catching her arm, holding her when she would have pulled away. "Yes, damn it, married," he ground out. "M-A-R-R-I-E-D. What the hell do you think *'An phósaidh tú mé?'* means?"

"*That's* what you were saying? You were asking me to *marry* you?" She was horrified.

His fingers bit into her arm. "Of course I was asking you to marry me! My God, Annie, you're not going to pull this again, are you?"

"Pull what?" She was pulling away from him at that very moment, struggling with him, prying his fingers off her arm with one hand, trying to tug on her shorts with the other.

Jared raked his fingers through his hair. "I don't believe this! I bloody don't believe this!" He looked at her, agonized. "What the hell are you trying to do?"

"Get dressed." She was pulling on her shirt as quickly as she could, hopping around, looking for her sandals. "I just want to get dressed. And you'd better get dressed, too," she said. "So you can leave."

But Jared stayed right where he was. Naked and furious, he sat in the middle of the bed and glared at her. Annie, frantic, furious, too, glared right back.

"I don't know what you expected," she gabbled finally. "I mean, I thought it was perfectly clear. I told you back in St. Louis—"

"You told me damn all back in St. Louis. You were like the bloody Sphinx back in St. Louis!"

"Because I didn't want to talk to you! Because I was afraid you'd start this marriage business all over again and, damn it, I was right!"

"What's wrong with marriage?"

"Everything!"

Jared rolled his eyes. "Ah, there's lucidity. There's clarity. Would you care to expound a bit, Ms. D'Angelo? Maybe shed a little light?"

"Yes. Yes, I would. What's wrong with marriage is men like you. Men like my father. Men who think that women will drop everything and follow them! Men who expect that their wishes, their desires, their needs are paramount and women don't count for a thing!"

"And you think that's what I want?"

Annie slapped her hands on her hips. "I know it's what you want! You proved it! You were perfectly satisfied to go along together the way we were as long as you couldn't put on the pressure, and once you landed damned old Reid McCullough, you wanted to change the game!"

"I—"

"Exactly the way my father always ran things when I was growing up. He got a job in Philly. We moved to Philly. He got a job in Dallas. We moved to Dallas. He got a job in Chicago... You get the point? And wherever we went, whatever we did, he chose and my dutiful mother traipsed along behind!

"Well, my dutiful mother isn't me. And no man on God's green earth is going to do that to me! Not ever! I am myself. I am an actress. And not you or anyone else is going to stop me!"

"I never—"

"And even if I wanted to marry you—which I don't—I wouldn't marry a man who sold out!"

Jared stood up, all naked power and ferocity, glaring down upon her. The words he said were harsh and Gaelic, and Annie would never in a million years mistake them for a grocery list.

"Sold out?" he bellowed. "What in the hell do you mean by that?"

Annie lifted her chin. "Just what I said. You are the most talented actor I've ever seen. You have incredible range, incredible power. You can make me laugh, you can make me cry, you can make me hunger. And you are wasted—positively wasted—playing that ridiculous smarmy TV cop! I don't care that no one was waiting with a contract at the very moment they offered it to you! You weren't starving! I would've supported you!"

"You'd been supporting me," Jared said tersely. He grabbed his briefs and then his jeans and yanked them on. "For almost two damned years you'd been supporting me, and I was sick of it! I wanted to support you for a change!"

"I don't need support!"

"Oh, no?"

"No!"

"But I do?" His tone cooled suddenly. His words bit. "Thanks very much."

"I didn't mean—"

"What you meant was crystal clear." He jerked his shirt over his head.

"Jared! For heaven's sake! I only wanted the best for you! I didn't want you to have to settle for less. And it is less," she added helplessly in the face of his wrath.

"Well, forgive me for offering to share it with you! Forgive me for sullying your great expectations. Forgive me for getting in the way of them. I had no idea. But I'm not your father, damn it. And I never thought you were your mother. In my foolishness, I thought we had something special, you and me. I thought you loved me. And sure as hell I loved you!" He bent and grabbed his shoes from beneath the bed.

"Jared!" She stared at him, stunned.

"The more fool I," he went on bitterly. "Well, I know when to quit. I retract my proposal. I'm sorry I made it. I never realized how offensive it was."

"Jared—"

"May you succeed beyond your wildest dreams. May you be Juliet, Ophelia and ever other damned woman in theater. But frankly, Annie, I doubt if even that will make you happy. I don't think you know what happiness is!" He stuffed his feet into his shoes and headed for the door.

"Jared!"

He jerked the door open, then turned to glare at her. But his gaze was icy now. "What?"

"I . . . I'm sorry. I . . . didn't want . . . didn't want it to end like this."

"Oh?" A dark eyebrow arched. "How did you want it to end?"

She shook her head, despairing. "I . . . I didn't mean to hurt you. I . . . care. I do care. Really, no matter what else you believe, you must believe that."

"Must I?"

"Yes." Her tone was fierce. "It's just that I . . . I—" She bit her lip, desperate, knowing she wasn't making it right, wasn't helping matters, unable even to help herself. "It wouldn't work, Jared. I'd be a terrible wife."

Jared didn't say a word, just looked down at her. Then, at last, a corner of his mouth lifted in a sardonic smile. "And of course, as usual," he said, "Annie knows best."

Then he turned and walked silently out of her life.

SHE WAS RIGHT. She knew she was right.

So why in God's name was she so miserable? Why couldn't she pick up her life and get on with it, putting Jared Flynn right out of her mind?

But for all that she tried to, for all that she told herself she was perfectly justified in her actions, nothing seemed to work.

She had the rest of the week off. Her vacation, she reminded herself. The one she'd been so desperate for.

And she tried to do justice by it. She decided, since she didn't want to go anywhere else, that she'd see New York.

So she did the tourist things. She went to the top of the World Trade Center, she went to South Street Seaport. She rode the Staten Island Ferry and she took the Circle Line Tour. She climbed the Statue of Liberty and checked out Ellis Island.

And wherever she went, Jared was there.

Not in body. Heaven only knew where he was in body. But in spirit he was with her. She saw places he would have loved. She heard snatches of conversation he would have cherished. She longed to share them with him, and she hated him because he wasn't there.

She hated him more because he'd made her wish he was.

She'd survived losing him once. She'd had anger on her side then. She'd had righteousness, determination, focus, a goal.

Now she was lost, tumbled about by his words, by his declaration of love followed by his fierce rejection of her.

"It's what you get for wanting things settled," she told herself as she dragged back up the steps from a four-hour walking tour of Greenwich Village.

The phone was ringing as she opened the door. Hurrying across the room, she snatched it up.

It was her mother. "You remember Julia?" Lucia began without preamble. "My cousin Julia, from St. Louis. Her nephew Carmine just got a job with Chase Manhattan and is moving to New York."

Annie groaned, seeing it coming. "No, Ma. No. I can't…"

"You always 'can't,'" Lucia complained. "What's the matter with you, Annie? Don't you want to fall in love?"

The matter was, Annie could have told her, she already had.

BUT IT WASN'T until she was at the church Tuesday afternoon, preparing for her one hundred and twentieth marriage, that she began to understand the implications of that love.

It wasn't until her bridesmaid, Helen, poked her head in the door of her dressing room and said, "Welcome back to make-believe. How was the real world?" that she knew what honoring that love required her to do.

She put the finishing touches on her makeup and looked at herself in the mirror.

She looked every bit the blushing bride, just as at other times she'd looked every bit the distraught Juliet, the slightly mad Ophelia, the seductive Maggie. It was her talent: she could act with a whole range of emotions, stir an audience to passion.

And then she could walk away.

Because Helen was right; acting was make-believe. It could inform, it could incite, but it couldn't replace.

Roles were not reality, nor were they ever meant to be. She saw Jared for the first time as a man, not simply as an actor. His talents were great, certainly. But they were not the whole of him. And she knew now that her gifts were not the whole of her.

There was more to life than being someone else.

Or, Annie thought, there should be.

Her own life, by her choice, had been directed, dedicated, and decidedly empty.

It was time to change that.

Once Diane had said to her, "Without Nick, nothing makes sense." Once her neighbor Jack had told her he would always make time for Frances because he needed to, he couldn't imagine life without her. She made him real.

Jared made Annie real.

He made her feel. He made her laugh and cry and dance and sing. Each role tapped a part of her. But only Jared brought out every subtle nuance of her personality. He was the other half of her self.

She remembered asking her mother during that last phone call about Carmine-of-Chase-Manhattan just why it was her mother was pushing marriage so hard.

"Because I want you to be happy."

"Are you happy?" Annie had asked doubtfully.

"I've never been happier in my life," came her mother's prompt reply.

"But . . . what about Dallas? What about Philadelphia? Chicago? Dad just uprooted you. You went everywhere!"

"Because he wanted to," Lucia said simply. "And I didn't mind. Besides," she added, "we didn't go to Los Angeles or Seattle or Duluth."

"L.A.? Seattle? Duluth?" Annie had been baffled.

She could hear the smile in Lucia's voice. "Those were the places we didn't go."

"You could have moved all those other times?"

"Yes."

"Why didn't you?"

"Because I didn't want to. So your father turned them down."

She hadn't wanted to. He'd turned them down. It sounded so simple. So obvious.

And Annie said hollowly, "I didn't know."

"There's a lot you don't know, my Annie," Lucia replied quietly. "But you're not stupid. You'll learn."

Well, she wasn't a quick study, Annie thought wryly now. But perhaps she'd got it in the end. At least she meant to try.

She gave her veil one last tug and lifted her chin, then headed off to find Dan, the director.

"QUIT? YOU WANT TO QUIT?" Dan looked at her aghast.

"I want to quit," Annie repeated.

"But we need you! You're essential! You're—"

"Leaving." The more she said it, the more right it sounded. "You don't need me. Helen will be a lovely bride."

Helen had every bit the same focus Annie'd always had. But Annie's focus was different now. Broader. She felt as if she'd been cured of a lifelong case of tunnel vision.

"Well, you can't quit yet," Dan said. "We've got a new groom. I need you to break him in for me."

Annie rolled her eyes. "Another one?"

"What can I say? They're all afraid to commit. Anyway—" Dan grinned "—this one's a hunk. Who knows? You might just want to stay." He gave her a lascivious wink.

But Annie just shook her head. "No," she said. "I'm committed, too." She crossed her fingers and hoped to God it was true.

She didn't know where Jared was, but she intended to find him. And when she did, she prayed he'd be willing to take a chance on her.

If he didn't...well, if he didn't, she'd probably survive. But she wouldn't survive, not really, if she didn't try.

"Suit yourself." Dan shrugged. "But you gotta stay the week, at least."

"Thanks, Dan." Annie gave him a bright smile.

He shook his head, reached out and adjusted her veil. Then Helen stuck her head in the door. "Two minutes."

Annie took a deep breath.

Dan winked at her. "Sock it to 'em, kid."

It wasn't exactly a bridal send-off, Annie thought as she made her way to the back of the church. But under the circumstances, she supposed it was fair enough. She wasn't a bride. Not yet.

Maybe not ever, she cautioned herself.

But she couldn't believe that, wouldn't let herself believe it. Instead she stood quietly at the back of the church and tried to imagine what a real wedding day would be like.

She remembered what Diane had looked like waiting to start down the aisle toward Nick. White-faced. White-knuckled. Nervous. Determined.

So very, very determined. Ready to take on the Hoffmanns, the Bauers, the Granatellis, her estranged father and mother, most of St. Louis and half of Italy to marry the man she loved.

But first, Annie remembered, Diane had had to take on Nick.

"He loves me," she'd complained to Annie once. "I know he does. He knows he does. I've just got to make him admit it."

Then she had looked at Annie, her normally serene brown eyes alight with amber fire. "And I will," she'd vowed and had given her friend's arm a squeeze. "Because you taught me to believe in myself. You taught me how."

Those who can, do. Those who can't, teach, Annie remembered some wag saying, and she hoped to God it wasn't true.

The organist began to play. Her "father" took her by the arm and whispered in her ear, "Pizza at Helen's after. BYOB."

And then, at last, Annie began her march down the aisle.

She remembered Nick, strained but steady, waiting for Diane. She tried to imagine Jared waiting there for her.

He was.

"I WHAT?"

"You fainted," Jared said. And she didn't look so hot right now, either, lying there in her dressing room on the lumpy sofa and staring up at him through glazed and glassy eyes. The wedding and reception had been over for twenty minutes, and still she looked dazed.

He felt her cheek. It was cold and clammy, distinctly worrisome.

And Jared was worried, no doubt about that.

Of all the reactions he'd anticipated—horror, disgust, defiance, anger—he'd never ever expected Annie to take four steps down the aisle, meet his gaze and faint dead away.

"I . . . I don't understand," she said haltingly. "Wh-what are you doing here?"

"Marrying you?" He said it with a quick glibness that belied everything he felt. But he couldn't help the rising inflection that made it the question it really was.

Annie looked at him, dazed, but unblinking.

He shrugged awkwardly. "Acting," he said in a low voice after a moment. "I was acting. Facing a challenge. Stretching. Like you said."

She blinked then. But she still didn't say a word.

He licked his lips, then pressed them together in a thin line. "I thought about what you said," he told her. "About selling out. There's a kernel of truth in it. But it wasn't only for me."

Her eyes widened and she opened her mouth to speak, but he forestalled her.

"Mostly I wanted it for you. It was a matter of pride, I guess. I'd depended on you so much since we met. If it hadn't been for you I'd have long ago gone back to Ireland."

Annie frowned, but Jared shook his head. "It's true. You gave me the courage to think I could do it, to fight for roles. You gave me the courage to come to New York after Boston. You supported me, literally and figuratively the whole time. You had a lot more faith in me than I ever did. Faith I didn't really think was justified. And I felt guilty the whole time.

"So when Reid McCullough came along—" he shrugged "—I didn't think, I just jumped at it. I thought I could do the providing for both of us for a change. I never thought—*never*—" he looked straight at her now "—of expecting you to continue backing me. On the contrary, I wanted to back you."

Annie swallowed. She opened her mouth, but for long moments no sound came out. Then she simply wailed, "Oh, God! Oh, Jared!" And she threw her arms around him.

Once, when Jared was ten, his mother had scraped together the money to send him and his brother to spend the summer with a cousin who'd married a farmer in Sligo. It had been a summer to remember, but what he remembered most was coming home.

He remembered the longing he'd felt, the hunger for familiar warmth, familiar faces and places. He remembered it building, growing. And finally, after six long weeks in Sligo, he remembered getting off the bus and seeing his mother. He remembered running to her, throwing his arms around her and pressing his face into her breasts, smelling once more her scent of strong soap and lavender while she held him close and kissed the top of his head.

Once again, more now perhaps than ever, Jared Flynn felt he had come home.

He almost hadn't dared. He'd almost walked out of Annie's apartment last Tuesday morning and got on a plane to

Mexico. Only the fact that he still had to unload all Nick's tools made him stay.

And unloading the truck, setting up Nick's workbench, weighing the tools in his hands had settled him, made him think. He thought about Nick and Diane, about the rocky, roundabout road their love had taken. He thought about Annie's words, about the fears they'd exposed. And about how, even at the end, she'd insisted that she cared.

He cared, too. He cared, at last, too much to let his pride stand in the way. He'd come back to show her she was right.

"You're the new groom?" she asked him now. Her eyes were smiling at him a little shyly.

He nodded. "Do you mind?"

"I don't mind. Of course I don't mind." Her smile widened. "But I don't know how to tell you this."

Jared frowned. His heart quickened. "What?"

"I quit."

He jerked in surprise. "You quit? Why? You loved it. You were grand. Even tonight—once they revived you."

Annie laughed. "Thank you. I appreciate hearing it. I'm glad you think so. But it isn't enough for me."

He felt suddenly scared. "You found another role?"

She nodded and ducked her head. Then she lifted her gaze and looked right at him. "Your wife."

He opened his mouth, but no sound came out.

"I may have had a point," she said quickly. "But you had a better one. I did love you. I do love you. But I was afraid. I'd worked so long and so hard for so many years to be what no one else thought I could be, that I wouldn't let anything— anyone—stand in my way."

"Annie," he began, but she touched her finger to his lips.

"You had your say," she told him. "Now let me have mine. Being an actress is important to me. But it isn't everything. I know that now. It opens up parts of me that otherwise I might never touch. But no one makes me more myself than you."

She smiled at him, her eyes dark and shining with a love he'd given up hope of seeing. "So, I quit," she told him. She reached for her purse, unzipped it and pulled out an airline ticket to Los Angeles for next Monday.

"I'll be damned," Jared breathed. "But why Monday?"

She grinned. "I had to give Dan a week and break in his new groom!"

"You did, did you?" Jared said slowly, smiling. "And are you thinking I'll get it down in a week?"

Annie feigned shock. "An actor of your caliber? Without a doubt. The ceremony will be a piece of cake."

"And the marriage?" Jared asked her between kisses.

"The marriage is something else," Annie murmured against his lips. "The marriage I hope we'll be working on for the rest of our natural lives."

HARLEQUIN
American Romance®

THE ROMANCE THAT STARTED IT ALL!

For Diane Bauer and Nick Granatelli, the walk down the aisle
was a rocky road....

Don't miss the romantic prequel to WITH THIS RING—

I THEE WED
BY ANNE McALLISTER

Harlequin American Romance #387

Let Anne McAllister take you to Cambridge, Massachusetts, to
the night when an innocent blind date brought a reluctant Diane
Bauer and Nick Granatelli together. For Diane, a smoldering
attraction like theirs had only one fate, one future—marriage.
The hard part, she learned, was convincing her intended....

Watch for Anne McAllister's I THEE WED, available *now* from
Harlequin American Romance.

ITW

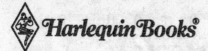 **Harlequin Books®**

GREAT NEWS...

HARLEQUIN UNVEILS NEW SHIPPING PLANS

For the convenience of customers, Harlequin has announced that Harlequin romances will now be available in stores at these convenient times each month*:

Harlequin Presents, American Romance, Historical, Intrigue:

> May titles: April 10
> June titles: May 8
> July titles: June 5
> August titles: July 10

Harlequin Romance, Superromance, Temptation, Regency Romance:

> May titles: April 24
> June titles: May 22
> July titles: June 19
> August titles: July 24

We hope this new schedule is convenient for you.

With only two trips each month to your local bookseller, you'll never miss any of your favorite authors!

*Please note: There may be slight variations in on-sale dates in your area due to differences in shipping and handling.

*Applicable to U.S. only.

HDATES-RR

A CENTURY OF
1890s AMERICAN 1990s
ROMANCE

A CENTURY OF AMERICAN ROMANCE has taken you on a nostalgic journey through time—from the turn of the century to the dawn of the year 2000.

Relive all the memories... the passions... of
A CENTURY OF AMERICAN ROMANCE.

1890s #345 AMERICAN PIE by Margaret St. George
1900s #349 SATURDAY'S CHILD by Dallas Schulze
1910s #353 THE GOLDEN RAINTREE by Suzanne Simmons Guntrum
1920s #357 THE SENSATION by Rebecca Flanders
1930s #361 ANGELS WINGS by Anne Stuart
1940s #365 SENTIMENTAL JOURNEY by Barbara Bretton
1950s #369 STRANGER IN PARADISE by Barbara Bretton
1960s #373 HEARTS AT RISK by Libby Hall
1960s #377 TILL THE END OF TIME by Elise Title
1970s #381 HONORBOUND by Tracy Hughes
1980s #385 MY ONLY ONE by Eileen Nauman
1990s #389 A.>LOVERBOY by Judith Arnold

Back by Popular Demand

Janet Dailey

Americana

A romantic tour of America through fifty favorite Harlequin Presents®, each set in a different state researched by Janet and her husband, Bill. A journey of a lifetime in one cherished collection.

In April, don't miss the first six states followed by two new states each month!

Available wherever Harlequin books are sold.

JD-AR